ALSO BY LINDA FAIRSTEIN

The Alexandra Cooper Novels

Death Dance
Entombed
The Kills
The Bone Vault
The Deadhouse
Cold Hit
Likely to Die
Final Jeopardy

Nonfiction

Sexual Violence: Our War Against Rape

BAD BLOOD

Linda Fairstein

DOUBLEDAY LARGE PRINT HOME LIBRARY EDITION

SCRIBNER

NEW YORK LONDON TORONTO SYDNEY

This Large Print Edition, prepared especially for Doubleday Large Print Home Library, contains the complete, unabridged text of the original Publisher's Edition.

SCRIBNER
1230 Avenue of the Americas
New York, NY 10020

Manufactured in the United States of America

ISBN-13: 978-0-7394-7873-8

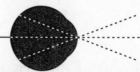

This Large Print Book carries the
Seal of Approval of N.A.V.H.

For Hilary Hale
Whose loyalty, encouragement and editorial gift
have taken Alex Cooper around the world

The voice of thy brother's blood crieth
unto me from the ground . . .

—GENESIS 4:10

BAD BLOOD

1

I was alone in the courtroom, sitting at counsel's table with a single slim folder opened before me. I had studied the photograph inside it hundreds of times in my office, but this morning I stared at it again for a different purpose.

The overhead shot of Amanda Quillian on a steel gurney had been taken at the morgue, shortly before her autopsy was performed eight months ago. Circular bruises were clustered on her throat, and crescent-shaped abrasions ringed the discolored areas of her skin, outlining the exact place where someone had ended her life by crushing her neck with his hands.

"Loneliest seat in town. Prosecutor in a domestic standing up before twelve good men and true—plus a few whacky broads mixed in—with a wee bit of circumstantial evidence, a snitch with a rap sheet longer than a roll of toilet paper, and no idea who actually squeezed the breath out of the late, lovely Mrs. Quillian."

I looked up at the sound of Mike Chapman's voice. "I didn't hear the door open. Is it unlocked already?"

Mike's smile was readiest at any chance to tease me. He brushed back his dark hair from his broad forehead, even his eyes laughing as he shook his head while reminding me of the uphill struggle that was about to unfold at trial.

"No. Artie Tramm let me in. Said to tell you the judge gave him orders to admit the riffraff at nine fifteen. Get rid of your coffee and say a little prayer to Our Lady of the Perpetually Hopeless Case."

"It gives me such a warm feeling in my gut when the detective who made the arrest

lacks conviction before even one of my witnesses is cross-examined."

"*Conviction?* This may be the last time
you get to use that word for a while, Coop."

Mike walked toward the well of the courtroom as I stood and took the last slug of
cold coffee. "Three cups should do it," I
said, tossing the cardboard container into
the trash can. "Three cups and several hundred butterflies floating around inside me."

"You still get 'em?"

"Put me out to pasture if I'm ever trying a
major case and tell you I don't."

He looked at the blowup of Amanda Quillian's face. "She talking to you, Coop? That
why you slipped up here at eight thirty?"

I didn't answer. Mike Chapman and I had
worked together on homicides for more
than a decade, well familiar with each
other's habits. We were professional partners and close friends. Mike knew that yesterday I had asked Artie, the officer in
charge of Part 83 of the Supreme Court of
New York County, Criminal Division, for permission to come up early to spend an hour
in the courtroom before the day's proceedings began.

The large shopping cart that had become

the favorite conveyance for prosecutorial case files over the last twenty years was parked behind my chair. It was loaded with Redwelds, part of every litigator's organizational system, and within them an array of colored folders—purple for each civilian witness, blue for NYPD cops and detectives, green for medical and forensic experts, and a few yellow ones for the names my adversary had turned over as part of the defendant's case. The lower rack held the dozens of physical exhibits I planned to introduce into evidence, all of which had been pre-marked for identification to save time during the trial.

"Hey, Mike," Artie Tramm called out as he stepped into the back of the room. "You see the game last night? The Yankees were hitting like it was a home-run derby."

"Ms. Cooper had me hand-holding witnesses till ten o'clock. I only caught the last inning. Good thing they can hit 'cause the pitching staff is having a problem finding the plate this year."

"You got a crowd growing out there, Alex," Artie said, pointing in the direction of the door. "I guess that's why they moved you to this part, so there's enough staff to control 'em. Lucky you came up when you did. Need anything?"

"I'm set, Artie. Thanks." I started to arrange my folders and notepads on the table.

"She needs a killer. She needs a stone-cold murderer I can drag in here in hand-cuffs before she makes her closing argument in three weeks," Mike said. "Do Coop a favor and keep your eyes open for one."

Artie laughed. "I think you got a few pos-sibilities in the peanut gallery."

The long corridors at 100 Centre Street were bookended with oversize courtrooms, and this case had been assigned to one. The Quillian matter had been high-profile since the victim's body was found in her town house in the East Eighties, half a block away from the Metropolitan Museum of Art, and the supervising judge had known from the time of the arraignment that the trial would draw spectators. Murder, money, and marital infidelity brought out the curious, who would fill the benches and choose sides to root for like fans at a wrestling match.

"Too bad you couldn't hear the openings

yesterday. They were both good," Artie said to Mike, twisting the ends of his handlebar mustache with his right hand as he walked to the judge's bench. His left thumb was hooked on the waist of his blue serge pants, which drooped below his paunch. "Both real good."

Because Mike would testify as a witness, he was not allowed to be in the courtroom for any other parts of the trial. "Scale of one to ten, how would you rate them?"

"Mike, please don't—"

"Go about your business, Ms. Cooper. Ignore us. Don't tell me you didn't read your own reviews in this morning's papers?" Mike grinned at me, running his fingers through his shock of black hair.

Artie was taking the judge's water pitcher to be filled. "Trust me. She was a lot better than that columnist said in the *Daily News*. I mean, it's not exactly like they're criticizing Alex. It's the facts that don't seem so strong. I'd give Alex a nine, but I'd give her case a three," Artie said to Mike. Then he seemed to remember that I was also there. "I hope you're saving some surprises for us."

"And Howell?"

"Ten. A perfect ten. He's so smooth. I tell

you, Mike, I ever get the urge to kill some-body? Lem Howell's my mouthpiece." The door swung closed behind Artie Tramm.

"I didn't mean to stir the pot, Coop."

"Artie's right."

"About our case?"

"About Lem Howell. Did Laura give you the list of calls to make this morning?"

"She wasn't in yet when I got to your of-fice." Mike was dressed in his trademark navy blazer and charcoal gray slacks. His pale blue shirt was unbuttoned at the collar and his rep tie unknotted and casually criss-crossed under the jacket. Both of us—Mike, taller than six feet, and me, five ten without my heels—seemed swallowed up by the large, empty courtroom.

"It's on her desk." I liked the flow of a trial to be seamless. Witnesses were lined up days ahead of time, placed on standby, and asked to juggle busy professional sched-ules to appear as needed. Most jurors be-came annoyed when unnecessary delays extended the length of their service. There would be things none of us could control—the juror whose subway train gets stuck or whose babysitter doesn't show or who claims his cat swallowed a hair ball and has to go to the vet—but Mike and my paralegal, Maxine, would monitor the lineup I had organized to keep my presentation tight.

"Anything else I—"

"See you at one."

"Don't get short with me, kid. I'm with you on this. You just got to be realistic about our chances. I'm sorry if I broke your concentration."

"That's not all you're trying to break."

I put Amanda Quillian's photograph back in the folder and replaced it on the cart.

"So you got up here early to avoid running the gauntlet into the courtroom, you brought all the exhibits with you—and I guess you've made your peace with Amanda."

It was something I did at the beginning of every murder trial, just my own quiet way of getting ready to go into battle. Within the hour, every aspect of this woman's personal life would be exposed to the jury—and to the public. The most intimate details of her daily affairs would be offered up for dissection—by me as well as by the defense— most of them things she had talked about, if at all, only with people she trusted and loved.

As soon as the doors were unlocked, the

first two rows behind me, on both sides of the aisle, would be crammed with reporters from each of the city's newspapers, and the television and radio stations, as well as stringers for the national media. The bench after that one was reserved for the victim's family—her elderly mother, two sisters, and several of her closest friends. The rest of the audience would be a mix of locals who braved the intense heat of the June day, some who were courthouse regulars who liked the show—no matter what the crime—and others because cameras aren't allowed in New York State trials, meaning no gavel-to-gavel coverage of the case on Court TV. And, of course, also attending would be the young Legal Aid lawyers and my colleagues from the Manhattan District Attorney's Office, slipping in between their own calendar calls to study Lem Howell's style or lend me moral support.

I knew my case cold. I knew its weaknesses and more of its strong points than the twelve jurors and four alternates would ever hear. Some of the state's evidence had been suppressed by the judge in pretrial hearings as inadmissible or potentially prejudicial, and Howell would do his best to limit me even further with every application I made. I had already prepared for the testimony that would be elicited today. I didn't need this time to do any work.

I had used the last half hour to think about Amanda Quillian. Mike was right—she had talked to me, over and over, through the various forms of evidence he and I had gathered in the months after her death.

I looked at the morgue photograph to remind myself of how eloquently she had told her story, from the outset, by the horrific damage done to her strong, healthy body. I looked at it to remind me of the outrage I had felt when Mike Chapman had first called to ask me to meet him at the medical examiner's office to see his victim—one of three homicides that had occurred in Manhattan on that cool fall afternoon. I looked at it to remind me that I had been invested with the trust of those who'd loved her to seek some kind of justice for the killer—the killers—of Amanda Quillian.

"Detective Michael Patrick Chapman, Second Grade, Manhattan North Homicide Squad, do you swear to tell the truth, the whole truth, and nothing but the truth—so help you God?" The powerful voice of my adversary boomed from the doorway that one of the court officers had unlocked for him.

"Lemuel Howell the Third. My very favorite black panther," Mike said, swinging open the gate that separated the well of the courtroom from the gallery. His reference described Howell's lean, elegant frame and his skin color, not his politics.

"Alexandra, my friend, good morning." Lem rested his monogrammed leather briefcase on the floor beside his chair, then stepped over to shake hands with Mike. He reached out his arm to grasp my elbow, leaning over to kiss me on the cheek. Lem had always been a toucher—the arm-stroking, back-rubbing, hand-grasping contact kind, all the while locking eyes and willing you to engage with him.

"Hi, Lem."

"Looking cool, collected, and with a faint scent of jasmine in that perfume today," he said, lifting his nose to sniff the air near my ear.

"Lavender, actually. But thanks."

"You might find this a bit of useful information for your off-duty life, Detective. Coco Chanel believed that women ought to dab perfume on themselves wherever they might like to be kissed," Lem said, pinching my arm before he let it go.

"Then you should be sniffing a little closer to Coop's ass than her ear," Mike said, as Lem winked at me—tapping his long fingers on my pile of folders before returning to his table. "You're looking mighty fine yourself, Counselor. Guess it's that razzle-dazzle moment for the jury."

Lem was as strong on substance as he was on style. He had been one of my first supervisors when I'd arrived in the office as a rookie prosecutor, before he left for a lucrative partnership in the litigation department of a midtown law firm.

Lemuel Howell III had the eloquence of the great black preachers, the brain and wit of a superb trial lawyer, and the looks of a leading man in a 1940s noir film—his wavy hair pomaded into place, straight back without a part. By the end of voir dire—in this matter a four-day exercise weeding through 182 prospective jurors—he had most of them ready to eat out of his hand before they'd heard the first prosecution witness.

He opened the brass locks on the briefcase and placed a sheaf of papers on his desk before removing a thick, gold fountain pen from his breast pocket. Then he smoothed the front of his beige suit.

"And you, Michael Patrick? You've detected, deduced, and done Alexandra's bidding for the better part of a year, and still no perpetrator?"

"If only your client would loosen up and let me know who he paid to do the kill, maybe I could twist Coop's arm to cut him a deal."

"He can't tell you what he doesn't know, can he?"

"Save that line of bull for the jury." Mike slapped Lem on the back as Artie Tramm returned with the water pitcher and told us that he was ready to open the doors. "And go easy on her, Mr. Triplicate, you know how Coop hates to lose."

Triplicate was what the courthouse reporters called Lem Howell, not for the Roman numeral III in his name, but for his habit of phrasing his descriptions in threesomes. Yesterday, in his opening remarks, Amanda's death was "admittedly savage, barbaric, and the cowardly work of a dangerous madman"; his client was "innocent, falsely accused, and horribly distraught by his wife's untimely demise"; and the People's case was "dreadfully flimsy, paper-thin, a gossamer web of fabrications."

"Both sides ready?" Artie Tramm asked.

I nodded while Lem gave him a firm "Yes, sir."

Tramm opened the door on the far side of the judge's bench, which led to the small barred holding pen to which Brendan Quillian had been delivered earlier this morning from his cell in the Tombs. I watched as one of the officers removed Quillian's handcuffs and walked behind him into the courtroom, to place him next to Howell so jurors would not know he had been incarcerated pending trial.

The defendant was dressed in one of his elegant Brioni suits, probably for the first time since the day of his arrest. He was as tall as Mike Chapman but with a beefier build, and his brown hair was showing streaks of gray, despite the fact that he had just turned thirty-five. He fixed on me with an icy look as he crossed behind his table, a glare made all the more sinister by the cast of his right eye. Brendan Quillian had been blinded in that eye by a childhood accident, and I swiveled away from its glassy, dead stare as he squinted at me.

"Smart move," Mike whispered, oblivious to the quick exchange. "Howell's the perfect lawyer for this case."

Quillian and Howell were animatedly talking to each other.

"He's the perfect lawyer for any case."

"Your middle-class white jurors won't want to think Quillian did it—don't understand domestic violence when it happens outside the ghetto. Your upper-class white women will think he's too handsome to be guilty, and your upper-class white men—"

"When's the last time you saw an upper-class white man on a Manhattan jury?" I asked. "They use every excuse in the book to avoid service."

"And your blacks—dammit, I guess everybody in the room—will fall under the spell of the silver tongue of Lem Howell."

"I'm ready to open the doors, Mike," Artie said.

"My money's on you, kid. Make 'em believe, okay?" Mike said, slapping the table and heading to the courtroom door. "See you at the break."

He walked out against the flow of incoming traffic, while I seated myself at the table with my back to the benches. The first five reporters made a beeline for Howell. The district attorney, Paul Battaglia, had firm rules that forbade each of us from talking to the press while a case was pending. Lem Howell, however, would leak like a sieve from now until the moment of the verdict, feeding the media tidbits helpful to his client that the jury would never be allowed to hear. So I sucked it up and sat quietly in place while the officers filled the rows with curious onlookers and tried to keep order in the court.

"Put your newspapers under your seats," Tramm roared at the two hundred spectators. "No reading materials, no food or beverages, no cell phones, no talking among yourselves.

"All rise," Tramm continued, "the Honorable Frederick Gertz presiding."

The door from his robing room opened and the stern-faced Gertz, five foot six, strode into the well and climbed the three steps to his bench.

"Good morning, Ms. Cooper, Mr. Howell."

"Good morning, Your Honor," we both answered.

Jonetta Purvis, the court clerk, was standing at her desk close to the defense table.

"The defendant and his lawyer are present, the assistant district attorney is present. Shall we bring in the jurors, Your Honor?"

"You both ready to go forward? Any housekeeping to attend to?"

"Ready," I said. I pushed the indictment aside—the written instrument that charged Brendan Quillian with "Murder in the Second Degree and Conspiracy to Commit the Crime of Murder in the Second Degree"—and reached for the thick purple folder beneath it.

Artie stood by the door next to the judge's bench and opened it. "Jurors entering."

The group of sixteen—the first twelve chosen and four alternates—filed in, taking their seats in the two rows closest to my desk. They fidgeted as they settled down, some staring at Quillian and Howell, others focusing on me and the full shopping cart behind me.

It was impossible to imagine how jurors had been able to obey the judge's instructions not to listen to television accounts or read stories about the case. I stifled my desire to scan the group to see what reading materials each had brought along. Last evening's news had led with a summary of the opening-day arguments, and this morning's *New York Post* banner—DIAL M FOR MOGUL: HUBBY HIRES HITMAN—would have been visible on every subway and bus route that carried these folks downtown.

I lifted the flap of the folder and squinted at the bright yellow Post-it note stuck to my punch list of questions. It was in Lem's handwriting, slipped onto the file when he had stepped over to greet me minutes ago. *Alex—take your best shot. If you remembered half of what I taught you, you wouldn't be leading off with Kate.* Beneath the warning he had scrawled another word: *SHOWTIME.*

Gertz's eyes swept the courtroom, making sure he had everyone's attention before he pointed his gavel in my direction. "Call your first witness, Miss Cooper."

My voice caught in my throat as I stood, and I coughed to clear it as I started the People's case. I didn't need to look over at Lem to let him know he had scored his first hit.

2

"Would you please state your full name for the jury?"

"My name is Katherine Meade. I'm called Kate."

I was standing against the rail at the end of the jury box, trying to draw Kate Meade's eyes in my direction. "How old are you, Ms. Meade?"

"Thirty-four. Thirty-four years old."

The jurors had watched Artie Tramm lead her into the courtroom and onto the witness stand. They had all scrutinized her appearance while she stood, fidgeting slightly, facing the clerk as she was administered the oath. Most of them had probably seen her bite her lip and flash a glance in the direction of Brendan Quillian, who returned it with a broad smile.

"Are you single or married?"

"Married. I've been married for twelve years. My husband is Preston Meade. He's a banker."

There was little about Kate Meade that these jurors would relate to. The nine men and three women who'd been impaneled were a mix of working- and lower-class New Yorkers—white, black, Hispanic, and Asian—ranging in age from twenty-seven to sixty-two. The four alternates—three men and one woman—were equally diverse. The business clothes most of them had worn during the selection process had been replaced by T-shirts and cotton blouses, chinos and jeans and capri pants.

"Where do you live, Mrs. Meade? In which county?"

They stared at her well-made-up face, auburn hair pulled back and held securely in place with a tortoiseshell hairband. The pale pink suit—with its short-collared jacket and pencil-thin skirt—seemed as rigid as my witness. I tipped my head toward the jury box, a signal I'd arranged to make her remember that it was to the people sitting in it that she had to tell her story. I wanted her to warm up to her audience and speak more naturally, but her expression was frozen and her anxiety was palpable.

"In Manhattan. New York County. On the Upper East Side," she said, turning to Judge Gertz. "Do I have to say exactly where—?"

"No, no. No, you don't."

Kate Meade exhaled as though relieved not to have to tell anyone who wasn't a member of the Knickerbocker Club what her address was.

"Do you have any children?"

"We do," she said, smiling at the foreman for the first time. "We have three children, all in elementary school."

"Do you work outside the home?"

"No, ma'am. I mean, I volunteer on several boards, but I haven't been employed since I married Preston."

I extended my right arm in the direction of the defense table. "Do you know the defendant in this case, Brendan Quillian?"

"Yes, I do. For a very long time."

"For how long, if you can tell us exactly?"

"I met Mr. Quillian—Brendan—when I was sixteen. He was seventeen at the time."

"Would you tell us where you met?"

"Certainly." Kate Meade was comfortable with this part of the story, and she shifted her body to face the jury box to talk. "I was in high school, here in Manhattan. Convent of the Sacred Heart."

Some of the jurors would know that Sacred Heart was the city's premier private school for Catholic girls, promising an education that intertwined intellect and soul. They might have some idea of what it had cost to educate Kate Meade and her friends if they knew that the current tuition was upward of twenty-five thousand dollars a year at the old Otto Kahn mansion on the corner of Fifth Avenue and Ninety-first Street.

"I attended Sacred Heart from kindergarten through high school. It's where Amanda Quillian—well, Amanda Keating then—and I became best friends, since we were five years old. We were together, Amanda and I, the day we met Brendan. It was at a game, a football game. He was a junior at Regis, and we were sophomores."

The all-male Jesuit high school was also on the Upper East Side, and because of the largesse of its original founders, it offered tuition-free college-prep education to Roman Catholic young men who passed rigorous tests for admission.

"You were present when Amanda and Brendan Quillian were introduced to each other?"

"Yes, I was. It was my brother who brought Brendan over to meet her." Kate Meade smiled again at the jurors. "He had seen her across the field and asked who she was."

I handed a photograph, pre-marked as People's Exhibit #1, to Willy Jergen, the court officer standing beside the witness box. "Would you look at that photograph, please, and tell me if you recognize it?"

Jergen passed the picture to Kate Meade. "Yes, I do. I gave it to you several months ago, Ms. Cooper."

"What does that photograph represent?"

"It was taken the afternoon Amanda and Brendan met. It's a picture of them talking with my brother, who was on the team, after the game. It's from our yearbook."

"Your Honor, I would like to offer the photograph into evidence at this time."

"Any objection?"

Lem Howell didn't bother to rise. "No, sir." He wasn't objecting to anything at this point. He knew the benign—even romantic—backstory of the young Quillians wouldn't do anything but reinforce his client's good character.

"Entered into evidence then," Judge Gertz said, starting to make notations in his leatherbound log that would grow to record the dozens of police and medical reports, photographs, and diagrams that both Howell and I planned to introduce during the trial.

"Mrs. Meade, I'm going to come back to that time period shortly, but I'd like to jump ahead for a few minutes. I'd like to direct your attention to a more recent date, to Wednesday, October third, of last year. Do you recall that afternoon?"

The young woman angled her body away from the jury, her eyes widening as though she'd been frightened by an apparition. "I do," she said, her voice dropping.

"What happened on that day?"

"Objection."

"Sustained. Ms. Cooper, you can't—"

"I'll rephrase my question." Kate Meade was nervous again. I could hear the sound of her thumbnails as she picked at one with the other. "Did you see Amanda Quillian that day?"

"Yes, yes, I did. I did. I had lunch with Amanda on October third. I had lunch with her an hour before she died—before she was murdered."

Howell didn't like the answer my question elicited, but he was too smart to keep objecting to information that he knew I would get before the jury anyway. All twelve, and even the alternates, were leaning forward in their seats. They obviously wanted to know what occurred in the last hours of the victim's life.

"I'd like you to take a look at another picture, please. People's two." I reached to the bottom level of the cart and removed an enlarged photograph—two feet square—mounted on posterboard. Again, I passed it to Willy to hand to the witness. "Do you recognize this?"

Meade inhaled audibly and lowered her head. "Of course I do. I took it."

"When did you take it?"

"October third. About two o'clock in the afternoon."

"Where?"

"At a restaurant called Aretsky's—on Madison Avenue at Ninety-second Street. It was an unusually warm day, so we sat outdoors, Amanda and I. I had just shot a roll of film on a disposable camera at my daughter's class play. She's also at Sacred Heart now. I had one exposure left, so I snapped a photo of Amanda."

"Your Honor, I'd like to offer this into evidence as People's two."

Gertz pointed a finger at Howell, who smiled and nodded his head.

"It's in evidence, Ms. Cooper."

"At this time, I'd like to display both of these to the jury."

Lem Howell had not been quite as passive as he was now when we'd argued a week ago, before voir dire, about the last photograph taken of Amanda Quillian. Irrelevant, prejudicial, and prosecutorial overkill, he'd maintained, sparring with Judge Gertz over and over.

But the snapshot of Amanda Quillian was ruled admissible. This was the only case I'd ever handled in which a picture had been taken an hour before the murder occurred, showing the long, bare neck of the victim— the exact focal point of the injury that caused her death—without a mark on it.

While the jurors were circulating the two photos among themselves, I asked Artie Tramm to set up the stand with the easel that was leaning in the corner. Day in and day out, Brendan Quillian would sit before these jurors. He'd been coached by Howell to put on his best game face—smile at them and bond with them in every way that did not involve direct communication. I had seen too many trials in which the prosecution never brought the deceased to life in the courtroom, never allowed the twelve people making the most important decision about her life to feel her presence and understand that the murder victim had as much at stake in this trial as did Quillian himself. For any semblance of justice to be achieved, I needed jurors to see Amanda Quillian vibrant and cheerful and alive, mere hours before she was posed on the steel gurney for a different camera in the autopsy room.

Willy returned the exhibits to me. I put the small photo on my table and helped him mount the blowup of the smiling Amanda Quillian on the easel between the witness stand and the jury box.

"Let's go back now, Mrs. Meade. I'd like to return to the story you started to tell us, when Amanda began to date the defendant."

"They went out together for the first time a week after they were introduced. I saw them at a movie theater the very next Saturday."

"Did you have occasion to spend time with them during the rest of your high school years?"

"Constantly. Neither my parents nor Amanda's wanted us dating alone at that age, so we usually went out in groups, or at least two couples. Since she was my best friend, we were together a great deal of the time. Amanda never dated anyone else seriously. Not during high school, not when she went away to Princeton. I mean, you can see how attractive she was, so she had lots of offers. But she was mad for Brendan—he's the only guy she ever cared about."

The jurors were taking it all in. Some were watching Kate Meade as she testified, a few stared at the face in the photograph while Kate talked about her friend, and many were glancing over at Quillian, hoping for a reaction to the testimony but getting none.

"And the defendant, do you know where he attended college?"

"Yes. Brendan went to Georgetown. In Washington, D.C. He had a full scholarship there."

"Were you present for the marriage of Amanda to the defendant?" For every time that a witness—or my adversary—would personalize the man on trial by using his Christian name, I would refer to him instead by his status in these proceedings.

"Yes, of course. I was Amanda's maid of honor."

"When did that take place?"

"The week after her college graduation, twelve years ago this month. Amanda had just celebrated her twenty-second birthday."

Through Kate's narrative I got much of the pedigree information about my victim and her husband before the jury. I had structured the direct exam carefully to avoid Howell's hearsay objections by eliciting facts my witness knew firsthand.

Amanda's father was the sole owner of a real estate empire started by her grandfather more than forty years earlier. Keating Properties had been responsible for much of the development of Manhattan's SoHo district, transforming vast commercial space into fashionable residential lofts and apartments. Then they repeated that trend in TriBeCa and on into Dumbo, restoring the charm of the streets and old buildings in the part of Brooklyn "down under the Manhattan Bridge overpass."

Because Amanda was the only one of the three sisters to marry someone interested in the family business, her father had welcomed Brendan Quillian into the company. After he completed his studies at Georgetown and received an MBA from New York University, Brendan learned the art of the deal from Richard Keating himself. By the time the Quillians celebrated their tenth anniversary, shortly before Keating succumbed to a chronic and severe case of congestive heart failure, he had made Brendan his partner in all his real estate ventures.

"Did Amanda Quillian work, Mrs. Meade? Did she have a job?"

"For the first three years after her wedding, she was also employed at Keating Properties. She handled some public relations matters for her father. But once Brendan was promoted to a management position, she wanted to get out of his way. Sort of take the pressure off him, the attention from other employees that he was the boss's son-in-law."

I knew the answers to the questions I was asking as well as Kate did. What I didn't know, what distracted me now with the persistence of a small hammer pounding inside my brain, was the warning that Lem had laid out for me, the land mine I was certain to encounter as Kate and I moved forward together.

"What did she do after that?"

"Volunteer work, mostly. Four days a week. She was on one of the hospital boards, and she devoted a lot of her time to a project for literacy." Kate came through with a smile. A forced one, perhaps, but several jurors responded in kind.

"Did Amanda have any children?"

"No, she didn't. They didn't."

"To your knowledge, was she ever pregnant?"

"Yes, she was. Amanda had three miscarriages, Ms. Cooper. I was with her at the hospital when she had the third one, just about four years ago." Any trace of that smile was now gone. Kate's lips tightened around her teeth and she drew in a deep breath. "It was a—a very painful time for her."

"How often did you and Amanda speak, Mrs. Meade?"

"Every day. Well, practically every day," she said, smiling at juror number three, an elementary-school teacher in her forties. "Some days we talked two or three times. And I saw her several times a week. She's the godmother—she and Brendan are the godparents of my oldest daughter. She was often at our house."

"Did she confide in you?"

"Objection."

"Sustained."

"Ms. Cooper knows better than to characterize, to lead, to—"

"I'll take your reasons at the bench, Mr. Howell," Judge Gertz said. "Not in open court. I've already ruled in your favor."

I turned my back to the judge and walked to the railing behind me, pausing before I returned and continued questioning Kate Meade.

"After Amanda married the defendant, did she ever spend the night at your home?"

"No, no, she did not," Kate said, looking down at her lap and again nervously clicking one thumbnail against the other. "Not until shortly before her father died. Then there was a time—several times—that she did."

"Can you tell us why she came to stay with you?"

"Objection. Hearsay, Your Honor," Lem said, rising to his feet and circling his right hand in the air, catching the light with his gold pen. "It calls for—"

"Sustained, Mr. Howell. I don't need three of your arguments when one suffices."

Lem grinned broadly as he sat down, claiming his victory to the jurors.

"Well, Mrs. Meade, the first time Amanda Quillian came to spend the night with you, was it at your invitation?"

"No, it was not. Certainly not."

"Can you tell us when this visit occurred?"

"It was about five years ago, in April, I believe. On a weeknight. One o'clock in the morning, to be exact." Kate was emphatic about the hour, as if no person of manners would confuse the time of night with a social invitation.

"Did she call you before coming over?"

"Yes, from a taxicab. She was on her way to a hotel, she told me."

"Objection!" Lem Howell was on his feet now, all business, ready to rein me in. From this point forward, he would hold me to the rules of evidence. The insidious growth of the marital conflict I wanted to lay before the jury would be difficult to show without a victim who could tell her own tale.

Judge Gertz looked down at Kate Meade on the witness stand adjacent to his bench, cautioning her against the hearsay testimony she was trying to deliver. "Don't tell us what Mrs. Quillian said to you, young lady. You may testify about your observations and your actions, but not about conversations she had with you."

I had prepped Kate for the manner of this examination—and for the fact that Howell would fight to keep out parts of the story—but she was visibly upset that the judge had chastised her.

"Can you describe Amanda Quillian's appearance when she arrived at your home that night?"

"She was crying. Crying hysterically. May I say that, Your Honor? I had never seen her as upset as she was that night. I held her and talked to her, but I couldn't get her to stop crying."

"Don't tell us what she said, Mrs. Meade," I guided her, since Amanda's words themselves would violate the hearsay rules. Kate could be cross-examined by Lem about her observations, but Amanda's statements to her could not be offered for their truth. "But did she explain to you why she was crying?"

"Yes, she did," Kate said, turning her head to grimace at Brendan Quillian.

"Did she appear to have any injuries?"

"No, no, she did not. Not that I could see on her face."

"Did she spend the night at your home?"

"Amanda spent five nights with us. She refused to go out of the house. I could barely get her to eat."

"Did you see the defendant during those days?"

"Once. Brendan came to our door two days later, first thing in the morning."

"Did you let him in?"

"No. I talked to him in the hallway. I told him that Amanda didn't want him there."

"Do you remember any specifics of your conversation with the defendant?" These statements by Quillian were not considered hearsay.

"Certainly. Of course I do."

"What did he say to you, as best you can recall?"

"He asked me to let him in. No, he begged me to let him in."

"Once?"

"Three—maybe four times."

"Did he ask you how Amanda—how his wife was?"

"No. No, he did not."

"What else did he say?"

"The only other thing he wanted to know was whether Amanda had told her father that she had left home."

"What answer did you give him?"

"I told him that she had not. Not yet."

"And then?"

"He wanted to know if I was sure of that. He asked me to promise him that I wouldn't let Amanda admit to her father that she had walked out on him. Brendan said he'd do anything to get Amanda back." Kate Meade was speaking softly now, trying to hold back the tears that had formed in her eyes.

I let the jury observe her for several seconds. I was relieved to have gotten this much of the story told without the backfire that Lem had hinted at to scare me. Maybe his warning had just been a scam to unnerve me as I started my case.

"What did you say to the defendant?"

She spoke to the foreman. "I told him to get out of my building. I told him I couldn't make any promises to him."

"When was the next time you spoke with the defendant after that?"

"It was on the sixth day. A Saturday, I think. Amanda had spent a lot of time talking with him on the phone the night before. He convinced her to come back home. He picked her up around ten o'clock that morning."

"Did you talk with him then?"

She shook her head from side to side before she answered. "Only to say good-bye to Amanda as they left."

I took Kate Meade through four more years of Amanda's sudden visits, at least one every six months. The episodes of tearful nocturnal flights made little sense without the substance of the revelations that my victim had made to her best friend over the years, but the pattern of conduct established before the jury the profound unhappiness in her relationship with her husband.

I tried to lay the foundation for the expert witness whom I planned to call later in the case, the one who would explain some of the dynamics of domestic violence. I expected her to be able to answer the question of why Amanda Quillian did not simply leave Brendan, the question I had been asked about my spousal-abuse victims more times than I could possibly count.

Kate Meade had been responding to my queries for more than ninety minutes by the time I caught her up to the last lunch the two women had together on October 3 of the previous year.

"You told us that you snapped this photograph—People's two in evidence—at about two o'clock in the afternoon?"

"Yes, just before we paid the check."

"And for the record, it's fair to say that Amanda is smiling, am I right?"

"She was very happy that day." Kate nodded to the jurors.

"If you know, Mrs. Meade, where was Brendan Quillian on October third?"

"He was in Boston, Ms. Cooper."

Lem Howell didn't mind that tidbit of hearsay. It helped him to have his client as far away from the scene of the crime as possible.

"Do you know why Amanda was so happy?"

"Yes, I do. I certainly do. She had made some decisions about her future, about ending her marriage. She told me that—"

"Objection."

"Sustained. You can't tell us what she said."

"Sorry, Your Honor. I gave her a business card—the name and phone number of a locksmith. It was a man I'd used when my children's nanny lost her keys the week before. I made an appointment for him to change the locks at Amanda's house the next morning, before Brendan was due back in town."

Kate Meade had blurted out the sentences in rapid-fire sequence, then slumped back in her chair as though satisfied she had done her best for her friend without a chance of interruption from Howell.

"What time did you and Amanda Quillian leave each other on the corner of Madison Avenue and Ninety-second Street?"

"Ten or fifteen minutes after I took this photograph." Kate Meade lifted a handkerchief embroidered with pink flowers out of her pocket and dabbed at her eyes. Then balling it up in her hand, she pointed at the life-size picture of her friend on the easel beside her.

"Did you speak to Amanda Quillian again after that?"

"Yes, I called her shortly before three o'clock. Preston suggested to me that we invite her to dinner that evening since she was alone, and so I called to tell her what time to come over."

"At what number did you call her?"

"On her cell phone. I called on her cell because I wasn't sure whether she would have reached home yet."

"Did she answer?"

"It went to voice mail. She picked it up a few minutes later and called me back."

"Was that the last time you heard from Amanda Quillian?"

Kate Meade's fingernails clipped each other more loudly than before. "No, ma'am."

"What happened next?"

"I was opening the door to our apartment when my own cell phone rang again," Kate said, tearing up as she hung her head. "She must have hit redial, it was so fast."

"Objection, Your Honor. This speculation, this guesswork, this 'must have,' 'should have,' 'could have' business is—"

"Sustained. Keep your voice up, will you, madam?"

Kate Meade lifted her head, picked out her favorite juror—the teacher—and locked eyes with her. "I flipped open my phone and I could hear Amanda screaming. Just a long, terrifying scream."

"Did she say anything, any words you could understand?" This excited utterance, as the law called it, was an exception to the hearsay rule. I was confident that the judge would allow Kate's testimony about this last call.

"First Amanda screamed. That's the only awful noise I could hear. Then she started crying and speaking to someone at the same time."

I lowered my voice and waited for Kate Meade to stop hyperventilating a bit. "Do you have any idea with whom she was speaking?"

Kate shook her head.

"Did you hear what she said?"

"Very clearly. She said, 'Brendan sent you, didn't he? Brendan sent you to kill me.' They're the last words I ever heard Amanda say."

"Did the other person ever speak while your phone line was open?"

"He didn't speak, Ms. Cooper. He just laughed. Amanda screamed one more time and the man just laughed."

I paused, letting the jury absorb the impact of the image Kate Meade had just recreated. "Was there anything distinctive about the laugh? Anything that you recognized or can describe to us, Mrs. Meade?"

"I remember he had a deep, gruff voice. He sounded like a madman, like he was enjoying the fact that he was torturing poor Amanda," she said, again pressing the handkerchief to her eyes. "I could still hear her screaming—more muffled at the end. And then the phone line went dead."

3

"I'm Lemuel Howell, Mrs. Meade. I'm sorry we haven't had the opportunity to meet before today, but I have some questions to ask you as well," he said to the witness, following a twenty-minute break given the jurors to refresh themselves. Howell wanted to make it clear to them that I had an advantage he had been denied.

He was polite and charming to Kate Meade, but whatever brief period of comfort she had achieved in recalling her friendship with Amanda during the first part of the direct examination had been wiped out by the last. Her body tensed up, and she wrung the handkerchief in her hands as her eyes darted back and forth between Brendan Quillian and his lawyer.

"So you've known Brendan for more than half your life, haven't you?" Howell had been standing behind his client, hands resting on his broad shoulders, and patted him on the back before walking closer to the jury box. He was telling the panel that he not only represented Quillian, but liked him, too.

Kate smiled wanly and nodded.

"You'll have to speak up, for the record," Judge Gertz said.

"Yes. Yes, sir. I'm thirty-four now. I met him when I was sixteen."

"Spent time with him during your high school days, did you?"

"Yes."

"Saw him often throughout your college years?"

"Occasionally."

Howell ticked off a litany of social events at which Kate Meade and the Quillians had spent time together. There were intimate family gatherings and celebrations of every variety, countless business functions in which the Meades had participated, and enough philanthropic work that both couples had engaged in that might have allowed the defendant to call on Mother Teresa as a character witness.

I had figured that Kate Meade would present the opportunity for Howell to put as much of Brendan's pedigree before the jury as Amanda's, and that she would establish for the defense some of his best qualities. It might even weigh in the decision that Howell would later have to make about whether to let his client testify. If he could establish enough of the defendant's good nature through the prosecution witnesses, he might not expose him to the cross-examination I so dearly wanted the chance to do.

But I had no other choice than to use Kate in my direct case. She gave me facts—the repeated separations that occurred in the middle of the night, the revelation that Amanda had chosen to end the marriage, and the last phone call before Amanda's death—that were among my strongest evidentiary links to Brendan's motive and role in the murder of his wife.

"I believe that you served on several nonprofit boards over the last decade, some organizations that do great work for the people of this city, am I right, Mrs. Meade?"

"Yes, I have."

One art museum, one major medical center, two diseases in need of a cure, and the junior committee of the best public library in America. Howell called out the name of each, his mellifluous voice investing them with even greater dignity.

"And was Brendan on any of those boards with you?"

"Yes," she answered quietly.

"I'm so sorry, Mrs. Meade," Howell said, cocking his head so that the jury could see how pleased he looked. "You did say yes to that, didn't you?"

"I did."

"And, let me see, God's Love We Deliver," he said, referring to a well-regarded New York City organization that delivers meals to terminally ill people in their homes. Lem was holding out one of his well-manicured hands as he counted fingers to mark Brendan's good works.

"No, no."

"No, ma'am? You're saying Brendan wasn't involved in that very noble cause?"

Howell said, pressing his arm across his chest in a false sign of distress.

"No, Mr. Howell, you're mistaken about *me*. I've never served on that board." Kate Meade was becoming flustered. She held out a hand with the crumpled handkerchief in the defendant's direction. "Brendan did."

"So, I am also correct that my client found time for even more community involvement than someone such as yourself, Mrs. Meade?" Howell asked, ticking off the names of four other charitable groups that Brendan helped.

"The Quillians were both very generous. It was Amanda's way."

Howell had made his point and moved on. "Your eldest daughter, Mrs. Meade, that would be Sara?"

Kate stiffened again, peeved that her child's name was being brought into the proceedings. She pursed her lips and stared at the defendant. "Yes."

"And you told us, in answer to Ms. Cooper's question, that the Quillians are her godparents, isn't that right?"

Her answer was another clipped "Yes."

Howell took the witness through another list of personal duties that established the close relationship between the nine-year-old girl and her parents' best friends—shared holidays, overnights when the Meades had other engagements, vacations together on ski trips and to beach resorts.

"In fact, with whom did Sara attend her first Yankee game last spring?"

"Brendan."

"With or without Amanda?"

"Without."

"And whom did you call to take Sara ice-skating in Central Park when your husband had the flu a few months before that?"

"Brendan."

Howell was getting nothing from Kate Meade. One-word answers seemed barely able to escape from her lips before she clamped them shut again.

"With or without Amanda."

"Without."

"So, I take it you never said to your daughter as you sent her out the door—and we all assume you love her dearly—'Now you watch out, Sara, 'cause your uncle Brendan, well, he's a murderer, did—'"

"Objection, Your Honor. Amanda Quillian was very much alive then."

Some of the jurors were chuckling along

with Howell—and with the defendant himself—always a bad thing to hear at a murder
trial. The hammer in my brain had resumed
its dull thud, reminding me that Lem had
something in store for Kate Meade.

"I'll allow it."

"No." Kate Meade was looking to me to
rescue her, but there was nothing I could do.

"And by the way, you never took stock
around the boardroom at the Museum of
Modern Art—or when he was raising millions of dollars for Mount Sinai Hospital—
you never said to any of your colleagues at
either institution that your dear friend Brendan Quillian wasn't to be trusted with your
money—or your life, did you?"

"Objection."

"Sustained," Judge Gertz said. "Let's
move on."

"Now, Alexandra—sorry, Ms. Cooper,"
Howell said, winking at me as though to
apologize for slipping into the familiar, so
that the jurors would know we had a friendship outside this arena. "Ms. Cooper asked
you about the night that Amanda Quillian
first appeared at your door, at one a.m. You
told us that you didn't see any injuries on
her face, isn't that right?"

"Yes."

"Well, did you call a doctor—that night or any day thereafter during the week?"

"No, no, I did not."

"Did you take Mrs. Quillian to an emergency room?"

"No."

"Did you call the police?"

"No."

"Was your husband at home with you that night?"

"Yes."

"And apart from him—that would be Preston Meade, am I right?—apart from your husband, did you tell anyone else about Amanda's visit?"

"No."

"Her parents?"

"No."

"Her sisters?"

"I've told you that I didn't," she snapped. "No one."

Howell was setting himself up nicely for his closing argument, three weeks away. He didn't want to ask Kate *why* she had told no one, because he was aware that the answer would be that Amanda had pleaded with her not to. Rather, he would leave the impression that things hadn't been serious enough to require any intervention. I made notes to try to clarify that question on my redirect of Kate Meade, hoping that the judge would think Howell had opened the door far enough to let me go there.

"Not even your nanny?" Howell asked. "Surely, Mrs. Meade, you have a nanny for your girls?"

"We do," she said, ruffled again. "I simply forgot about her, Your Honor. I—uh—I didn't mean to hide it."

Howell used his softest expression to try to calm her. "I didn't think you were doing any such thing. I'm sure your memory of those events isn't quite as clear now as it was back then. Did you tell the nanny why Amanda Quillian was staying at your apartment?"

"No. She knew Amanda was my best friend. I didn't have to tell her anything."

"Because she just worked for you, isn't that right?"

"Exactly," Kate answered, in a way that would not endear her to most of the jurors.

Howell was clever about subtly creating even more distance between them and my young socialite witness.

"Let me understand this, Mrs. Meade. When is the very first time you told any-one—anyone at all—about the night Amanda Quillian left Brendan to come stay with you?"

Kate paused to think. "The day I met Ms. Cooper. The detectives took me down to the District Attorney's Office the morning of October fourth. I told Ms. Cooper about it then."

"So, that was—my goodness—that was four—no, four and a half years after the night you've described, wasn't it?"

"I guess so."

Howell wasn't going to question her certainty about the timing. I had turned over Kate's datebook entry that confirmed she had made a record of her friend's brief estrangement from Quillian.

"And we all know how our memories of events, of conversations, of details—how they change over months and years." Howell was walking in front of the jury box now, one hand on the railing and the other adjusting his tie.

"I remember everything that happened with Amanda. I have a very good memory."

"But for telling me that your help—your

nanny—was at home that week, isn't that right?"

Kate was smart enough not to keep the battle going, and Howell knew he could weave her five-year silence into a suggestion that nothing had been more serious between the couple than an occasional lovers' quarrel.

"Now, when Brendan came to the door of your home, that first week, more than five years ago, didn't you ask him, Mrs. Meade—didn't you ask him to explain what he had done to upset your best friend so?"

"No."

"Didn't you ask him to tell you his side of the story?"

"I didn't need to ask him. Amanda had already told me."

"But surely, you would agree that there are two sides to every story, wouldn't you? Whether you wanted to hear what Brendan had to say or not?"

Howell was scoring twice. Not only was he making Kate Meade seem obstinate and small-minded, but he could later argue the same principle in the event the defendant didn't testify on his own behalf.

"Possibly."

"But you didn't even bother to ask, did you?" Howell said, speaking slowly and emphasizing each of the words in that short question with obvious disapproval.

Kate Meade was pouting in silence.

"You must answer the question," Gertz said to her.

"I did not."

"Ms. Cooper," Howell said, standing to my side and holding out his hand. "May I see People's Exhibit twelve?"

I removed the pile of photographs that had been admitted during my direct exam of Kate and handed him the one he asked for.

"Would you look at this again for us, Mrs. Meade?"

"Of course."

"Now, this is the actual photograph—the entire photograph—that you took at your lunch with Mrs. Quillian the terrible day she was killed, isn't it?"

"Yes."

"And this enlargement, on the easel, that's a close-up of her face made from this exact picture, am I right?"

"Yes, you are."

"This smaller picture actually captures a

bit more of the subject, of the entire scene, wouldn't you say?"

"Yes. You can see the restaurant awning behind Amanda's head, and the little bistro table we were sitting at. Her coffee cup, the sunglasses on top of the menu. Is that what you mean?"

"Exactly." Howell leaned on the edge of the witness stand and looked over Kate's shoulder at the image. "There appears to be a ring on Mrs. Quillian's finger, am I correct?"

I knew where Howell was going and I could have kicked myself for not pointing it out on my direct exam of Kate Meade. I intended to bring up the issue of the ring through the first cop on the scene and the Quillian housekeeper. Howell had taught me many years ago to gain the jury's trust by introducing any weakness in a case through the state's own witnesses, before the defense could expose them. I knew the ring was missing—stolen—by the time the police found Amanda's body. It hadn't occurred to me to introduce that fact through Kate.

"Now I know Ms. Cooper wouldn't neglect to notice a fine piece of jewelry, but I don't believe we've discussed this ring here today, have we, Mrs. Meade?"

"No. No, I wasn't asked to."

"Let me ask you then, do you recognize the ring Mrs. Quillian was wearing that day?"

"Yes. Yes, certainly."

"Now, I know it's big, and I know it's brilliant, and I know it's blue," Mr. Triplicate said, smiling at the jurors as he turned his back on Kate Meade. "What kind of stone was in that ring, if you happen to know?"

"A sapphire, Mr. Howell. It was a sapphire ring."

"And how many carats was it—or maybe I'm asking you to guess, in which case—"

"It's not a guess. I was with Amanda when she went back to the Schlumberger salon to have it sized. Six carats. It was a six-carat sapphire."

Howell let out a soft whistle as he stepped back. "So, that was her engagement ring?"

"No, no, it was not. Brendan couldn't have afforded anything like that when he asked Amanda to marry him."

"Well, do you know when she received the ring, or whether she bought it herself?"

"He gave it to her," Kate said, dipping her head in the defendant's direction.

"He? You mean Brendan? And when was that?"

"Two years ago. They had a tenth-anniversary party—Preston and I were there—and Brendan gave it to her then."

Howell twisted his shoulders and smiled to the jurors to show them he liked that fact. "Did she wear it often?"

"Every day."

"Was she wearing that ring when she stood up from this very table in the photograph and said good-bye to you on October third?"

"Yes, sir."

"And you're aware, are you not, that when the police and the housekeeper found Mrs. Quillian's body shortly after that—after your call to 911—the ring was missing?"

"That's right."

Howell would want to argue to the jury that the serious anniversary gift was a sign that the Quillians had reconciled their differences in a sentimental, and expensive, manner. And he would use the theft of the ring by the killer to argue robbery as the motive for Amanda's death. Mike Chapman referred to the over-the-top bauble as a guilt gift from the defendant, and he explained its disappearance as an obvious staging of the scene—the taking of a significant jewel and the superficial ransacking of drawers and tables near the victim's body meant to encourage police to think first of a push-in robbery as the killer's plan.

Howell was jumping from topic to topic now, rattling Kate Meade with the uncertainty of what direction he would next take.

"I'll get back to that 911 call in a minute, but let me ask you a few more questions about the day you sent your daughter skating with Mr. Quillian."

Kate stiffened again, I assumed at the second mention of her child in this public forum. "Your Honor, may I speak with my lawyer?" she asked, turning to Judge Gertz.

"Are you talking about Ms. Cooper? She's not your lawyer, Mrs. Meade—she represents the state," the judge said, trying to calm her. "Let's finish your testimony and get you on your way."

I clasped my hands together on the table, waiting for Lem's warning to strike its target. Kate wanted to tell me something and I feared that my adversary knew exactly what it was.

"I'm talking about a day in February of last year, do you recall that?" Howell said softly but firmly.

Kate seemed suddenly drained of all color, her jaw again locked tightly in place. "Yes."

"Did you go to the Quillian home for the purpose of picking Sara up after the skating party, at about five o'clock?"

"Yes."

"Objection, Your Honor. May we approach?"

Artie Tramm led Kate off the stand as Howell and I walked before the judge and I whispered the reasons for my objection.

"This is beyond the scope of my direct. Way beyond. There's no reason to bring the Meade children or a spin around the ice into this."

"I gave you a lot of latitude on direct, didn't I, Alex?" Gertz asked.

"I'll get right to it, Your Honor," Howell said. "It's not about the little girl. It's about a conversation this witness had with my client and his wife. Ms. Cooper brought some of those out on her case. I'd say it's relevant, it's probative, and it's admissible."

"Step back. Let's see where you're going with this."

Artie Tramm walked up behind us and spoke to Gertz over my shoulder. "This gonna be much longer, Judge? The witness isn't feeling too good. Maybe it's the heat or something. You don't want her getting sick in the courtroom."

"Keep it moving. We'll break for lunch as soon as Lem is done with her."

Kate reluctantly climbed the two steps to the stand, and I perched on the edge of my seat, ready to interrupt if the cross went off subject.

"Now, your memory of events of a year and a half ago, would you say that's as good as your memory of events of five years ago?"

She dropped her head. "Yes."

"Were you alone when you went to the Quillian home the day of the skating event?"

"No. I was with my two little girls and their nanny."

"Was Amanda there?"

"No, no. She had gone on a museum trip to Vienna."

"You knew she was out of the country when you called Brendan to ask your little favor, didn't you?"

"Yes, but—"

"Did your nanny and the children stay on there with you and Mr. Quillian?"

"No." I could barely hear the word. "She took them to a movie."

"But you chose to remain?"

No answer.

"Did you stay at the Quillian home?"

Kate Meade was having a meltdown before my very eyes. I'd asked her about every one of her conversations with Brendan Quillian, and she had not remembered—or not offered to me—the details of this one.

"Yes. To talk about Amanda."

I glanced across at Lem. He was standing next to his client, one hand resting on his shoulder, the other jabbing through the air at Kate Meade. He had his most serious expression on display as he savored his moment, the witness pinned to the ropes as Howell made it clear to the jury that he was fighting for his client's life.

"Did you indeed talk about your best friend, Amanda Quillian, that early evening?"

She swallowed hard and coughed to clear her throat. "Yes, we did."

"By the way, in which room did you have this discussion?"

She coughed again. "Brendan's den. On the second floor of the house."

Howell paused, letting go of Quillian and taking a few steps closer to the witness stand. He poured a cup of water from my pitcher—Kate had not touched the one in front of her—and held it out to her. "You seem parched, dry, thirsty, perhaps. May I give you this?"

She pushed his arm away and shook her head from side to side. The internal butterflies seemed to be multiplying at a furious pace in my gut. Kate Meade, Brendan Quillian, and Lem Howell knew facts that I did not.

"Did you ask my client for something to drink that evening?"

Kate looked at Brendan with contempt, almost sneering at him in full view of the jury. "I did."

"And what did you drink?"

"Wine. Too much red wine."

"Did there come a time when your conversation stopped?"

"Yes."

"Is that when you left, Mrs. Meade? Is that when you left Brendan's home?"

Artie Tramm moved closer to the stand. It looked as if my witness was going to faint.

"Did you leave the Quillians' house after your chat with my client, to go home to your ill husband and your precious little girls?"

"Not immediately."

"You remember what you did next?"

"I was drunk, Mr. Howell. I can hardly remember—"

"I'm relying on the fact that you told all of us today what a very good memory you have, Mrs. Meade. Isn't that when you—"

Kate clamped a hand on the railing in front of her and raised her voice. "He—he took advantage of me—of my condition, Mr. Howell."

"Would you tell these good people, please." Lem stood behind me, sweeping his left arm in a wide arc across the front of the jury box. "Isn't that when you quite voluntarily engaged in an act of sexual intercourse with Brendan Quillian, the husband of your lifelong best friend?"

4

"The sign on the door still says ladies, doesn't it?" I asked Mike.

The four stalls behind me were empty in the dingy gray-tiled bathroom around the corner from my eighth-floor office. I had filled a sink with ice-cold water and was splashing it on my face while he watched.

"I just came in to make sure you hadn't flushed yourself out of the building. What the hell's taking you so long?"

"I needed a quiet place to think. No Monday-morning quarterbacks, no phone calls from the boss, no excuses from Kate Meade. I'm trying to cool down."

"It's like a hot box in here."

"I'm adjusting my temper, not my body heat. Keep that woman away from me or I'll kill her."

Judge Gertz had recessed the proceedings for lunch and I was trying to regroup after the shock of Meade's testimony. I dried off and picked up my pale yellow suit jacket from the wooden table below the mirror.

"I thought broads don't sweat."

"We don't. I *perspired*. I sat in front of those jurors while my star witness was eviscerated in silken-smooth form by Lem Howell, turned crimson from the top of my scalp to the soles of my feet, and willed the tears I was holding back not to fall so that they trickled out through every pore of my body instead."

"I got lunch sitting on your desk. C'mon."

"I'm too nauseous to eat."

I had waited in the courtroom until the judge declared a recess and Artie Tramm had cleared it of all spectators. I called my paralegal, Maxine, from my cell phone and asked her to send Mike up with Mercer Wallace, the six-foot-six first-grade detective who was Mike's closest friend and former partner.

They had flanked me as I walked down the long corridor to the elevator, past the more aggressive members of the press corps who wanted my reaction to the testimony.

I obeyed Mercer's direction to walk on without turning my head, ignoring the questions reporters tossed at me about Kate Meade and whether the shocking information would affect the rest of my case.

"Hey, Alex—you look like you just got hit by a Mack truck. You call that leading off with your best shot or what?" one reporter yelled out as he tried, with no luck, to thrust a microphone past Mercer's arm, while another asked if I expected to keep things as lively as this every day of the trial.

Mike opened the door of the restroom and walked me the short distance to my office. My secretary, Laura, would screen my calls while I'd try to regroup with the advice of the two detectives, who had as much experience in the courtroom as I did.

Mercer was standing in the doorway talking to Laura but grabbed my arm as I walked by. "I've got Kate in the conference room down the hall. You've got to see her."

"What I really have to do is revise my strategy for the afternoon. This witness blew up in my face, taking her dignity—and all her credibility—with her. Lem stuck it to me right before we started this morning, and now I've got to think about the wisdom of using any of Amanda's other friends on the stand. I need to get some forensics before this jury today. I've got to make them understand what a brutal killing this was. Kate Meade can take a hike."

I picked up the phone and dialed the medical examiner's office.

"You've got to calm her down, Coop," Mike said. "You can't just let her walk out the door to the wolves."

I shook a finger at him. "I should take lessons in etiquette and interpersonal relationships from you? Forget it. You deal with her. You be the diplomat for a change."

Jerome Genco, the pathologist who had autopsied Amanda Quillian, came on the line. "Sorry to do this to you, Jerry, but I need you in one hour. You're going to have to testify this afternoon."

"You told me next week. I have it on my calendar for Thursday."

"Is there a body on the table?"

"No. I'm working up some frozen slides—"

"Jerry, I've got to have you today. Max is sending a patrol car from the Fifth Precinct to pick you up—lights and sirens. Put the slides back on ice and save me, okay? You're going on right after the first cop who found the body."

I hung up and headed for the file cabinet that held the rest of the medical evidence.

"Alex," Mercer said, "Kate's your witness. She'll be wailing all afternoon."

"A little time for reflection might be good for her conscience. I'll put Genco on first and then you have to help me figure out something else that will make a strong impression before the end of the day."

"Don't be stubborn, now. She's hysterical and she's scared to death. Can't even imagine facing her husband tonight."

"She should have thought about that before she gave it up to Brendan Quillian."

Mercer held out his hand to me. "Get it done."

I followed him down the corridor, with

Mike trailing us. The slim woman appeared to have shrunken even more inside her suit. Her chest was heaving between sobs, and the tears running down to her chin had streaked through her makeup.

"I hate you!" she shrieked as she looked up at me. "I hate all of you! You've destroyed my life. Why did you let that man do that to me?"

"Mrs. Meade, there was only one way for me to protect you from that—that piece of information. I told you from the outset," I said, although the idea that she had been sexually involved with Quillian had never occurred to me, "that there was nothing more important in this case than your candor, your honesty."

"But I told you the truth. I swear it's all true."

I put both my hands on the table, at the far end facing Kate. "I said that I needed to know *every* conversation you ever had with Brendan from the time Amanda first tried to leave him—the night he smacked her across the face. You never mentioned being alone with him, sipping wine in his den by the fireplace after the blizzard—not to mention—"

"That—that encounter had nothing to do with Amanda's murder."

"It had everything to do with Brendan, though, didn't it? How could you possibly think he wouldn't use that—what would you call it, Mercer?" I looked over at him before turning back to Kate. "*Encounter* just doesn't nail it for me. That *tryst*? That betrayal of your best friend?"

I was trying to control my temper and hold my tongue. We ruined her life? How long had she been waiting, been thinking, about getting into bed with Quillian?

"Amanda didn't love him anymore. I've told you that. Their entire reconciliation was an accommodation to keep Brendan in the Keating business. To stop Amanda from telling her father about the fact that she wanted to leave Brendan, while Mr. Keating was still alive. Then she had to keep the charade going after his death or Brendan would have walked off with half the Keating fortune." Kate grimaced and barked out the last sentence. "It was all about the money."

"And you? What was it about for you?" I tried to make eye contact with her, but she put her hands over her face.

"I was having my own problems at the

time. And they are none of your business," she said, pointing her finger at me and then repeating the gesture at Mike and Mercer. "And you, Ms. Cooper, why didn't you get up when that—that—shyster was done and ask me to explain the circumstances of that evening? You should have—"

My eyes widened. "How could I possibly have known you had something to say that would have restored any credibility to your testimony when I didn't even know that one-night stand had occurred? It was as though you handed Brendan Quillian a loaded gun, aimed to blow my case apart and take both of us out with it. Did you think for one minute he wouldn't use that night to discredit you?"

"Never."

"Whatever drugs you're on, Mrs. Meade," Mike said, "I'd like a handful."

"There . . . are . . . rules, Detective," she said in a clipped, angry voice. "There are just some things that one never—"

"Dream on, lady. Maybe they got regs in the Social Register that I don't know about, but this scumbag's on trial for friggin' homicide. Quillian paid or hired or leaned on some bastard to kill his wife, and if you thought he was gonna let you sit there and nail him for all the world to see like you didn't flop down on your back for him and throw your legs up in the air, you're insane."

Kate Meade had never been addressed that way, I was sure. She sat up straight and directed her venom at Mike. "I never asked for any of this. I never wanted to come here and talk about these things in a court of law. This wouldn't have happened if you hadn't forced me to come down to this office that day in October. Now how am I supposed to go on with my life?"

"Mrs. Meade, you're the one who called 911," I said. "You're the only person in the world who heard what Amanda said to her killer. You hurled yourself at me last fall, telling me you'd do anything in the world to help find the man who murdered her. Nobody forced you to do this."

"I'm sorry I ever told any of you what I heard," she said, dissolving into tears again.

"What I most need to know from you right now is whether every word you said in that courtroom is true."

Her answer was smothered as she cradled her head in her folded arms.

"What did you say?"

"Why would I have lied?"

"Because it seems to me your feelings about Brendan Quillian are a bit complicated, at the very least. Mr. Howell is going to tell the jurors to disregard every single fact you gave to them because—trust me, he'll think of a reason—because you hate Brendan for what he did to you that night or you hate him because he didn't do enough for you after that night. He might even tell them you want to see him convicted because of your own guilt for betraying your best friend."

She lifted her head, shaking it as though she had never thought of any of these things. "Why don't they despise Brendan as much as I do? He's the one who was unfaithful to Amanda, lots of times."

Kate knew that I had other evidence of the defendant's philandering. But I certainly hadn't needed her to make that point so dramatically and so personally before the jury.

"And what do you get?" Mike asked, anticipating the next morning's tabloid take on my first witness. "The Park Avenue Neighborhood Association Desperate Housewife of the Year award? You've cratered our whole case. There's not a word you said today that the jury'll give any weight to."

Mike's beeper went off and he opened the door to step out into the hallway.

I could hear Kate Meade draw breath. "You mean I've done this for nothing? I've— I've exposed myself to all this public humiliation for no reason?"

"You have something more serious to think about right now," I said. "We've got to get you out of here by the back door so the photographers don't ambush you. My paralegal will get police officers to take you home."

"Photographers waiting for me? Why in the world would they—" The answer seemed to hit her as soon as she formed the question. She stood up and walked toward me. "You've got to come with me, Ms. Cooper. I can't face my family alone."

"I'm due back in court in forty-five minutes. I won't be able to help you with this. I'm a prosecutor, Kate, not a social worker."

"I'll take you. I'll stay till your husband gets home," Mercer said. He had worked in the Special Victims Unit for almost ten years, one of the only African-American detectives in the NYPD to hold the rank of first grade. Like me, he thrived on the highly charged emotional connections in this category of crimes, which required extra sensitivity on the part of the investigator. Mike Chapman, on the other hand, worked best when there was no one to hand-hold, when the cold, hard facts were teased out of the victim's remains and the physical evidence. He loved being a homicide cop.

Kate Meade tugged on Mercer's sleeve like a child hoping not to get lost in a crowd. "You've got to make sure there are no pictures in the newspapers."

"I'll allow Detective Wallace to take you home, Mrs. Meade. But only on the condition that you tell him every detail—I don't care how intimate, I don't care how embarrassing—about what went on between you and your friend Brendan. By the time I see Mercer later tonight, if there is anything Lem Howell knows about you that I don't, there'll be hell to pay."

I turned on my heels to go back to my office to wait for Jerry Genco.

"Slow down," Mike said, pulling me into the alcove next to the conference room. "Do me a favor—don't buy any lottery tickets today."

"Now what? Genco's stuck in traffic?"

"Someone got to Marley."

"How? What do you mean? He's on Rikers Island." Mike had come up with a witness, a thirty-two-year-old burglar from the island of Jamaica who was awaiting trial on a string of break-ins when Amanda Quillian was murdered.

"Got out of jail free. Went directly to the operating room at Bellevue Hospital."

"What for?" It had taken me weeks to negotiate a cooperation agreement with Marley's lawyer, whose client would testify that six months before Amanda's murder, Brendan Quillian had offered him twenty thousand dollars to kill his wife.

"Snitch fever."

The only prisoners lower on the totem pole than pedophiles were rats. "He's sick?"

"You would be, too, if someone stuck a shiv between your fifth and sixth thoracic vertebrae while you were working out in the yard."

"You think it's related to the case? Will he live?"

"It's all about the case. Count on it. Critical but stable."

I shook my head and continued on my way. "Yeah, maybe it's just a jailhouse—"

"I mean they cut off a clump of Marley's dreads and shoved them in his throat to try to choke him to death. The message was pretty clear that somebody doesn't want him to talk."

5

The cops in the patrol car who got the message from the 911 dispatcher to respond to the Quillian home were there within six minutes of the call. Although they were the closest unit to the location, they had been double-parked in front of a deli to buy sandwiches and lost more time while stuck behind school buses stacked to pick up students from trips to the Metropolitan Museum of Art. Police officer Timothy Denton referred to his memo book, with the court's permission, as he recited the times he had recorded in it.

"When you turned into the block between Fifth and Madison Avenues, did you observe any unusual activity?"

"No, ma'am."

"Did you see any pedestrians?"

"Yes, ma'am. Mostly kids. A few adults, all women."

"Did you see anyone running from the location?"

"No, I did not."

The rookie cop wasn't much less nervous than Kate Meade.

"Were you able to enter the Quillian residence?"

"Not right away. The door was locked. My partner rang the bell while I tried the service door to see if it was open," Denton said. I was accounting for more critical minutes that had elapsed while Amanda Quillian lay inside on the living room floor. "Then I climbed up on the railing of the stoop to check if I could force open a window, but they had bars over the glass, so there wasn't any use."

"What did you do next?"

"I'd already radioed once for a backup unit. I called again and asked for ESU."

"Would you please tell the jury what those initials stand for?"

"Sorry. Yeah. It's the Emergency Services Unit. They do all the rescues and stuff. People stuck in elevators or jumpers on bridges. Called for them 'cause they have the battering rams to open doors."

"Who was the next person to arrive at the Quillian house?"

Denton looked at his memo pad and repeated the name he had written there. "It was maybe ten minutes later. This young woman came—with a set of keys. Said she worked for Mrs. Meade, the lady who called 911. She was the babysitter."

"Did you enter the town house?"

"Yeah, me and my partner. He opened the front door with the keys. We made the girl wait outside and we went in."

"Can you tell us what you found?"

Denton ran the back of his hand over the top of his buzz cut and down his neck. He swallowed hard. "My partner—Bobby Jamison—he was ahead of me. We went in the entryway. Something must have caught his eye—"

"Objection."

Judge Gertz admonished the young cop, "Just tell us what you observed and what you did."

"Yes, sir." Denton turned back to the jurors. "He stepped off to the left, into—well, like a parlor, I guess. I walked straight ahead. Then, I—um—I heard this kind of noise. Sort of a gagging noise. I doubled back."

"What did you see?"

"That's when I saw the body—the lady on the floor."

"She was making a gagging noise?" Gertz asked, incredulous, because he thought he was familiar with the facts of the case.

"The sound you heard," I interrupted to ask Denton, trying to keep control of the witness in the face of jurors who had already seen me sabotaged by a character in my own case. "What was the source of that?"

"Was she?" Gertz said again.

Denton's head moved back and forth between me and the judge. "No, sir. The corpse was already dead." Yogi Berra couldn't have said it any better. Denton sheepishly looked to the jurors for some sign of understanding, then answered me. "That was my partner, Officer Jamison, making the noise. Throwing up. It was his first DOA."

Despite my many hours of prepping Denton for his court appearance, he had always seemed more focused on Jamison's reaction than Amanda Quillian's condition.

I walked him through the events that followed, trying to leave as little room as possible for Lem Howell to paint the pair of rookies as Keystone Kops. Bobby Jamison's physical response to encountering the murder victim had obviously contaminated an area of the crime scene. No, neither man had worn rubber gloves or booties in the house; yes, Denton had moved the body a bit to keep clear of the problem his partner had created; and, no, they hadn't called to report the homicide until after they had cleaned up Jamison's mess.

"Were there any signs of forced entry?"

"No, ma'am."

Howell would argue that the killer was a street person who had pushed in after his victim unlocked the door. It was Chapman's view—with Brendan Quillian conveniently out of town and the housekeeper on her regular day off—that the defendant had given the killer access to the home, so that he could lie in wait for Amanda as she entered alone after her luncheon date.

Howell's cross-examination was a well-organized punch list of activities that the most casual of television viewers had come to expect of crime-scene responders. Tim Denton had been oblivious to just about every rule as he tended his unsteady partner on that fall afternoon, and the volley of *No*'s he gave in response to the questions seemed endless.

"I have no redirect of Officer Denton," I said when Howell ceded the witness back to me and nodded at me with a smile.

The entryway of the town house and the area surrounding Amanda Quillian's lifeless body had been hopelessly compromised by the first two cops on the scene. If the killer had left any trace evidence near her, he couldn't have asked for more than the timely arrival of Jamison and Denton.

"You want a recess before you call your next witness?"

"May I have ten minutes?" I didn't need the time, but I counted on it to let the jurors stretch their legs and come back fresh to a more compelling witness.

"Sure," Gertz said. "Why don't we give the jurors a short break."

Max signaled me from her third-row seat that Jerry Genco had arrived and was waiting in the witness room. Artie Tramm let me slip out of the courtroom to the small cubicle off the locked hallway, and I confirmed with the pathologist the points that would be covered in his testimony.

"Dr. Genco," I asked as the trial resumed, after he had completed the details of his medical education and training as a forensic pathologist and been qualified in his area of expertise, "for how long have you been employed at the Office of the Chief Medical Examiner of the City of New York?"

"Three years."

"I'd like to direct your attention to a date last fall, the late afternoon of October third. Do you recall that day?"

"Yes, I do."

"What was your assignment at that time?"

"I was catching cases," he said, speaking to the jurors in the manner of a professional witness who had testified many times before, and explaining the steps that he was obligated to perform at a crime scene. "I was on call to respond to any homicides reported between eight a.m. and six p.m."

Jerry Genco, expecting a day in the morgue's lab, was casually dressed in a sports jacket and chinos. He was in sore need of a haircut and a small screw to replace the Band-Aid that held one earpiece of his glasses to the edge of the frame, but his smart, studied answers were in sharp contrast to the nervous manner of Kate Meade.

"Would you tell us, please, what time it was and who was present when you arrived at the Quillian town house?"

"It was four thirty, and I was admitted to the home by Detective Michael Chapman, Manhattan North Homicide Squad. There were two uniformed officers from the Nineteenth Precinct there, three other homicide detectives, and Hal Sherman, from the Crime Scene Unit."

"Any civilians?"

"There was a woman identified to me as the housekeeper, but we never spoke. Someone had called her and she was brought in just as I arrived."

"What happened when you entered?"

"Chapman led me through the vestibule into an adjacent room, like a small sitting area with several armchairs and a sofa. In the middle of the floor, on the carpet, was the body of Amanda Quillian."

"Would you describe for us what you observed?"

Genco faced the jury box and gave a clinical description of the scene. "I saw the body of a Caucasian woman who appeared to be in her midthirties, fully clothed, lying on her back, apparently dead."

He was more artful than Tim Denton in talking about the grotesque bruising on the slim neck of the victim, the protruding tongue hanging to the side of her mouth, and the pinpoint hemorrhages that dotted her still-open eyes.

Genco carefully described what he set about to do to pronounce the manner of Mrs. Quillian's death, the legal classification that made it a homicide, rather than a natural event. The causation—the medical finding of the mechanism responsible for the death—was fairly obvious to anyone looking at the victim's throat, but not able to be legally confirmed until autopsy.

This was not like the many cases in which the determination of the time of death played a critical role in the case, making measures of postmortem rigor, lividity, body temperature, and ocular changes significant. Here, instead, the parameters were tightly drawn by the hour and minute stamped on the digital photograph taken at the end of the ladies' lunch, the phone records from Amanda Quillian's cell as she was confronted by her killer, and the 911 call from Kate Meade.

So Dr. Genco moved his audience from the exquisitely appointed parlor in which he first saw the body of the deceased to the formaldehyde-scented room decorated only with a cold steel gurney in the basement of the morgue.

He described photographing his charge, undressing her, washing her body, and autopsying it. He didn't need a receipt from the tony bistro where the friends had dined to assert that the victim's last meal had been a Cobb salad with blue-cheese dressing. Stomach contents visible to the naked eye underscored that death had occurred within a short time after the ingestion of food. The two glasses of white wine she had

sipped might have made it even more difficult for her to resist her attacker.

"Were you able to determine, Doctor, to a
reasonable degree of medical certainty,
what caused the death of Amanda Quillian?"

"Yes, Ms. Cooper, I was."

"Would you please tell the jury about your
conclusions?"

"Mrs. Quillian died as a result of asphyxia,
and in particular in this matter, by compression of the neck—or strangulation."

"What is asphyxia, Dr. Genco?"

"It's actually a broad term referring to
conditions that result in the failure of cells to
receive or to utilize oxygen, along with the
inability to eliminate carbon dioxide. Body
tissues simply cannot function without oxygen. Most especially the brain, since it uses
twenty percent of the body's total available
oxygen."

"Is there more than one category of asphyxia?"

"Yes, in general there are three. One
would be chemical asphyxia—things like
carbon monoxide or cyanide poisoning,
which operate by excluding oxygen from
the brain. A second would be suffocation or
obstruction of the airways."

"Let me stop you here for a moment, Dr. Genco, at these first two categories. In the case of both chemical asphyxia and suffocation, is it correct to say that the resulting death might occur homicidally?"

"Yes, Ms. Cooper. You're right—in some circumstances. But in both instances death might also be accidental. And in the case of suffocation, it's frequently self-inflicted." Genco went on to give examples of each to the jury. "One may have a choking fatality because of the unintentional inhalation of an object—a wine cork or the cap of a pen that someone puts in his or her mouth temporarily, but then it gets sucked in and occludes the airway. Same thing happens with a piece of food."

Several jurors nodded their heads in understanding.

"Now, Doctor, what is the third form of asphyxial death?"

"Compression of the neck, Ms. Cooper—usually by strangulation."

"Are there different methods of strangulation?"

"Yes, there are. Again, we usually break these down into three varieties. Those would be hanging, ligature strangulation, and manual strangulation."

"Can you distinguish between accidental, intentional, and homicidal deaths in the case of asphyxia by strangulation?"

Genco spoke confidently to the jurors farthest from the stand. "Most of the time, of course. The overwhelming number of hangings are suicides—it's not a method frequently used as a means of killing someone."

The jury was following his analysis. "With ligature strangulation, although you do get a few accidents, virtually all the cases are homicides—probably the most common form of homicidal asphyxia."

"And by *ligature,* tell us what you mean exactly."

"Certainly, Ms. Cooper. I'm referring to a bond of some kind—electrical cord, rope, wire, necktie—an object used to encircle the neck horizontally, occluding blood and oxygen from reaching the brain."

"That's distinguished from manual strangulation, is it not?"

"Quite easily, in fact. Manual strangulation—death caused by using one's hands to compress the neck of another—can never be anything but homicide."

"Would you please tell the jury why, Dr. Genco?"

He straightened his glasses and looked earnestly at the people in the box. "It's not possible to use your own hands to strangle yourself. Pressure on the neck is a very intentional, deliberate action. The first thing such excessive pressure causes is a loss of consciousness. So that if you were holding your own throat until the point at which you passed out, you couldn't possibly continue to keep the grip on. You'd regain consciousness as soon as your hands dropped away."

I wanted him to go through every second of Amanda Quillian's final agony. I wanted them to understand that her last moments were spent face-to-face with her attacker, at less than arm's length, while he purposefully squeezed the life out of her body.

"Can you estimate for us, with a reasonable degree of medical certainty, how long it was that Mrs. Quillian remained conscious while her neck was being compressed?"

Genco took his time with the answer, trying to explain the dynamic of this death mechanism without drawing an objection for any prejudicial statement. "Strangulation, you must understand, does not cause death as quickly, say, as a bullet to the brain or a stab wound to the heart. There is evidence here that despite her small stature and weight, the deceased put up a struggle—a fierce struggle—for her life."

Several jurors began to wriggle in their seats as they followed his testimony. Genco paused, asking permission of Judge Gertz to step to the easel and refer to an enlargement of one of the autopsy photographs I had introduced through him half an hour earlier. I handed him a pointer and he got back to work.

"These marks on the neck of the deceased represent the force used by her assailant to subdue her, and then to cause her death." He tapped at several large bruises on her throat as he spoke. "Repeated applications of force, actually, suggesting that she was struggling against him while he tried to fasten his grip more tightly. All of that fighting prolonged the process of the strangulation."

The finger marks of the killer looked enormous to me, causing not only the external bruising but the hemorrhaging deep into the musculature that Genco's dissection of the throat had revealed. I had studied the images for months, thinking constantly of someone with hands big enough, strong enough, to cause that damage. Someone with hands much larger than Brendan Quillian's, which detectives had examined at the time of his arrest.

"Is there any other physical evidence to suggest that unconsciousness did not occur immediately after Mrs. Quillian was attacked?"

"Yes, Ms. Cooper. All the medical hallmarks of manual strangulation are present."

"Would you identify those to the jury?"

Genco pointed to the small, crescent-shaped marks that bordered the larger discolorations. "Can you see these small semicircles?" he asked the jurors, most of whom were nodding. "These abrasions weren't made by the killer. They were left there by the fingernails of the deceased herself."

Brendan Quillian had assumed a posture of faux anguish. His shoulders were slumped and he held his head in one hand, shaking it from time to time as though incredulous that someone could have done these things to his wife.

A few jurors seemed surprised, until Genco went on with his explanation. "Mrs. Quillian was struggling against her attacker to breathe, fighting for her very life. Like every victim of strangulation whose arms aren't bound, she tried to free her airway of the hands that were restricting it. She didn't mean to scratch herself, but each time her assailant increased the pressure on her neck, she fought to claw his hands off her—unsuccessfully despite a number of attempts.

"This is a very slow and deliberate way to kill someone," Genco said. His glasses were cockeyed on his nose and he adjusted them again. He looked up. "Strangulation is an especially painful way to die."

Howell knew better than to object. The damage had been done with the forensic pathologist's assertion, and the defense position was simply to distance Brendan Quillian from the murderous act of whatever lone thug had committed the crime. Howell leaned over to stroke his client's back, to suggest that he needed to be comforted during this graphic description of Amanda's death.

I took Genco through each set of finger-nail scratches, hoping jurors could imagine the fourth, fifth, and sixth times that Amanda Quillian scratched at the massive pair of hands to gasp for air. I looked for their reactions out of the corner of my eye as the doctor explained the abrasion on the tip of the young woman's chin, which he said had been injured when she lowered it in the vain effort to protect her fragile neck.

"Back to the question I asked, Doctor, about whether you can estimate the length of time you believe Mrs. Quillian fought before losing consciousness?"

"Yes, Ms. Cooper, I can. Were there constant compression of the carotid arteries, for example, one might become unconscious in fifteen or twenty seconds. But that isn't the case here."

Genco repeated the rest of the autopsy findings: the congestion of Amanda's face, which had become cyanotic—tinged with a blue cast—above the site of the compression; the pinpoint hemorrhaging in the whites of her eyes and densely spread throughout the eyelids themselves; and the fracture of the hyoid bone, a horseshoe-shaped structure at the base of the tongue, crushed by the deadly reapplications of force.

"I would say that the nature and number of injuries to Mrs. Quillian's neck and face, as well as those she sustained internally, suggest that the struggle may have lasted for as long as two or three minutes. Perhaps even four," Genco said, looking up at the clock above the doors at the rear of the courtroom.

In my closing argument, I would repeat the medical findings and stand silently in the well of the courtroom while the second hand swept slowly around the dial four times, reminding the jurors how very long that time took to elapse. The death throes of Amanda Quillian had been excruciating, and I would make that point at every possible opportunity.

I would also have the chance, then, to suggest to them our theory that as Brendan Quillian had ordered, the enormous sapphire ring was wrenched off Amanda's finger, and the area around the still-warm body was ransacked to create the illusion of a botched burglary. The killer had the great good fortune to be out the door and away from the town house with barely two minutes to spare before the first cops came within half a block of the scene of the crime.

I was almost at the end of Jerry Genco's direct exam, with just a few points to clean up. The jurors and indeed the spectators seemed sobered by his testimony, following the morning's unexpected entertainment from Kate Meade. "Did you have an opportunity to meet Brendan Quillian?"

Genco lifted the damaged eyeglass frame and focused his attention on the defendant, who sat upright and returned the stare. "Yes, I did. He came to my office the following day, October fourth."

I didn't bother with questions about his demeanor. I would argue that it had been part of his plan to play the grieving widower. "Did he tell you where he had been on October third?"

"Yes, he mentioned that he was in Boston. That he took the shuttle back to New York late in the evening, after Detective Chapman had notified him of the death of his wife."

"Did you examine any part of the defendant's face or body?"

"Yes, actually I did."

"What were you looking for?"

Quillian's hands were folded in front of him, resting on the counsel's table. His fingers were long and slender, unlikely weapons in this matter, which we'd known from the outset.

"Detective Chapman and I were convinced the killer would have been injured in this struggle as well. I expected if we found him early enough, there would be lacerations—probably numerous cuts and scratches—caused by the victim's frenzied fight for her life, on his face and hands," Genco said, looking squarely at the defendant. "Mr. Quillian had no such injuries."

I was about ready to relinquish my witness to Lem Howell, running my eyes down the checklist of facts that I had planned to cover on direct before I asked the judge to issue the grim photographs to the jury.

The silence occasioned by Genco's recounting of Amanda's last minutes alive was broken by loud voices coming from the rear of the courtroom. As with all high-profile trials in Manhattan, every seat in the house was filled, and a line of onlookers queued in the hallway to fill the place of any departing spectator.

The lone court officer in charge of the flow was pushing and shoving a tall, pale-faced man in a blue seersucker suit who was trying to break past him.

I glanced over my shoulder again as Judge Gertz banged his gavel to restore order.

Preston Meade, the cuckolded husband of Kate, was shouting my name as he charged toward the railing that separated the benches from where I stood.

6

"He only wanted to publicly humiliate you, kid. Like you did to him this morning."

"Me? I didn't do anything to him except—"

"Except completely misjudge the character of your first witness," Mike said. "Mr. Meade was probably hoping that if he made a big enough stir inside the courthouse, it would trump the news story of his wife's infidelity."

Judge Gertz had quelled the commotion and allowed Lem Howell to end the session—keeping the jury later than planned—

with his cross-examination of Dr. Genco. It was after six when Mike and I returned to my office to make the phone calls confirming the appearances of the next day's witnesses.

"You changing the batting order?"

I was scratching out names and shifting some of the civilian witnesses to the next week. "You bet. I'm sticking with forensics at the moment. Cold, clinical facts."

I dialed the beepers and home numbers of the crime-scene analysts who had scoured the Quillian town house unsuccessfully for fingerprints, photographed the entryway and the parlor, and tried to give the lab techs something to work with, as well as the forensic biologist who had spent painstaking hours vainly trying to find nanograms of DNA on items that had been on or around the victim's body. By seven fifteen, I had restructured my case presentation and was ready to quit for the night.

"Let's check the tube and see how they play the day," Mike said, starting out for the public relations office on the main corridor of the eighth-floor hallway. The press secretary, Brenda Whitney, had the responsibility of monitoring media accounts—on television and in print—of all the office cases that attracted attention for daily reports to Paul Battaglia, the longtime district attorney of New York County.

"Did Brenda leave you the key?" She had a bank of television sets that ran all day so that her staff could follow national news stories—Battaglia's creative white-collar investigations that frequently shook up the financial industry—and feeds from the local networks that replayed around the clock.

Mike dangled the key over his shoulder as he walked out my door. "Follow me. One cycle of breaking news and then you can feed me. Mercer will meet us for dinner in an hour."

"I've told you I can't eat," I said, picking up some folders to take home and turning out the lights.

"We need to keep your strength up for the rest of the battle. I think Lem's been chewing steak knives to sharpen his teeth for the kill."

We let ourselves into the pressroom and Mike flipped on one of the TVs. The local all-news channel repeated its headlines three times an hour, and it took only minutes until they reran the end-of-the-day broadcast from the courthouse steps.

Mercer had done his job well. He had spirited Kate Meade out the back door so the press had no photo ops, no footage with which to tell her story. Instead, they got shots of Preston Meade being led away from the building by three uniformed officers who had surrounded him when Judge Gertz ejected him from the proceedings.

The telegenic Lem Howell smoothed his hair back and smiled for the cameras. He'd never met a microphone he didn't like. "I think you'll see that the state rushed to judgment in this tragic matter," he said to the reporter, who was eager to get a quote from a principal in the case.

"You have any idea who the killer actually was?"

"No more so than the prosecutor does, I'd have to say."

"Give those glib jaws a rest," Mike called out to the image on the screen as he switched channels. "You didn't come off too badly in all that."

"Only because Preston Meade hasn't found a path to Battaglia yet to complain."

"C'mon, blondie. The way your luck is

blowing, I got a shot at *Jeopardy!* tonight and then we're off, okay?"

For as long as I'd known Mike Chapman, it had been his habit to watch the last five minutes of the perennially popular quiz show in order to bet against whoever was in his company on the final *Jeopardy!* question. Mercer and I were the usual combatants, wagering twenty dollars or more, depending on whose favorite subject was the topic of the evening. Squad commanders, prosecutors, morgue attendants, and dead bodies had all been kept waiting while Mike tested his wits against the on-screen players.

Alex Trebek was smiling at us as the commercial break ended. "Tonight's category is Greek Mythology. Let's see what the answer is, folks."

"Double or nothing," Mike said. He had majored in history at Fordham College before joining the NYPD and had encyclopedic knowledge of military figures and events, both American and worldwide. If the subject was an ancient Greek warrior, he would beat me cold. "You can always hope for Leda and her swans."

"Do I have any choice?" I asked, removing the bills from my wallet.

Trebek revealed the answer on the giant blue game board as he spoke it aloud. "Iconic desert figure whose original Greek name means 'the strangler,'" Trebek said, repeating the word I had hoped not to hear again tonight. "The strangler."

"Brendan Quillian isn't Greek, is he?" Mike said. "I'm totally stumped. Where's there a desert in Greece?"

"Out of my league," I said, waving the bills at him. "We'll use this for drinks."

"I'm sorry that none of you guessed it correctly," Trebek said to his three dejected contestants. "The Sphinx. The Great Sphinx at Giza, which for many people symbolizes the country of Egypt, is named from the Greek word for a fantastic creature with the head of a woman, the body of a lion, and the wings of a bird. Legend has it that she strangled travelers who couldn't solve her riddle."

Mike zapped Trebek off with the clicker. "I'll give you a hundred bucks if you work that image into your summation. 'Ladies and gentlemen, the defendant testified in this courtroom, no longer silent like the

Sphinx, the great ancient strangler of the desert—'"

"'Half-man, half-beast.' You're on. And it's all providing I survive Lem's motion to dismiss at the end of the People's case. Where are you meeting Mercer?"

"Primola," Mike said, referring to my favorite Upper East Side Italian restaurant on Second Avenue, not far from the high-rise building in which I lived. The consistently great fare, the casual ambience, and the personal attention we received from the owner and his crew made it one of my regular haunts. "My car's on Baxter Street. Wait in the lobby and I'll come around for you."

We rode down together in the elevator and I chatted with the Fifth Precinct officer who had been assigned to lobby security, a quiet post on this warm summer night. When Mike's car pulled in front of the orange cones that kept Battaglia's parking space reserved, the cop walked me out and opened the car door. I threw the paper bags full of empty coffee containers and soiled napkins onto the seat behind me and settled in on the passenger side for the ride uptown.

Mike Chapman and I made an unlikely

pair. I had turned thirty-seven at the end of April, six months after he'd celebrated the same birthday, but we had few other traits in common beside our age. His father, Brian, had been a legend in the NYPD, known for his street smarts, his guts, and his investigative style, who'd retired after twenty-six years on the job only to die of a coronary forty-eight hours from the time he gave up his gun and badge. His widow, born in Ireland, made good on her promise to see that Mike graduated from college, but was just as proud when he used those qualities of his father's that seemed to have passed to him through the genes and joined the force the day after completing his degree at Fordham.

I rested my head against the back of the seat. The bright lights over the sign at the entrance to the northbound FDR Drive beat down at me from above, so I shifted and stared at Mike for a minute or two before closing my eyes. He had all the instincts of a great cop plus the benefits of a good education. The coveted gold shield of the detective division had been awarded to him early in his career, for his role in arrests in a drug-related massacre on Christmas Day of his first year in uniform, followed by the daring rescue of a pregnant teenager who had threatened suicide from atop the George Washington Bridge.

"You fading out on me?"

"I'm tweaking my summation."

"That's weeks away, if you're lucky."

"One of things I learned from Lem Howell," I said. "You write your closing argument before you ever open to the jury. It forces you to organize your case more thoroughly, to structure it with a logic that the jury can follow as you put the pieces of the puzzle together."

Mike looked over and smiled his great wide grin that warmed me no matter how bad my mood. "Back to the drawing board, huh, Coop?"

"Forget my 'Kate Meade, pillar of the community' remarks. I'll have to toss them. Did you get an update on Marley Dionne, or do I write him off, too?"

"The Rasta disaster? He may not talk, but he'll live." Mike ran his right hand through his hair. "He's out of surgery."

I hadn't seen much of Mike's humor in the last six months. His fiancée had been killed in a freak skiing accident, and he had withdrawn from Mercer and me—the two friends whose personal relationships had become as close as our professional ones over the last decade.

My passage to public service had come from an entirely different direction. I had been raised in Harrison, New York, an affluent suburb of New York City. My parents had melded their diverse backgrounds into a strong, happy marriage—she the descendant of Finnish immigrants who had settled on a dairy farm in Massachusetts at the turn of the nineteenth century, and he the child of Russian Jews who'd fled political oppression before World War II and come to this country with his older brothers, my grandmother giving birth to her first "American son" two years after their arrival.

From my mother, Maude, I'd inherited more than her green eyes and long legs. She had gone to college for a degree in nursing, and although she had given up a career she loved to raise my brothers and me, her superb nurturing skills and great compassion for people in need had found its way into my work with victims of sexual violence, who required more than a law school education from their advocates.

My father, Benjamin, was completing his post-medical-school internship in cardiology when one night he and three friends waited in line after a twelve-hour shift at the teaching hospital to spend the evening listening to jazz at the most famous Manhattan nightclub of its day—Montparnasse. Dozens of people were killed when a kitchen fire swept through the lower floor of the crowded restaurant, the flames fueled by the starched table linens and the gauzy costumes of the chorus girls. For the next several hours, my father and the other young docs rode the ambulances that responded to treat the scores of injured patrons, alongside the beautiful but unflinching young nursing student—who escaped from the inferno with her date to join the small band of volunteers—with whom he fell in love.

Our middle-class, suburban lifestyle changed dramatically when I was twelve years old, the year that my father and his partner in medical practice invented and patented a half-inch piece of plastic tubing that became known as the Cooper-Hoffman valve. The miraculous little device became an essential part of cardiac bypass surgery, used in operating theaters all over the world for more than a decade, and modified to keep current with medical advances to the present day.

This lifesaving invention had supported my education at Wellesley, a first-rate all-women's college where I majored in English literature, followed by my studies for a Juris Doctor at the University of Virginia School of Law. The trust funds established for my siblings and me had not only allowed me the luxury of buying a home on Martha's Vineyard, but also made it possible for me to devote a career to public service while maintaining a more privileged lifestyle than many of my colleagues.

I had thought that my own encounter with tragedy—the death of my fiancé, Adam Nyman, in a car accident as he drove to our wedding weekend on the Vineyard—would help me relate to Mike when Val was killed. But Mike had shut down on every emotional front, and my own memories of great happiness cut short by the senseless loss of life roiled up again with fresh pain that belied the passage of so many years.

"I've been meaning to find the time—the right time—to ask, you know, how you've been doing lately," I said. Mike's strong profile was outlined against the car window, backlit by the overhead lights as we sped along the drive. "You want to talk?"

"Not now." His eyes never left the road.

"I worry that you're—"

"Worry about yourself. Worry about your case for the next few weeks. You got creatures imploding on you inside and out of the courtroom. Me? I'll still be on the last stool at the end of the bar at Forlini's when the verdict comes in, win or lose. We needed someone sticking Marley Dionne like you need another pair of shoes."

Mike still wasn't letting me any closer on the personal side. He was telling me something, though, by the way he snapped at me and refused to engage. We were back to the business of the trial, and I trusted he knew I was available for him to lean on whenever he was ready.

"You going to try to talk to Marley tomorrow?" I asked.

"I'll be bedside in the intensive care unit before I start down to your office, pinching that IV tube from time to time to jog his memory. I'm hoping we got a Samson effect going on."

"You mean—"

"Someone cut off his dreads and maybe his balls shrunk in the process," Mike said, wheeling the car off the drive and onto York Avenue, circling the blocks to get to Second.

We parked across the street from the restaurant and walked over, making our way through the crowd at the bar to get to Mercer and Giuliano, the owner, who were sitting together at a table against the front windows.

"Ciao, Alessandra," Giuliano said, rising to greet us. "Detectivo, *come stai?*"

"*Benissimo,* now that I'm here," Mike said, slapping the taller man's back.

"Fenton, *subito,*" the owner called out to the bartender, snapping his fingers to get his attention. Giuliano winked at me as he pulled out my chair. "I think Signorina Cooper needs a double tonight, from what Mr. Mercer has been telling me."

Our cocktail preferences were so well-known here that we had only to enter the restaurant before the good-natured waiters—Adolfo, Tony, and Dominick—delivered them to our places.

"Give us some fried zucchini to nibble on with our drinks," Mike said to Giuliano, who offered to take our order himself. "The princess here has been giving me a hard time about eating all day. Do up a vat of ziti, with some of that tomato-basil sauce. She's been working too hard to consider cutting her food or even chewing it. This'll just slide down her throat, no effort at all."

"I've got some delicious striped bass tonight, gentlemen."

Mercer nodded and Mike continued ordering. "Two of those, and give us some prosciutto and figs. Blondie'll just watch."

"Nice job of getting Kate Meade home without paparazzi," I said to Mercer as I lifted my glass of Dewar's to click against each of their drinks.

"I'm not sure she'd ever seen the service entrance of her apartment building or even knew there were handymen who work in the basement, but I'll be surprised if she doesn't tip them well come Christmas."

"How was the ride uptown?"

"Human tear ducts must hold a lot more fluid than I imagined. She never stopped crying."

"Did she have time to talk before her husband got home?" I asked.

"Alex, that woman was so damned distracted, thinking about what was going to happen to her marriage and her kids and her life, there wasn't any way to do a serious interrogation."

"Did you get anything at all?"

"Seems like Preston Meade had been caught with his pants down a few months earlier. They'd been in marriage counseling for a while, but both of them were too uptight to talk their problems out in front of a therapist."

"So Kate took the more direct route," Mike said as he moved the ice around in his vodka glass. "Payback, don't you think? One shot with the guy she's probably had the hots for since high school. You got to look out for those mousy little ones, I'm telling you. Bad-tempered ballbreakers like Coop let it out now and then, but think about how long all this has been seething inside the very proper Mrs. Meade. Some of those nuns who taught her math, manners, and morals must be doing overtime on their rosary beads tonight."

"What happened when Preston arrived?" I asked.

Mercer started to answer and I cupped my hand, leaning over the table to try to hear his answer. The chattering customers standing at the bar behind me were competing with the group of eight over my other shoulder that had just come in to wait for a table, and from the street outside came the sudden screeching noise of sirens passing by.

Mike pulled back the white voile café curtain. "Fire engines."

"What did you say?" I repeated to Mercer.

"Wait till they pass," he said, pointing to the window.

But the noise didn't abate. I lifted the curtain on my side as a block-long, red hook-and-ladder wailed its urgent noise, stuck behind several cars that were jamming the intersection. It was joined by a backup chorus of whelping vehicles, so Mike stood to walk to the door, attracted by the growing fleet of patrol cars and ambulances.

Mercer's waistband beeper started to vibrate just as Mike flipped open his cell phone and hit a single button—speed-dialing his office, I assumed.

Mercer unclipped the beeper and frowned as he looked at the illuminated numerical message. "Ten thirty-three."

I knew too well the numbers of most of the NYPD emergency codes, from the extremely urgent ten thirteen to assist a fellow officer to the familiar ten thirty-four of an assault in progress.

I reached for Mercer's arm as he pushed away from the table. "What is it?"

"Possible bomb, Alex. Report of an explosive device."

Mike had covered one ear with his fingers as he listened to someone on the phone before turning back to speak to Mercer, ignoring me altogether. "Big explosion midtown, somewhere in the West Thirties. Get Coop outta here, will you? She has to be sparkling in the morning to make up for today's fiasco. I gotta go. My whole squad's been mobilized."

I thought the day's events had drained the adrenaline from my system, but somehow it began coursing through me again. "That's Manhattan South. It's not even your jurisdiction."

Dreadful memories of 9/11 were seared in my brain, and I knew Mike was quick to put himself in harm's way for anything the department asked of him.

"They're calling in everyone on the terrorist task force. Could be a hit. Take a slug of your Scotch, kid, and head for home."

7

I could barely keep up with Mercer's long strides as we hustled to his unmarked car, parked on Sixty-fourth Street, for the short ride uptown to my apartment.

Pedestrians seemed oblivious to the parade of emergency vehicles heading south, but customers were flowing out of bars, where televisions were undoubtedly flashing the same news alert that we could hear on the radio.

New Yorkers were being urged to stay calm by the all-news-station announcer, who was waiting for specific reports to broadcast. Police helicopters were circling overhead, engines droning and searchlights sweeping the streets below, put in the air almost immediately as if to guard the northern rim of the midtown perimeter.

"What do you think it is?" I asked Mercer.

He glanced over at me and smiled. "You know I don't like to be critical, girl. Just pretend Mike's here and imagine what his answer would be."

"He'd start with a derogatory remark about how stupid my question was, tell me to stop thinking worst-case scenario, and remind me of how much he admired the way the Brits handled themselves during the Blitz, the years of IRA attacks, and the Al Qaeda subway bombs."

Mercer parked in the far end of the driveway of my high-rise building and stuck his laminated police identification plate in the windshield.

"Aren't you going home?" I asked. Mercer lived in Queens with his wife, who was also a detective, and their baby son.

"Vickee's got Logan down in Georgia, visiting her folks for the first week of her vacation. Let's hang till we hear from Mike."

The doorman opened up for us as we approached. "Hey, Ms. Cooper. We got a call from the management company. Just thought you'd like to know, the city's terror alert has been raised to orange. Something happened about an hour ago."

"Thanks, Vinny." We walked to the elevator and I hit the button for the twentieth floor.

Mercer went into the den and turned on the television. I followed him, poured us each a drink to replace the ones we'd left behind, and we settled in to watch the news.

". . . reporting live to you, this is Julie Kirsch," the chic young reporter said, with plumes of smoke rising into the night sky from the scene behind her. "We'll be back in a few minutes with an important message from the mayor of New York City."

Julie clapped a white plastic mask over her mouth as toxic-looking fumes swirled around her head, and the station went to commercial break to fill the airtime. Mercer flipped the channels, but each network had taken the same opportunity while the politicians readied themselves to speak.

When the live feed resumed, Kirsch

shouted into her handheld mike over the commotion of men yelling orders at each other and vehicles continuing to stream into the general area, with revolving red lights flashing on their hoods. "We're back on West Thirtieth Street, just off Tenth Avenue," she said, pointing to the phalanx of fire trucks in the distance, "about half a block from the site of this enormous blast."

The network anchor spoke. "Who's in charge of the operation now, Julie?"

"The police commissioner is the top official here, but we've also got Fire and Emergency Medical Services. You may recall that after the terrible events of 2001, and the confusion about which agency should be supervising the mission, it's the NYPD that was given the lead position in these situations."

"Any word on possible loss of life yet?"

Kirsch pursed her lips and shook her head. "The fire was still raging when the first responders got here. It will only be after they contain the flames that they can get down inside and assess the damage. We're hoping that the time of night will be in our favor on that issue—not as many workers around the area."

"Down inside what?" I asked.

Mercer was sitting on the edge of his seat, his glass on the floor between his legs, trying to pick up the background conversation and looking for faces of his colleagues. "Must be the tunnel."

The cameraman found the public officials setting up on a platform in the middle of the street, which had been blocked off by fire trucks.

"Which tunnel?"

Manhattan sat above a maze of underground connectors. Roadways stretched beneath the Hudson River across to New Jersey in the Holland and Lincoln tunnels; Brooklyn was linked by the Battery Tunnel; Long Island by the Queens Midtown Tunnel; and more than fourteen underwater tubes comprised the network of subway tunnels that were the vital infrastructure of New York City.

"Right there. Thirtieth Street," Mercer said, hushing me with a finger over his lips.

I didn't recognize the mayor until Mercer pointed him out to me. He was dressed in a yellow slicker, with a bright green plastic hard hat, and heavy rubber rain boots that covered his trousers up to his knees. The police commissioner mounted the podium next to the mayor, and the fire commissioner, clearly unhappy to be second banana, was grim-faced as he stepped to the rear.

"Good evening, my fellow New Yorkers. The commissioner and I are here together at the mouth of Water Tunnel Number Three. As most of you know, almost two hours ago, shortly before nine o'clock this evening, an explosion was reported inside the underground entrance at this site, a place unknown to many of you, even though it will play an essential part in every one of your lives.

"There is absolutely no cause for panic or alarm," the mayor said, giving what had become the traditional post-9/11 exhortation for calm and equanimity in the face of the unknown.

Five minutes of reassurance were followed by introductions of all the parties who were playing a role in this crisis. The mayor was clearly stalling for time, for someone to give him a better understanding of the potential danger to the city.

"As of now, there is no reason to believe this event is the result of a terrorist act. The brave men who have worked underground since this project began its development almost forty years ago—in 1969—have faced death in ways most of us have never contemplated. This subterranean world that provides New York with all the water it uses daily has been created out of sheer bedrock by dynamite. We expect that tonight's blast and the resultant damage will prove to be simply a terrible accident, not an intentional act—not part of a scheme intended to cripple our city.

"But," the mayor went on, summoning the man he'd appointed to lead the NYPD to step forward beside him, "but I'd like Commissioner Scully to tell you what precautions we've taken to keep you and your families safe."

"It's the damn *buts* I hate so much," Mercer said. "Give us the bad news."

The commissioner was a head taller than the mayor. He removed his hard hat and handed it to an aide, then leaned over to speak into the mike. I had known Keith Scully when he had been chief of detectives more than five years ago, and I had watched his hair whiten and fine lines become etched in his brow since the time of his appointment two years earlier.

"We have been keenly aware of the vulnerability of our tunnel systems in this city since the tragedies of September eleventh. Our counterterrorism plans have included increased manpower at all entrances and exits, upgraded with video monitors and intercoms," Scully began, then referenced additional sophisticated techniques adapted and improved after Moscow's subway explosions in 2004, the Madrid commuter train bombings that same year, and London's 2005 coordinated Tube attacks.

"One of the repeated threats we've picked up from international surveillance and through the Department of Homeland Security," Scully went on, wiping sweat from both sides of his face, "has been to the aging system providing water to the five boroughs of this city. The original structures—Water Tunnels Number One and Two—have been in service for more than a century. They are"—he paused for emphasis—"they are extremely antiquated and terribly fragile."

Scully turned his head to the mayor, who gave him the nod he was looking for to be the bearer of bad news. "If one of the old tunnels is breached, if one is damaged in any substantial way, then the collapse of the system will be catastrophic."

We could hear reporters calling out to Scully from behind the wooden barricade, asking what he meant. Clearly, he was not ready to take questions from them.

"In cooperation with the Department of Environmental Protection, we have dispatched teams to every site throughout the five boroughs of the city in this monumental construction project. We are urging you at this time, however, to conserve your water usage in every way possible." Scully went on to list how households and businesses could do that, encouraging people to stock up on bottled water as well.

The reporters were rowdy now, trying to get an explanation that would make sense to their viewers.

The mayor elbowed Commissioner Scully aside and regained the mike, speaking in his folksy way, as if his more relaxed manner would do anything to downplay the possible dangers.

"If you ladies and gents don't remember your history, then perhaps you may not understand that New York is a great city—but it simply doesn't have the one element we all need to survive. We can live without a lot of things, but water is not one of them. And on this island, we don't have any source of fresh water. None at all."

"Better learn to drink your Scotch neat," Mercer said, leaning back and sipping his vodka. "People open their faucets every morning and never even think about where the water comes from. That's the goddamn *but* about it—*but,* if the old tunnel system that is literally our lifeline blows up or implodes anytime soon, the NYPD has a one-word plan for the island of Manhattan."

"And what's that?" I asked him.

"Evacuate."

8

"This is Teddy O'Malley," Mike said, introducing Mercer and me to the man who followed him into my apartment a few minutes after midnight. "He's one of the workers from the blast site. The commish teamed each detective up with one of them so we can learn our way around the tunnel system pronto."

"Pleased to meet you," Teddy said, standing awkwardly to the side of the Oriental rug in the hallway. "Sorry to be bringing in so much soot with me."

"It's not a problem. Make yourselves comfortable." I led them into the dining room so that Mike could put the two large pizza boxes down on the table. "You must be starving."

Teddy's T-shirt, jeans, and steel-tipped work boots were caked with mud. His freckled skin was smudged with dirt on both his face and well-muscled arms, but his curly orange hair must have been shielded by a hard hat while he had been in the vicinity of the explosion.

"Teddy's gonna be my guide dog for the week, starting tonight. We're on our way to the Bronx now, so I figured we'd stop here for a snack. Can you live without me in court tomorrow?" Mike asked me.

"Absolutely. This is a hell of a lot more serious than the Quillian trial. I expect half my jurors will go into hibernation over these news accounts. You okay, Teddy?"

"I'm fine, ma'am. Wasn't there when it happened. I'm a union rep, so I came back into town to make sure the cops had what they needed from us. Shooed me right out of there, they did, and assigned me to this character," he said, pointing a finger at

Mike. "He's trying to make a copper out of me already."

"May the force be with you, Teddy," Mike said, turning to Mercer. "She hasn't packed her bags yet, Mercer? How'd you keep her from skipping town? Any minute now I'd expect Coop to step out of those leggings and—let's see—whose monogram is on the cuffs of that fine-looking shirt? Some jerk she kicked out of bed must have left that behind. I figured by this time she'd have traded in her civvies for the hazmat suit she keeps under her bed and headed for the border."

"I briefly entertained the notion of leaving town, but Mercer reminded me that I'd have no one to badger me if I left you behind. Imagine how lonely I'd be."

"What do you guys think happened?" Mercer asked, while I went into the kitchen to get plates. "Teddy, what are you drinking?"

"I'd give my right arm for a couple of beers."

"Coming up."

Mike took the lead answering Mercer. "Too early to tell. The shaft into the tunnel is so narrow and the smoke was so intense the fire department couldn't even get a man in the hole by the time we left."

Mercer served the drinks while I handed out napkins and Teddy opened the first pizza box.

"Don't give the blonde any anchovies, O'Malley. Coop's fine with dead bodies, but she's squeamish about oily little fish. Pepperoni's for her."

"Bomb squad there?" Mercer asked.

"Running the show," Mike said, adding crushed red pepper to his slice. "You've got a school day tomorrow, little girl. You'd better get some sleep. Lem Howell's probably deep into his REMs by now, dreaming about ways to make you look bad."

"You must be kidding. Nobody'll be closing their eyes tonight. I'm glued to the news. What's going on out there?"

"Unfortunately, you got some folks taking this terror stuff seriously. Whichever idiot at City Hall came up with sending that message public has screwed us up completely."

"Yeah," Mercer said, "but heads would be rolling if they didn't put it out since there have been actual threats to the water system."

"Now there's already a lot of traffic heading for the bridges, and the PD's doing car checks at all the tollbooths and tunnel entrances so every skittish New Yorker trying to get to his bunker in the Hamptons or her secluded corner of Connecticut is going nowhere very fast."

Teddy O'Malley was on his second slice.

"You don't buy the terrorist theory?" I asked.

Mike looked at Mercer as he talked through his impressions. "I don't know. It doesn't fit the pattern of what we've been expecting, but nobody's ready to rule it out yet. I would have thought the Al Qaeda signature would be multiple blasts in different parts of the system timed to go off at once, or following each other an hour or two apart. Besides that, it's the original old tunnels that are their best targets. A good hit to either one of them would be cataclysmic. There'd be no water in this city for at least a year."

Teddy's arms bulged like those of a weight lifter on steroids as he lifted the bottle to his lips before speaking. "It ain't outsiders. We got enough turmoil going on among ourselves to blow each other to kingdom come. I'd like to see a bin

Laden–type bastard with a towel on his head try to get past the guard gate with the Daugherty brothers and the McCourts on the watch."

"Spoken like a true sandhog," Mike said, laughing as he reached for his second slice.

"A what?"

"Teddy's a sandhog, Alex. It's like Skull and Bones for micks. A very secret society that does its best work underground. You never met one before, did you?"

"No."

"We'll tell you about 'em, but before I forget, maybe Mercer can take over for me and stop by the hospital in the morning. One of us needs to keep the heat on Marley Dionne. Make sure he's still with us."

"Will do," Mercer said before turning back to Teddy O'Malley. "What did you mean when you said bad stuff is going on among yourselves that could lead to this kind of thing?"

"You know our business?" Teddy asked, letting his third pizza slice rest on his plate while he wiped his mouth with the back of his hand.

"Not well."

"First of all, you can't ever rule out an accident when you're working six hundred feet under the surface, blasting through bedrock with dynamite."

"Six hundred feet below city streets?" I asked.

"Yes, ma'am. Sixty stories down. What we do for a living is dangerous. And then there's the politics of it. We've got a powerful union on one side, and you got your usual crop of corrupt officials on the other. A lot of hands have been greased to keep the men moving. There are scores of unhappy people on both sides—union guys, city councilmen, clubhouse politicians, mobsters trying to get a foothold in the union. Goes round and round like that, and bribery's been standard operating procedure for a very long time."

"Anything else?" Mercer said.

Teddy looked to Mike before answering.

"Nothing he hasn't heard before, Teddy. You think Mercer could rise to the top of the detective division and not know what racism is?"

"Old news. Tell me about it. I thought you hogs were all very clannish—very band-of-brothers."

Teddy exhaled and seemed to be through

with his meal. "We are. Mostly. It's two very different bands, and lately there's been some ugly business going on."

"Don't Irish-Americans have a stranglehold on the sandhog work?"

"'Twas that way from the start, Detective, more than a hundred years ago. Who else would want it?" Teddy asked. "Uneducated immigrants with no skills and thick heads. They made great money doing the digs. But in short order they brought in some West Indians, for the very same reasons. In the old days they were known as the iron men. We were the miners and muckers—we did the shoveling—but the strong workers coming in from the Caribbean bolted together all the curved iron sections that formed the tunnel linings."

"And there was never tension between them before this? Hard to believe."

"From time to time, sure. But once you're hundreds of feet down in the hole with someone, you trust him with your life every time you start a new shift, even if—you'll excuse me, Detective—you wouldn't necessarily want him marrying your sister."

"What's the beef now?" Mercer asked.

"So many of the jobs in the dig have been

replaced by new, advanced machinery that not all the men can promise work to their sons anymore, like we did for generation after generation. The blacks are complaining that they're being forced out first, even though as many of them have been there for generations, like we have. I'll be giving Mike the names of guys he needs to talk to. It's not everybody, you know."

Mike went to the refrigerator and helped himself to a large glass of milk. He walked behind me and leaned against the dining room wall.

"You may think you know what you're dealing with, but believe me, you don't," Mike said, trying to imitate someone, although I couldn't make out who it was. He went on with the accent. "That's what the DA used to tell me—in Chinatown . . . Forget it, Jake, it's Chinatown."

I rubbed my eyes. "What does this blast have to do with Chinatown?"

"Now you really do sound like a dumb blonde. Didn't you get my best Jack Nicholson impression? My John Huston? *Chinatown*—the movie, not the neighborhood. The flick was all about stealing water to get it to Los Angeles, don't you remember? You could tell the same story about New York—we had to steal the water from somewhere, only nobody remembers that."

I walked to the den and checked the television before returning to the table. Julie Kirsch was still live from Tenth Avenue and still speculating wildly about the cause of the explosion.

"Can you put on a pot of coffee for Teddy and me before we get back to work?"

"Sure."

"How old are you, Teddy?" Mike asked.

"Forty-three."

"Same as Mercer. You married?"

He nodded and picked at the crust of another slice.

"Be on the lookout underground for a man who likes black coffee, English muffins, and a dinner of strong runny cheese and stale crackers. That's all she knows how to cook. Coop's available, and maybe a guy who packs a mean sledgehammer could handle her. Your wife from a hog family?"

"Course she is. Father, grandfather, brother," Teddy said, smiling. "Nobody else understands what it's like."

"What exactly *are* sandhogs?" I asked.

Mike said, "Tunnel Workers Union. Maybe fifteen hundred guys total."

Teddy gave the more elaborate answer. "Local 147, Compressed Air and Free Air Shaft Tunnel Foundation, Caisson, Subway, Cofferdam, Sewer Construction Workers of New York, New Jersey, and Vicinity."

"So you save time just saying *sandhogs*— but why that name?"

"You know the Great Bridge?" Teddy answered my question with a question.

You couldn't be a New Yorker if you hadn't ever had a love affair with the Eighth Wonder of the World, the magnificent result of John Roebling's 1867 plan to build the world's longest suspension bridge across the East River, connecting what were then the separate cities of New York and Brooklyn.

"The Brooklyn Bridge, of course. I can see it from the window of my office."

The bridge played a vital part in the life of the city, standing grandly at the foot of the harbor, its gigantic stone towers and elevated promenade remaining one of the most beautiful vantage points from which to enjoy the ever-changing Manhattan skyline.

"You know what a caisson is?" Teddy asked.

"Not really."

"Roebling's idea was a mighty risky one, Alex. The whole design plan balanced on the strength of the towers, and to build them meant sinking huge wooden boxes— 27,500-ton caissons, each of them more than half the size of a city block—into the riverbed."

"How did that work?"

"They were open at the bottom, these great chests, and then boulders were laid on top of them to force them down and keep them in the water. What was so radical at the time is that Roebling decided to use compressed air to sink them, then pack them with concrete so they'd be solidly in place forever."

Teddy stopped to take a swig of his beer. "The men were then lowered into the caissons to excavate the foundations of the towers."

"I don't understand how they could do that."

"Teddy, my lad, this is a girl who finds the toaster oven to be a real challenge," Mike said. "The only tools she's good with are an ice-maker and a razor-sharp tongue, so explain it to her nice."

Teddy smiled and got up from his chair, turning it around and straddling the seat so that he could rest his crossed arms on its high back.

"Look, Alex, for as long as man had been building aboveground and tunneling below, nothing as large as these caissons had ever been seen—monstrous boxes they were—no less sunk into the treacherous waters of the East River. They needed men—really fearless men—to climb into steel cylinders—man locks, they called them—long metal tubes that were fed into the caissons. Once down there, the guys would dig out the river bottom in order to lay these foundations."

"But what about the water?"

"Well, that's it precisely, isn't it? The compressed air I'm talking about was forced into the caissons from the top, also in tubes, meant to displace the water, meant to hold it back from coming in and drowning the men. That air was searing, like it came out of a blast furnace, like white-hot needles were pricking at your lungs and your eardrums, they used to say."

"Nothing they could see or smell or

touch," Mike said, "but it was the compressed air that kept them alive."

"Or killed them," Teddy added. "You hear stories about working in the air from any of your folk from the other side?"

Mike nodded.

"Men would tell you their chests swelled to twice the size, their voices were high-pitched, if they could speak at all, and the headaches were blinding. Worst of all was what they called the caisson's disease."

"The bends," Mike said.

"Crippled the joints, terrible abdominal pains, bad fever and sweats. Every shift in those boxes, only three or four hours was all they could stand, seemed a lifetime."

"But why—" I started to ask.

"'Cause if you just got off the boat and had no way to put food on the table," Mike said, "it's what you did. It's all you could do."

"And when the air didn't hold or the men struck a boulder fifty feet down, there'd be a great blowout spurting back the water like a geyser, and taking the workers with it," Teddy went on. "Drowning them, squeezing them into the mud below, crushing their lungs with the pressure—hell of a lot of ways for a man to die down there, and many of them did just that."

Teddy paused. "Work got under way on the Hudson River tunnels a few years later, our boys were digging out rock and earth— and then worst of all was when they got to the sand below the riverbed. Like quicksand it was, shifting and sinking—have you up to your neck in slime before you could count to five. They didn't have a name for us until then. Sandhogs it was a hundred years ago and sandhogs it is today."

Mike took his blazer off the back of his chair and slung it over his shoulder, his fore-finger looped beneath the label. "There's an entire empire built beneath New York by sandhogs for more than a century. Subway and train lines, water tunnels, car tubes, train terminals. They're what keeps us in business, Teddy. They're what makes this place possible. But it's a city we don't often think about, and it's a city most of us never see."

"There's a reason for that, Mike—a good reason," Teddy said, pushing up to leave the table. "That beast beneath us? It's a city of death."

9

Artie Tramm had been schmoozing with me since I walked into Part 83 at ten thirty in the morning. I had driven downtown, leaving my apartment at 7 a.m., although traffic aboveground was as slow as the West Side subway routes, which were tied up because of the investigation into the explosion. My normal twenty-minute ride had taken more than one hour.

"You wouldn't catch me in one of those tunnels," Artie said, leaning against the railing behind me, picking at something between his front teeth with the tip of a small pocketknife. "I'm a real—what do you call it? Claustrophobe? Papers say that dig is as far down in the ground as the tip of the Chrysler Building is high. Sixty stories deep. Could you stand being in someplace like that every day?"

I was organizing my files in the empty courtroom, waiting for the players to arrive so we could get on with the trial. It was Thursday, and we were already scheduled not to work tomorrow because of a personal day off that I had requested weeks earlier.

"Nope. I'm with you. Fresh air to breathe and lots of daylight," I said, remembering my own reaction to being trapped briefly in an enclosed space during an investigation in Poe Park the previous winter. It chilled me even to think about it.

"A few years from now, we'll be drinking water from that pipeline, wondering if those guys' fingers or toes are still swimming around in it."

"What guys?"

Gossip traveled through the corridors of 100 Centre Street faster than the speed of sound. I had listened to the car radio all the way downtown and heard nothing more about any loss of life in the blast.

"The poor schmucks that got blown up. The hogs whose DNA is gonna be dripping out of the H_2O and into your kitchen sink before very long," Artie said, licking his teeth and folding the knife.

"What?"

"You know Billy, the captain in Part 62? He's got a cousin whose wife's brother is one of them sandhogs. Says there's three guys missing. Says the cops found some pieces of flesh when they went down inside this morning."

The door that led to the judge's chambers opened and Gertz came in, lifting his robe up over his shoulders as he took the bench shortly before eleven o'clock.

Lem Howell followed him into the empty courtroom and perched on the edge of my table. There was no use complaining about whatever ex parte conversation he had been having with the judge. Their friendship went back longer than mine, and they would both deny that their conversation had included the Quillian case.

"Artie, how many jurors have we got?"

"Nine, so far."

"Any of the missing call in?"

"Yeah, number two," Artie said as he approached the bench. "She got as far as Penn Station on the IRT, then she had a panic attack while the cops were stopping kids all around her to search their backpacks. I told her to get out and take a cab and we'd reimburse her. The others must be stuck underground, Judge. The radio's reporting lots of delays."

"So, Mr. Howell, how do you propose we pass the time? Miss Cooper?"

Lem liked to use the subterfuge of personal chitchat to stick his nose in my pile of papers, hoping to pick up some clues to the nature of the evidence I'd be presenting in days to come.

"I'm hoping, Your Honor, that Ms. Cooper will tell us how she pulled that sleight of hand last night. Whatever *did* you do, girl, to create that midtown miasma? My Kate Meade moment lost in the headlines to this commotion in some big ol' hole in the ground. I know Alexandra had something to do with it." Lem lifted a blue folder from the table and waved it over his head. "Right here, Judge, it's her 'dirty tricks' file."

"The first of many, Mr. Howell. Something

stayed with me from those early days under your tutelage," I said to Lem before responding to the court. "Do we have a stenographer? Would you be willing to hear argument now, Judge, on the domestic violence expert I plan to call?"

"Good idea. Artie, see if the court reporter is in the hallway."

Lem walked up to the bench and tried to sweet-talk the judge before we resumed the formal proceeding. "Seems to me there's nothing beyond ordinary understanding that these jurors need to hear. We're not talking scientific methodology, are we? She has no business calling an expert on this issue. Alexandra doesn't have a scintilla, not a shred, not a speck of medical evidence suggesting any violence in the Quillian relationship. No injury, no police reports."

"Help me make my argument, Lem. That's precisely part of the reason I need this witness."

Artie Tramm returned with the official stenographer, who carried her compact machine and its tripod toward the front of the room.

Lem was wise to ask for an offer of proof to try to knock my witness out of the case.

By forcing my hand early in the trial, I would have to give the judge—and the defense—a preview of the points I hoped to make. If I lost the argument, it would be a major blow to the case I was trying to mount.

"Let's have the defendant," Gertz said, waving his robed arm at Tramm again. "Bring him in."

Now, without jurors or spectators present, the court officers opened the door on the far side of the bench and I could see them unlocking Brendan Quillian's handcuffs as they led him from the holding pen. He was compliant and cooperative with his jailers, unlike most felons being brought to court, offering up his wrists to them like a gentleman and thanking them as they freed him to enter the room.

Jonetta Purvis called the case into the calendar, the judge made a record of the reason for the late start to the day, and I rose to begin my argument. The legs of Quillian's chair scraped the floor as he positioned it to look at me, and as I picked my head up at the sound of it, I fixed briefly on his cold, dead eye.

"Who's this expert you want to put on the stand, Ms. Cooper?" Gertz asked.

"Her name is Emma Enloe. Dr. Enloe. She's a physician with the New York City Department of Health."

"I thought you told Mr. Howell the deceased was never treated for any injuries?"

"That's correct, Your Honor. Dr. Enloe neither met nor examined Amanda Quillian. Her expertise is the subject of intimate-partner violence."

The law had come late to respect and recognize this area of specialty. In most courtrooms all over America, as recently as the 1980s, domestic assaults had most often been considered private matters. Husbands and wives, boyfriends and girlfriends, ex-lovers whose quarrels had escalated to physical abuse were told by prosecutors, police, and judges to go home and work out the problems between themselves. Rarely was the known assailant considered the same risk to the victim as a stranger, and rarely was any attempt made to consider the lethality factor—the potential for future harm—in setting bail or issuing a protective order.

"What's to know about it?" Gertz asked. "The crime is the same on the books— homicide, assault, rape—whether the bad guy is married to the victim or never saw her before."

"It may read that way in the penal law," I said, "but the fact is that most people don't treat victims of domestic abuse in the same manner. Not in law enforcement, not in the criminal justice system, not in the medical community—and not in the general public, the people who make up our jury pool."

"So what's this lady going to tell us?"

"Mumbo jumbo," Lem Howell said. "Gibberish. She's not going to tell you anything you don't already know."

"Dr. Enloe issued a formal report two years ago, which was the result of a research project conducted under her supervision. Scientific research, if that makes Mr. Howell any happier. She used a four-year period before that to study the causes and manner of death of every woman murdered in New York City."

"How many was that?"

"More than twelve hundred killings in just that time range—femicides—all women over the age of sixteen. And in more than half of those cases—the ones that were solved—they were able to establish what the relationship was, stranger or acquaintance, between the victims and their killers."

The landmark report had been front-page news in the *New York Times* and widely disseminated in the legal community, but Gertz cocked his head and looked at me in a way that suggested he hadn't read it.

"Go on, Ms. Cooper."

"Half the women in the study had been killed by their husbands or boyfriends. Fifty percent of them."

"I think the judge knows that fifty percent is half, Alexandra," Lem said.

"I'm not done, Mr. Howell," I said. "This isn't psychobabble, Your Honor. Enloe's findings are based on autopsy reports, crime-scene photographs, toxicology, and ballistics. It's completely fact-driven."

"What's the relevance here, Ms. Cooper?" Gertz asked.

"There is a lot of information in regard to domestic violence—a number of things that are well beyond the general knowledge of the jury, or, may I say, most respectfully, even of the court."

Lem was pacing behind his client now, trying to distract the judge from the points I wanted to make. He chuckled in a blatantly artificial way. "Something the court doesn't know? I taught you a long time ago never to dis the judge like that, Alexandra."

"First of all, while the rate of every other violent crime in this city decreased steadily throughout the years of the study, the rates of domestic homicides did not." I checked my notes to begin my list of the project's findings. Effective community-policing efforts cut down street crimes and crack dealing with enormous success, but were useless at reaching beyond the closed doors of an intimate relationship.

"Last year, the NYPD responded to 247,000 incidents of domestic abuse—that's almost seven hundred calls a day."

"But Mrs. Quillian never called the police nor did she report any crime. Not last year nor any other year. I'd object, Your Honor, to Ms. Cooper even bringing that useless little factoid to the jury's attention."

"Well, then, I'll move on to something about which Mr. Howell, in his opening—and in his cross-examination of my first witness—made a big fuss. Something *he's* put at issue in this case. That's the fact that Brendan Quillian has no criminal history, no known violent behavior prior to this arrest.

In Dr. Enloe's study, in thirty percent of the murders the offender had exhibited no previous physical violence."

Judge Gertz rested his chin in his left hand and started to take notes with his right.

"Women are actually murdered in different ways than men," I went on. "Male victims of homicides are most often shot or stabbed to death. They are killed on the street or in the workplace or in any kind of public space, while women are attacked inside the privacy of their homes. When women are killed by a partner, it's usually in a very personal manner—hands on, if you will—exhibiting far more force than necessary to cause death, and far more rage. They are beaten and burned and thrown out of windows," I said, glancing at the defendant. "And they are most frequently victims of strangulation."

Quillian took advantage of the jury's absence to smirk at me. His good eye cut through me like a laser.

"In addition, Your Honor, Enloe's study identifies two times in intimate relationships when women are at greatest risk of victimization. These findings have been confirmed, in fact, by all of the data available nationally."

"Let's have them," Gertz said.

"The leading cause of death for pregnant women in America is homicide, Your Honor—which is a fact not generally known—"

Lem Howell stepped up to the table and slammed his hand against it. "That has nothing to do with this case, Judge. Nothing at all to do with my client or Amanda Quillian."

The door to the holding pen opened and a court officer waved to Artie Tramm, summoning him out of the courtroom.

"Calm down, Mr. Howell. Ms. Cooper, you're not suggesting that the deceased was pregnant, are you?"

"No, sir. Not at all. The autopsy report is clear on that."

"But it's quite a claim you're stating. Makes us sound like a third-world country. The numbers back you up?"

"Yes, Your Honor. That's my point. Again, I'm trying to demonstrate for you that the latest studies in this field have had some astounding results. Certainly, if this court isn't aware of the facts, I would hardly expect a jury to know them. Most people assume that pregnancy is an event to celebrate, while the maternal mortality studies prove that the stressors added to the intimate relationship put the woman at far greater risk during those nine months if she is in an unstable situation."

"You said there were two bad times, Ms. Cooper." Gertz pointed his finger at me. "What's the other one?"

"Separation, Your Honor."

Gertz held up his hand—palm outward—to stop another outburst from Howell. "But the Quillians were living together."

"Amanda Quillian had told the defendant the marriage was over, Judge. Dr. Enloe's study proved that *seventy-five* percent of the women who'd been murdered by their partners or exes had tried to terminate—or had announced their intention to terminate—the relationship."

It was clear from the expression on Fred Gertz's face he was hearing this information for the first time. Had the facts been so well-known—say, such as Madison Avenue is one block due east of Fifth—that the court could have taken judicial notice of them, I'd have no need to introduce them through an expert. But the study was new enough, and shocking enough, to warrant my effort to do it this way.

"When did you plan on calling Dr. Enloe?" the judge asked. "How far into your case?"

"Probably next week, when I've completed the forensics."

"Judge, you're going to have to take that testimony subject to connection," Howell said, gesturing with his gold pen. "If Ms. Cooper fails to provide any evidence that links my client to the murder, then the prejudicial nature of this woman's testimony would far outweigh any probative value."

Howell could tell that Gertz was beginning to lean in my favor. His best hope was to force me to save the expert until the end of my case, hoping—or knowing—that Marley Dionne, my snitch, might be lost to me.

"I don't mind holding Dr. Enloe until that link is established," I said. I wasn't about to let Lem Howell dictate my order of proof, but I was confident that leaving the jurors with Enloe as their last witness could be a powerful way to arm them for their deliberations.

"I'll reserve decision on your application, Ms. Cooper. At the moment, I'm inclined to take the doctor's testimony, so have her on standby once you've proved the elements of your case."

"Yes, Your Honor."

"Get Artie back in here," Gertz said to one of the two officers standing behind the prisoner.

It was unorthodox to leave a homicide defendant in the care of one guard. And Lem would normally have been the first to remark on how different the rules were for a white businessman who had no violent criminal history. The short, stocky woman in the crisp white shirt and tight navy serge pants that bulged at the hips with her holster and gun pointed to her young colleague and sent him to find Artie.

The judge stood up and flipped his papers impatiently. "You have any witnesses here, Alex, if we get our panel in by the afternoon?"

"Yes, sir. I'm ready to go."

"Just to be clear, Judge," Lem said, "we have the day off tomorrow, isn't that right?"

"Yes. We promised that to Ms. Cooper. She's moving in on my turf, Lem," Gertz said, signaling to the reporter that we had gone off-the-record. "Is this legit, Alexandra? This is going to be legal?"

"Chapter 207, Section 39, of the Massachusetts General Law. One of my dearest friends is getting married, at my home on Martha's Vineyard, and the governor has granted her request to allow me to perform the wedding. It's a one-shot deal—your job is perfectly safe."

We were talking about the ceremony I had written for the event when Artie Tramm came back into the courtroom. He was twisting the end of his mustache with one hand and motioning to Lem and me to stay back.

Artie went directly up the steps to the bench and pulled on Gertz's arm to turn him away from us while he whispered something to the judge.

Gertz remained standing and glanced from Lem to me, shaking his head from side to side. "Ms. Cooper, Mr. Howell. Would you approach the bench?"

"You want this on the record?" the stenographer asked.

"No," Gertz said, "not yet. Artie, you want to have the crew take Mr. Quillian back inside for a few minutes?"

Lem and I walked toward Gertz to see what had him looking so sober, while the court officers walked the defendant back to the holding pen.

"Artie, tell them what you heard," the judge said. "I don't know how to deal with this."

"It's his brother. It's his brother that's one of the dead."

"Whose brother?" I asked.

"The defendant's brother, Ms. Cooper."

"I didn't know he had one, Your Honor. Was he—"

"You know about this, Lem? How do you want me to handle this?" the judge asked.

"I'm in the dark, too," Lem said. "Exactly who is his brother and how did he die? I certainly don't intend for Brendan to hear this news in a public courtroom."

"Artie says there's a rumor—"

"It's not a rumor anymore, Judge," Artie said. "The mayor's gonna have another press conference at one p.m. to announce it. Duke. Duke Quillian. It's your client's brother, Mr. Howell."

"What about him?" Howell asked, taking a few steps toward the door that led to the pens. He looked flustered and truly surprised.

"They've found body parts at the blast site, Lem," the judge said quietly. "It seems that several workmen were killed in yesterday's explosion."

My master-of-the-universe perp, the Upper East Side millionaire who passed in New York society with as fine a pedigree as his late wife's, had a brother who was a sandhog?

"Hog heaven, Mr. Howell," Artie said, walking over to open the door for him. "Duke Quillian is one of the guys who was blown to bits in the tunnel last night."

10

"Did I wake you?" I asked Mike, after dialing his apartment from my office.

"Nope. Came home from the Bronx around six a.m. Napped for a few hours. Got the call from Lieutenant Peterson," Mike said, referring to the commanding officer of Manhattan North's Homicide Squad.

"Did you know Brendan Quillian had a brother?"

"Never came up in the investigation. I thought I knew him inside out, Coop. Now

Peterson tells me he had three brothers—
including the late Duke—and a sister. All the
men are sandhogs, like their father before
them. I don't know what to say to you. I
don't know how I missed them."

There wasn't a more thorough investigator than Mike Chapman. "I'm not blaming
you for anything."

"Didn't surface in any of the background
checks, nothing on the phone records, not
on the radar screen in weeks of surveillance. Didn't sign the funeral-parlor memorial book for Amanda. Not even jailhouse
visits. Like they were separated at birth.
Knowing how close these sandhog families
are, it's really weird. How'd he react to the
news?"

"Gertz was smart enough not to let me in
on the session. He dismissed the jurors
who'd shown up until after the weekend.
Excused me, too. Then gave Lem the jury
room and had Artie bring Quillian in there so
he could tell him about it privately."

"And the trial?"

"Adjourned till after the funeral. If I
thought I had a chance to win up to this moment, watch when the news breaks. Talk
about a sympathy vote. I can see it now.

Lem will stand there wringing his handkerchief while he sums up. He'll find some way
to bring this tragedy right into the well of the
courtroom."

"Let me talk to Mercer."

"He's gone back to Bellevue," I said. The
hospital had a prison unit, where Marley
Dionne was being guarded after his
surgery. "Your snitch said he wasn't into
conversating this morning. Mercer wants
to try to get a rise out of him with a mention of Duke Quillian's death. See if he
knew anything about the brother."

"I'll catch him there."

"What are you going to do?"

"Peterson's setting it up for us to meet at
the union headquarters near the entrance to
the hole. Get a briefing on what they've
found since the recovery began this morning. You want in?"

"Sure."

"Four o'clock. Be there."

"They using the FRV?" I asked, referring
to the NYPD's experimental Forensic Response Vehicle, a mobile lab that could actually be driven to the blast location to
analyze evidence, turning around DNA results in less than ten hours.

"Yeah. They expect to have positive IDs on some of the remains by then. Dress down, kid. I've taken you to some dives, but this joint is really rough."

"I've got my crack-den crime-scene jeans ready to go."

"Brendan Quillian might be the luckiest guy in the world if this whole thing is just one great big coincidence and he skates right out of the courtroom 'cause people feel his pain. Me, I'm more of a master-plan kind of guy. This thing stinks of trouble. See you later, Coop."

My secretary, Laura, stuck her head in the door. "I'm ready to go to lunch. I'll bring you back some tuna salad, okay?"

"Fine, thanks."

"That young woman who works at Chase Bank? You know, the one who's being stalked?"

"Yeah. Carol Goodwin."

"She's here, Alex."

"I told her I couldn't see her this week. She knows I'm on trial."

"She really sounds desperate."

"Did you call around the unit to see whether—"

"Catherine and Marisa are both interview-

ing witnesses. Nan Toth is lecturing at Co-
lumbia Law School. You said Goodwin
needs somebody senior, right? I couldn't
find anyone else," Laura said. "Anyway, she
only wants to talk to you."

Our pioneering Sex Crimes Unit had forty
lawyers, most of them with caseloads so
heavy that they were often on trial or evalu-
ating new matters.

I looked at my watch. "She can't be much
more desperate than I am at this point. One
fifteen. Okay, I'll see what this is about. I'm
out the door at three thirty to meet Mike and
Mercer."

Laura ushered Carol Goodwin into my office. "I'm sorry to do this to you," she said,
sniffling and reaching for my tissue box as
she sat down. "Just show up, I mean. But
I'm getting frantic about this investigation,
and the detective from my precinct just
doesn't care. He hasn't done a thing for
me."

The twenty-eight-year-old woman worked
in private banking. She was intelligent and
well-spoken, but obviously high-strung, and
I doubted that the time she had spent in
counseling for an eating disorder during
college had completely cured the problem.

She was several inches shorter than I and rail thin, nervously fingering the strap of her designer handbag while I shuffled through a file cabinet for her case folder.

"I don't think that's fair, Carol. They've been working with you on every angle of this for two months."

"Then how come they haven't caught the guy? What if he—what if he hurts me before they do? I'm the one at risk here. They need to be taking this more seriously."

"Why don't you calm down? There's no point discussing any of this when you've got yourself wound up in such a state."

Carol Goodwin had been referred to me by a victims' advocacy group. She was reluctant to press charges when she first encountered her stalker, but once I'd offered to monitor the case, she had agreed to cooperate with the detectives to try to nail him. The man she described to us had taken to following her from work once or twice a week, showing up at events she attended for business purposes, sending her menus from restaurants she frequented that arrived in her mail a day or so after she had been to one of them, calling her in the middle of the night from phone booths in her neighborhood—all the activity following a note that had been slipped under her door one night this spring, with the words I'LL GET YOU cut out from a newspaper and pasted onto a textbook photograph of a corpse.

"You think this is easy, living in fear all the time? Have you ever been the victim of a crime?"

I needed a high-maintenance witness right now like I needed my wisdom teeth extracted without anesthesia. It wasn't my practice to talk about my personal problems with them, either. I had stories that would make Goodwin's silent stalker seem like her best pal.

"My update from the detectives only carries me through last weekend. I apologize for that, Carol. I've been on trial with a murder—"

"Is that what it's going to take to get your complete attention, Ms. Cooper? Would you prefer that this man murders me?"

I stood up from my chair. "I think you'll be happier dealing with one of my colleagues, Carol. I've obviously let you down. I'm going to reassign your matter to someone else in the unit who can devote the time you require to it."

"No, no. That's not it. I really want you to handle my case yourself." She stretched out her arm to me. "I'm sorry—it's just that I'm losing control and I feel so helpless all the time. My counselor told me to trust you. Please don't give up on me."

I sat on the edge of the desk, scanning the file. "You still have no idea who might be doing this?"

"I can't seem to help the cops with that at all," Carol said, shaking her head. "I was sure it was my ex-boyfriend—the guy who broke up with me two years ago—but they've ruled him out."

The man she referred to had married and moved to Connecticut. The police reports detailed his whereabouts on the dates in question, and the investigators excluded him unequivocally. His physical characteristics matched the description of the mystery man—but so did those of millions of other five-foot-nine-inch, sandy-haired white men with an average build.

"What brought you here today?" I asked the questions but could barely concentrate on the woman's answers. No matter how many times the detectives had followed her to and from her office or planted themselves undercover at evening social encounters or meetings, the stalker never appeared. I was so focused on the Quillian connection that I knew I had given Carol Goodwin short shrift.

"Last night. It happened again last night, and whoever answered the phone in the detectives' squad didn't want to do anything at all for me."

"What time last night?"

"Ten thirty. I had stopped in the corner deli to get some milk for my coffee. He—he, um—he was waiting for me outside the door." She blew her nose with a tissue. "He looked so menacing, like he was going to attack me this time."

"What did you do?"

"I ran back inside and used the phone in the rear of the store to call the precinct."

"Did he have a weapon?"

"I don't know, Ms. Cooper. I didn't get close enough to find out."

"Did he follow you in? Did the counterman see him?"

She looked down at her shoes. "No. He said he never did."

"That's too bad. It would be useful to have another witness."

"Why? Why is that? Because you don't believe he was there?"

"Of course I believe you. It would be helpful if someone else could confirm an identification—it always is—once we get the guy."

Her voice quivered as she seemed to lose control again. "Well, how the hell are you going to get him if the police don't even respond to my call? How?"

"Carol, are you aware of what happened in midtown last night? Do you know there was an explosion? People were killed? Every precinct in the city had to direct manpower to the scene, can you understand that?"

"So my case means nothing to them, right? I'm the bottom of the pecking order, aren't I? You think the newspapers won't be interested in that? You think I can't get some reporter to do a story on how this has impacted me both emotionally and professionally?"

"Tell your story to anyone you think will help you, Carol," I said, rising again, aware that I'd be losing points on the sensitivity scale today. "Threats don't work very well with me, so now I'm going to suggest that you leave and let me get back to business. You got home safely, didn't you?"

"I had to wait in that damn place until one of my neighbors came in and walked me home. I guess the police wouldn't have cared if I had to stay there all night." She got up from her chair and fumbled in her bag to find lipstick to apply.

"That's a silly thing to say, Carol. They've been very concerned about this. I'll give the cops a call, but I think you've got to cut them a break about last night. Where are you going now?"

"Back to work."

"Would you be more comfortable if I had one of the detectives from the DA's squad give you a ride?"

"Yeah. That would be great."

"Then have a seat in the waiting area, okay?"

I led her out past Laura's desk and returned to my office, closing the door behind me. I dialed Steve Marron in the squad, one flight above me. "Steve, have you got twenty minutes?"

"Every time I give you twenty you manage to turn it into an hour. Five hours. Ten."

"Come on down. I need you to drive a witness to her office on Wall Street. Tell Joe Roman to stand outside our building entrance and get a good make on the young woman who'll be coming out with you."

"Be right there, Alex."

When Steve Marron knocked on my door and came in, I explained the situation. "I need Joe to do surveillance on her. I don't want to wait for her to call the next time the stalker shows up. I want Joe to follow her from her office when she leaves tonight, onto the subway, then to her house. And then he needs to take her in the reverse direction, from home to work, the next few mornings."

"Aren't there detectives assigned already?"

"Yes, but I don't want her to know we're doing this. She's met those guys. I want to use a team she doesn't recognize. If this is for real, then the perp also must have figured out who the cops are by now."

"And if it's not for real?" Steve asked. "Don't roll your eyes at me."

"We have to assume it is. Give it a try."

Few investigations were more frustrating than stalking cases. Victims were rightly terrified by criminals or psychos who lurked outside their homes and offices, following them for months, often without making any overt gestures. Law enforcement agents and judges had traditionally responded to complaints with a cavalier and dismissive attitude that "nothing" had happened over time. But when the behavior might escalate was often unpredictable, and until resolved, every break had to go in favor of the victim. Threat assessment had burgeoned since stalking had been recognized as a crime category only a decade ago.

I introduced Carol to Steve Marron and saw them to the elevator, then returned to my office to grab my jeans and driving moccasins before heading to the ladies' room to change.

Artie Tramm was sitting in Laura's desk chair when I got back, flipping through the copy of *Cosmo* that sat on top of a pile of the unit's latest indictments.

"What do you need?" I asked.

"I think you dropped something on your way out of the courtroom. Thought I'd bring it to you myself," he said, giving me a small white business card with a handwritten notation on the blank side.

I hadn't any cards with me when I went

upstairs to Part 83 this morning, so I was puzzled as I reached for it.

The name that had been written on it was not familiar to me. It was in a bold script that I recognized from looking at hundreds of documents signed by Brendan Quillian and said simply *Lawrence Pritchard.*

I flipped the card, surprised to see the logo of Keating Properties.

I reddened as I handed it back. "C'mon, Artie. You know this isn't mine. We'd better go back up to the judge and make a record. It could be Brendan Quillian's."

"It don't belong to anybody. I told you I picked it off the floor. It's garbage, wouldn't you think? Just garbage."

I shook my head at Artie.

"Besides, Gertz is gone until Monday, after the funeral. Meantime, Alex, the least you could do is find out who this guy is—the one whose name is written here. You never know, maybe he's somebody who could be useful to you." Artie pocketed the card and walked to the door. "And your case needs all the help you can get."

11

I parked at the corner of Eleventh Avenue and walked east across Thirtieth Street to the front of the barbed-wire entrance to the construction site at three forty-five in the afternoon. I had called Mike on his cell phone and he was waiting for me at the gate.

"I can't believe you told Lem about this Lawrence Pritchard business before you even found out who the guy is."

"It's a little thing called ethics, Mike. If it has anything to do with our case, Lem would be likely to move for a mistrial. This one won't get any better the second time around."

"He's baiting you. That's all it is."

"What do you mean?"

"Lem Howell? Dropping a piece of paper on the floor by mistake? There's a guy who never had a spit curl where he didn't want it to be and he's playing loose with a clue or a potential suspect's name? Not his style, Coop. You know your players better than that. You know he wanted you to be misled by that business card. What'd he tell you?"

"He was very gracious about it. Said it had nothing to do with the trial. Thanked me for the call and said I could make a record of it when we resumed next week."

"Sucker," Mike said, and started to walk through the yard.

"I googled this guy Lawrence Pritchard," I said, stepping over enormous pieces of mechanical equipment and walking between two tall cranes to keep up with Mike. The site was a beehive of activity. The sandhogs were in work clothes, the detectives had eschewed sports jackets for T-shirts, and the officials from a mix of city agencies were the only ones standing around in suits, kibitzing with each other. I hadn't smelled this much cigarette smoke in any one place since my first midnight visit to a homicide squad.

No one seemed happy to see me, but that was hardly a new crime-scene experience.

"What'd you get on him?" Mike asked, calling to me over his shoulder.

"Former chief engineer on this project. Fired two years ago. Has his name come up?"

"Watch your step," he said, waiting for me and holding out his hand. "It gets really sloppy over here from the fire hoses last night. Never heard of him."

"There are a few articles about it. Max is going to pull them for me. Looks like he was involved with kickbacks. Pocketed more than a hundred thou, took lots of expensive gifts, went on a few gambling trips and boondoggles."

"And Quillian knows him?" Mike was standing at the bottom step of a trailer, a dust-covered double-wide that seemed to be the headquarters of the operation. He climbed the four stairs and held open the door, which was draped with black bunting. "Welcome to hog house. No kidding, that's what they call it."

"Thanks," I said, pausing at the threshold. "That'll be your job to figure out, don't you think? We'll be looking for a link between Duke Quillian and Pritchard. Obviously, I think Brendan was trying to put Lem Howell on Pritchard's trail for some reason. Lem said it has nothing to do with my murder case, but he must figure there's a connection to Duke's death."

"We've got the main man from the Department of Environmental Protection here. The entire tunnel project—everything having to do with the water supply in New York—is under their watch. He's supposed to tell us what we need to know. Later, we can ask him if he's got the scoop on Pritchard."

Several desks and lots of folding chairs were in the long room. Stacks of paper, small tools, lunch boxes, and ashtrays covered the tabletops. Stained yellow slickers and protective gear were hanging from hooks on every side. Several workers were clustered near the entrance, manning a bank of phones, and appearing to be exhausted from long hours of vigil for their lost colleagues. A few more were glued to the local all-news channel on the television set mounted on a stand in the corner. Most of them stared at me as I passed through but offered no greeting.

Mercer introduced me to George Golden, a senior geologist with the city's DEP. "Four of your task-force detectives are already in the tunnel. Are you expecting anyone else?" Golden asked. He was about fifty-five years old, with a deep tan, hooded eyes, and a sharply pointed nose that looked like a hawk's beak.

"That's it," Mike said. "Start from the top. What have we got here?"

"We're standing directly above the main artery of Water Tunnel Number Three. I'm talking about a sixty-mile-long tube that sits six hundred feet below street level and is going to cost more than six billion—not *million*—six billion dollars before it's completed. And we don't expect that until 2020, if we get lucky."

"Why so deep?" Mike asked.

"Construction on New York's first tunnel began in 1911. For more than a century, we've been building a subterranean city under your feet, a whole maze of pipelines that nobody but these workers will ever see. You've got subways and electrical systems and sewers down there, and farther below that is the second water tunnel. So there was nowhere for this one to go but deeper underground."

"How much water does it take to quench our thirst?" Mercer asked.

"And bathe you? And flush your toilets? Start with 1.4 billion gallons every day."

I could tell from Mike's pensive expression that his fascination with history was driving his need to know more about this dig.

"I'm missing something here. When the island of Manhattan was settled in the seventeenth century—when they kicked the Indians off to the mainland—weren't those Dutchmen smart enough to know they needed something to drink?"

"Sure, they knew they were completely surrounded by salt water, Mike. But it wasn't so much a problem a few hundred years back," Golden said. "The major settlements were all on the southern end of the island, as you're probably aware."

Most New Yorkers were familiar with the tale that Mannahatta had been purchased from the Lenape Indians by the West India Company for sixty guilders—the equivalent of twenty-four dollars. New Amsterdam was colonized close to the tip of the waterfront, and the population pushed northward slowly over the next two centuries.

"In those days, there were a lot of fresh-water streams and brooks all over the island," Golden went on. "Sherman's Creek up in Washington Heights, Harlem Creek, Lispenard Meadows. And there were several kills—like the Great Kill, right at Forty-second Street, and the Saw Kill in Central Park."

"Yeah, we happen to know some of the kills pretty well," Mike said, looking over at Mercer. The Dutch word for "channels" had given its name to inlets and waterways all throughout the New York harbor.

"The greatest natural feature of Manhattan was probably the Fresh Water Pond. Seventy acres of perfectly pure spring-fed waters. Added to the neighborhood wells that were dug near many of the residences and the cisterns that folks filled with rainwater, it seemed like more than enough for everybody."

"Fresh Water Pond? Never heard of it," Mike said.

"How about the Collect?" Golden replied.

"That's what it was called when the English took over. *Kolck* is Dutch for a small body of water."

Mike shrugged. "So where is it today?"

Golden pointed to me. "You work in the courthouse, Alex? One hundred Centre Street?"

"Yes."

"Well, right about there. The pond covered most of the area east of Broadway, from Chambers to Canal streets. Your offices were built right on top of the Collect."

That acreage now encompassed the grid of concrete government buildings in lower Manhattan, from City Hall to Federal Plaza to all of the civil and criminal court structures that exist today—the ones the original city planners had called the Halls of Justice.

"It doesn't make sense," Mike said. "Why build over a water source when the stuff was so scarce? Did it dry up?"

"Easiest to say a combination of population expansion and sanitary implosion did in whatever fresh water there had been. The wells were stressed by the growing numbers of people arriving in the city every day, and it didn't take long for the streams to become putrefied by carcasses of dead animals and human waste. Totally polluted," Golden said. "Then throw in some plagues— it was yellow fever in the 1790s that caught the city fathers' attention about clean water, followed by a typhoid outbreak from time to time. And the cholera epidemic of the 1830s that got them off their asses."

It embarrassed me to realize I had never given much thought to these things. I knew that cholera patients developed an insatiable need for drink, and that ironically, the disease is caused by exposure to contaminated water in the first place.

"You know how many New Yorkers died of cholera in 1832?" Golden asked.

"No idea," I said.

"More than thirty-five hundred people. Thousands more fled to the country just to avoid the spread of the disease. There simply wasn't any clean water in the city by that point in time. Not a drop."

"So what did they do to get it?" Mercer asked.

"Same thing the Romans did, three hundred years before the birth of Christ," Golden said. "It's been our model for all this time—the eleven ancient aqueducts built by Roman slaves, all working from the basics of gravity and the downhill flow of water, brought millions of gallons a day into that city from rivers and lakes in the faraway hills."

"So we've got the Croton watershed," Mike said, referring to what was today a twelve-reservoir system, created in West-chester County by harnessing the Croton River.

"Exactly."

"But that's almost fifty miles north of the city," Mercer said.

"It's a piker, compared to the distance covered by the original Italian aqueducts," Golden said. "The Croton River starts much farther north, in Dutchess County. Its water-shed covers more than three hundred and sixty square miles, capable of putting out four hundred million gallons a day."

Mike gave out a low whistle. "And what gets it to Gotham?"

"First they had to create a plan to dam the river, by flooding acres and acres of homes and farmland in the area. Breaking the hearts and spirits of everyone who had set-tled in that fertile part of the state. Just like the government does today—pay them a few bucks and claim eminent domain."

Golden continued, "Miles of pipeline were laid, zigzagging south through Westchester County, cutting through rock ridges and valleys, water being forced down the hills by the sheer force of gravity and then entering Manhattan in very dramatic fashion via the High Bridge."

That fabulous structure, the oldest remaining span connecting the island to the mainland, must have been spectacular when it was built in the 1840s. It had sported fifteen of the same elegant arches that characterized the Roman aqueducts and had carried water to New York County over the Harlem River.

"How big were those tunnels?" Mike asked.

"Only eight feet wide."

"And how was the water distributed once it reached Manhattan?" I asked.

"Well," said Golden, "it flowed into the Receiving Reservoir, which looked like a giant fortress, capable of holding one hundred and eighty million gallons of water."

"But where was that?"

"It was built on York Hill, Alex. You know where that is? The land all belonged to one gentleman, a fellow named William Mathews, and it was pretty prime real estate, both then and now."

Mercer laughed, but the name meant nothing to me. "A brother, if I'm not mistaken. Deacon of the African Union Methodist Church, back in the 1840s. That neighborhood was the Harlem of its day."

"Where?" I asked.

Golden answered, "Smack-dab in the middle of Central Park. The Receiving Reservoir fed fresh water to Manhattan until 1940, when it was drained and completely filled in to create the Great Lawn."

"So recently—just a few generations ago? That doesn't seem possible."

"Take it one step further. The water flowed downtown from that facility to what was called the Distributing Reservoir. That's where it was provided to homes and businesses in the city. Fifth Avenue and Forty-second Street. Imagine that where the New York Public Library now stands was once another enormous fortification filled with water."

"And it's come to us that way for almost two centuries," Mercer said.

Golden stroked his beak and nodded. "Croton sort of maxed out at the beginning of the twentieth century. So the engineers just kept digging farther north, reaching into the mountains above the city, tapping into the Catskills and the Delaware River."

Mike said, "I got a whole new respect for all the liquid gold."

The door to the shack opened and a workman stuck his head in and called out, interrupting Mike, "Hey, George! You got an all-clear in the shaft."

"Thanks a lot. The cops tell you anything else?"

We all turned to listen to the answer. "They've been doing that test all day—what do you call that stuff?"

"DNA," I said. My three favorite letters of the alphabet. The science hadn't even been reliable enough to be admissible in any courtroom in America until 1989, when it took six months for a lab to return a preliminary result to police and prosecutors who submitted evidence to the few facilities then capable of doing the work. Now it had reached the point that we could get a positive identification by dusk on human remains found at daybreak at a homicide scene like this.

"Yeah, they're working on those—um,

those pieces of flesh in a truck down the street. It's got to be Duke. Duke and those two guys from Tobago."

"What two guys?" Mike asked.

George stood up and reached for a slicker from a peg on the wall. "Tough break. There's nobody any one of our men would rather have working shoulder to shoulder with them than Duke Quillian. Third generation in the hole—a real lifer. And these other two were just kids. Cousins who came up from the Caribbean to work in London with their uncle. Did a big piece of the Chunnel dig. Moved to the States just a couple of months ago."

"Who reported them missing?" Mike asked. "Their families?"

"Nope. Neither one had any relatives here. Shared an apartment in Queens. They were set to work the evening shift yesterday. Landlord says they never came home."

"These guys work evenings, too?" I asked. It was hard enough to imagine being so far down in the bedrock in daylight, but even creepier to think of being in that tunnel in the dark.

"Twenty-four/seven, Alex. We're a few years behind our due date."

Mike followed George toward the door. "What's the difference, Coop? There's no natural light down there anyway."

"You game to go down with me?" George asked, pointing a finger and sweeping it around from Mike to Mercer to me.

The answer caught in my throat, but Mike and Mercer were quick to say yes.

George stood next to the solemn group of sandhogs who had just heard the news about their Tobagonian colleagues. "I need one of you guys to take us in, okay?"

Five of them stood up as though they hadn't heard the question and excused themselves to get out the door. The others, elbows on the table and their chins resting on their hands, ignored Golden and listened to the commercial for hemorrhoidal cream as intently as they had followed the news stories of the blast.

"Bobby—Bobby Hassett," Golden said to the man leading the group out the door. "Be a gent, will you? One way or the other, we're going down there."

"Sorry, Georgie. I've been helping since daybreak. Got a ride home waiting for me," Hassett said, holding the door open for some of the others and then following them out.

"C'mon, somebody step up to the plate," he said to the ones who remained. "Give me a hand. These detectives are here to figure this out, make us safe."

Water Tunnel #3 had been designated a crime scene for the purpose of the investigation—to determine whether the blast was intentional or accidental. Even an accident could be declared a criminally negligent homicide.

No one responded.

Golden patted the back of the sandhog closest to him. "Get your gear on and come along."

The surly-looking workman kicked back from the table and stood up, letting his chair fall over on its side. "Not if she's comin' down," he said, cutting the air with a thick brogue and a sneer in my direction.

I started to say I'd prefer to wait right here, my usual eagerness to visit a crime scene—in order to understand every dynamic and detail of it—overcome by my fear of journeying so far into the ground.

"What's your problem?" Mike asked. "She's been places you wouldn't have the balls to go to if I walked in front of you with an AK-47."

Golden waved off the hog with one hand and pulled on the doorknob with his other.

"Ignore him, Alex. It's an old wives' tale. These guys all cling to their myths and their macho bullshit. Bad luck to let a woman in the tunnel."

From the reaction Golden's request had drawn, it was a tale that still had legs.

"'Tisn't bad luck," the man said to him, striding past Mike out the door. "It's no luck. No luck at all. It's death to us down there, Georgie. We've already lost over thirty men since we started the dig for this job. How many more have to die?"

12

"I'll wait up here if we all won't fit in," I said.

Three wooden crates were near my feet, each stamped on the side with the words EXPLOSIVES—30 LBS. In front of me was an eight-foot-tall metal cage that looked like the kind in which divers are lowered into the ocean to photograph sharks. Its open gridwork was painted red, and it dangled over the top of the hole from a giant winch. The sign on its door read: DANGER: AMPUTATION— KEEP HANDS AWAY FROM DOOR.

George Golden smiled at me. "Step in, Alex. It can hold us."

Mike nudged me in the back and I reluctantly entered the Alimak—the tiny elevator that would carry the four of us to the floor of the deep shaft below. We were all wearing the obligatory yellow slickers, plastic hard hats in a variety of primary colors, and steel-tipped rubber boots that George had appropriated from the shack. Mine were way too big, and I shuffled forward to avoid stumbling out of the borrowed footwear.

The fifth man was at the controls of the machine, which ran up and down along the inside of the gaping, thirty-foot-wide mouth. He was dressed as we were and had large plugs protruding from his ears. "Do we need those?" Mercer asked.

"Only according to the law," George said. "The guys never use them inside the tunnel, even though they're supposed to. In the long run, they'll have permanent hearing damage anyway—the blasts can split your eardrums. But it's even more dangerous to take a chance that they can't hear what's going on down there."

I clasped the honeycombed grid with one hand, bracing my back against the rear of the cage. The metal box rattled and shook when Mercer and Mike added their weight to it, and then again as the chief geologist entered last.

"You look nervous," George said to me. "There's nothing to worry about, really. You've got to keep your fingers in though."

He reminded me of the DANGER sign and I dropped my hands to my sides. Mercer took one of mine in his own and squeezed it tightly.

Mike saw the gesture and laughed. "Coop's tribe? Let's just say it wasn't the Stoics."

The operator of the Alimak flipped the switch and the machine lurched into its descent.

Golden ran a finger down the length of his nose, watching my reaction as the noisy cage picked up speed. I didn't want his attention centered on me, so I leaned my head back, concentrating on the circle of daylight over my head.

"You can always tell when someone isn't going to like it in the hole," he said.

"I'll be fine."

"If you got room down there for a wet bar,

a mirror, and a tube of lipstick, then Coop is good to go," Mike said.

By the time we had descended a hundred feet, the opening above had narrowed considerably and I felt constricted by the thick, dark wall surrounding us. I closed my eyes and lowered my head. Pinpoints of light— probably the naked bulbs at the bottom— were all I could see through the metal grating.

"You don't want to look down, Alex," George said, his voice echoing off the surface of the rock, which glistened with water.

"Are there guys who have trouble working here?" Mercer asked.

"Plenty of them. It's gotta be in the blood. There are men who come down once, realize that this creaky elevator that might squeeze eight of us in at best is the only way out from that hellhole, and that the tunnels stretch for miles in both directions, full of sandhogs. Some would crawl up the walls if they could. And then there's the dripping. Constant sound of dripping water. That's what gets the rest of 'em."

The Alimak operator called out, "Two hundred feet."

I craned my neck upward but could no longer see anything above.

"Is the dripping from cracks in the old pipes overhead?" Mercer asked.

Another fear I hadn't considered. I could hear the pinging sound but wondered what could possibly be leaking this far below the surface.

"There are leaks all right. But the water you see here is a natural phenomenon. It's all in the landscape above us, pouring down through the earth and rocks, from riverbeds and underground streams. Another two minutes you'll be five hundred feet below the Hudson River."

I shivered at the thought of the weight of an entire city pressing down upon me. There was nowhere for me to look but straight ahead, at the point of Golden's nose.

"You're not cold, are you?" he asked.

"Just a bit."

"People always think it's gonna be freezing. The odd thing is that it's mild the entire year all this way down. Fifty-five degrees."

"Three hundred feet," the man at the controls said, and I knew we were halfway through the four-minute ride to the bottom, the Alimak creaking as we seemed to hurtle on our descent into the darkness.

"So what do the guys do for fresh air?" Mike asked.

"*Fresh* isn't exactly the operative word. But air is pumped in all the time by fans, and then the stale air is pumped out through ventilation pipes. Got to be tested constantly for toxic gases and stuff like that."

Gases. Check. Something else to add to the short list of ways I hadn't thought about to die in this water tunnel.

"The ones that can't take it," Golden went on, "they just blanch before they're out of this cage. Turn green, some of them, on the ride. Like a kid on his first crack at the giant roller coaster. Get all queasy inside."

Queasy would have been a good feeling. I was nauseous at this point, clinging to Mercer's hand as the cage seemed to bounce against the wall and vibrate.

"Four hundred feet."

"Think about it," George said. "You go up to see that fabulous view from the Rainbow Room, over at Rockefeller Center. You can look up the Hudson and practically touch Canada from there. Another minute and you'll be farther in the ground than that sky-scraper reaches into the sky."

Smoke and dust, the residue from last night's explosion, were still heavy in the air. I covered my mouth and coughed, hoping not to be sick in the crowded elevator.

Golden reached in his jacket pocket and pulled out several small plastic bags—the kind used to store sandwiches or food—with something folded inside each. "You might want a mask," he said to us, holding out his arm. "The fire will make it tougher to breathe today."

In another bag he had a package of cough drops, which he offered to me. "Everything has to come down here in plastic—the guys' lunch, their cigarettes, their identification. The constant dripping gets to everything—and everybody."

"Five hundred feet."

The droplets had turned into running rivulets of water, streaming through the wire of the cage from the reinforced-concrete walls of the hole.

I was willing myself to stay on my feet, thinking of the beautiful June day that was awaiting me on my return to the surface. As we neared the end of the descent, the artificial light source below us cast an eerie glow against the scarlet mesh of the Alimak.

The operator cranked back the lever to bring us to a stop, blowing a shrill whistle to clear the landing platform and announce our arrival to the men in the tunnel. The cage shuddered on the enormous chain that tethered it to the winch.

Golden reached back and unlatched the door, stepping out onto the top of a wooden staircase that led down to the floor of the shaft, six hundred feet below midtown Manhattan.

"Welcome to the center of the earth," he said, as Mike followed him out and started down the steps. Golden ran his hand across the wet surface of the wall as he walked. "Nobody but the sandhogs—and you investigators—will ever see this—this bedrock, this tunnel that will keep everyone in New York alive for generations to come."

Mercer kept hold of my hand and led me out behind him. I stopped to look up toward the top of the hole—the great void to the side of the Alimak—trying to discern the source of a terrible clanging noise over my head.

"You okay?" he asked me, trying to disengage from my grasp. "C'mon, Alex. Let's keep up. I promise to get you back up there in one piece."

I grabbed the banister, reluctant to take the first step off the wooden platform, struggling to keep from walking out of my borrowed boots.

Golden was pointing out the tunnel structure to Mike, who was behind him, and to Mercer, who had started to descend the staircase after them as I stood frozen in place. The Alimak jerked upward from the base and started its noisy climb while the other dreadful banging in the hole seemed to get even louder.

"Hurry up," Mercer said, coming back up toward me and stretching out an arm to coax me down.

Then I saw the expression on his face as he screamed at me to duck.

I leaned over, my hard hat crashing down the steps, falling into the mudpile at the bottom. Behind me, a lethal metal spear—a tire iron that had fallen, or been dropped, from street level at the mouth of the hole—landed inches from my back and impaled itself into the wooden floorboard.

13

"Get her out of the way!" Golden ordered.

I straightened up and plodded into the mud as fast as I could move away from the shaft at the bottom of the hole.

"What the fuck was that?" Mike yelled at him. "Bring that Alimak back—I'm going up. The damn thing nearly killed her."

"Nobody could have seen Alex from up on top. It must have been—"

"Don't give me that crap," Mike said, wrapping the end of the metal weapon in his handkerchief. "Somebody was sending a very clear message. You were the last guy to step on and the first one off, so whoever was watching knew you wouldn't be the target. I'm guessing this was meant for one of us."

My heart was speeding again, the beat as loud to me as the tire iron had sounded as it had bounced off the rock walls. Mike was going nose to nose with Golden.

"You stay and get this done," Mercer said, separating the two men. "I'll check out who's up there."

"I'll go with you. Let me get the cab back down," Golden said, heading for the control booth at the head of the staircase. He pointed into the tunnel. "O'Malley's waiting for you."

I squinted into the long black tube that stretched out in front of us—laid with train tracks as far ahead as I could see—and then made out Teddy's hulk emerging from the haze about twenty feet away.

"Step lively, Alex," he said. "Last guy we lost had a bad habit of lingering near the Al-imak door. Spring thaw came along and an icicle broke off in the shaft above him. Point of it split his head in half, like a water-melon."

Everything about the operation was dangerous. This was a world shrouded in darkness and mist, the occasional bulb hanging from wire that was taped overhead. The vivid colors of the hard hats and rain slickers were in sharp contrast to the tones of black and gray that dominated the landscape.

"Sorry. I can't go any faster."

"You've got to watch yourself on these railroad ties," Teddy said. "It's nothing but puddles in between."

"Why the tracks?" Mike asked, each of us trying to lift one foot at a time over the railroad ties, in single file, sinking into the mud as we tried to advance.

"Can you see ahead?"

We both looked up into the shadowy cylindrical tunnel that seemed to be about twelve feet in diameter, with side-by-side tracks running through it.

"Yeah," Mike said.

"This leg will go nine miles to the south of us," Teddy said. "It'll connect the water supply to an identical piece in Brooklyn. Everything moves around here on railroad cars, lugged down the same hole you came in, and then assembled once on the ground."

Mike turned to check on my progress. He looked over my head. "And behind us? What's that?"

"The other half of the tunnel—a thirteen-mile piece. It comes via the Bronx from up-state—that entrance we looked at last night—and connects to here through a tube under Central Park."

More than twenty treacherous miles of cavernous tentacles and only one way to get back out to Thirtieth Street. I looked down again as frigid water sloshed over the top of my boots.

Teddy pulled a plastic bag from his pocket and removed a cigarette, lighting it as I caught up to him. "The crime-scene guys are waiting for you farther inside the tunnel, at the mole. That's where the explosion was."

"What's a mole?" I asked.

"It's the machine that actually bores the hole through the rock. Never been used in the States before," Teddy said. "It's how the Chunnel was dug between England and France. Until then, every tunnel in the world was built the same way the Romans did centuries ago—blast and drill, drill and blast. Slow as molasses."

"And with this?"

"It's a monster," he said, his huge feet swallowed by the soft mud, water dripping from the ancient schist over our heads. "Weighs three hundred tons. Brought it below in parts and put it together just like we build the trains. You'll see—it drills its way through the rock, leaving the walls as smooth to the touch as ice, and it's three times as fast as the old system. That's how come so many hogs are out looking for work."

I could see a moving beam in the far distance. It looked as if someone was holding a flashlight, waving it slowly around and around in a circle. Behind me a machine rumbled into motion.

"Get off the tracks," Teddy said. "Off to the side. That's the signal to send one of the trains down to the mole."

I grabbed for Mike's shoulder and stepped over to the rounded wall of the tunnel, pressing myself against the cool, wet surface. I coughed again as the residual dust from the blast was stirred up by the wheels of the railroad car. The small mask that Golden had handed me hung on a string around my neck. I couldn't bear to put it over my mouth for fear—which I knew was irrational—that it would muffle any sound I might try to make.

"Where's he going?" Mike asked.

"It's a muck car. Once the mole drills into the bedrock, the debris—the muck—has to be hauled out of here. Goes up a conveyer belt behind the shaft."

"Why not just repair the old water tunnels?" I asked. "Wouldn't that be easier than doing all this?"

Teddy shook his head. His voice boomed back at me. "Call it metal fatigue or whatever you want, but the entire infrastructure that brings the water to the city could go at any minute."

I looked overhead at the giant bolts—supersize like everything else in this dark dungeon—that seemed to hold the bedrock in place above me.

"They were built with valves back then, Alex. Think of big floodgates inside the tunnels that were supposed to be opened and closed whenever they needed fixing."

The mud was covering my boots up to the ankles. It felt as though I were walking in quicksand. "So—?"

"Gets to the point, a hundred years later,

where the valves can't take the pressure of billions of gallons of water. Nobody's even sure that if they could be turned off at this point, they could ever be turned on again. And nobody wants to try to find out," Teddy said. "Hell, the aqueduct that services the old tunnels upstate leaks so bad it's made a sinkhole that could swallow up half the town."

Check and check again. Manhattan without a drop of water, and the entire island sinking back down below the Hudson and East rivers.

"So Duke Quillian wasn't scheduled to man the evening shift last night?" Mike asked.

"Nah. He wasn't set to work again until next week. I don't know what he was doing down here. But you'll see the list of names. We gave it to your buddies this morning. Those two kids from Tobago were in working the blowpipes. They were the only ones signed out to be in this stretch of the tunnel."

"What's a blowpipe?" I asked. "What were they doing?"

"We did some blasting yesterday morning. When that's done and it's mucked out, then the next crew comes in with blow-pipes. They wash the dirt out of the holes by blasting water and air into them. That's what those cousins were doing when the explosion happened. No clue what Duke was up to, though."

We seemed to be walking for the better part of a mile, slogging through mud while water dripped everywhere. Huge ventilation pipes snaked along the curved walls of the vault, and below them, row upon row of black cable—the source of electricity that powered the dig—hung from hooks that had been drilled into the bedrock.

I stopped when another coughing fit seized me.

"You all right?" Mike asked, again expressing his concern but obviously anxious to press forward.

"She'll live. It's just the dust, Mike," Teddy said. "You need to be down here longer than this to get a real lung disease, like the rest of us have."

I knew he meant well, but his humor wasn't comforting.

"That odor," I said, stifling a gag at the sweet, pungent scent. "Is that gas?"

"Dynamite. Gelatin dynamite, it's called,"

Teddy answered. "Water-resistant. We use tons of it down here."

"Thank Alfred Nobel," Mike said. "Nitro-glycerin and diatomaceous earth. Now all you have to do, Coop, is figure out why the dynamite made an unscheduled appearance last night."

We were getting closer to the scene. Shovels and rakes and sifting screens, the tools of the bomb-squad investigators, were stacked against the wall.

"There's KD," Mike said, calling out as he recognized another of the task force cops, Jimmy Halloran, a guy whose baby face had earned him the nickname Kid Detective.

Mike and Teddy finished greeting the team that had been brought in for the site briefing, and I added my wet handshake when I caught up.

The large men were dwarfed by the enormous piece of machinery that loomed behind them in the tunnel. This was the fantastic mole that was eating its way through the ancient bedrock under New York at the rate of one hundred feet a day.

KD was bringing Mike up to speed. "Nope. No blast was scheduled last evening. So far as anybody knew, you had the two cousins up on this end with blow-pipes, cleaning up the day's mess. We got the names of the eight other men who worked the shift, but they all say they didn't hear anything before the explosion."

"Somebody been talking to them?"

"Yeah, they've been in interviews with guys from the squad the whole day."

"What would you expect them to have heard before it went off?" I asked.

"You gotta excuse her," Mike said. "Digging ditches wasn't a required course at Wellesley."

"There are blasts in the tunnel almost every day," Teddy said, reaching in his plastic bag for another cigarette. "The guys prep the walls by jacklegging a drill ten feet in and making a grid. It ain't exactly a haphazard occurrence."

"And the site is cleared of all workmen, right?" KD asked.

"You bet. You gotta be three miles down the tracks if you don't want to wind up airborne to Brooklyn. There's a three-minute warning that's sent out, and a follow-up with a minute to go. Nobody in his right mind doesn't get the hell out of range."

The empty railroad train that had passed

us on the way down to this spot had coal cars like those on a Lionel train set. They were open on top, and when ready to dump their load, they tipped over on one side and poured out the coal.

KD Halloran stepped sideways and tapped Hal Sherman on the back. The NYPD's best crime-scene investigator was kneeling in the mud, meticulously photographing the splintered remains of the wooden ties that had caught fire in the blast.

He looked up at Halloran—spotted us—and blew me a kiss. "What next?"

KD told him the workmen were ready to load the already processed debris into the cars to be removed from the dig.

One sandhog walked to the far side of the tracks and picked up a long black hose. He turned a spigot and water—more water—poured forth from the nozzle. The muck cars rolled on their sides to receive the first loads.

As two other men began to shovel piles of rubble, the hog with the hose started to spray it all down.

KD asked, "What the hell are you doing?"

Teddy interrupted him, "They gotta keep

the crap wet or we'll choke to death. It's routine."

"Yeah, well, we've got to sift through this again when we get it upstairs," the detective said.

Teddy raised one of his arms to stop the guys. "I thought you were finished."

KD looked to Mike for help. "We've gone through it twice the best we can in this light. We got a couple of tarps spread out behind the crane up in the yard. This all has to be examined more carefully."

"What have you found so far?"

"Pieces of flesh," KD said. "Can't even smell it in here over the dynamite."

"Salt and pepper?" Mike asked, referring to the mixed races of the victims.

"Yeah. Got some teeth, some strips of clothing. I'm telling you, shoot me the next time I complain about working a scene in some roach-filled ten-by-twelve room in a flophouse. This explosive stuff is a nightmare." KD pointed down the tunnel behind me. "The bomb squad makes the focal point of the blast about twenty feet back, but the fragments go a helluva long way from that."

"You locate any device? Got any ideas?"

KD bent over and with his gloved hand lifted a stick of dynamite from a cardboard box between the two sets of tracks. It was about eight inches long and one and a half inches in diameter, wrapped in a waxed paper that seemed to be oil-stained from the nitroglycerin inside.

"We've got some detonating cord in the mess," he said. "It was probably laced through the sticks of dynamite. All on its way to the lab."

Mike looked around at the remaining piles of debris. "So what do you want these guys to do?"

"Shovel it onto the car and take it to the conveyor belt," KD said, his annoyance obvious in his tone. "I just don't want them hosing it down yet, destroying any evidence."

Mike nodded to Teddy, and the men resumed their work.

KD stood next to the second muck car, running the beam of his flashlight back and forth along its length as the rubble was thrown onto it. Something glinted from the ashes and he called out for the guys to stop.

"What is it?" Mike asked, stepping forward to watch as KD picked up the object.

"Looks like a belt buckle." He held it up for us to see, a silvery metal clasp with bits of shredded leather extending from its sides.

"Give me that light again," Mike said, pulling a pair of rubber gloves from his rear pocket and practically sticking his nose into the soot-filled car. "Right here."

KD focused his powerful beam over Mike's shoulder, as I squatted beside him.

I covered my mouth with the plastic mask that hung around my neck as I stared at the thick, white finger that sat atop the pile.

"Bag it, KD. It's no bomb that ripped that digit off," Mike said. "Look at it, Coop."

He scratched the ashes away from it, exposing the tip of the dirt-encrusted nail down to the beefy knuckle that had caught his attention.

"What do—"

"Too even. Damage from an explosion would be much more ragged. My money's on a serrated knife," Mike said. "Somebody sliced this guy's finger off while he was still breathing. Sawed it off like a hunk of steak."

14

"What do you figure, Mercer?" Mike asked. "You think the minute she's through making love, Coop gets out of bed and heads for the locker room?"

Mercer was pouring drinks in my den as I walked in from the bedroom. I had changed into a collared T-shirt and jeans and was toweling off my wet hair. "Clean is good, Mr. Chapman," he said. "I wasn't down in the shaft half as long as you two and I can't wait to get that smell out of my nose either."

"You take more showers than any broad I

know. Don't you like it with a little dirt on your uniform, like you just stole second, sliding into base? Be a little daring?"

"I'm taking a break from daring for the long weekend. What did the ME say?"

"Ah, Ms. Cooper is going into her Vineyard tranquillity mode. A walk on the beach, late-afternoon massage, sunset swim. Enough to make you forget the island of Manhattan is about to implode. You remember the drill, don't you, Mercer?"

"This is all about Joan's wedding, guys. It's not too late to change your minds. I can make room for you at the house."

Joan had come to know Mike and Mercer almost as well as I did. And although the small guest list was a mix of her family and friends, she had sincerely wanted them there with us. Mike was still trying to cope with Val's sudden death when the invitation came and told Joan that he didn't want his mood—gloomy and remote—to put a pall on her happiness. Mercer wouldn't think of going without Mike.

Mike steered the subject back to the water-tunnel death investigation. "Dr. Kestenbaum says antemortem amputation. Hemorrhage in the adjacent tissue. Believes it's this one," he said, flexing the first knuckle next to his thumb. "Duke Quillian—that's a confirmation on the DNA from the mobile lab—was alive when that finger took a walk from the rest of his hand."

"Any prints on file?" I asked.

"Nope. Never been collared."

"You figure how we missed a connection to Brendan yet?"

"I've been going over and over the possible links all day, since I heard the news. It intrigues me as much as it does you. But there's not even one damn phone call that suggests that the brothers talked to each other in the last year."

"Any word on the tire iron?" I asked, sitting on the sofa with my Scotch.

"Like the proverbial hound's tooth, Alex," Mercer said. "Nothing on it."

"Don't take it too personally, kid," Mike said, switching the channel from the news to the final few minutes of *Jeopardy!* "That was just a get-out-of-our-hole signal to all of us interlopers."

"Those hogs don't want us down there," Mercer said. "It's like they think they're going to handle this entire investigation themselves. What happened in Water Tunnel

Number Three stays in Water Tunnel Number Three. No one we talked to saw people near the shaft at the time the damn thing fell, there's no video cameras on top, and the cops were all so busy keeping the reporters out of the yard that they weren't any better at figuring what went on."

"We've got subterranean jurisdiction, don't we?" Mike asked, restoring the sound with the clicker just as Alex Trebek turned to the big board for the last question.

"Battaglia? If there was an intergalactic crime and a light beam from another planet bounced off the sidewalk in Manhattan, he'd claim jurisdiction. Six hundred feet down? Not an issue."

"I'm counting on it. Nothing worse than finding a suspect, convicting him of the bombing, and watching while some legal asshole takes this all the way to the Supremes claiming we got no standing south of the subway system. Those are your people, Coop. That's what they do with a friggin' law degree."

"Feathered Friends," Trebek said. "We haven't seen this subject in a while, gentlemen. Feathered Friends."

"I'm out," Mike said, getting up and walking toward the kitchen. "I'm a city boy. The only bird I know is the pigeon. DNA all over my car and occasionally on the top of my head."

"Twenty bucks," I said. "Everybody plays."

"Speaking of birds, you got anything to eat? Cheese and crackers?"

"Not even that. Sorry. I'll order in from P. J. Bernstein's whenever you're ready."

"Known as the Lord God bird for its stunning plumage and great wingspan, it was thought until recently to be extinct," Trebek read aloud from the square blue answer board.

Two of the contestants couldn't even fake their expressions into a bluff. The third scrawled a short answer on his screen.

"You got it, Coop?" Mike asked, leaning in the doorway of the room.

"Not a clue."

"Peking duck," he said.

"Great wingspan and stunning plumage?"

"Not Trebek's bird. The question is, what do I want Mercer to buy me for dinner?"

"You two need to get a little more religion in your lives," Mercer said as Trebek subtracted two thousand dollars from the winnings of the Nashville firefighter who had taken a stab at the dodo. "What is the ivory-billed woodpecker?"

"The Lord what?" Mike asked. "You bird-watching on the side?"

"You have to know the swamps and tupelos of Alabama," Mercer said. "My granny Wallace told me all about it when I was a kid. Got its name 'cause that's what folk use to cry out when they saw the creature. She had a stuffed one in the attic that she got at a flea market, used to scare me half to death. *Lord God bird* is right."

"You can do better than dinner from the deli, can't you now, Mercer? Shall we upgrade to Chinese?" Mike asked.

"Fine with me," Mercer said, and I opened the drawer of the side table to find the Shun Lee Palace menu.

Mike's beeper vibrated on the bar as I took a food order from each of them. There was no point in placing it until he returned the call. He stepped into the living room and came back several minutes later.

"Don't light any candles or dust off the crystal, Coop. I'm out of here."

Mercer was on his feet at once. "Where to?"

"Westchester County Sheriff's Office. Two

guys were picked up an hour ago at the Kensico Dam," Mike said. "It's a major stop on the Croton Reservoir system that brings water to the city. Used wire cutters to get through the chain-link fence."

"Sandhogs?" I asked.

"Hardly. Saudi nationals. One of them had a map of the entire system, right down to the hole on West Thirtieth Street."

"Explosives?"

"No sign of any blast equipment on or around them, and the driver who was waiting for them got away. They're not talking, but someone called in an anonymous tip fifteen minutes ago. Says the men were planning a chemical attack—dumping a bacterial pathogen in the New York City water supply."

15

I had cleared security for the nine-thirty flight from La Guardia to Martha's Vineyard. It was Friday morning—still no update from Mike—and although I had looked forward to my friend Joan Stafford's wedding for several months, it was hard to think about anything except the events of the last twenty-four hours.

Most of the passengers in the lounge were watching the television monitor that was mounted on the wall. The same reporter who had covered the tunnel-explosion story,

Julie Kirsch, was now on location on a thickly wooded hillside in Valhalla, the West-chester suburb in which Kensico was located.

"Too early to know yet," Kirsch said, in re-sponse to a question that the anchor had posed. "New York City police officials have been working through the night with local authorities to get answers to some of those questions, but there's just no way to say whether the two incidents are connected."

Glancing at her notes, Kirsch went on, "While the threat of biological and chemical terrorism has been of great concern to the government, most experts are telling us to-day that the risk of individuals succeeding at some kind of deadly mass dissemination is quite small."

"Why is that, Julie?" the studio voice in-terrupted.

"Simply because of the enormous volume of water that flows into the city from up-state. The counterterrorist agents I've talked to this morning agree that the toxic effect of the chemical would most likely be diluted by the billions of gallons before any real harm was done. I'd like to take the viewers back to the news of the grim discovery made inside the tunnel in Manhattan yesterday."

Most likely were not the two most encouraging words I'd rely on before drinking from the tap in my apartment anytime soon.

Julie Kirsch's cross-examiner pressed for more detail. "Before you do, would you tell us exactly what kind of agent might be used for such a chemical attack? We all recall the deadly sarin gas in Tokyo."

"Well, I've been asked not to alarm our viewers unnecessarily," she said, hesitating before she went on. "For example, one gram of typhoid culture dropped into a water system would have an impact roughly equal to forty pounds of potassium cyanide. Or, a person drinking a few sips of untreated water from a reservoir this size that had been contaminated by *Salmonella typhi* would become deathly ill."

I was grateful when the U.S. Airways gate agent interrupted the news program with her boarding announcement.

The fifty-minute flight over Long Island Sound on the cloudless morning offered spectacular views of the seascape that was so familiar to me from years of commuting to my favorite retreat—the coastline of the

North Fork, Montauk Point, the short hop to Block Island, and the descent to the Vineyard as the forty-two-seat turboprop crossed Cuttyhunk and circled the cliffs of Aquinnah.

My caretaker had parked my convertible at the airport, and I put the top down for the short ride to my home. The path curved alongside the bike trails that cut through the forests of West Tisbury, then climbed the gently winding slopes of Chilmark, lined with stone walls that had been built hundreds of years ago to separate each farmer's land from the next.

I was so pleased to be hosting the wedding for Joan and Jim, even though it was a bittersweet reminder that my own engagement had ended so tragically shortly after I'd graduated from law school. Once it wouldn't have been possible for me to think of standing on the site where Adam and I were to have been married and celebrating someone else's happiness. But in the last couple of years, I had found solace and strength in great friendships, and fortitude from the experiences of the women who entrusted their lives to me every day that I went to work.

I parked next to the barn, pausing before going into the house, looking out over the meadow and the sea, a view that never failed to restore my spirit.

The answering machine was choked with messages. I kicked off my shoes, opened the French doors that led to the deck, and sat on the steps surrounded by pale blue hydrangea bushes while I played them back.

"It's me. We got here last night. Call me the very minute you get in." Joan's voice was as vibrant as she herself had been ever since Jim had proposed.

Her second message asked whether I had room at my house for one extra guest, a friend of Jim's who had, at the last minute, decided to make the trip from Europe.

There were the voices of the caterers and the florist, well-meaning mutual friends who didn't want to miss any of the events that Joan had planned for the weekend, the photographer who was going to shoot the ceremony, and the captain whom Jim had hired to take his friends shark-fishing in the afternoon. An update from Max, at the office, was sandwiched in the middle.

The final call had come in moments before I arrived. My beloved college roommate and best friend, Nina Baum, had phoned as she boarded the 8 a.m. flight from Los Angeles to Boston. I hadn't seen her in months, and as with Joan, I could confide in her about everything that was going on—or not going on—in my life. Nina confirmed that she'd make the connection to Cape Air and be with us by the time dinner ended. Her husband had a screenplay in production and couldn't accompany her after all.

The phone rang as I walked into the kitchen to check the decorations and floral arrangements that had been set around all the rooms of the house.

"Why haven't you called me?" Joan asked.

"I've only been here five minutes."

"Do you believe this is happening?"

"I'm beginning to. Do you?"

"If I don't drive Jim out of town first. I've got to come over. The poor guy is trying to write an article about an Iraqi insurgent who beheaded four hostages today, and between the spectacular view from our room and my constant chatter, he may just put himself on the next ferry off-island. Can you make him marry me in absentia?"

Jim Hageville—the groom—was an expert on foreign affairs whose syndicated column was the first opinion piece with which most intelligent readers started their day. Joan was an accomplished playwright and novelist who split her time between their homes in Washington and New York. She was known as well in both places for her salonlike dinner parties—mixing intellectuals, politicians, writers, and old friends like Nina and me—and for staying impossibly au courant on the social crimes of the rich and famous with whom she had been raised, while I covered the street-crime beat.

"Are you at the Outermost?" I asked, referring to the inn at which she and Jim were staying. "Come right now. I'll put some coffee on."

"Did you get my message about Luc?"

"Who's Luc?"

"Jim's friend. Maybe I forgot to tell you his name. Anyway, there are three weddings on the island this weekend—not a hotel room to be had. I'm desperate to find him a place."

"Of course he can stay here, if he doesn't mind being surrounded by women. Nina's in the big guest room, Lynn and Cathy have the suite at the top of the stairs, so Luc can have the little bedroom overlooking the garden." It was the room I'd been saving in case I had convinced Mike and Mercer to change their minds.

"I think he'd rather fancy those odds. What a relief, Alex. He won't get in until tomorrow, I don't think. Be there in ten minutes, okay?"

I called Laura and she reassured me that the office was quiet. I filled the coffeepot and took the portable phone out on the deck.

I dialed Mike's cell. He picked up on the second ring, so I knew he was neither in the water tunnel nor attending an autopsy. "What's new from the chapel of love?" he asked.

"Joan's wired. Very excited, as she should be. She's on her way over and I'm going to try to distract her for the rest of the day. Tell me about last night?"

"Pretty scary scenario to see how close people can get to those reservoirs. These two guys they picked up are tough. Couldn't get squat out of them."

"You think they're connected to the blast in the city, too?"

"I'm fresh out of crystal balls, sweetheart. Westchester's holding them on a trespassing charge for now, while we try to sort it all out. And your trial slows down another step."

"Why?"

"Duke Quillian's funeral is set for Monday. Canonical law—can't be done on Sunday and there just wasn't any way for the family to get it together for tomorrow."

"So I lose another day? How do you know? The judge's secretary hasn't even called Laura yet."

"Lieutenant Peterson got the notification from the Corrections Department. Gave me the detail for two take-out orders. He's letting your perp go for a visit to the wake on Saturday afternoon. Just the family—no outsiders. Back to the Tombs. Then we've got to take him to the funeral on Monday morning. Church and cemetery."

"In shackles, I hope."

"Temper, temper, Coop. That's a photo op you don't want your jurors to have—the graveside shot of the grieving brother in cuffs and leg-irons."

"Well, doesn't the lieutenant think somebody from the squad ought to be interviewing these siblings we didn't even know Brendan Quillian had?"

"Nothing your buddy Lem Howell didn't think of first. Not one of the Quillians has any interest in answering our questions. The only thing they claim is that little brother Brendan has been estranged from all of them for years."

"Did they give a reason for that?"

"Suppose you take care of what you're supposed to do this weekend and I'll try to have all these answers by Monday."

"I don't get to nudge you about one more thing?" I asked.

"Shoot."

"Lawrence Pritchard. The engineer who was fired from the water project for taking kickbacks. I know you were peeved at George Golden yesterday, but you've got to talk to someone about exactly what that involved."

"Relax, blondie. Reset your coffeepot with decaf for a change. Get off the high-octane juice, okay? Teddy O'Malley has the skinny on that. It all happened when Duke Quillian was the union rep three years back.

A bribery scheme that Pritchard tried to engineer with one of the bureaucrats. Not good for the union, so he and Duke went head-to-head on it."

"But Max checked with the rackets bureau this afternoon," I said. "There was never an indictment—not even any record of an investigation."

"Bronx County, Coop. Battaglia never got his hands on this one."

A large portion of the tunnel construction was completed in the Bronx before work had even gotten under way in Manhattan. I should have thought of that myself. "And Duke never cooperated?"

"Cat got his tongue. Might have had something to do with the fact that Lawrence Pritchard threatened to put big Duke's lights out if he ever squealed. Maybe that's why Brendan Quillian wants to find him."

16

"You really ought to get some sleep," Nina said. "It's almost midnight."

"How often do I have the chance to sit up all night and talk to you?"

Joan and Jim had organized a sunset clambake for the thirty guests who had arrived for the wedding. The glorious stretch of Black Point Beach was on the Atlantic Ocean, and with bonfires ablaze, we had feasted on local shellfish taken right out of Tisbury Great Pond, hot clam chowder from the Bite, burgers from the Galley, and dozens of lobsters from Larsen's Fish Market.

When I returned to the house after the festive evening, Nina—who had randomly been assigned as my roommate from our first day at Wellesley—was settling in after her long trip from California. We had taken different paths in both our personal and professional lives—Nina marrying a college boyfriend and mothering her young son, Gabe, while also making partner at a powerhouse L.A. law firm, with an expertise in packaging large entertainment projects for screen and television movies.

Nina had opened a bottle of Sancerre and nestled into the oversize armchair in a corner of the living room, and I filled my glass and settled in on the floor in my sweatshirt and leggings, resting my head on a pillow at her feet.

We caught each other up on family, I listened to Nina talk about the contract negotiations of her latest deal, and she indulged me while I tried out my response to Lem Howell's motion to dismiss Brendan Quillian's murder indictment for failure to make the People's case.

"So, cut to the chase, Alex," she said,

yawning and pulling a cashmere throw over her robe. "Didn't you tell me that you were bringing a guy to the wedding? For almost a month his name was in every e-mail you sent me. Then he dropped off a cliff."

"Easy come, easy go. I got in a bit over my head, and our pal the bride didn't exactly help."

"This was your airplane pickup?"

"Yup. Dan Bolin. Met him in April, when Joanie was up here with me for the weekend. Came on way too strong but even she thought he was charming." I reminded Nina of the story of our meeting.

"Did you . . . ?" Nina said, lifting her eyebrows as she tried to tease an admission out of me.

"No. Never got that far."

Her leg straightened out and she poked her toe against my knee. "It's me you're talking to. Tell the truth."

I smiled and sipped my wine. "Turns out he wasn't quite as separated as he told me he was when we started dating. Couldn't ever see me on Thursday evenings. I bought the story that it was his standing racquetball game and dinner with the guys."

"What was it?"

"Marriage counseling. They were still trying to find a way to put things back together. Dan's one of those guys who just can't stand being alone for a minute."

"Thank goodness he told you before you got in any deeper."

"He didn't tell me. The florist did."

"What?"

"Way too many flowers. The Dan Bolin signature. All flowers all the time. About six weeks into our dating frenzy, there must have been a particularly heartwarming session with the counselor. The estranged wife got a magnificent bouquet, and mine must have been pretty nice as well."

"You never saw it?"

"Nope. The florist mixed up the delivery. I got hers with a note promising reconciliation as soon as his head cleared, and whatever enticing words he penned to lure me into bed landed in her hands. She called him while I was still up in court. The whole thing was over before it began."

"Sometimes, when I'm dealing with the PTA and playdates and car pools, I'm so envious of your lifestyle I want to scream. And then I think of how miserable it would be to be back on the market and wouldn't swap with you for all the money in the world. Didn't Joan have a fix-up for you months ago?"

I rolled on my side and stared out the window at the nearly full moon that lit the lawn and the surface of the water at the bottom of the hill. "She's always got a prospect for me. I just can't stand blind dates. I've got nothing to talk about but my work."

"That's ridiculous. You've got great friends, you do interesting things, you're a voracious reader, and you happen to have a job that gives you enormous emotional satisfaction. Talk about those things."

"Yeah, but most guys really think the job is strange. That I must stay in the office because I hate men or something."

"Don't they understand how rewarding it is to take victims into court and help them regain their dignity?" Nina said. "Guys like Mike get it. Why couldn't you convince him to come up here this weekend?"

I got up from the floor, kissed Nina on the crown of her head, and embraced her.

"It's only been six months since Val was killed. It's still way too raw for him. I keep trying to find ways to—you know—ways to get him out of his morose mood, bring him *back.* It's like I've lost my right arm."

I started toward my bedroom as Nina corked the bottle.

"I know what you can do to bring him back, Alex. You know it, too, don't you?"

I waved her off.

"You fly up here with Mike one weekend, to this incredibly romantic setting. A few logs in the fireplace, more of this great wine. You'll both be better for it. You haven't forgotten *how,* have you?"

"I'm cutting you off, Nina," I said, wagging a finger at her and laughing. "I work with the man. We're partners on some of the most serious cases in the city, and you know as well as I do that our professional relationship would have to end if—if—"

"If you got smart and took a chance? Worst that happens is that somebody else will work the big trials."

"I need the judge and jury to speculate about my sexual escapades, too? You've met Lem Howell—Mr. Triplicate. That would be a really sweet cross-examination, wouldn't it?" I paced the floor, doing my best imitation of Howell's manner and delivery. "'Isn't it true, Detective Chapman, that

Ms. Cooper asked you—no, ordered you—
demanded that you come up with some
kind of confession from my client? Isn't it
true that you fabricated this statement in order to get yourself into her arms—into her
pants—into her bed?'"

I stopped and shook my head. "I can't believe I actually worry about how complicated my friendship is with Mike."

"Bad news and good news."

"What? That with my track record the romance won't work, and I'll also be out of a
job for going after it?"

"The bad news is that you're dead-on
about the line of questioning from a good
defense attorney," Nina said. "The good
news is that you even think about it."

17

"Isn't rain supposed to mean good luck on your wedding day?"

Nina and I were helping Joan dress, in my bedroom, at six o'clock on Saturday. Our friends were gathering on the wide lawn, and there wasn't a cloud in sight anywhere in the brilliant blue sky.

"There were a few sprinkles just after midnight," Nina said. "Make do with that. My hair would be a nightmare if there was even a hint of precipitation."

"Here you go, Joan. Borrowed and blue in

one fell swoop." I unhooked the sapphire bracelet that Nina's husband had given her on her tenth anniversary and clasped it on the bride's wrist. "You look absolutely drop-dead gorgeous."

"I can barely breathe in this thing," Joan said, adjusting the strapless ivory dress and looking out the window at the couples ambling toward the tent where the ceremony would be performed. "I should never have had that lobster roll for lunch yesterday. Where's my Jimmy?"

"He's right out there, talking to your mother," Nina said.

"Is he wearing socks?" Joan asked.

"Why . . . ?"

"No cold feet, right?" Joan walked into the bathroom to finish touching up.

"He looks deliriously happy, darling. It's either the three-hundred-fifty-pound thresher shark the guys caught today or he really does want to get hitched. You ready to make this legal?" I picked up the leather-bound folder that held my remarks. The certificate from the secretary of the Commonwealth of Massachusetts authorizing me to solemnize the marriage was on top.

Nina and I looked each other over, head

to toe, as we had done scores of times before we'd set out on the town together.

She put her arms on my shoulders and squared off in front of me. "Are you sure you can do this?" she asked.

When Adam's car had crashed on the way to the Vineyard, it was Nina who had had to break the news of his death to me. This very hilltop that was supposed to be the site of our own wedding represented for a time my greatest heartbreak. Now it would be invested with new joy.

"Don't ever forget him, will you?"

"Not a prayer."

"Then this is the perfect thing to do for Joan and Jim. Thanks for asking."

"You're mush under all that tough stuff you put on in court," Nina said as Joan came back to us for a second look. "Here comes the bride. Okay, you're ravishing this time. Good-bye, Ms. Stafford, and hello, Mrs. Hageville. See you shortly."

We could hear the music playing. It was my turn to give the bride a last prenuptial hug and walk out to the tent. Jim offered his hand and I stepped up on the platform, happy to see that so many of our friends had made the trip to my island paradise to witness the happy occasion.

I scanned the rows of guests as everyone turned to follow the bride's procession toward the makeshift altar. Nina winked at me, and I noticed a man I'd never seen before leaning down to whisper something in her ear. Joan and Jim broke into irrepressible smiles as they locked eyes and she glided into place by his side.

"Dearly beloved, we have come together here today, on this magical island—on a perfect June evening—to celebrate the marriage of Joan and Jim.

"How fitting it is that the Vineyard is the place you chose to formalize your union. The first trip you took together was to this island, finding pleasure in its glorious natural setting, finding sustenance in the magnificent waters that encircle its shores."

I had written a short service for them, after which I was ready to take the bride and groom through the classic vows—simple words that belied the profound commitment they represent.

". . . as I ask you, Jim, do you take Joan to be your wife? To have and to hold, from this day forward—for better, for worse, for richer, for poorer, in sickness and in health, to love and to cherish, so long as you both shall live?"

His strong basso voice resonated throughout the tent when he said, "I do."

Now all the ladies' tissues came out. Joan affirmed her vows as rings were exchanged and I ended the short ceremony. "It gives me great pleasure, by virtue of *whatever* authority is vested in me by the laws of the Commonwealth of Massachusetts, to now pronounce you man and wife. Jim, you may kiss the bride."

The devoted friends were all on their feet applauding the long embrace and the recessional, before moving to the two larger tents that had been set up, one for a seated dinner and the other for dancing.

Champagne corks popped as waiters filled our glasses and Jim made a toast to his dazzling bride. Nina snaked her way to me after greeting old friends and stopping to chat with Mrs. Stafford.

"Add this talent to your résumé, Alex. You did just fine."

"I'll pass on that, but thanks," I said, touching my flute against hers. "It's even more nerve-racking than giving an opening argument. I kept waiting for someone to stand up in the tent and object."

"Mrs. Stafford almost did. She can't bear the thought of Joan living in Washington."

"Neither can I. Now, who's your new best friend, darling? You were tête-à-tête through the whole ceremony."

"The poor guy didn't know anybody, so I was pointing out all the players. I never got his name, but he said he goes way back with Jim. Catch your eye, did he? I didn't think he was your type."

"What would that be?"

"Aloof. Unavailable. Self-centered. Any or all of the above. Who did the seating for dinner? Maybe I can play around with the place cards," Nina said. "His looks are so uneven, aren't they? Makes it more interesting."

"Don't mess with Joan's tables. It's all very carefully calculated."

I could see Jim's friend just a few feet away, conversing with two other journalists I'd met last night. Nina was right about his features. One wouldn't describe him as classically handsome—a slim, chiseled face with what my mother called a Roman nose, long and straight, and wire-rimmed glasses that shaded his blue-gray eyes. But he exuded a strong, attractive presence, and I blushed when he turned and caught me staring at him.

"How old do you think he is?" Nina asked.

"Who?"

"The guy in your sights."

"Sorry. I was just daydreaming—nothing serious. Maybe forty-five or so."

"A mature man would be such a good change for you. Better mingle, Alex. Here comes Mrs. S."

"That was such a sweet thing for you to do," Joan's mother said as she approached me to introduce a gaggle of relatives. "You've absolutely got to be the next to go. Aren't your parents frantic that you're still single?"

"I figure they've just given up on me."

"Married to her job," she said to the others. "That's what I always say about Miss Alexandra."

I circulated among our friends and guests for more than an hour, until the sun slipped behind the Aquinnah ridge and the groom asked us all to be seated.

"You're with us," Joan said, looping her arm through mine and walking me to the table, to the seat next to Jim. "We'll never be able to thank you enough for doing this. I'm delirious, and everyone else seems to be having a great time."

"Congratulations. I hope I'm gaining a husband and not losing one of my best friends."

"That's a deal," Jim said. "Have you two met yet?"

I turned to find his friend standing behind me. "No. No, we haven't. I'm Alex. Alexandra Cooper."

He gave me a crooked smile—sexy and warm—and set his glass down on the table before reaching for my hand. "Luc. Luc Rouget. Joan tells me you've graciously agreed to put a roof over my head tonight. I'm very grateful."

"I know how pleased they must be to have you here," I said as he pulled out my chair and waited for me to sit down. "I'm delighted to do it. When did you get to the island?"

The French accent was an added starter. "About an hour before the ceremony."

"From?"

"A very long trip, actually. My home is in Mougins—the south of France. Do you know it?"

"The Côte d'Azur. I've only been there once. It's quite beautiful."

"Then you must come again. I shall have to repay your hospitality."

The seating plan was no accident. Joan's playfulness amused me. "And you've traveled all this way for the wedding?"

The waiter refilled our glasses as Luc leaned in to talk to me. "It was a perfect opportunity for me to get some business done in New York this week. Jim and I go back twenty years—when he was assigned to the Paris bureau of the *Washington Post*. I didn't want to miss this affair."

Nina was standing behind the waiter, trying to get to her seat to Luc's left. He rose to greet her again as she bent over and tried to whisper discreetly in my ear.

"I've got a little more intelligence on your houseguest. Add three years, an ex-wife— but really ex—and two kids," she said. "And he's G.U."

The translation meant that Luc was forty-eight and divorced, but geographically undesirable.

"Were you in on this plan?"

"Totally Joan. There's an ocean and an Alpine mountain range between the two of you. I haven't lost my mind completely," Nina said, straightening up and handing the handkerchief she had borrowed from Luc during the ceremony back to him. "Thanks for the loan. I know you're Luc. I'm Nina Baum."

"Enchanté," he said, kissing her out-stretched hand. "Without you, I wouldn't have had any idea who all these people are. You and Alexandra are the only two I got a full advance briefing on."

"You did?" Nina asked.

"Well, Jim told me that your husband couldn't make the trip, so I'm to be certain that your glass is always full and to expect that you'll need a dance partner from time to time," Luc said, as expressive with his hands as he was with his eyes. "And I'm afraid I have to admit, Alex, that Joan had planned to introduce us a few months ago, when I was in the city. I think you—how shall I say? You protested, is that right?"

Joan had urged me to accept a setup with a guy whom she had befriended after one of her readings. I remembered it was for a Valentine's Day museum benefit. "So you're the writer, then?"

"No, no," he said, shaking a finger. "After

him. Joan told me about him. She said she couldn't move you even to have that dinner. I think she decided to try a little—well, foreign intrigue. You were investigating a murder at the time. Some terrible thing at Lincoln Center, and it seemed rather foolish to try to take you away from that. Did you get your man?"

"I wish I could say she always does."

"Yes, the police solved it."

"So what kind of business are you in?" Nina wasn't the least bit subtle in trying to get Luc's pedigree.

"I own a restaurant. In Mougins. I do some consulting in Paris and New York. That's why I'm here so often."

"So, you wear the toque and the white jacket and sprinkle pepper in the pot and go *'Bam!'*?" Nina asked.

Luc laughed. "No, *chère madame,* I'm not an entertainer. I own the restaurant. I'm the executive chef, as we say, but I don't do the cooking."

"How many stars?" Nina asked.

"Michelin? Three stars, naturally," he said playfully, feigning surprise that she even needed to inquire.

"Excellent," she said. "I'm not going all

that way to sample any one-star joint. Truffles?"

"In season, of course. From Périgord, not those ridiculous American ones you try to cultivate in North Carolina."

"Your wine cellar?"

"Superbe."

"It's a very tough business. It's so competitive," Nina said. "How did you get into it?"

"The easy way," he said, pocketing his glasses, so that the blue-gray eyes appeared to be more vivid. "I was born into it. Did you two ever know Lutèce?"

The landmark French restaurant that had closed its elegant doors a couple of years ago had been the center of the culinary world in New York for four decades.

"Very well. Alex took me there the first time I came to the city on a business trip."

"André Rouget?" Luc asked.

"America's first superstar chef," I said, thinking of the many special occasions in my life that had been feted in that wonderful town house on East Fiftieth Street.

"He's my father. So you see, I had rather a good head start."

"How divine it was," Nina said. "I wish it hadn't shut down."

"Well, perhaps we can do something about that," Luc said. "One of the things I've been exploring on these trips is the possibility of re-creating the restaurant."

The music had started and the bridal couple made their way to the adjacent tent, which had been set up for the small band. When others joined in on the second number, Luc asked Nina to dance. She tried to resist and turn him over to me.

"When I hear a Smokey Robinson song," he said, sounding ever so French as he pronounced my favorite Motown name, "then I understand I'm to come back for Alexandra."

The next few hours were a seductive mix of dancing and dining, talking while trying to keep myself grounded as my heart fluttered for the first time since my ill-fated romance with Jake Tyler.

By the end of the evening, after Joan had tossed her bouquet and driven off with her groom, only a dozen of us were left on my deck.

"Would you like to take a walk?" Luc asked.

I stepped out of my heels and rested my empty glass on the ground, leading him to the footpath beyond my caretaker's cottage. "Let's go down to the water."

I hadn't felt this kind of electricity in a long time, but I knew I had to get off this one spot, this piece of earth that still called up Adam's memory whenever I stood on it. I wanted to kiss Luc, I wanted to be held by him and caressed, and yet I wanted to pace this newfound excitement just as badly.

Nina saw us start to walk away and followed me to the top of the steps. "See you in the morning, *mes amis,*" she called out to us. "She's really gotten rusty, Luc. Her French—I mean her French is rusty. Make her work on it."

He picked up my hand as we walked down the grassy slope, neither saying a word until we reached the edge of the pond. The sand felt good underfoot, and I let go of Luc to wade into the shallow water, refreshed and a bit sobered by the cold June current that lapped over my feet.

I turned around and Luc took my face in his hands. Moonlight bounced off the surface of the pond, and for three or four minutes we just drank each other in while he held on to me and stroked the outline of my features. Then he started to brush at the tendrils of hair, wisps that had broken loose from my ponytail as we'd danced, that had curled around my forehead and the nape of my neck.

Gently but firmly, he put his lips down against my mine, kissing me over and over until I opened my mouth and kissed him in return. For more than an hour, we walked the shoreline and climbed slowly back up to the yard, stopping to taste each other from time to time, trying to slow ourselves down.

The lights were out in the guest bedrooms and my other friends had departed. I started to lead Luc back out to the deck. The night was too beautiful to waste on sleep.

Instead, he opened the screen door into the living room. "I know you won't turn into a pumpkin, but I have very strict orders from Joan to send you off to sleep before it gets to be too late. She said you're in the middle of a big trial and you must absolutely be tucked in by—"

Luc looked at his watch and uttered a completely Gallic "Ooof. You see? I lost all sense of time."

"But we can sit up for a little longer."

He put a finger up to my lips to quiet me. "I've got to pay attention to the rules or maybe I won't be invited back. Your room is here?"

"Yes," I said, walking through the kitchen and study. Luc followed behind me and took my arm as I opened the bedroom door to go inside.

He pressed me against the wall and kissed me again—harder this time—on my mouth. Then he nibbled at the top of my ear, smiling as he pushed me over the threshold and backed away. *"Bonne nuit, ma princesse. Bonne nuit."*

18

"Sorry to bring you back early," Mike said, closing the car door outside the shuttle terminal at noon on Sunday. "I think I need you for this interview. Festivities over?"

"Mostly." I had been sitting on the deck of the Chilmark Store with Luc, drinking coffee, eating a blueberry muffin, and reading the Sunday *Times* when Mike had called. Switching my flight from evening to midday was simply a reality check. Holding people's lives in our hands as we did with every serious case we handled, I never questioned

the urgency of an interruption from Mike or
Mercer. Today—leaving the Vineyard, and
Luc—I felt as if I'd been wrenched out of
paradise.

"Tell me about the call," I said. I needed to
focus on Mike's new information, but last
night's hours with Luc had been one of
those encounters that struck like a thunder-
bolt. "You think she's for real?"

"The first one came in this morning. Peterson said she sounded legit."

"Caller ID?"

"Yeah. Just a pay phone. But it's right
around the corner from the funeral home in
the Bronx where Duke Quillian's being
waked, so that fits."

"She asked for you specifically?"

"'Detective Chapman. The man who
locked up Brendan Quillian.' That's how she
put it."

"Did she give a name?" I knew I was
missing a chance to let Luc's magic work itself on me back in Chilmark, and I couldn't
help but wonder if that was a moment that
would ever present itself to me again.

"Nope. Said she wouldn't talk to anyone
but me. Peterson told her to phone back in
an hour, then called and told me to get my-

self back to the squad," Mike said. "Something wrong? You look distracted."

"Just tired. Has he got anyone sitting on the phone booth?"

"Iggy grabbed somebody to go with her." Ignacia Bliss was one of a handful of women to have penetrated the ranks of Manhattan's elite homicide squad. She had the skill and intelligence necessary for the job, but was usually short on charm and humor. Still tacked to the windowsill behind her desk was the sign with which Mike had reluctantly welcomed her to the mostly macho unit—IGNORANCE IS BLISS.

"Were you there when she called back?"

"Yeah. But it was a pretty short conversation. She asked me a few questions and for whatever reason seemed satisfied that I was the right guy. Told me she has information about Duke Quillian's death. Said she knows the explosion wasn't an accident."

"Wouldn't give her name?"

"Nope. And she refuses to come into the office to talk. Not mine, not yours. Won't give it to the bomb squad or the task force. She wants me."

"Did Iggy eyeball her?"

Mike shook his head. "She made the second call from a different phone, different neighborhood. Iggy cruised around the funeral parlor for a while, but she says that won't tell us anything. Every sandhog and his wife, every parishioner from Duke's church—the place is expected to be a mob scene by three o'clock."

"So what kind of deal did you make with your lady?"

"The wake starts at three. She wants to meet me at two, a few subway stops away, in a bar—El Borricua—in Soundview."

"Where's that?"

"Between the Bronx River and the parkway. No view of the Sound at all, in case you're looking for one, and a completely Hispanic neighborhood. I think we're going someplace that none of her peeps will recognize her."

Mike had told me to hide my blond hair under a baseball cap and wear sweats or something that would call no attention to myself. Iggy would be our backup outside the bar.

We drove from the airport in Queens, over the Triborough Bridge, to the Bronx. Mike knew the territory and steered us to the neighborhood, which seemed to be a clumsy assortment of tenements wedged between redbrick housing projects. We found the bar and, a block beyond, saw Iggy waiting for us in her car.

Mike pulled up alongside. "You scope it out yet?"

"Yeah. I been in. Sleepy little place. I'm not sure you'd want to eat anything there, but there's enough rum behind the bar to float a navy."

"Anybody home?"

"A bunch of old guys wearing polyester guayaberas and watching soccer on the tube. A few roosters in the back and I'd think I was in Humacao," Iggy said, referring to the small town in Puerto Rico where she'd been raised. "There are four booths along the wall. That last one is where you want to be."

"Thanks. We got some time to kill. I'll take Coop for something to eat."

"Pelham Parkway. You could get some good bacalaitos. We'll sit on the place," Iggy said, pushing herself up off the car seat to look at me. "You taking her in with you?"

"Yeah. That's the plan."

"Well, I better set myself up at the bar with the boys," the petite detective with straight black hair and dark brown skin said to Mike. "If you think you've camouflaged that white-bread prosecutor with a Yankees hat and workout clothes, you're thicker than I thought. I'll keep the old geezers occupied inside. Give me ten for a couple of Coronas."

Mike passed her a bill and we drove off for a late lunch.

This kind of thing—a mysterious caller offering useful information—had happened to us scores of times before. Once, the night before my closing argument, a woman who lived in a penthouse apartment on Central Park West had called to tell me she had seen the real killer while walking her dog just minutes before the murder inside the Rambles had occurred. If we ignored the information, we might be missing an essential clue, a possible witness, or a piece of exculpatory evidence. The dog walker had been a whack job and a waste of time, but one of us had to follow up on every lead and evaluate its usefulness.

We discussed that old case while we ate at the counter of the diner. Mike told me about Brendan Quillian's short reunion with his family—quiet and uneventful—at the funeral parlor yesterday afternoon. Mike and the other detective had waited at the door of the small chapel in which Duke's body was laid out, and for an hour Brendan had been allowed to visit with his relatives. I described Joan's wedding and extended regards from the friends who had asked after Mike. Neither of us talked about anything more personal that had happened over the weekend, which had been the nature of most of our conversations since Val's death.

"Let's go get comfy at El Borricua," he said, getting off the stool to pay the check.

We doubled back to the narrow street and walked into the dingy restaurant. The men at the bar all turned to look as we slowly made our way to the back of the room. Mike was fooling himself if he thought no one made him as an NYPD detective.

Iggy, whose tight black jeans and slinky white shirt had caught the eye of the regulars, was standing among them and drinking. As we passed by, she said something in Spanish about *policía* and waved us off as she encouraged them to ignore us. Mike wasn't the one trying to hide his identity. It was the caller who preferred this spot to her home or a police station.

Mike sat with his back against the wall, facing the door. We each ordered a beer to make the proprietor happy, and I sipped the soda chaser as we waited.

When the woman came in, she must have noticed Mike immediately in the darkened room. I saw him sit up straight as the footsteps approached our booth.

His mouth fell open as she revealed herself to us at the table, untying the black scarf that she had wrapped around her head.

"I'm Trish. Patricia Quillian. Brendan's my brother—Duke was, too."

Mike was on his feet. "I'm Mike Chapman. I saw you there yesterday. I—uh, I'm sorry about Duke."

"It's no accident at all, Mr. Chapman. He was murdered in that tunnel, that's the truth. I can tell you who did it and I can tell you why it happened. But you've got to help me, Mr. Chapman. They'd kill me for talking to you."

19

"This is Alexandra Cooper, Ms. Quillian. She's the assistant DA on—"

"I know very well who she is." Trish's speech was sharp and clipped, and if she could have spit at me, I think she would have. "She'll have to leave."

The woman was younger than I but had hard features, pale skin lined prematurely with creases, and eyelids reddened from crying. She was tall and gaunt—unlike her brothers—and her shoulders slumped, perhaps from the weight of the week's events.

"Alex is working this investigation with me. There's nothing you can tell me that I won't be telling her."

"She's railroaded Brendan, that's what I know. I won't have her here."

"We're a team, Trish. You think you've got something to help us on Duke's case, give me another call," Mike said.

"She's not one of us. She won't understand me." I assumed Trish was referring to the Irish Catholic bond she expected to make with Mike.

"C'mon, Coop. Let's move on."

I was halfway out of the booth as Trish Quillian stopped chewing on her lip and told me to sit down. Mike had heard the desperation in her voice and knew that as much as she must have hated both of us, she needed something only Mike could do for her.

"Will you sit?" he asked.

She looked at the door and then down at me. I slid over to the wall and she sat beside me, clutching the black cloth coat that seemed way too heavy for the warm afternoon.

"Are you okay here? We can go somewhere else."

"Back when I was a kid, this was McGinty's Pub. Had a cousin who worked here till the whole neighborhood turned over. No one knows me here anymore."

"Who are you afraid of, Trish? We ought to know that before we get started."

The question provoked the hint of a smile. "I'd have to start with my own blood. I've got two brothers left now—that's besides Brendan, even though he doesn't really count anymore. The both of them would kill me just for talking to you."

I wondered why Brendan didn't count.

"Any others?" Mike asked.

"I take it you know something about sandhogs? Not a one of them wants you people snooping around their business. They'll be promising me Lord knows what to just be still and let them find out what happened in the hole, what got Duke killed, themselves. Screw the cops."

"Is that because you think whoever murdered Duke is also a sandhog?"

"Of course he is."

"And the young men from Tobago?" I asked. "They were part of the murder plan?"

"I don't know what they were, Ms.

Cooper. I'm not here to talk about them. Maybe they just got in the way."

"Does this have anything to do with Brendan's case?"

She hesitated when the bar owner came back to ask if she wanted a drink. "Also a beer, lady?"

"No. I'll take a shot of whiskey. Straight." Trish then answered me without turning her head to me, "I can't prove that yet, but I'll bet that it does."

"So, why don't you tell us your theory? Tell us who did it and why," Mike said, waiting as the shot glass was placed in front of her and letting her take a drink.

I could tell from his tone that Mike was skeptical of Trish's usefulness. She seemed to be the bitter voice of the hapless Quillians, and he wouldn't want to head off on a wild-goose chase just to assuage her while his task-force colleagues were following solid leads.

She looked up at Mike from the small glass she was rubbing between her fingers. "Do you know the name Hassett?"

We exchanged glances. I let Mike answer. "I think there was a Hassett—Bobby Hassett—working at the tunnel site on Thursday."

He was one of the workers who had refused George Golden's request to take us down in the shaft. But so had a dozen others.

Her eyes widened. "Doing what? Not getting in the way of my brother's investigation, was he?"

"No, no, no. What's he to you?" Mike asked.

"There's no polite way to say it, Mr. Chapman. He's scum. The Hassett boys—that's just what they are."

"I'll try to take your word for it, Trish. But it would help if you could explain why."

"I could give you more reasons than you've got time to listen to. I raised quite a row at the wake last night, after you were gone. The three of them dared show up, dared walk in there like decent souls to pay their respects with the rest of the crowd. I told Bobby—he's the oldest Hassett, must be twenty-four now—I told Bobby we knew they'd done the killing," Trish said, working herself up, her cheeks flaming red and her lips taut, chafed from the way she'd nervously been chewing on them. "I told them to get out of there before I had them dragged out by their boots."

Mike let her rage on until she completed her tirade. With as much patience as he was able to maintain, he tried to coax a sensible story from her.

"Trish, you said you know the Hassetts killed Duke. Is there any evidence you can point me to? I understand how you feel, but so far, if all you've got to give us is—"

"I'm not a damn detective. I'll tell you the facts and you find the evidence. The Irish are good at grudges, aren't we, Mr. Chapman? Stubborn lot. Sometimes it takes a hundred years to right a wrong. But none of us have got that much time. You got to do something before they take the two brothers I've got left."

"Your family, Trish, tell us about them," Mike said.

She shrugged, as though they were no different from any other family. "Fifth-generation tunnel workers. My great-great-grandfather came from Ireland in 1906 to build the Pennsylvania Railroad tunnels under the Hudson River. I don't know that he liked the work, but he liked getting paid every week, and he must have been fearless. His kin followed like sheep, and the Quillians have been down in the hole ever since. Brothers, uncles, cousins, in-laws."

"What about your brothers, Trish?" Mike asked.

"Duke," she said, then paused to close her eyes. "Duke was the oldest. Named John Wayne Quillian for my dad's favorite tough guy. Called him Duke long as anybody can remember. He'd be two years older than Brendan. Thirty-seven, may he rest in peace."

"Did he have a wife? Any kids?"

"Married a girl from the neighborhood. One of *them*," she said, tossing her head in the direction of Ignacia and the Latino men sitting at the bar. "She didn't understand the life. Walked out on him four or five years ago. No kids. Maybe that had something to do with his health, too. Had cancer—bad run of it—back in his twenties. Almost didn't make it. Breaks my heart he pulls through that to be cut down by these bastards."

"How old are you?" Mike asked.

"Twenty-eight."

I looked at her again, wondering whether it was something besides grief that had given her such a hard look so early on.

"And you live . . . ?"

"With my mother. She's got the Alzheimer's. Only thing the damn disease has been good for is not knowing she lost Duke. I told her all about it last night when she saw me crying, but she doesn't understand what it means. Five minutes later she asks me if I've seen Duke today."

"Do you work?"

"I used to help out in the parish office. Secretarial work and such. But the last three years I can't be leaving her alone. That's why we needed Duke. He always helped with the money so I didn't have to leave her with no stranger."

Mike signaled to the owner to bring Trish a refill.

"How about your other brothers?"

"Richie—he's thirty-three. His wife's third-generation. Got three little ones. And Marshall—he's thirty. Named for Marshall Mabey. Ever hear of him?"

"No," Mike said.

"My great-great-grandfather was working next to him, tunneling the East River in 1916, building the BMT." Every time Trish mentioned a different sandhog project my awareness of the city beneath our city expanded. "There was a big blowout, if you know what I mean."

Mike asked, "When the water breaches the caisson under the riverbed?"

"Yeah, exactly. Old man Quillian heard that terrible screech that signals the blowout, the story goes, and he's one of the lucky ones. Scrambled back into the air lock. But three of them others were sucked down into twelve feet of riverbed, as the air escaped and propelled them out like a cannon. Two are buried under all that cement until kingdom come. Marshall Mabey—he was shot out by the burst of compressed air, through the mud and up out of the water like a geyser, five stories high."

"Makes a good tale, Trish."

"It's true. There's a lot of sandhog babies named for Marshall. Went back to the job the very same week. Everybody's hero. Survival of the fittest, I guess."

"What about Brendan?" I asked, wondering how the defendant in my trial had emerged from this underground fraternity to wind up in such a totally different social and professional milieu. "Why did you say he didn't count anymore?"

Trish looked at me for the first time since

she had started answering Mike's questions. "If you're hoping I'm going to say something bad about him, you'll be mightily disappointed."

Mike took the reins back from me. "I dropped the ball, Trish. I'm the guy who locked your brother up and I never knew any of you even existed. What's that about?"

Trish stiffened now and took a deep breath. She seemed to be trying to decide whether to talk to us about him.

"Brendan got out, Mr. Chapman. He was the one of us meant to escape from the kind of lives the Quillians had chosen for themselves for as long as they've been in America."

Her voice had an edge, and she started again to chew on her lower lip.

"That's what you call it? He escaped?"

"My mother was very religious. Devoutly so. She believed that God had a different design for Brendan, that he wasn't going to be like the rest of us."

"And your father?"

"Blamed my mother for everything. Said it was her plan, is all. Nothing to do with God. Nothing but her grandiose ideas for the boy, come back to bite her in the ass—to be as blunt as he was. Even blamed her for the accident."

"What accident?" Mike asked.

Trish frowned as she answered him. "Surely you know Brendan's got only one good eye?"

"Yes," Mike said, and I thought immediately of the chilling stare-downs Brendan gave me in court that were probably no more than the vacant gaze of his blind eye.

"He was five when it happened, before I was born. My mother took him out to her cousin's place at Breezy Point. Him and Duke. It was Fourth of July and there were fireworks on the beach," Trish said. "Nobody talked about it much to the kids by the time I came along. Dad blamed my mother for letting Brendan get too close, for not watching him that day. Got his eye put out by a stone that kicked up from the discharge. She was too hysterical to help him. It was Duke who dragged him out of the way. Could have been worse."

"Lost his sight?"

"The right eye. Mama babied him something terrible after that. Made up her mind she was going to find him a better way.

Make him study real hard, get him into a better school so he wouldn't be bullied all the time by the local toughs. She loved books, Mama did—that's how she traveled to different worlds without ever leaving the house very much. As long as Brendan had one eye, she was determined to keep it in books, too."

That explained how he wound up at Regis, the parochial school that offered free education to students who had scored well on the entrance exams.

"And your father never tried to make a sandhog out of Brendan?" Mike asked.

"Sure he did. Took him down every chance he could, but the kid couldn't take it." Trish turned her empty glass upside down on the table. "I remember them coming home one time—Brendan must have been eighteen, so I guess I was almost eleven. Dad got him a summer job with the union, thinking he could keep a hold on his son before he went off to college, made a life for himself. Quit and came home the second day. My father got there an hour later and tore him apart in front of all of us. Called him a sissy—told him he wasn't good enough to work in the hole. Would have hit him, I think, if Duke hadn't been there to step in the way."

"Sounds like Duke took good care of him," Mike said softly.

"He thought like Mama. He knew Brendan had other possibilities."

"Did you know what had happened on the job that day?"

"Sure, all us kids wanted to find out. First, it was no secret that Brendan had always hated it down there because it was so dark, so hard for him to see. Things were going on all around, creating a racket in every direction, and it frightened him not to know what was coming at him. But it was the blasts that got to him most when he showed up to work that week. The guys would rig the dynamite and set off the explosion, and whenever Brendan heard that dreadful sound, he'd be reliving the noise of the firecrackers that took his eye."

"So he never went back in the tunnel?"

"Not once. Duke and Richie and Marshall, they live and breathe like sandhogs. Brendan, well, he's something else."

"And he had a scholarship to Georgetown?" Mike asked.

"I cried so hard I thought I was gonna die,

the day he left," Trish said. "My father wouldn't even come out of his room to say good-bye. He knew he had a son who was just rejecting everything his own life had been built on."

"But Brendan lived at home after that, didn't he?"

"First year he did. Holidays and like that. Then he'd be getting with his fancy room-mates and all, staying in their homes on Fifth Avenue or traveling with them for sum-mer jobs over in Europe. And Amanda—his entire life revolved around Amanda by the time he was finishing high school. It was as though her family adopted him, even before they got engaged."

"What was Amanda like?" I asked.

Trish looked at me quizzically. "You're asking me?"

"You must have gotten to know her a bit," Mike said.

"One time. I only ever met the girl once."

"Why was that?" Mike asked. "I thought your family was so tight-knit."

"All's I can figure is that Brendan was ashamed of us." Trish took a deep breath. "There he was, mixing with all these fine, rich people—wanting to become one of them. Not that I ever had the feeling the Keatings wanted anything to do with the likes of us, either. There was never any talk of inviting them over to the house or taking any of our holidays together. They must have figured they could have Brendan without bothering with his low-life relations. And it seemed to have suited him fine, too."

"Was it at the wedding when you met Amanda?" I asked.

Trish cleared her throat and drank some water. "It was like a year before the wedding, when Brendan and Amanda became engaged. He called my mother and asked her to come to lunch—to bring me, too—to meet Amanda and Mrs. Keating. I was fifteen years old—so excited I was. I actually thought it was gonna be a chance to get the two families together, to make things better. We were to meet at the Boathouse in Central Park, real pretty in the springtime, right on the water. I was sure it meant we'd be getting Brendan back.

"Two days before we were supposed to go, Brendan mailed a package to the house. I'll never forget how it looked when Mama removed the brown wrapping paper. Two bright red boxes tied with white satin ribbon, from a department store in the city I'd never dreamed of setting foot in. One was an expensive knit suit for my mother—with gold buttons and grosgrain trimmings—and the other was a lovely yellow dress for me, all lacy and soft."

"To wear to the lunch?"

"That's what Brendan wanted. My father exploded when he saw them. Told my mother that if her own clothes weren't good enough for Mrs. Keating, she could go to the park naked or she couldn't go at all."

"So there was no lunch," Mike said.

"Mama didn't go. My father wouldn't let her." Trish bit into her lip and stared at the whiskey glass. She shook off the image and smiled at the memory that took her back to that long-ago day. "Me, I put on my yellow dress the minute he left for work that morning. Sneaked out of the house to meet my best friend, 'cause she wanted to see what this Amanda looked like, too. We played hookey from school, took the train into Manhattan so I could be at the lunch, and I gave Bex—my friend Rebecca—gave her a couple of dollars to go for a boat ride so she could watch me getting to meet Brendan's new family. Like it wasn't going to be real if someone didn't see me there."

"What did you think?" Mike asked.

"Brendan was so nervous—about me, I guess—I thought he'd have a seizure. I watched my manners and was careful about my language." Trish was smirking as she twisted the glass around and around. "Mrs. Keating was very kind to me. Warm, actually. Amanda didn't care about anything but Brendan—and once he saw Bex in the rowboat, ten feet away from the table, I think he was petrified we kids were going to do something to mortify him. Make a scene or something. But it was fine. I was only sad that my mother was too insecure to come herself. Really sad."

"And the wedding?" I asked.

"Brendan was twenty-three, a year later, after Amanda's graduation. My father died a month before the wedding."

"How?" Mike asked.

"Painfully, Mr. Chapman. The way sandhogs do," Trish said, looking up at him. "Silicosis it was. Too many years of breathing in the black dust. Silicosis killed him slowly—ate away at his lungs."

"Sorry," Mike said, pausing briefly. "But the wedding went on?"

"For the Keatings it did. And for Brendan. But my mother refused to go out of respect for my father. Kept all the boys home, too. Bex and me, we slipped into town and sat on a bench across from the church, just so we could see them when they stood out in front, all dressed up and such, posing to have their pictures taken before they went off to the reception at some club the Keatings belonged to.

"Brendan had called my mother one last time to urge her to come, but she told him to get on with his new life, to just act like we all had died when Dad did, if we embarrassed him so much."

"And that's what he did?" I asked. It seemed unthinkable to someone like Mike or me, to whom family was paramount.

"I never saw him again until yesterday, at the wake," Trish said. "Can't blame him too much, can I? He really made it, my big brother. Really crossed the tracks and created a fine life for himself without all our baggage. Until somebody set him up for Amanda's death."

"So now we know something about the

Quillians," Mike said. "I still don't follow why you think the Hassetts killed your brother Duke. You never mentioned—"

"Did I give you a flavor of my father, Mr. Chapman? Could you get the sense he might have crossed a few folk along the way?"

"Sounds very proud, very tough," Mike said, struggling for words.

"Feared and despised. I heard them words pretty often growing up. About six months or so before all this happened with Brendan, when the digging began in the Bronx for Water Tunnel Number Three, there was a dreadful accident in the hole."

"A blast?" I asked.

"Not like that," Trish said. "Old man Hassett—the boys' father—he was somehow pinned against the side of the wall and crushed to death by a piece of machinery."

"You called it an accident," I said. Another painful way to die added to the tally.

"I was only a kid at the time. I grew up believing it was. But that was the last time the Quillians and the Hassetts ever went down in a shaft together. It was my father who was foreman of that job—it was Duke who was working the shift with Mr. Hassett."

"It's been more than twelve years, Trish," Mike said. "What makes you think . . . ?"

She reached under her coat and removed a folded envelope from the pocket of her skirt. "I guess for some people patience really is a virtue."

She opened the letter and handed it to Mike, who flattened it on the table so we could read it together.

"See the date?" she asked, pointing to the postmarked envelope. "That's the morning after you arrested Brendan, when the story that he hired somebody to kill Amanda was all over the newspapers."

"It's written to Duke," Mike said. "Where did you get it?"

Trish wiped her mouth with the back of her hand. "Cleaning out his things yesterday morning. Found it in the top drawer of his dresser, under the watch my father left him."

I read the note again, thinking of the sign affixed to the side of the Alimak that had taken us down the shaft last Thursday. *Duke—The one-eyed wonder is gone. Keep your hands away from the door. Danger of amputation.*

20

"Trish," Mike said. "There's nothing here to connect this to anyone named Hassett."

"The 'one-eyed wonder'—that was their nickname for Brendan—that's how they teased him because of his blind eye. They're the ones that called him that."

She pushed up the sleeve of her coat and looked at her watch. "I've got to be at the wake," she said, folding up the letter and replacing it in the envelope. "You don't believe me, they'll be more deaths to follow. Suit yourselves."

Mike took the envelope from her. "We'll give it a run. No promises, but it's something to work up. When you saw Brendan yesterday, did you tell him about this?"

"See that rip in the piece of paper? He wanted to keep it himself. Didn't want me anywhere near you."

"You mentioned you were going to call me?"

"I asked him whether I should. He was furious with me. Told me it was a stupid idea and it wouldn't help to open all those old wounds," Trish said. "What the hell—it's not like I owe Brendan anything. I got to do what's right by Duke."

Mike pulled his steno pad from inside his jacket pocket. "How many Hassett kids are there? Where do they live?"

"There's three boys," Trish said, listing their names. "Bobby's twenty-four, like I mentioned, and the twins must be twenty-two by now. They all live in Queens. Douglaston. Moved away from here after their father's accident."

"That's a good neighborhood," I said.

"It's not like the old days," she said.

"Sandhogs make a pretty decent wage. My younger brothers do okay for themselves. Duke had the same damn curses my father did, though. Horses and hooch, my mama used to say. A little less of both and we'd have been on easy street."

"So these guys weren't in the tunnel when their father died, were they?" Mike asked.

"No, no. They were all in grade school at the time."

"They couldn't have witnessed anything then?"

"Tall tales. That's what they're going by."

Mike flipped the page. "You know any other men who were down there at the time Hassett died, with your father and Duke?"

She thought about it for thirty seconds. "Nobody who's a friend."

"Trish," Mike said, "I'm not looking for Duke's friends or his enemies. I'm looking for an eyewitness who might tell me the truth."

She put her elbows on the table and covered her eyes with her hands. "My mother knew every one of the crew. Too bad those memories are all locked up inside her head now."

"Think, Trish," Mike urged. "You've heard this story so many times."

She remembered the names of two of the older men who had died of the same black-lung disease that had killed her father, and two more who'd retired out of state. She recalled some common surnames—Powers, Ryan, O'Callahan—that Mike would have to find by checking through union records going back more than a decade. Reluctantly, she decided to give us someone who might have been an eyewitness.

"Phin—Phinneas Baylor. If he's still alive, maybe he'll talk to you. Phin was crippled that day in the crash. Never got back to work so far as I know. He never blamed Duke—everyone said it was my brother who saved Phin's life." Trish's attitude was growing in defiance. "Used to live over in Throgs Neck with his daughter. I knew her from school. She and Bex and me—we were all good friends in junior high."

"You remember what address?" Mike asked.

"Right next door to St. Frances de Chantal. Hollywood Avenue, just to the left of the church. I don't know the number, but the house is right there," Trish said. "Too bad Bex is dead. She'd have kept the boys' heads on straight. She knew better than to blame Duke."

Trish slid out of the booth and stood next to Mike. "I've got to be going now."

"Bex?" I asked. "Your best friend? What did she have to do with this?"

"She was a Hassett, too. Rebecca Hassett, the boys' older sister. Bex was my age—we were like sisters from the time we were four or five."

"What did she know about the accident?" Mike asked.

Trish hesitated. "You think she would have stayed so close to me if she thought anyone in my family had killed her father?"

Mike's impatience was beginning to show. "Look, Trish. That's just—just . . . I don't want to say it's of no value, but—"

"It's the truth, Mr. Chapman. You just want it all made easy for you, don't you?"

Trish started to walk past the bar. Mike and I followed. "Can I give you a ride?"

"I told you I can't be seen with you," she said to him.

"When did Bex die?" I asked. I couldn't remember a modern urban culture like this world of tunnel diggers—and their families—in which lives seemed so constantly at risk.

"We were sixteen," she said, wrapping the black coat around her. "It was about five or six months after her father got killed. She sort of spun out of control when that happened. Had to be like a second mother to the three boys and she was too young to deal with that. Bex liked her freedom."

"What became of her?"

"My mother used to say she was a wild child. I'd get a beating if I skipped school and got caught. Bex just stopped caring, and there was nobody to rein her in. Hung out on the street, spent more time at my house than she did at her home. Then she got in with a crowd—older kids mostly—who used to stay out late at night in the park."

"Which park?" Mike asked.

"Pelham Bay. The golf course was where they found her. Bunch of hoodlums used to practically live there, smoking and drinking, making trouble all night. She got in over her head with them. That day we sneaked downtown to Brendan's wedding together? It was the last time I saw Bex Hassett alive."

Trish was making her way to the door of the bar while Mike paid the tab.

"What happened to her? How'd she die?" I asked.

"Some—some animal tried to rape her, I guess. We came back from Manhattan and I remember we had a big argument on the train, her asking me all about how come my family wouldn't go to the church, and how could Brendan do that to us—give us all up for some rich, fancy girl. Wanted me to run away with her 'cause her mother tried to get crazy strict with her after her father died," Trish said. "Wasn't any use by then. I don't think she ever went home that night. Her brothers came to get me the next morning—we went everywhere looking for her."

"She didn't even go back to school that week?"

"Bex didn't care about school," Trish said, frowning, chewing her lip furiously again. "The very night she was killed she called the house."

"What did she want?"

She met my eyes with hers. "I don't know. My mother wouldn't let her talk to me. Told Bex that I was already asleep and she'd give me the message. But Mama never told me about it until after the police found her body. I always thought I could have helped her, you know, the way kids do? Blamed myself for it. Thought that if she was looking for a place to stay or something, she wouldn't have been murdered that night. I could have done something to save her if she hadn't gotten so agitated, so—"

"That's a heavy burden to live with, Trish," I said. "Whatever happened to her wasn't your fault."

"She must have been very scared that night to call me. The last day we were together she did nothing but argue with me—was so spittin' mad at me about my family and the wedding she didn't call me or come over the whole week."

"You were with her brothers when they found her?" I asked.

"No, ma'am. We went looking, I told you. It was cops who actually found her body, way out in the middle of the golf course. Those bastards choked her to death and left her body right there in the park. Over what? It had to be rape, 'cause there's not much else she would have bothered to fight about. Strangulation—you wanted to know? That's how Bex died. I still remember when the detectives came to the house to ask about her—when we had seen her last and such. They called it a soft kill, the way she died. Sounds like anything but that to me."

21

"*Soft kill.* That's the most oxymoronic phrase in forensic medicine," Mike said, brushing his dark hair off his forehead. "Nothing soft about strangulation. Right up there among the most painful ways to die, fighting for enough air to breathe while someone squeezes the life out of you for four or five minutes."

They were murders without weapons, murders without the guns or knives or tire irons that made other homicides "harder." The designation was as baffling to Mike and me as it had been to Trish Quillian when she'd learned the fate of her best friend.

"Am I crazy to be thinking about a possible connection to Amanda Quillian's death?" I asked. "Is it just coincidence that both she and Bex Hassett were strangled?"

"What connection do you mean—the Quillians? You always want it both ways, Coop. I thought your expert was primed to tell the court that ligature and manual strangulation are among the most common methods of homicidal deaths with female victims. Especially if they've been sexually assaulted."

"That's why I can't go too far with that statistic in front of the jury. There wasn't even an attempt at a rape in Amanda's case."

"Well, according to Trish, the cops thought it was the motive with Bex. If it makes you happy, we'll pull the file on her investigation. Meanwhile, you game to try to find Phinneas this afternoon?"

"You think it's worth the chase?"

"Trish's half-right," Mike said, talking as he dialed his cell. "Somebody had it in for Duke. I think she's grabbing at straws, but we got a nice June afternoon to kill. See what the Hassett-Quillian grudge is about."

I opened the car door as Mike spoke into the phone. "Who's this? . . . Hey, Spiro—it's Chapman. Need a favor. Go back twelve years, give or take a few months. Find me a file on a sixteen-year-old girl, Rebecca Hassett. Called herself Bex. Asphyxial in Pelham Bay Park. Yeah, I know. I'll owe you a great big juicy sirloin at Patroon with a steep bottle of red."

Mike got in and started the engine as the detective on the other end of the phone responded to him.

"What do you think I want, Spiro? Everything on paper, as fast as you can put your mitts on it. Yesterday if you can do it. Case folder with the DD5s," he said, referring to the detective-division documents that would have every detail about the old investigation. "Autopsy report, photographs, any record of an arrest or suspects. Call me back when you've got it."

The ride to the outermost peninsula of land in the East Bronx, an old community in the shadow of the large modern bridge that crossed Long Island Sound, took another twenty minutes. Mike used the time to show off his mastery of the history of the city, which I never tired of hearing. "Throgs Neck. You know how it got its name?"

"I have no idea."

"John Throckmorton. Settled a farm there—hundreds of acres—while the Dutch had control of New York in the 1640s. We're looking for Phin Baylor's place next to a church on Hollywood, right? That's got an interesting namesake, too."

"You've been there?"

"Let's just say the final *Jeopardy!* category for the afternoon is Doo-Wop," Mike said. "An audio daily double. The answer is 'Girl group with 1958 hit—"Maybe."'"

He began to croon to me. "'May—ay—be . . .'"

I had danced to that a few times at college parties when the deejays were spinning oldies. *Maybe, if I hold your hand . . . maybe, if I kissed your lips,* I thought to myself. I knew the lyrics as well as Mike did, but if he wanted me to sing to him, I wasn't going there. And I just didn't know who had recorded the song.

"The Shirelles?"

"Not even close."

"The Sequins?"

"I gave you the whole damn clue, Coop. Who are the Chantels?"

"From this church? St. Frances de Chantal?"

"Yup. Just changed the spelling by a letter. They practiced by singing in the choir and doing Gregorian chants. Performed in the parish at a school dance when they were teenagers, got noticed by a big promoter, and were one of the first girl groups to hit it big with doo-wop."

We turned off Harding Avenue at the corner of Hollywood. The bright stained-glass windows of St. Frances gleamed in the late-afternoon sun. Two young women—about Trish Quillian's age—were sitting on the stoop of a narrow brick house adjacent to the church. They stopped chatting and stared at the car as we came to a stop at the curb.

"Let me do this," I said to Mike.

I walked up the path and introduced myself to the pair, asking if this was where Phinneas Baylor lived.

"Yes, and I'm his daughter, Janet," the fairer one said, standing to come toward me. "Something wrong?"

"No, we'd just like to talk to your father."

"Depends on what it's about. I don't need you bothering him."

"We're actually with—"

"I know it's not a courtesy call. Your automobile kind of gives the both of you away in this neighborhood," Janet said, trying to back me down the path, putting distance between our conversation and her friend. I could hear the door slam behind me and figured Mike didn't like the dynamic he was watching.

"Mike Chapman here. NYPD," he said, both hands in his pants pockets. "Nothing to get perturbed about. You're . . . ?"

"Janet. Janet Baylor." She looked back and forth between Mike's face and mine and made her choice. "This a problem for my dad?" she asked him.

Mike took her arm and steered her toward the car, smiling at her to reassure her. "Ancient history, Janet. We need a lesson. Hear your pop has some stories about the old days that might be a help in something we're doing."

She cocked her head. "Quillians it'll be, won't it? They're all over the news. You won't be mixing him into that stuff, will you? He don't know the first thing about it."

"Fair enough. We're just trying to get a handle on some of the background."

"That's all? Honest?"

Mike held up his hand and smiled again. "Blood oath."

"Phin took a walk down to the water, at the end of Pennyfield Avenue," Janet said. "Fort Schuyler. Sits up on the ramparts there every day he can, May to October, until sunset. Silver hair—and I think he's got on a black T-shirt and baggy pants. Got a bad gimp. You'll know him by the cane."

"Do you mind my asking whether you know Patricia Quillian?" I said.

Janet looked up. "Went all through school with Trish. Haven't seen her since we got out."

"Any reason why?"

She shrugged. "Just went separate ways, that's all. We had another friend—Bex—and—"

Mike wanted to show her we knew about Bex. "Rebecca Hassett, right?"

Janet paused. "Yeah, yeah. Guess you've got a good start on your history lesson already, Detective. Well, her murder shook up our whole crowd. Just never knew what happened. Me, I used to keep all the news-paper clippings about the case."

"You still have them?" I asked.

"Nah."

"Why did you save them?"

She pushed the hair off her forehead. "Bex's murder made her the most famous person we knew. Had her name in the paper every day for a couple of weeks. Seemed like the cops were coming around talking to us all the time at first. Seemed like the most important thing in all our lives. Then they just stopped coming. Stopped caring about Bex. Most people did. They always figured it was the druggies in the park."

"And you?" Mike asked. "What did you think?"

She shrugged again. "Same as everybody else. She should have stayed with our crowd. Bex, I mean. Started running with hoodlums. People who weren't like us. Lots of people thought she was asking for it."

I closed my eyes, stung by words I had heard far too often about victims of vio-lence.

"How well did you know Brendan Quil-lian?" Mike asked.

Janet Baylor frowned. "Not at all. Too

much a pretty boy for me. Never really saw him around here anyway."

"And Duke?"

She didn't answer.

"Did you know Duke?"

"Had firm orders from my mother to keep away from him. We all did. Now that was a nasty boy, Duke Quillian."

Mike was standing as close to Janet Baylor as he could get. "Tell me what you mean. Tell me why you say that."

She hesitated again and licked her lips. Then she shook her head from side to side.

"Janet?" Mike said, trying to get her attention again.

"I don't know. Maybe I'm remembering wrong."

"He's dead now. He can't hurt anybody."

"Terrible things, he did. At least that's what I used to hear."

"What? Like shooting squirrels and skinning cats?"

Janet laughed and pointed a finger in Mike's face. "You've been watching too many of them serial-killer shows, Detective. Not that stuff."

"What then?"

She took a deep breath. "It's only stories I heard, mind you. Nothing I witnessed."

"Tell them to me," Mike said.

"Duke had a fight with a kid once," Janet said, pointing down the street. "A boy who lived over there, but the family moved right afterward. Duke tied his one arm to the fence in the backyard to keep him still. Had a pair of pliers—big, rusty old things he carried around in his pocket to break locks open and such. Pulled all the fingernails out of the kid's other hand to teach him a lesson."

My stomach heaved, but I tried not to show any reaction, hoping that Janet would keep talking.

"And one of the girls who made a fool of him in front of his friends? He doused her hair in some kind of oil and set fire to it."

"I can't believe he was never locked up for these things," Mike said.

"Please, Detective. Nobody dared call the cops. We've got our own way of settling things. Duke Quillian didn't need to practice on squirrels and cats, Mr. Chapman. It was people he liked to torture."

22

Mike followed Schurz Avenue down to Pennyfield, an eclectic mix of row houses and white stucco buildings that resembled the sides of small cruise ships, with railings that fronted on the unusual waterfront setting. The smell of the salt sea air was a refreshing change from the odors of the liquor and beer in the dark bar.

"You seem to know this area well," I said.

"Fort Schuyler. Built in 1833, named after General Philip Schuyler. You probably don't

know anything about our seacoast fortifications," he said.

"Guilty as charged."

Mike always shifted into high gear when
he could display his knowledge of military
history.

"After the French revolution," he said,
"the Founding Fathers were afraid we'd be
drawn into the European wars that broke
out all over. They started to build military
forts for defense along the coastline, calling
them the First System. They started the
Second System in 1807, when Great Britain
became a threat, too."

"Not much help, I guess, if you count the
War of 1812."

"Brilliant deduction, Coop. You can tell
they hadn't been very successful with the
first two stages. So this one—and Totten,
across the sound in Queens—were built as
part of the Third System, later on." He got
out of the car and slammed the door, pointing as he surveyed the vista. "The idea was
to be able to use cannon fire from these two
fortifications to stop any enemy ships that
tried to enter the Sound in order to approach New York City."

The monumental building across the

strait, an impressive partner to Fort Schuyler, had its granite bastion jutting out toward the water like the prow of an ancient Roman sailing vessel. I caught up with Mike, marveling at another cityscape that was fresh to me, fascinated by the locals so obviously enjoying this slice of beach life on the walkways and porches of the small cottages that bordered the road.

He led me through the entrance to the interior courtyard of the enormous pentagonal fort. There were a few visitors, some of whom were descending the large stone steps that took us up to the top of the ramparts.

The solid mass of building was punctuated by eyebrow-shaped windows on each of the three sides that faced the waterway. "See those? They were the casements for two tiers of guns. The men could fire from every angle on those sides. It's a brilliant location for the protection of the city."

Several kids were shooting at imaginary pirate ships from the top of the dramatic walkway, and alone on a bench at the very tip of the battlement was a man who fit Phin Baylor's description—a sixteen-ounce beer bottle in one hand, a week's grizzle on his face, bedroom slippers on his feet, and a wooden cane resting beside his out-stretched leg.

He turned to look as we approached him but said nothing. "Mr. Baylor?" Mike asked, showing him the blue-and-gold badge. "Mike Chapman. NYPD. This is Alexandra Cooper, with the DA's Office."

"My daughter put out a missing person's report?" he asked with a laugh, looking back out at the view, small sailboats slicing through the blue water and powerboats creating wakes below the span of the long bridge.

Mike stepped in front of Baylor, balancing against the wall of the old fortress. "She expects you home for dinner, I think. May I call you Phinneas?"

"Phin. Just Phin. Who're you looking for?"

"We're fishing right now. Looking mostly for information. I'm working on that accident—"

When Mike said that word, he got Phin's attention.

". . . that accident in the tunnel midtown. Water Tunnel Number Three. Duke Quillian, you know they're waking him today?"

Phin lifted his bottle in the direction of the

sun, sinking in the sky to the west. "What goes round comes round, like they say. Seen it on television the other night and can't say I lost any sleep over him. I'll take a pass on the receiving line at the funeral home. Seen you on TV, too. You're the woman prosecuting his brother, aren't you?"

"Yes, I am."

"Brendan Quillian. Now there's a boy who should never have grown so high and mighty. Strange kid, he always was. Wanted no part of his family, no part of any of us. Guess he won't have Duke to fight his battles anymore," Phin said. "That's the only thing that kept Brendan alive on the street as a kid, was his big brother. He's gonna need some protection if he winds up where you're trying to send him."

"Did you know Brendan well?" I asked.

"Nah. He had no stomach for the hole, hard as his father fought him about it. Even tried to make the kid a pencil. Let him use his head if he wanted to, but stay in the business."

"A *pencil*?"

"Men who can't do the physical labor. The engineers, the contractors—the guys who push pencils all day," Phin said with a trace of disdain in his voice. "Tell me, Mike, will you? Duke's death wasn't no accident, was it?"

So far, the police and the medical examiner had not released any details of the severed finger to the public. It would only be a matter of days before too many insiders knew about it and the news leaked, but for now it was a crucial piece of information, intentionally withheld until further leads were developed in the case.

"What have you heard?"

"I've learned to mind my own business. Not many of his friends even remember I'm alive. I was already too long in the hole when I got hurt, and that's going on more than a dozen years ago."

"I was hoping we might trouble you to tell us about that—that day," Mike said.

Phin squinted into the sun as he looked up at Mike. "You weren't going to say that word *accident* again, were you now? That *day,* as you called it?"

"We don't know what happened. We only heard you were there—that you got hurt— the day old man Hassett was killed."

"Who's blabbing to you?" Phin asked.

Mike didn't answer.

"Must be one of the Quillian boys. Tell 'em not to worry, Detective. I'm long over my tunnel days. I look out at the sea and the sky and don't know how I lived so far underground as I did for so long."

Mike looked to be trying to think of another way to ask Phin to talk, but the sandhog code of silence seemed to be thicker than the walls of the fortress.

"Is it fair to say it was a bad place to be—between a Quillian and a Hassett—when they had a beef to settle?" Mike asked.

Phin's expression didn't change.

"Nothing to the rumor, then, that Duke Quillian saved your life?"

Phin threw back his head. "Gave yourself up there, Mike. That's the crazy sister you're talking to, isn't it? What's her name? Trish. That girl has never been right in the head."

Mike looked at me and shrugged his shoulders.

Phin Baylor smiled. "I'll tell you about 'that day,' as you call it."

He was ready to talk. He liked Mike, and something Mike had said moved him off the starting block.

Phin nodded and took a swig from his

bottle. "I was working the first piece of the dig for the new tunnel, right here in the Bronx, over in Van Cortlandt Park. Must have been six of us down there that day— me and Hassett, Duke Quillian and his father—he was supervising the drill—maybe two other guys left by the end of the shift."

"What did you do exactly?"

"We were building the rib cage, you know? After the hole is bored in the tunnel, we've got to build a concrete hull around the sides. Support the walls, smooth them out as the tunnel goes forward." Neither of us wanted to interrupt him, so we let him go on with the details we had learned firsthand last week about how the cylinder was created.

Phin pulled a pair of shades out of his pocket and put them on. I didn't know whether it was the glare from the sun on the water or simply to make it impossible for us to see his eyes.

"The shift was just about over. That's why so few of us were left," he said, getting back to the narrative, pausing as a mother dragged her two whining children off the battlement and over to the exit. "You know what an agitator is?"

I looked to Mike, who answered, "Those giant cement mixers?"

"Yeah. That's what we were working with at that point. Hassett and I were down at the bottom of a steep incline—you know how the water has to flow downhill, all the way into the city? So three of the railroad cars at the top of the slope, inside the tunnel, had been fitted as agitators." Phin tapped his cane on the cobblestone walkway. "So that we could do the work down in the shaft.

"One of those mothers broke loose— twenty tons of steel loaded with cement steaming away on a sharp downhill grading. Hassett didn't have a prayer. Crushed him into the bedrock like he was an ant."

"And you?"

"I was up on a ladder with my trowel. Last thing I remember is the noise of that frigging thing barreling down at me."

Mike started to ask, "Couldn't you—"

"Get out of the way? Forget it, son. There wasn't nowhere to go. I was already flat up against the wall." Phin leaned forward and stowed the bottle under his bench, putting his head in his hands.

Mike swallowed. "So it caught you, too, along the way?"

"I don't have any recollection of being hit. Doctors say I never will. I can see that damn thing coming down the track, picking up speed for more than half a mile, and it's screeching like a banshee. But that's all I know and I gotta thank God for that. Doctors say I'll never have any memory of it, the way the brain works. The agitator car must have slammed into my ladder and wedged me against the concrete side of the tunnel." Phin paused for a minute. "No lights, no noise, till I began to make it myself. All I could hear was the sound of my own screams."

"Was anyone around to come to help you?"

He looked away. "Duke Quillian. First man to get to me. First one I saw when I came to after passing out. Couldn't even get close in, Duke. Had no way to move the agitator car. You'd have needed a derrick to do it."

"Where was Duke's father? Wasn't he supposed to be supervising?"

"Went back up in the Alimak to get help. So he said. Seemed like forever."

"And you . . . ?"

Phin was rubbing his left thigh while he talked.

"Pitch-black in there. Nearest lightbulbs had been crushed along with Hassett's body. But my left leg was pinned behind the railroad car, split open down the middle." Phin made a line down his calf with his hand. "Too dark to see the blood, but it was seeping out of me like a steady stream. I could feel it covering me, all thick as it was. I could smell it, too."

Mike bowed his head. "What did Duke do?"

Phin picked up his voice and tapped his cane. "I guess you could say he saved my life, if that's what you want to hear, if that's what you want to tell little Trish Quillian. Duke did what I told him to do. First we waited and waited for an ambulance—maybe four minutes, maybe six. I was getting dizzy and light-headed, and all I had the strength to think about was that I damn well wasn't gonna die in that hole. Gave my entire life to digging tunnels and I sure as hell wasn't gonna bleed to death in one of them."

"So, what . . . ?" I asked.

"I asked Duke for a flashlight, a bottle of beer, and a knife. Took him a few minutes to run up the track to where I had my lunch box and back." Phin slowed his pace now, tapping the cane against the stone. "I drank as much of the beer as I could, held the light on my leg, and put the lip of the bottle between my teeth. I told Duke to cut off whatever part of my foot was stuck behind the agitator."

Neither Mike nor I could speak.

"Sawed off my heel and some of the foot," Phin said, raising his left knee with his hands, so that the black leather slipper slipped off. I could see that the lower part of his leg was a prosthetic device.

Mike started to say something about how tough Phin must have been, but the old sandhog didn't want to hear it.

"I don't recommend beer as an anesthetic, young man. Didn't help worth a damn. And when I bit down on the bottle to fight the pain, the glass broke and a big piece of it lodged in the roof of my mouth. Sure as hell took my mind off my foot for a while."

Phin Baylor refused Mike's offer of a hand up from the bench, steadying himself with the cane, then limping to the edge of the rampart.

"So Duke got me out of the hole alive—that's all I asked of him. Lost the rest of the foot at the hospital. Too much damage had been done to save it."

"The Hassett boys are wrong about Duke, are they?" Mike asked. "Wrong about blaming him for their father's death?"

"Now you're asking two different things of me, aren't you, Mike?" Phin said, looking overhead at a plane making its approach to La Guardia, across the Sound. "You wanted to know if Duke saved my life, so I guess the answer has to be yes to that. But first you gotta know how that agitator car got uncoupled in the first place. You gotta know how it got loose from the brake car, don't you, before you reach your next conclusion?"

"You mean, you think it was Duke Quillian who—who did that? Intentionally?"

"There, you said it yourself. It isn't a very good idea to wind up between a Quillian and a Hassett, especially when one of 'em's armed with a twenty-ton weapon."

I couldn't understand how Phin could be so calm if he thought Duke had engineered Hassett's murder and his own near-fatal injury. "But didn't the police investigate this? Didn't you tell them you thought Duke was responsible?"

His face wrinkled as he looked at me

quizzically, as though he couldn't fathom why I was asking what the police thought.

"Like I told the cops when they came to the hospital, I couldn't see anything that far up the tunnel. I didn't have no proof anybody tinkered with the cars. Besides, Duke couldn't have known I was even in the hole. Just my dumb luck that Hassett asked me to go back in with him after I signed out for the day. He wanted to finish up the last part of the job before he knocked off. Needed a hand and I gave it to him. Didn't know what it would cost both of us."

Phin turned his back to me, pulled a cigarette from his pocket, and lit up. "If you haven't learned it yet, you'll find we don't put much stock in cops five hundred feet underground. We're used to taking care of ourselves."

"I'm surprised Duke lasted this long, with so many Hassetts around," Mike said.

"The Hassetts thought they were getting some powerful help from above, Detective. Duke got real sick, maybe a month after all this happened. Had cancer so bad he almost died. What's that hospital in Manhattan?"

"Sloan-Kettering," I said. The world-renowned medical center specialized in treatment of cancer patients, one of whom had been Mike's fiancée, Val.

"Duke spent a few months there. Never thought we'd see him again. By that time I'd cut all my ties to the job, had no need to look back." Phin came as close as he had so far to a smile. "One thing I was always damn sure of—Duke Quillian wouldn't die of old age."

Phin Baylor swiveled on his good leg and leaned on the side of the battlement, looking over the water. Mike was beside him, shoulder to shoulder.

"Can you tell us *why,* Phin? Why you think Duke might have done such a thing?"

Phin took a long drag on his cigarette.

"You've had more than enough time to figure it out, haven't you?"

"He was a mean bastard, Detective. What's the difference why he did it? I'm not ever going dancing again, even if I knew. Got me out of the hole, in the end, which probably adds twenty more years to my life."

Mike wouldn't give up. "But why was he after old man Hassett? Why did Duke hate him?"

"Might be no more than the grief Hassett gave Duke—gave his father, really—about Brendan. Taunting them constantly about how weak Brendan was, how he couldn't make it in the tunnel. Used to say he wasn't even half a man. Stuff like that. Used to drive the Quillians crazy because Brendan's goals were such a rejection of their roots in this country and the work they'd been bred to do. Here's two families that for generations have dedicated their lives, if you will, to building New York from the very bottom up. That's part of the irony of them destroying each other. Taking pleasure in it as well. A real blood feud between them, that's what it was."

"Did they fight about—"

"They fought about everything, Chapman. Maybe it was money at the root of all this, maybe it was the girlfriend that old man Hassett and Quillian once shared, and maybe it was simply the fact that Duke Quillian knew every one of these stories and simply liked to hurt people. There's miles of trouble beneath these city streets, making it all work up above—and some very rough dealings go into staying alive."

Phin crushed his cigarette and flicked the

butt over the side of the fort. "That's all I have for you. Better push on and do your work."

Mike motioned to me that he was ready to leave. "Can we give you a lift over to the house?"

"No, thanks. The air here is good for me." Phin leaned an elbow on the massive granite battlement and exhaled a row of smoke rings. "You see that crazy Quillian girl, Mike, you give her a message for me."

"What's that, Phin?"

"Tell her she'll live a lot longer if she keeps her yap shut, will you? Tell her nice as you two are, I'm not interested in any more company, thank you very much. She ought to dig for the bones in her own backyard."

23

I waited for Mike at the car. He had waved me off and stayed behind to talk to Baylor.

"What did Phin mean by that last shot?" I asked when he joined me ten minutes later.

"Just what he told us. That the Quillians always made their own trouble—he's got no use for any of them. Says Trish ought to mind her own business before she goes pointing fingers at anyone else."

"That's all you got from him? He must have been making a point."

"Like your interrogation techniques are

any better than mine? The g   322
squealed in more than a decade-
fortitude to hold the flashlight whil
body amputated half his foot—an   u
think he's going to go belly-up 'cause I'm
butting heads with him over something that
nitwit said to us back in the bar? I'll let you
out, blondie. Try playing footsie with him
and call me tomorrow."

Mike saw there was a message on his cell
phone and held it to his ear.

"Sorry," I said. "It just sounded like he had
more to say. Did you ask him if he remembered Bex?"

He flipped the phone shut. "Yes, ma'am.
Says he used to scare his own daughter by
reminding her of what happened to the Hassett girl for hanging out with those bums in
the park. 'Lay down with dogs, you're
gonna have fleas.' Life according to Phin."

"That's a tough old bird."

Mike made a U-turn. "Want a look at the
file?"

"You serious?"

"The message is from Spiro. If we stop by
Bronx Homicide right now, he'll take us into
the Cold Case Squad. The Hassett file is sitting there, waiting its turn in the middle of a

pile for one of the guys to pick it up and see whether any of the old evidence is suitable for DNA analysis."

"I'm in. It's only six thirty," I said, looking at my watch. "Why not?"

Although prosecutors in America had been introduced to DNA technology in the mid-1980s, before I'd even dreamed of a career as a prosecutor, no court admitted evidence of genetic fingerprinting in a criminal case until 1989. The accuracy of this scientific technique revolutionized the criminal justice system, linking perpetrators to crime scenes with complete certainty, and allowing the exoneration of others mistakenly accused or wrongly identified.

Not until the start of the twenty-first century—after DNA testing methodology had undergone a decade of refinement—were state and national data banks established. In the infancy of this forensic breakthrough, evidence that had yielded enough DNA to create a unique human profile could only be compared to a specific donor—suspect or witness—who surfaced on the radar screen in an investigation.

But data banks offered a much broader capability for solving crimes. In every state, legislation mandated the creation of arrestee or convicted-offender DNA files, filled with profiles of growing numbers of miscreants, against which crime-scene evidence could be searched by computer. Matches were now being made daily all over the country—unsolved cases being connected to others in different jurisdictions by "linkage" data banks even as jailed felons and parolees were regularly being identified for crimes most law enforcement officials had assumed would go unpunished.

Homicides, in particular, were being reexamined by police and prosecutors with new forensic tools not available when the cases had occurred. Unlike violent felonies in most states, no statutes of limitation exist for murder cases, and detectives everywhere began digging through old files and forgotten pieces of evidence in unsolved cases in hopes of striking the ever-satisfying "cold hit"—the match to a DNA profile of a known subject in a constantly growing network of data banks.

We left Throgs Neck for a less gentrified section of the borough—1086 Simpson Street—home of the Bronx Homicide Task

Force. Sunday night in the squadroom was as quiet as I had expected. The approaching days of summer in the city, when asphalt streets were more likely to come to a boil and the murder rate usually spiked, would bring more weekend action to this group of specialists. For now, Spiro Demakis and his partner, Denny Gibbons, seemed content to be catching up on the tedious paper-pushing that was a hallmark of good detective work.

"You don't got enough to do in Manhattan?" Spiro asked, walking us down the hallway and turning on the lights in the small, empty office that housed the borough's cold-case files. "I'm sitting on four unsolved shootings—all drug-related, without a single witness who could put his hand on a Bible and be believed. I got two domestics—one guy took out the girlfriend's mother and three kids just for spite. And last week I picked up a drive-by with a dozen spectators on the sidewalk who saw zilch. It ain't the bright lights of Broadway, but if you're into making cases in the Bronx, I'll take the help."

"Coop may be looking for new digs if she blows her trial."

"You got that rich boy that hired someone to off his wife, don't you? Thin ice, Alex. Newspapers read like you're on thin ice."

"Stay tuned, Spiro. I've still got a few surprises left."

"I don't envy you going up against Lem Howell. He wiped the floor with one of the Bronx prosecutors a few weeks ago. Three-month trial and deliberations barely lasted through lunch."

Spiro unlocked a file cabinet and tossed a couple of manila folders on one of the desks. "Whoever the squad boss was at the time must have dumped this one. Guy who had it wasn't one of our sharpest. Retired about a year later. Doesn't look like he did all that much detecting."

Mike dragged a second chair over and sat beside me. "You know him?"

I started to skim the first few pages of documents.

"Only by reputation," Spiro said from the doorway. "Looks like he had a confession and all. Perp skipped back to the Dominican Republic, so nobody went after him. Might keep it myself. Sounds like an easy collar. Help yourselves. The Xerox machine is over on our side."

"Where's the confession?" Mike asked, sliding the folder over as he picked through it.

"'Rebecca Hassett. Female Caucasian. Sixteen,'" I said, reading aloud. "'Found in a drainage ditch off the side of the fairway on the eighth hole of the golf course.'"

"There's your girl," Mike said. He studied two photographs that were in a small envelope stapled to the side of the folder, then passed them to me.

The first was from a school yearbook, probably taken just months before her death. Bex was unsmiling, with dark brown eyes and thick black hair—the color of Mike's—framing her pale face in a layered cut. She looked older than her age, or perhaps it was the makeup she used to achieve that effect. She was rail thin, wearing a black turtleneck sweater with a plain crucifix on a chain around her neck.

"Pretty kid," I said.

The second picture was one of the Polaroids taken by the detective at the crime scene.

He had obviously stood over the body, shooting down at Bex's face and upper torso. I would never have recognized the solemn young woman who had earlier posed for the camera at school. Her head was turned to the side, against the ground—the once pale skin cyanotic and the swollen tongue protruding from her mouth. The sweater she was wearing was opened halfway down her chest, and abrasions lined the tip of her chin. Faint oval bruises were apparent on her neck, probably the fingertips of the killer.

"What's this mark?" I asked Mike, pointing to a pattern within the discolored patch of skin.

He leaned over me and looked again. "I can't tell. Your folder have the autopsy report?"

I turned several pages of DD5s until I came to the medical examiner's findings.

"Manual strangulation," I said, skimming the first page of the document. "The ME thinks those lines on the neck are caused by the zipper of her sweater, caught under the perp's hands and pressed into the skin. There must be close-ups of the injury in the morgue archives."

I looked at the Polaroid again. The thick metal zipper had left an imprint like miniature railroad ties as it was pressed against Bex's throat.

"Sexual assault?" Mike asked.

My finger ran down the paragraphs as I looked for the doctor's description of the vaginal vault. "No sign of it. Nothing completed, anyway."

"How does it read, Coop? Like they looked?"

I knew what Mike meant. A sixteen-year-old kid who'd been living recklessly the last few weeks of her life might have been presumed by investigators as well as acquaintances to have contributed to her own death. Perhaps the case had not been worked as aggressively as the murder of a teenage girl on the Upper East Side of Manhattan. Perhaps there had been so many homicides the same week that this one was relegated to the back burner by a detective with less interest in his victims than Mike Chapman had.

"Covers the bases," I said. "Detailed examinations of the external and internal genitalia. Vaginal swabs taken and prepared on slides. Both negative. The UV lamp showed nothing either."

The presence of seminal fluid or sperm inside the body or on the thighs would have been suggestive of penetration. Since semen fluoresces under ultraviolet light, it was routine to scan the body for matter not visible to the naked eye.

"They did a pubic-hair combing, too," I said. "Nothing loose, nothing foreign."

"Bite marks?" Mike asked, referring to one of the classic injuries that often presents in a frenzied homicide in which the motive was sexual assault.

"No. Doesn't look like there were abrasions anywhere else on Bex's body."

"Finger marks on the thighs? I mean, does it specifically say there were none?"

I shook my head. An attempt at a rape often resulted in minor bruising as the assailant tried to pry apart the victim's legs.

"No, but look at the chart," I said, referring to the outline of a human body that was part of the autopsy report. "The only notation of any focal point of injury anywhere on Bex Hassett is on her neck."

I could see Mike's expression changing as he evaluated the detective's reports while he listened to me. Bex Hassett was becoming one of his victims. He was Monday-morning quarterbacking the guy who had dumped the case—even after getting a suspect to confess—as Mike liked to do with every unsolved homicide he came across.

Mike was flipping the pages of the second folder. "How about fingernail scrapings?"

I thought of Amanda Keating and her frantic effort to get her killer's hands off her neck so that she could continue breathing.

"No."

"No, they didn't take any?" he asked impatiently.

"The doc scraped the nails. Negative findings."

He reached across and tried to take the folder from me. "There must be some signs of a struggle. It sounds like the girl didn't even fight. Why did Trish Quillian think she'd been sexually assaulted?"

"There's your answer," I said, passing the papers to him. "Third paragraph from the end. Bex's blood alcohol level was over .23. That's why she couldn't fight."

Mike answered with a whistle. "Jeez, the poor kid must have been dead drunk. What a target for any scumbag who happened to be hanging around."

The most commonly abused drug in America is alcohol. The pack that Bex Hassett was running with in the park, if Trish Quillian had been right, had encouraged her to get in over her head once she began to be alienated from her family and friends. If she had voluntarily intoxicated herself—and the ME's report had no findings of any other illegal substances in the toxicological studies performed—then she could have been either in a stupor or entirely unconscious when her life had been taken.

Mike had grabbed the autopsy report from me so that he could study it himself from top to bottom. I picked up the folder he had placed back on the desk to read through the detective's follow-up reports to see how his suspect had been developed.

The description of the crime scene included a canvass of the area within the park that surrounded Bex Hassett's body. An empty bottle of Courvoisier and several cans of beer were found a few feet away. DNA profiles had been developed from saliva left on the glass—including on the lip of the brandy bottle—and matched the genetic fingerprint of the deceased teenager. Results had also been compared to some of the street kids who had been picked up in the neighborhood for questioning, but none of them had been a hit.

"You can copy all this," I said to Mike, rubbing my eyes. "Maybe I'm just tired—and my heart breaks for this lost child—but can we save this for another day?"

Mike started turning pages more quickly. "Make sense of this for me."

"What?"

"The detective's notes from the confession. Nineteen-year-old kid—one of the park regulars named Reuben DeSoto." Mike stood up straight, obviously jarred by something he had seen in the case file. "Two of the other hoodlums fingered him as the last of the group to be seen drinking with the girl that night."

"DeSoto admitted killing Bex Hassett?"

"Don't get ahead of me, Coop." Mike squinted at the words as though he were trying to decipher them. "Says he knew her from the park. She'd been hanging out with his homeboys for a couple of weeks. Not involved with any of them. But that night Reuben came on to her—tried to have sex with her. She'd been drinking. But beer, he says—only beer."

"No mention of brandy? Wasn't her DNA on the Courvoisier bottle?"

"Yeah, but it doesn't sound like that beverage was within Reuben's budget. Says he tried to hook up with her but she refused. Not drunk at all—just a few pops of brew. Says he actually got on top of her and tried to penetrate." Mike looked up at me as he asked, "Wouldn't that have left some kind of physical evidence?"

"It should have. Unless she was so intoxicated that she wasn't able to offer any resistance. Her muscles would have been so relaxed you'd have no internal injury either. But you'd expect to find some of his pubic hair on her body or clothing, even if he didn't complete the act. There really should have been some kind of trace evidence if what he admitted is true."

"Yeah, well, either Reuben was hallucinating or the ME needs a refresher course."

"What's wrong?"

Mike slapped the folder closed and picked up the second one that I had left on the desk. "Reuben—the guy who's been the suspect for more than ten years while this case was sitting on a shelf collecting dust? He claims he killed Bex Hassett all right.

Reuben says he choked her to death with a ribbon that he pulled out of her hair when she started to scream."

"But the pictures of her neck—?"

"You can tell from that lousy Polaroid what those marks are on her throat? There's no mention of any ribbon in the crime scene report and the autopsy doesn't say a thing about any kind of ligature."

I was trying to get us on our way. "So?"

"So you shouldn't have stopped reading the file halfway through. Listen to this. Reuben had himself an *abogado* because of a burglary case he had pending. He skips back to the DR and the lawyer writes a letter to the commish, claiming the kid's confession was coerced. That's why the dick probably stopped investigating."

"Why?"

"The lawyer also made a complaint to the CCRB. It was probably easier for the detective to just let it go rather than cloud his pension hearing with litigation over the fact that maybe he beat the crap out of Reuben and wound up with a phony confession," Mike said, pacing the short room back and forth, worked up by the prospect of bad policing in the still-unsolved murder case.

The Civilian Complaint Review Board could have put intense pressure on the department if there was evidence that an officer had used physical force to get an admission.

"So you don't like Reuben as the killer?"

"You've got the day off from court tomorrow," Mike said. "I'll be at the cemetery with Brendan Quillian. Call the morgue and have them pull everything on the Hassett autopsy. Get your hands on the physical evidence, if they can find it. This report says there was a speck of blood on the top of the zipper of Bex's sweater."

"Could be hers, don't you think?"

"She didn't bleed, according to the autopsy. The report says Bex had abrasions, not lacerations."

"But they did DNA," I said.

"Not on that bit of blood. There wasn't enough of it for analysis at the time. Back then, a bloodstain had to be the size of a quarter for the lab to work it up. Maybe the perp nicked his finger on a rough edge of the metal."

Bex Hassett's death had occurred when the methodology of DNA had been more primitive, requiring far larger samples of fluid. In the last several years, the shift in technique to STRs—short tandem repeats—meant that the smallest droplets of blood could now be amplified, copying the unique genetic profile until there was enough of it to be mapped and identified.

"I promise you when the trial is over, I'll jump-start this one for you," I said. "Save some of your energy for the witness stand."

I opened the door and turned the light switch off and on to get Mike's attention.

"It doesn't interest you that the Quillians make a guest appearance in the case file after all?" he asked. "I knew I could get those eyebrows of yours up a few inches."

"What'd I miss? Trish told us the cops came to the house. She and Bex were great friends."

"Yeah, but the fact is, the reason the police knocked on the door is that they were looking for Brendan."

Mike spread out some papers on the desk and started tapping his fingers as he examined them.

"Why? What have you got?"

"Phone records. Over here are three months of them from Bex Hassett's house, right through the time she was killed. Every now and then, looks like someone was placing calls to Brendan Quillian's cell phone. Long conversations—four or five minutes each."

I walked over to stand beside Mike. I could see that certain numbers had been circled in red ink.

He read to me from the detective's report. "Says Mrs. Hassett and her sons deny making any calls. Outgoing volume seems to be heaviest in the month before Bex began spending her nights in the park. No way to track her comings and goings, which days she'd actually been in and out of the house."

"Is there an interview with Brendan?" I asked with renewed interest in the old case.

"Where's your sense of romance, Coop? Wouldn't you figure Brendan was on a honeymoon somewhere? Bex was murdered a week after he got married," he said, pursing his lips. "Forgot about that myself. That's why the cops went to the house, hoping to talk to him because of the phone activity. I was beginning to lick my chops."

"How about Duke? Didn't they question him?"

Mike brushed his hair off his forehead and

read on. "Mrs. Quillian was interviewed. Talked to two of her other sons at the house and spoke with Trish, too. Brendan was out of the country and his mother didn't know where he was or how to reach him. Double-check that honeymoon story with Amanda's family, will you, blondie? And Duke Quillian was a patient at Sloan-Kettering. He was being treated for cancer. The detective checked that out. Has a phone number at the hospital, too."

"Hey, it was a long shot anyway," I said.

"Maybe not as long as you think. You got a date tonight? You didn't even look at this set of phone records." Mike was leaning against the desktop, shoving another page of numbers under my nose. "The detective was obviously interested in Brendan—interested enough to subpoena his cell phone information."

"What is it?" I asked.

"The last phone call made from Brendan Quillian's cell phone the day before his wedding. It's to the Hassetts' phone number. Mrs. Hassett told the detective Brendan had called there looking for her daughter, Bex."

24

"I know it's an old case. I wouldn't be begging you for help if I could walk into the morgue and chat up the guy who did the autopsy," I said at eight fifteen on Monday morning to Jerry Genco, the forensic pathologist who had testified for me last week. I had called him from my desk. "Your Bronx office handled it."

"The doc who performed the postmortem is dead," he said. "Natural causes. He was an old-timer back then. No way you can talk to him, Alex."

"I'm not as interested in him as I am in the homicide victim. There are some anomalies in the investigative file, and Mike Chapman thinks it would be useful to look at the physical evidence again. He doesn't think the police work was kosher—doesn't like the suspect they were looking at. Wants to check the original ME's notes and photos—they're not in the detective's records."

"You two are killing me. Agita, that's going to be the cause of death. Agita by prosecutorial pressure to the gut. What's Mike after?"

"He found Brendan Quillian's name in the dead girl's case folder."

"Anything else? You know we don't have the physical evidence here."

"I understand. Mercer is going out to the NYPD storage facility in Queens to see what he comes up with." Pearson Place was where all the property from old cases was stored until it was either thrown away or, if it had any independent value, auctioned off to the public. "The case got stalled along the way. The detective settled on a suspect whose admission doesn't seem to square with the autopsy report."

"Oh, no. I see where you're going with this. Is Battaglia pushing you?"

"I haven't seen him since last week, Jerry. Pushing me where?"

"He called the ME himself. Wanted to know what he needed to allege in order to get permission to exhume a body. That case in Chelsea from a couple of years ago? The cops just caught a killer who said he shot the guy, but the autopsy findings showed knife wounds."

"You're way ahead of me here. An exhumation? That never occurred to me."

"Yeah. Well, it turns out they arrested the right guy anyway. He shot the victim in the chest—then tried to dig the bullet out with a penknife. The mistake was on our end. Missed the bullet hole on autopsy," Jerry said. "What's a little piece of lead between friends?"

"All I'm asking is if you can pull the Hassett file for me."

"That's the way trouble always starts for me. One of you young Turks is trying to be creative and do the right thing. Then Battaglia gets a whiff and takes it to the next level. Save yourself some paperwork. Does the deceased have any family?"

"She does," I said.

"Get their permission. The court likes it better if they're on your side before you go disturbing the peace."

I don't think an exhumation was what Phin Baylor had had in mind when he'd told us to tell Trish Quillian to dig for the bones in her own backyard.

"Jerry, are you suggesting this is a road I want to go down?"

"If you've got a reason to think something was overlooked when the autopsy was done, that the examination wasn't thorough, then as much as I hate to do these things, it might be worth another look. Nobody has better instincts about these cases than Mike."

"Let me talk to him about it, okay? Just call me when you find the file."

Mike had dropped me off at home last night shortly before nine o'clock. The exhilaration of the wedding, and my Saturday-night encounter with Luc Rouget, had carried me through the events of the day. But I was tired and knew that I was facing another difficult week in the courtroom, so I said good night to Mike and went upstairs to order in a salad from P. J. Bernstein's deli.

This morning, I spent the next hour on the phone, greasing the wheels to arrange the things that would need to be done in the forensic biology lab and medical examiner's office if Mercer was successful in finding the long-neglected case evidence. Messages from the end of last week were stacked on my desk, and I returned calls on the less urgent matters that still required attention, trial or no trial.

Rose Malone, Battaglia's executive assistant, buzzed me on the intercom the minute he arrived in his suite an hour later. "Pat McKinney's over here with the boss. There's some kind of emergency meeting with the police commissioner at City Hall and the district attorney wants your input."

McKinney was my direct supervisor in the Trial Division, a rigid bureaucrat who liked to try to micromanage the several hundred prosecutors in our section of the six-hundred-lawyer office, dealing with every street crime from homicide and sexual assault down to trespass and harassment. McKinney resented my unique relationship with Battaglia, who respected the work of the men and women in the Sex Crimes Unit and allowed me direct access to him without reporting up the chain of command.

I walked across the eighth-floor hallway, and the security guard opened the door to the administrative wing. "Good morning, Rose. Is this any way to start my week?"

She had been a loyal friend to me for years and was the most discreet person on the planet. She organized Battaglia's professional life with skill and precision—not a moment of his day wasted with nonessential meetings or visitors—and she quietly did what she could to protect me from Pat McKinney's frequent attempts at backstabbing.

Rose was leaning over a file drawer with a sheaf of papers in her arms. Always perfectly coiffed and dressed in slim skirts and high heels that showed off her great figure, she added a note of style to the grim decor of the front office. She picked up her head and nodded in the direction of Battaglia's office. "Pat was waiting for him when he got here. It's something to do with the water tunnel explosion, so I told the boss you ought to be in on this."

"Thanks, Rose. Let's have lunch when my trial ends." I turned the corner and smelled the smoke from Battaglia's Cohiba, probably his third of the morning by this hour, before I reached his room.

The district attorney was sitting at the far end of the long conference table, his hand on the receiver of the multiline phone that served as his mini–command center when he moved away from his oversize desk. McKinney sat next to him in one of the red leather chairs, both of them surrounded by dozens of Battaglia's framed awards and citations, which were hung around the office on the faux-wood-paneled walls, tributes to him from every legal organization and law enforcement agency in the country. For most New Yorkers, he was the only person in recent memory to have held this elected position, now serving in his fifth four-year term.

Battaglia replaced the phone in its cradle when I walked in the room. The thick cigar was planted in the middle of his mouth, like a cork in a bottle. He clasped his hands as he talked, the words emerging from around the Cohiba as he smiled broadly.

"The least you could have done was bring a soufflé with you, Alex."

"Sorry? Did I forget something?"

"A croissant. Some escargots. I had to go to a meeting at the Metropolitan Museum of Art this morning. Your friend Mrs. Stafford's on the board," Battaglia said, referring to Joan's mother. "She told me all about the wedding this weekend. Said there was a very determined French chef stirring the pot."

McKinney was staring at me as I blushed and tried to make light of Battaglia's joke.

Whatever incredible array of sources the district attorney had worldwide to give him breaking news on international business intrigue, banking scandals, terrorist financing funds, and crime cartels, they were light-years slower than word that came through his endless local pipelines. The man just liked to know everything, and he liked to know it first.

"I didn't think that was a felony, Paul. Am I wrong?"

McKinney's head was going back and forth as if he were at a Ping-Pong match. He didn't know what to make of the conversation nor why it embarrassed me, and I knew that Battaglia liked that angle, too.

"Shows how little you understand about

arson, Alex. A fire could be a good thing, if the flames don't get out of control."

"Obviously, you'll probably know before I do. Rose said you wanted me here."

Battaglia rested the cigar in an ashtray. "Pat's going to represent me over at the mayor's office. There's a meeting on updating emergency evacuation plans for the city. Worst-case-scenario kind of thing."

"Because of the explosion in Water Tunnel Number Three?"

"That's the catalyst. Whatever turns out to be the cause of the blast, and I was just getting the latest from the commissioner, it reminded everybody that the entire city will have to be evacuated if any of our tunnels experience an actual breach—whether from metal fatigue or terrorism or any kind of criminal action."

"Don't look so skeptical," McKinney said to me. "Think about the last few years and all the megadisasters. Hurricane Katrina and New Orleans. There wasn't a government official who didn't know a monster storm was going to hit, but no one had a plan in place."

"I know the terrorist task force is still working an aspect of the explosion, Paul, and I realize those two Saudi guys are in custody in Westchester, but Mike and I are certain the event on Thirtieth has something to do with the sandhogs," I said.

McKinney leaned over in an aside to Battaglia. "'Mike and I think.' If Mike Chapman told her to jump off the Brooklyn Bridge, she'd probably—"

"I'd check the homicide roster first before I went up on the bridge, just to make sure neither you nor your idiot girlfriend were on call," I said to McKinney. He had annoyed Battaglia—a devoted family man—by recently leaving his wife for a woman in the office with whom he'd been having an affair for years. "Nothing personal, Pat. I'd just prefer a careful investigation from a sensitive prosecutor if I were to meet an untimely end."

Battaglia ignored the quibbling. "I understand there's no court today because of the Quillian funeral. Have you got half an hour to bring Pat up to speed on what you've learned about the tunnel system vulnerability?"

"Sure."

"Sit down." Battaglia motioned to the chair on his other side. He didn't need to waste the time going to City Hall himself, but he clearly wanted to be in on any important developments. The cigar was back in his teeth, and he was already shuffling through the mounds of correspondence that Rose had stacked in front of him, more able to do four things at once than anyone else I'd ever met. "You do any homework on this, Pat?"

"I got the basics from the Office of Emergency Management. It's entirely different for a Category Four hurricane than a catastrophic event."

"Is that what you hear?" Battaglia asked, angling his head to me.

"Nobody's talked about this much in my quarters, boss. These guys are just trying to solve a crime."

McKinney's expression of disgust wasn't lost on Battaglia. "Apparently, the perfect storm could hit the financial district—and Kennedy Airport and half of Staten Island— with twenty-five-foot surges of water. The city's been divided into more than a hundred zones—trying to move people out of harm's way will make what happened in the Gulf Coast area seem like a picnic. We're talking more than two million evacuees."

Battaglia's crooked nose was hovering above a memo from someone in the office, his eyeglasses raised on his forehead. "I'm not asking about a flood, Pat. I want to know what happens if there's no damn water to be had. You're going to have federal and state hotshots at this meeting today. Look smart, will you?"

Objection, I thought to myself. Beyond the scope of the possible.

McKinney fidgeted in his chair. "We've obviously got the advantage over New Orleans and southern Mississippi of mass transit opportunities to move people out of the metropolitan area."

"Get some specifics about how those systems operate before you open your mouth. What about moving patients in hospitals on ventilators, people in nursing homes? What do the police and fire departments plan to do about looting and all the things that we'll be responsible for dealing with? Who's going to ride shotgun on water and gas deliveries so desperadoes don't hijack them? It's a strategic-planning meeting."

McKinney started making a list of Battaglia's concerns.

"Alex," the district attorney said, putting down the memo and eyeballing me. "What's got you and Mike thinking the way you do about the tunnel?"

I made my case presentation with the facts as I knew them, including my Sunday-afternoon excursion with Mike Chapman. McKinney was restless, too out of the loop to enjoy listening about an investigation in which he played no role.

Battaglia devoured detail as if it were essential to his diet, but then usually left his top aides alone to get the work done themselves, occasionally offering direction from his long prosecutorial experience. He listened intently to my description of the tunnel interior and dismissed the story of the tire iron that had narrowly missed my head—which he'd heard from the commissioner—with barely a question about my own fears.

"So Jerry Genco just told you about the exhumation order?" he asked. "I had to push you on that, didn't I, Pat?"

"Good idea, boss. It really was."

"Take Alex through it," Battaglia said, ready to get us out of his hair now, and hoping, as he always did, that we would work through our personal differences. "You ought to think about asking Fred Gertz to do the same thing in this Hassett murder."

I fingered the edge of the volume of criminal procedure law that sat on the table next to the phone. "I know it rarely stops you, but there's a little concept known as jurisdiction. Bex Hassett was killed in another county."

"Be creative, Alex. Maybe Quillian made the cell call from Manhattan. Get your toe in the door and make some noise here. I can always kick it over to the Bronx DA."

McKinney could barely suppress his smile as he watched me struggle to handle the boss diplomatically. He knew as well as I did that Battaglia hated to be told no when he came up with an idea he thought was a winner.

"It's a bit premature, Paul. Let's see what condition the evidence is in when Mercer gets back from the property clerk. I'd have to have some basis in fact to even raise the issue."

Battaglia's lips pulled back around the cigar in the mischievous grin that characterized his relentless prosecutorial drive. "Rattle your boy Brendan's cage, Alex. Use your imagination. Get under Lem Howell's skin if you can. Even if Gertz can't entertain the motion for an exhumation, the press hounds will love you for bringing it up."

"With all due respect, Paul, I don't think—"

"McKinney, go up to court with Alex this afternoon. Help her float this one past the judge."

"Will do," he said, sporting his smug attitude like a new suit. "Gertz practically eats out of my hand when I feed him enough law. I play him like a violin."

I followed Pat McKinney down the corridor, which was lined with the stern-faced black-and-white portraits of Manhattan's district attorneys going back more than a century. Dewey, Hogan, Banton, and the others seemed to gaze down at me, investing me with a sense of mission and duty.

Pat held open the door. As I stepped out past the security guard, I could hear a woman's screams coming from halfway down the wide eighth-floor hallway.

I broke into a trot as I saw Joe Roman, the squad detective, pushing open the door of the ladies' bathroom. I ran in behind him.

He reached the figure, collapsed on the

floor, before I dropped to my knees at her side.

It was Carol Goodwin, the stalking victim I'd assigned him to watch. The razor she had used to cut her wrist was beside her hand, blood pooling next to her on the cold gray tile.

25

The EMTs responded within minutes from nearby Beekman Downtown Hospital. They had stemmed the bleeding and bandaged the hysterical young woman, who had attracted the attention of dozens of staff members within earshot, before taking her out to the ambulance.

I had stood by the elevator doors as they closed, having tried for half an hour in the restroom to calm Carol Goodwin, to talk her down from her frenzied ranting while the

EMTs worked on her. She took that last opportunity to yell out her accusation.

"This is *your* fault, Miss Cooper! You're
supposed to help people like me. You're
supposed to believe in me. If I die, it's going
to be all your fault."

I rested my head against the wall, eyes
closed and arms crossed, waiting for the
gathering of lawyers, secretaries, witnesses, cops, and student interns to dis-
perse.

Joe ordered everybody to get back to
work.

"I'm not moving until they all go away," I
whispered to him. "Whatever fumes I was
running on to start this week, I'm out of
emotional gas. I don't want to talk to any of
them, I don't want to explain things to anyone. I've got a murder trial that I've got to
focus on, but life—such as it is—seems to
be going on for everyone else in all the old
familiar ways."

"Chapman's right. You do attract a lot of
whack jobs, don't you?"

"It's my specialty, Joe. What set this one
off?"

"Carol Goodwin's on me. I did just what
you told me to do. I followed her when she

got on the train after work on Thursday, picked her up at her house the next morning, and tailed her all the way to her office. Reversed it again on Friday, both directions. I knew by the time we got to her subway stop that she was making the whole thing up."

"How?" I asked, starting back to my office.

"Alex, she claims she's been stalked for months, right?" Joe was taller than I, with straight brown hair and an irrepressible smile. He was always animated, talking with both hands to underscore his points. "Terrified by some guy for a reason she can't fathom, but nobody's been able to flush him out. She complains about the police and everybody not doing enough for her."

"That's Carol."

"The girl gets on the subway with her book, sits down, and starts to read." Joe was imitating her now, opening a book with the palms of his hands. "The train stops ten times between her office and her home. She never looked up once—not a single time—to see who got on at any of the stops. Wasn't worried about who was sitting near her or who got off at her station. Kept right on reading, not jumpy and nervous like somebody who's truly in fear, waiting for the stalker to show up again. She doesn't have any way to know who I am, so that wasn't the reason. She had no way to make me. The girl is just a complete phony."

Laura had a hot cup of coffee waiting for me as we turned into my office.

"And I take it you chose this morning, on my doorstep, to break that news to her?"

Joe tried to keep a straight face. "Carol didn't go nuts on me until I locked her up."

"For?"

"Filing a false report."

"Help me here, Joey. We got something besides your hunch?"

He laughed. "When I tailed her home Thursday night, she stopped off at a Chinese restaurant. Walked in and came out five minutes later with her take-out bag and holding a menu in her hand. Lucky I waited around. Friday morning she dropped an envelope in the mailbox near her house. She called Steve Marron on Saturday, saying she was freaked out of her mind."

"By what?"

"Carol told him that when she opened her

mail, there was a menu from the restaurant she had eaten in on Thursday."

"The menu?"

"Exactly. Said she had dinner at the restaurant—which wasn't true—and that the guy had obviously followed her there while Steve wasn't doing anything to help and mailed her the menu to creep her out, show that he'd been stalking her. If ten or fifteen other clients hadn't had their mitts all over the menu, too, we'd have lifted clean prints, I can bet you."

"So you jumped?"

Joe raised his hands and shrugged his shoulders. "I had to lock her up. There was no stalker, and she obviously mailed the damn thing to herself, like she's been making up the rest of this nonsense, driving the cops crazy."

"Where'd you get her?"

"I picked her up in front of her house this morning. She came like a pussycat at first, until we got here and she asked to use the ladies' room. I shouldn't have let her go in by herself."

"The EMT says it wasn't a serious cut. He thinks Carol was just acting out."

"All she wanted to do was talk to you. I

read her the rights, asked her if she wanted to call a lawyer, but she just needed to explain things to you," Joe said. "I figured I'd come by to see whether you were in court or not—if you had a few minutes to hear her spiel—and let Laura give me someone to write up the case."

I looked at my watch. "Carol probably just wanted to distract me from what I'm supposed to be doing. Suck a little more time and energy out of me. It worked fine."

It had rattled me to see one of my own witnesses moved to the point of self-mutilation. I needed every ounce of concentration for the courtroom events of the coming week, and Carol's words—placing the blame for her arrest on me—had shaken me up.

"The ambulance is waiting for me to go with them over to have her stitched. You making a bail recommendation?" Joe asked.

I dug on my desk for the Goodwin file. The legal charge wasn't as serious as the young woman's psychological problems. I scribbled some notes to be attached to the arraignment papers and handed them to Joe.

"Let's ask for a remand for psych observation. Be sure they put a suicide watch on
her, too. Call me later and let me know how
she's doing."

I walked him out to Laura's desk.
"McKinney just called," she said. "What
time are you going up to see Judge Gertz?"

"Tell him Lem Howell is meeting me there
at four. Gertz wanted to check with us after
the funeral to make sure we're ready to go
in the morning. Mike expected to have
Brendan Quillian back in the Tombs by
midafternoon."

"I'll tell Pat to pick you up here at quarter
of?"

"Thanks, Laura. Would you hold everything, except Mercer or Mike?"

I spent the next couple of hours at my
desk, reworking my direct examinations of
Mike and several of the other detectives,
based on the rulings that Gertz had made
throughout the past week. I was hampered
by his indecision on my domestic-violence
expert and was hopeful he'd give me the
green light today.

Laura knocked on my door at one
o'clock. "I'm going out for a walk, Alex. I'll
bring you back a sandwich."

I took a bill out of my wallet and gave it to her. "Thanks. I'm starving."

"Here are your messages. This guy named Luc has called three times." She handed me the slips. "Should I have . . . ? Never mind. Your expression says it all. Next time I'll just ignore your directions and put him through."

I waited until she closed my door and dialed his cell number.

"*Bonjour,* Alexandra. I hope I'm not bothering you with my calls?"

"My secretary just told me about them. I'm delighted you phoned."

"Is it always this difficult to get through to you?"

"I think Laura will see that it's easier from now on."

"I want to thank you again for making the weekend such a pleasure. You may have heard by now that you have to charge me for another night."

I laughed. "Vineyard fog, I assume?"

"Exactly. Nina and I waited together at the airport for almost four hours until they shut it down. The fog was so thick you couldn't even see across the airstrip. We went back to the house and she grilled a couple of steaks that were in the freezer. I may know more about you than even you do."

"Sunday night was included in the package deal, Luc. I'm delighted you both got to enjoy it."

"So, I have some business dinners this week that I've got to attend, but one of my very dear friends has offered me the most impossible table in town. Will you be able to have dinner with me on Thursday, Alex? At Rao's? Do you know it?"

I hoped Nina had explained to him what life was like for me in the middle of a trial.

"I absolutely adore Rao's. And you're right, it's the hardest ticket in town."

The twelve-table restaurant in East Harlem was run more like a club, only open for five meals a week—dinner from Monday to Friday—with so many high-profile regulars that there was hardly any way to snag a reservation without being given a personal invite.

"Will you say yes?"

I wanted my enthusiasm for seeing Luc again to register in my voice. "I want you to understand how much I'd love to have dinner with you—and how especially delicious it would be to do it at Rao's—but Thursday night isn't going to work."

He was quiet, waiting for more of an explanation.

"We've lost time at the trial—my fault last week and with the funeral today—so the judge is going to start us earlier in the morning and keep us going until six, if he can, from now on. Prepping witnesses and all the catching up I have to do when we get out of court," I said, tripping over my words, nervous that Luc wouldn't understand the bind I was in, "I just can't make a dinner date during this week."

"Well, if I can rearrange my schedule to stay in New York over the next weekend, may I have the first bid on Saturday night?"

"Absolutely," I said, knowing that as I worked myself through the heart of the prosecution case, with or without my cooperating snitch, I'd probably look like a zombie by the time Saturday rolled around.

"I'll let you get back to work now. I'll try to find you again tonight. Let you know if I can change my plans."

"I look forward to that."

When Laura returned, I ate at my desk and redrafted my closing argument. The original version included points about the testimony of Marley Dionne, so I needed an alternative summation in case his refusal to talk to anyone since his attack at Rikers extended to the witness stand.

Mike Chapman called at three fifteen. "Packed house, Coop. Duke filled the church this morning. Brendan even managed to shed a few tears."

"Tell me he's back behind bars. Under lock and key again?"

"I just delivered him to the Tombs."

"Have you heard anything from Mercer?"

"Yeah. It took them five hours at the property clerk, but they found the evidence from Bex Hassett's case. Looks like it was stored properly. No reason they can't take a shot at analysis. He's on his way to the lab."

"The girl's sweater?" I asked.

"Uh-huh. There's a rough edge on the zipper. They'll work up the blood for a profile."

"Mike, I really need you and Mercer to go back at Marley Dionne. That's got to be the first order of business. I'm planning to try to use him on Wednesday, and then follow him up with your testimony."

"I didn't ask for this funeral detail. The lieutenant just stuck me with it. We'll pay a visit to Dionne tomorrow. Aren't you even curious about why Brendan Quillian called Bex Hassett the day before his wedding?"

I swiveled in my chair and stared out the window. I didn't want to snap at Mike, but I would take him on if he had jeopardized the case. "I've already had a rough day. Please tell me you didn't ask him about that?"

Lem Howell would raise a stink if Mike had even tried to question his client.

"Temper, temper, Madam Prosecutor. There were two uniformed cops sitting right there in the front seat of the car. I didn't ask him anything."

"But you said—"

"Now there are no rules that say I can't talk to the man, are there? Offer my condolences and the like."

"So you told Brendan what?"

"I just thought he'd want to know that I found his name in an old case file. Probably a coincidence is what I thought. Another homicide. Another manual strangulation. A sixteen-year-old girl named Rebecca Hassett."

I reached in my desk drawer for some aspirin. "If he responded to you, I really do not want to know what he said. Got it?"

"He didn't speak at all. I was sitting on the wrong side of him, so all I was looking at was the walled-up eye of the Cyclops. But I'm telling you, Coop, his whole body twitched so bad, I think if he wasn't cuffed to me, he would have thrown himself out of the car."

26

Lem Howell was talking to Judge Gertz at the bench when Pat McKinney and I entered Part 83. Lem's smooth voice boomed in the large, empty courtroom. "The big gun, the artillery, the cannon fire, Your Honor. It appears that Alexandra has had to call in the cavalry. Mr. McKinney, welcome to the fray."

"Gentlemen, good to see you."

Lem didn't like Pat any better than I did. They had often tangled before Lem left the

DA's Office for private practice—Lem, the personification of great style, and Pat, who exhibited none. He was a fine investigator, but his lack of interpersonal skills didn't translate well in front of jurors and adversaries.

"Everything go as planned today?" Fred Gertz asked me.

"Yes, sir. I understand the defendant has been returned to the custody of the Department of Correction."

"Do you have your schedule for the week?"

I handed my witness list for the next day to the judge, with a copy to Lem. "These are the detectives I'm calling tomorrow. The rest of the week is a work in progress. You'll know as soon as I do."

Lem was pleased to see there were no surprises. I had turned over all my discovery for these cops when jury selection began.

"You here to pick up some pointers, Pat?" Lem asked, brushing some flecks of dandruff off McKinney's shoulder. "For starters, whoever is choosing your ties is doing a badass job."

McKinney looked down at the ugly brown paisley pattern and snorted at Lem.

"We're starting at nine sharp, folks. Is that okay? Get this show back on the road," Gertz said. "Artie called all the jurors today. They'll be in early and ready to go."

"That's fine," I said.

"Judge, I'd like to give you a heads-up about something," Pat said, sidling up to the bench and squaring off to Lem Howell.

Gertz was already on his feet, taking off his robe to hang it in chambers for the night.

"What's that? Something to do with Alex's case?"

"Well, more to do with Brendan Quillian."

Lem glanced at me and I looked away. "What would that be?" he asked.

Gertz sat down again and McKinney talked directly to him. "I think you should be aware, Judge, that yesterday afternoon, Detective Chapman came—uh—came across an open case. An old one, Your Honor, from more than a decade ago. A homicide of a young woman."

"What do you mean, came across it?" Gertz asked.

"I don't think we're prepared to tell you exactly how that happened right now. But the important thing to know is that one of the persons of interest in that matter . . ."

Pat McKinney stalled, making sure he had Gertz's complete attention. My head was bowed, trying to avoid Lem's questioning expression. I didn't agree at all with Battaglia's suggested tactics and I didn't want to be part of this bench conference.

". . . one of the persons of interest in the manual strangulation of this teenager was Brendan Quillian."

Lem Howell scowled at McKinney. "What do you think you're up to, Pat? Your Honor, first of all, are we off-the-record? Is this some kind of joke that the District Attorney's Office is going to play with my client's life?" he asked, swinging an arm around the well of the court. "Are you grandstanding for some better ink in this case?"

"Tell me what you know," Gertz said, cocking his head and letting McKinney sketch an outline of the case for him, calling on me from time to time for details.

"Ask Alexandra why she's so quiet," Lem said. "Something tells me she doesn't have a dog in this fight."

Gertz checked me out, then turned back to McKinney. "What's your point?"

"I just thought you ought to know, Judge, that Battaglia may ask the Bronx district attorney to—um—to re-autopsy the case. New forensic technology, a more careful examination."

Lem's outrage was growing. For the eight hundred fifty dollars an hour that Brendan Quillian was paying for his services, the defendant would get more than his money's worth, whether he was here to see the action or not. There was no trace of Lem's good humor as he pointed his finger at McKinney and demanded some straight talk.

"Re-autopsy? Is that some kind of euphemism for digging up a body in the middle of my client's trial? Maybe happen to have a reporter trailing along with you, a photographer or two to make sure you hit the tabloids? Have you lost your mind, Pat? Alex, you've got better sense than this."

"I'm not saying it's going to happen, Lem," McKinney said in a soft, whining voice. "The DA just wanted me to let Judge Gertz know this might be taken out of our hands."

"Weasel words, Your Honor. Not the first time I've heard them from Mr. McKinney. This—this—this—" Lem said, struggling, as he rarely did, to express himself. "This is absurd. Quite frankly, Judge, I've got no idea what the law is on this issue, but even the mere suggestion of an exhumation is a ridiculous reach. I'd like the court to order the prosecutors not to go any further with this until I've had an opportunity to do some research."

"McKinney, this young woman—this teenager—does she have a name?" Gertz asked.

"I'm—uh—I'm not sure I recall," McKinney stammered, glancing over to see if I would give him up.

I was nodding my head up and down in response to the judge's question.

"Oh, yeah. Hassett. Rebecca Hassett. That's right, isn't it, Alex?" McKinney had recovered the memory quickly in the face of more potential embarrassment.

"That mean anything to you, Lem?" Gertz said, looking back and forth between the men.

"Nothing. Nothing, Your Honor."

"Ms. Cooper, where are you in all this?" Gertz asked.

"Mr. McKinney and I don't agree with each other about the propriety of raising this issue with you at this point in time. It has no place

in this case, Your Honor. You both need to
know that beyond the jurisdictional issue, it's
apparent that Brendan Quillian was out of the
country when the young woman Pat has referred to was murdered."

Lem Howell looked at Pat McKinney, and
I could lip-read his clearly articulated "You
motherfucker," which he whispered with his
back turned to Gertz.

McKinney didn't know when to stop.
"Now, Mr. Quillian was also out of town
when his wife, Amanda, was murdered. Ms.
Cooper and a grand jury—and this court
that reviewed all of Mr. Howell's pretrial mo-
tions to dismiss on the sufficiency of the evidence—didn't seem to think that was a bar
to prosecution."

"Pat, we're off-the-record here, so I won't
say this quite the way I would if a reporter
were taking down my remarks. Keep your
mouth shut, will you? Not a word of any of
this until you package it before some judge
in the Bronx, where it belongs—when you're
quite ready to do that. Alexandra, do you
understand me?"

"Completely, Your Honor. I think Mr.
Howell and I trust each other enough so
that he'll believe me when I assure him that

there will be no leaks from my office. He has my word on that."

Gertz was surprised to see me in agreement with my adversary. "Lem?"

"I do appreciate that, Alexandra, but I'd like the judge to exact that same promise from Mr. McKinney. Unfortunately, Pat has a little less respect for the law than some of his colleagues."

"Spare me the ad hominem attacks, Lem," Gertz said, not able to put his finger on what was going on among the three of us. "You listen to me, Pat. Not a word of this to any reporters. I don't know what your game is here, but I'm not having any of it in my courtroom."

Gertz stood up again and pounded his gavel for emphasis. "Nine o'clock tomorrow. Be ready to put your first witness in the box at nine fifteen."

I turned to leave. Pat McKinney was a few steps behind me, muttering under his breath. "I'm trying to help you here, Alex. If Gertz thinks Brendan Quillian is involved in another homicide, even the most subtle rulings would tend to go your way from this point on. It'll change his whole attitude."

"Sorry, Pat. You forgot to tell me which

hand it is you've got the judge eating from, and what it is you've been feeding him. I think I can guess, but I'd rather do it the old-fashioned way. Ethically, if it's all the same to you."

Lem picked up his briefcase and held open the wooden barrier that separated the well from the courtroom seats. "I wonder about the company you're keeping, Ms. Cooper. Try to shake loose from that devil before the morning, will you?"

"See you tomorrow, Lem."

Artie Tramm followed Pat to the door to lock it behind us. As we entered the dark-ened corridor, I recognized the man walking toward me. He was one of the most promi-nent litigators in the city—Justin Feldman—whose practice kept him active in the more refined setting of the nearby federal court-house. Distinguished-looking, in his late six-ties, he was taller than I, with thinning hair and a tan that looked as if he'd spent many recent hours on the tennis court. Feldman had mentored a good number of my friends at the bench and bar.

"Laura told me I might find you up here," he said. "May I take you away from Pat for a minute?"

"Of course." I stepped into the alcove outside Part 83 and let McKinney go on his way. "I owe you for that. What can I help you with?"

"I've just been brought in to represent a guy named Lawrence Pritchard. Do you know who I mean?"

Pritchard was the former chief engineer on the tunnel project, the man whose name had been written on the back of Brendan Quillian's business card and dropped on the courtroom floor.

"Yes, Justin. I know exactly who he is."

"An agent from the joint terrorist task force showed up on his doorstep this morning."

"I'm not in charge of any agents. I didn't send anyone to Pritchard's home."

"I know that. Apparently he's one of the Feds on the task force. He's working with a prosecutor in the Southern District."

Battaglia would have my head if he lost the tunnel investigation to the U. S. attorney for the Southern District of New York.

"The guy wanted to question Larry about his relationship with Duke Quillian, about the explosion in the tunnel last week. I've told him not to talk to anyone until I met with you. Battaglia said you're in charge of the investigation for the moment."

"We can get you someone to meet with while I'm on trial," I said, feeling thoroughly overwhelmed with the problems of my own witnesses, the untimely direction from Battaglia and McKinney about Bex Hassett's case, and my nagging concerns about Carol Goodwin's hostility, since she had blamed her suicidal ideation on me just a few hours earlier. "What are you looking for?"

I wondered how quickly I could get Battaglia to put a couple of junior assistants on the tunnel case without yielding control of the investigation to Pat McKinney.

"First of all, I'd rather work with your office than the Feds on this. It takes so damn long to run everything past Washington when you're trying to clear things up for a client."

Feldman was right. Battaglia was the court of last resort when decisions had to be made on office matters, but the federal prosecutors needed to get authority from the Department of Justice before going forward.

"What else, Justin?"

"Queen for a day, Alex."

Pritchard had chosen his counsel well. Feldman's request for a particular kind of interview session that would limit his client's exposure had come to be known by that flippant name within the criminal bar. His witness was essentially telling him that he had information that would be of value in our investigation. He was offering to cooperate with the state—and, in exchange, I would be giving up my ability to use any statements Pritchard made on that day in any future criminal prosecution against him. The witness may have been helping me build a case against one of the other suspects, but in all likelihood he was trying to protect himself because of some illegal conduct in which he'd been involved.

I was startled by the introduction of Pritchard's name and that he claimed to have a story to tell. I tried to read Feldman's face in the darkened hallway. "Lawrence Pritchard wants to talk?"

"He's got information about Duke Quillian, Alex. What do you say, will you give us queen for a day?"

27

I had gotten off the elevator and gone directly to Battaglia, confident that Pat McKinney was shut in his office with his girlfriend for their ritual of five o'clock tea behind closed doors. Once I made the DA aware that one of his traditional archrivals, the federal prosecutor, was trying to grab hold of the tunnel investigation, he was quick to accept my suggestion of assigning someone to oversee the case.

"I'd suggest you get Nan Toth to work with the team," I said. "She's done everything from high-profile murders to complex white-collar litigation. She can match wits with a guy like Feldman without being intimidated, and the detectives respect her."

"And she's loyal to you, too. You like that part of it, don't you?"

"I like it a lot, boss."

Battaglia leaned over his intercom, took the cigar out of his mouth, and told Rose to get Nan on the phone. He asked if she could free herself up from whatever she was working on and meet in my office in ten minutes.

Mike Chapman and I spent the next two hours going over everything that we had learned in the days since the explosion with Nan, one of the senior prosecutors, who had been on Battaglia's staff five years longer than I. Married, with two kids, the striking brunette had been successful with some of the most sophisticated cases in the office, and I had relied on her skilled guidance as much as her friendship.

"Can you hoof it uptown with Coop and me for an hour?" Mike asked, checking his watch.

"You don't need to take me home," I said.

"I wasn't making a social plan, kid. You've

been so wrapped up in yourself since Ms. Goodwin took a slice out of her wrist that you haven't even asked me about my day. I saw Teddy O'Malley at the funeral this morning. I couldn't talk to him until I put Brendan Quillian back in the car with the guys from patrol. You want a chance to check out the three Hassett brothers?"

"Where?"

"They're working the four-to-twelve shift in the tunnel tonight. Teddy'll call them up around eight fifteen, to hog house, while they're breaking for their meal. Figures they'll want to hear all about the funeral. I said I'd just show up."

"Let's not miss this one," Nan said, eager to get started. "My husband's turn to help the kids with their homework anyway."

"Can you imagine what Coop would do with a husband and kids during a trial? The only other living thing in her apartment is a cactus, and she barely remembers to water that once a year," Mike said. He kicked the leg of my chair. "Stop feeling sorry for yourself. Nan'll do the heavy lifting till you go to the jury. Let's check out Trebek and then we'll go uptown."

"You mean I get to lose money in this

deal, too?" Nan said. "I'm Mercer's stand-in?"

We walked around the corner to Brenda Whitney's office, where her assistant was still at work on the week's press releases. Mike switched from the local news channel to *Jeopardy!*

He left it on mute for several minutes through the end of the double-jeopardy section and a pack of commercials.

"I guess you were too busy carousing with Joan Stafford to watch on Friday night, weren't you? Movie trivia," Mike said, a favorite topic for all three of us. "I raised the ante a few times but Mercer whipped me. I was sure it was *Luke*."

"What was Friday night? Where were you and Joan?" Nan asked me, just as I blushed and tugged at Mike's sleeve.

"What do you mean about Luc?" I said.

"Back down, girl. Did I hit a nerve? *Cool Hand Luke.* I thought for sure the Oscar went to Paul Newman. He was Luke, remember? The antihero, the loner. But Mercer pegged George Kennedy for Best Supporting Actor. Eighty bucks down the tubes."

The longer I could keep my love life out of

the mix of office gossip, the better my chances for succeeding with a new guy. Battaglia's morning greeting suggested that it would be no easier a task than usual. I had jumped at the sound of the homophone of Monsieur Rouget's name when Mike had said it.

"The category tonight," Trebek said, as Mike boosted the volume, "is Foreign Affairs. Foreign Affairs. That's it, gentlemen— and lady—so place your wagers now."

"We start at twenty bucks," Mike said to Nan. "This one's probably a trick question. It's as likely to be how many babies has Prince Albert of Monaco fathered out of wedlock as some political stumper. Where's your money?"

"Across the street in my office, Mike. Trust me for ten minutes," Nan said, ruffling his hair.

"He doesn't trust his mother. We're all in."

"Then we'll let you see the answer," Trebek said. "Look at the board and there it is—'First occasion in which the United States government attempted to overthrow a foreign regime.' Which affair was that?"

The musical tick-tocking of the show's theme song counted down the seconds. I was mired in thoughts of the Spanish-American War and knew that it wasn't even worth mentioning when I saw Mike's wide grin as he rubbed his hands together.

"I'm clueless," said Nan. "Do you know?"

"*Semper fi,* you two heathens. Think of the 'Marine Hymn.'"

"I'm sorry you came up blank, dear," Trebek consoled the computer programmer from Kansas City who had bet the farm on the big question. He held his hand to his ear, getting advice from someone offstage, as he moved to the second contestant. "Okay, Kevin, we'll accept that answer, too. 'What are the Barbary Wars?' We'll take that, Kevin. The question we were actually looking for is—"

"What was the Tripolitan War?" Mike asked.

"—probably the least known conflict in American history, folks, 'What was the Tripolitan War?' Yes, indeed. President Jefferson sent forces to the shores of Tripoli because the pasha and his Barbary pirates were threatening all the merchant ships in the Mediterranean and taking our sailors captive. So that's all for this evening—"

Mike clicked Trebek off midsentence. "Double or nothing if you can name the hero who led the battle. Twenty-five years old, they made him the youngest captain in the navy."

"Humor him," I said, walking out with Nan. "John Paul Jones usually works when you need a naval hero."

"Stephen Decatur, girls. 'Our country, right or wrong,' and all that. Died in a duel."

"Yeah, but can you remember what you're going to testify about in the case this week?"

"Spontaneity, Coop. You need to lighten up. You got to rock and roll with the circumstances at hand."

"I'm rocking as best I can. What if the arraignment judge decides to let Carol Goodwin go instead of holding her for a psych exam?"

"You worried about her coming after you?" Mike asked.

"No, I'm concerned that she's going to do something more dramatic to hurt herself and blame that on me. I kept flashing to that snapshot of her bloody arm on the bathroom floor when I should have been concentrating on other work all day."

"Give me five minutes to close up my of-

fice and I'll meet you outside the building,"
Nan said. "Whose car?"

"I'm the wheelman."

I took a couple of folders, shut out the
lights, and headed for the elevator with
Mike. The brisk night air was refreshing after an entire day inside the courthouse. I
waited at the curb until Mike brought his car
around.

I leaned into the window. "Would you
mind checking with Central Booking as long
as we're waiting? See if you can get a status update on Goodwin?"

"You're really nervous, aren't you? Wait
here for Nan." Mike left the engine running
and walked to the rear of 80 Centre Street,
into the open garage through which prisoners were delivered for their first court appearance following their arrest and for
fingerprinting.

Nan joined me in the car, and Mike returned shortly and said, "Your fruitcake
won't see a judge until sometime tomorrow.
She threw a little tantrum in the ER over at
Beekman, so they had to restrain her for a
while to sleep it off. They'll keep her in the
psych ward tonight for observation, and

she'll be arraigned in the morning if she be-
haves. Feel better?"

"Yes. As long as she's in a locked facility
getting medical attention, it'll get my day off
to a better start."

When we reached Thirtieth Street, Mike
parked the car on Tenth Avenue and we
walked into the construction site. Patrolmen
were still guarding the entrance and the
perimeter, but all of the media were gone.

When we reached the double-wide trailer
that was the sandhogs' headquarters, Mike
entered first, holding open the door for Nan
and me. Teddy O'Malley and a handful of
men had their lunch boxes opened on desk-
tops. The conversation stopped dead as the
group stared at the three interlopers.

O'Malley got to his feet to greet us. "Hey,
Mike. C'mon in. Miss Cooper."

Mike stepped over and started shaking
hands with the first two workmen closest to
us. "Mike Chapman, NYPD. Nan Toth, Alex
Cooper, from the DA's Office."

The man we had seen on our first visit—
Bobby Hassett—was sitting near the rear of
the room with O'Malley. He closed the lid of
his tin box and stood up, jerking his head
toward the door. "Let's go."

Like his younger brothers—identical twins who stood up at his command—Bobby Hassett was about six foot two. All three Hassetts were strapping young men, with wide, moon-shaped faces and high foreheads, heads sitting atop thick necks that widened into barrel chests. All three wore work clothes covered with dirt.

Bobby's expression was stern and his voice sharp. "Emmet, Hal—I said, let's go."

The twins hadn't moved the first time. They were as curious as the other men about who we were and how O'Malley seemed to know Detective Chapman.

"Mike, here, was hoping to talk to you guys," O'Malley said, looking at Bobby Hassett as he spoke. There was no question who was calling the shots for the brothers. "He's on the team that's investigating the blast."

Bobby stowed his lunch box above a locker and put his hard hat back on his head.

"Can't help you, pal. I wasn't working that night. Emmet, bring some extra cigarettes. Let's get back to work."

He came at us, stuffing half a sandwich in a plastic bag and pocketing it in his overalls.

Mike had moved from the door, but I was standing next to it, with Nan a few steps farther away.

"It won't take long, Bobby," Mike said. "There's just some things you might be able to help us with."

The big man put his hand on his waist, and as he turned to answer Mike, his elbow caught the side of my chest, knocking me back a few steps. I tripped over the chair leg behind me, and a stack of papers tumbled off the nearest table.

"You okay?" Nan said, grabbing my hand to pull me up.

"Take the broads and get out of here, Mr. Chapman. There's a lot of accidents can happen around the tunnel, do you hear me? I've got nothing at all to say to you. Emmet, Hal—this isn't a picnic," Bobby said, reaching for the doorknob. "Hey, Teddy, since when are you doing the man's bidding? Next time you want to invite me for dinner, tell me who else'll be at the table."

Bobby and his brothers stomped down the steps of the shack in their mud-caked boots. Mike was annoyed, his lips clamped together and his eyes darting from Teddy to the door. He hadn't come this far to be dissed.

"Wait here," he said, holding his hand up at Nan and me as he headed out.

O'Malley was on his heels. "That's a bad idea, Mike. Let them be. Cop or no cop, you'll not make them talk to you. You'd best try to set up a meeting through the union rep."

Nan looked at me and we dashed for the exit, too. A couple of overhead lights helped us navigate around the giant machinery and over the pockmarked ground as we trailed behind O'Malley.

I couldn't make out the words but I could hear Mike's voice, badgering the trio of Hassetts as they made their way to the top of the cylindrical entrance to the tunnel shaft. They moved swiftly—more sure-footed on this rough terrain than either Mike or the two of us.

"They'll turn on you, Mike," O'Malley said. "Don't be riding them."

Bobby Hassett grabbed the wire cage opening on the side of the Alimak and slammed it shut as soon as the twins stepped on behind him. He flipped a switch and the bare lightbulb over his head glowed against the schist in the bedrock wall.

"You want to talk about the Quillians, Mr. Chapman? I'll make an appointment for you to come downstairs here to my office sometime. Leave your little girls at home," Bobby said, leering at us, his blackened fingers clutching the mesh of the cage. The grinding noise of the motor started up, Bobby raising his voice to shout over it. "Teddy knows how to find me, as you can see. Keep my brothers out of this."

"I want to know everything there is to know about Duke Quillian," Mike said.

"You shoulda been at the church, Detective. Teddy says Duke got himself a really deserving send-off," Bobby said, his white teeth shining as he threw his head back and laughed. He obviously had no reason to know that Mike had been at the funeral service.

"I need to talk to you about Brendan Quillian, too."

The Alimak started to move slowly off the platform.

"You got him in the right place, Mr. Chapman. Let's see if you can keep him there."

"And Bex," Mike said. All we could see of

the Hassetts were the crowns of their bright yellow hard hats. "Your sister, Rebecca. I want to ask you about her murder. I want to ask what you remember about how she died."

The groaning wire cage disappeared down into the deep black hole, and none of the three men aboard it—a true band of brothers—said a word.

28

We had a quick dinner together at Primola before Mike put Nan in a cab for her ride home to Brooklyn Heights and dropped me in front of my door.

I left the apartment at 7 a.m., driving myself to the courthouse and parking on the empty street behind the small park in Chinatown that Mike called Red Square. Fishmongers were packing ice chips onto their sidewalk display cases, filling them with wriggling crabs and lobsters and fish whose odor would grow less appealing with the heat of the June day, while Asian farmers from rural New Jersey were unloading mounds of fresh, exotic vegetables.

I stopped at the cart on the corner of Centre Street for two large cups of black coffee and a Danish—caffeine with a sugar boost of pastry to get me through the morning.

I didn't expect to see two detectives from the Special Victims Unit—Alan Vandomir and Ned Tacchi—waiting for me at my desk when I walked in the door at seven thirty.

"Don't worry, we know you're on trial," Alan said. "We've got Ryan Blackmer writing up the case downstairs. But he said you'll be the one to deal with the administrative end of this. That Battaglia would handle the politics. I was just leaving you a note. Hope that you don't mind that we let ourselves in."

"Of course not."

Vandomir and Tacchi were two of the best detectives in the department, in both investigative style and in their manner of relating to victims of sexual violence.

I dropped my case folders on the desk. "What have you got?"

"Viagra," Alan said. Neither one had a good poker face.

"What do you mean?"

"Around midnight last night, we locked up an old friend of yours. Derrick Ferris, re-member him?"

"I certainly do. We convicted him for three rapes in the Taft Housing Projects. Must have been one of my first patterns with you guys. That's going back."

"Yesterday, we got a hit to the data bank from these two new cases—the girls up on Adam Clayton Powell Boulevard in May. The one you assigned to Ryan."

"Great."

"Got a tip from Parole that his mama still lived in one of the buildings at Taft. We just staked out her apartment till he came home from his night's prowl. You know how these two victims said he never lost his erection—that each of them said the rapes went on for an incredibly long time?"

"I do." I had struggled to convince many jurors over the years that the sexual dys-function some rapists exhibited was usually quite different from consensual coupling. It was exhibited in a variety of behaviors, including—as with Ferris—the ability to maintain an erection for hours.

"Well, we patted him down at the scene for weapons—"

"Get the knife?" I interrupted.

"Nope, but CSU is searching the stairwell. We had a bit of a chase. Then Ned searched Ferris back at the stationhouse and took this out of his pocket."

Alan held out a baggie with a white plastic pill bottle inside.

"Viagra," I said, studying the label. "I guess I shouldn't be surprised. It's probably easier to get this on the street than smack."

"It isn't street stuff, and it didn't fall off the back of the truck. This is your tax dollars at work, Ms. Cooper."

"What?"

Ned handed me a piece of paper. It was a receipt for a prescription with Derrick Ferris's name on it—for Viagra—from a pharmacy that filled the request and received payment from Medicaid funds.

"It doesn't make any sense for the government to do this. Derrick Ferris is a level-three offender," I said. "I did the hearing myself."

Ferris was eighteen at the time of his conviction and had been released after serving
only eight years of his twenty-five-year sentence. But he had been designated the
most-serious-level sex offender, to be
tracked by the convicted-felon registry on
the underlying facts of his original case
and his risk to the community—far more
likely to commit similar assaults again than
most other criminals.

"I spoke to his parole officer yesterday,"
Ned said. "Ferris is actually supposed to be
on medication that—what do I say? Sup-
presses the urge."

"You know how this stuff works?" I asked,
shaking the bottle. "It increases blood flow
to the penis. If he was having any trouble
performing, this just enhances his ability to
complete an act of intercourse. How many
of our guys is Medicaid enabling?"

"Sit down for this one, Alex. We did a
check last night. All the level-three offenders are registered online. The sergeant's
calling in the names this morning to the
Medicaid office as soon as they open, but
there's more than two hundred convicted
rapists in this county alone, and they're all
eligible for the drug. He thought you'd want

to let Battaglia know this one's going to hit the media."

"Thanks a lot. Ask Ryan to do a memo to the boss for my signature. Remind him to emphasize that level-three offenders don't change their colors. I've never met one who's been 'rehabilitated' by a visit to jail."

"Good luck today," Alan said.

"My first witness is Curtis Pell," I said. They both knew the detective who worked Manhattan North, in the office adjacent to theirs, with Chapman. "I'll be prepping him as soon as he gets here and we go upstairs to Gertz before nine. If the jurors are all there on time, we'll be on at nine fifteen. If you hear anything from Medicaid on this by then, give me a heads-up."

Curtis Pell arrived half an hour later with more coffee and breakfast for himself and Laura. We had been over his involvement in the investigation and his written reports four or five times in the last month, so I just walked him through the trim version of his direct that I had fashioned yesterday.

The chatter of assistants arriving filled the eighth-floor corridor as Curtis helped me maneuver my shopping cart from my office to the first of two elevator banks that connected to the courthouse tower above the DA's Office.

The hallway outside Part 83 was already lined with spectators and a handful of local crime reporters. Two court officers were standing between the metal detector through which they all had to pass and the long wooden table on which handbags and backpacks and briefcases would be searched.

Curtis Pell opened the door for me and we walked down the aisle to counsel's table.

Lem Howell had the *Wall Street Journal* spread out before him. His cream-colored suit looked like the cleanest thing in the drab courtroom, a cool contrast to my slim turquoise sheath.

Lem didn't pick his head up from the market listings but heard the tap of my heels as we approached him. "Good morning, Alexandra."

"Morning, Lem," I said. "Hey, Jonetta, how are you?"

The court clerk waved at me, and Artie Tramm was on his way off the bench to fill the judge's water pitcher. "We got eight jurors, Alex. We should be able to get started on schedule if the next few mosey in on time. Mind if I put Detective Pell in the witness room?"

"He's all yours."

Pell followed Artie out the side door of the courtroom. The hallway behind the jury box had several small rooms—the one in which jurors gathered before proceedings and in which they eventually deliberated, and a windowless cubicle in which witnesses waited before they were called to the stand.

When he came back into the part, Artie called out to Lem and me, "Gertz wants to know if you're ready as soon as we get our full panel."

"Good to go," I said.

"You expecting a visitor?" Artie asked.

One of the court officers had let Alan Vandomir into the room. Lem Howell recognized the detective and got on his feet to sit on the edge of my table. "No more monkey business up your sleeve, is there?"

"It is monkey business, actually, but nothing to do with your case. This will only take a minute. You can listen in, Lem. You'll hear it on tonight's news anyway."

Alan and Lem shook hands. "The sergeant got through to the head of the

Medicaid office half an hour ago. These Viagra pills, they cost ten bucks a shot, and the government's been paying for released sex offenders to get them for *five years* before anybody happened to notice. The bill for keeping these pervs' private parts up, just in New York alone, runs over twenty-one million dollars. You better call Battaglia, Alex."

"Will do, Alan." He turned to leave the courtroom and Artie Tramm walked him out, locking the door behind him so that Gertz could take the bench without any further interruptions.

"Let me understand this," Lem said, pacing the well as though arguing to an imaginary jury. He was entertaining me and Jonetta Purvis, the court clerk, and Artie Tramm, the last bit of humor before we hunkered down for a day of testimony about Amanda Keating's homicide.

The two uniformed court officers who would be guarding Quillian for the remainder of the trial—a stooped older man, Oscar Valenti, and the short African-American woman, Elsie Evers, who had worked the part last week—were leaning against the door to the defendant's holding pen, also watching Lem perform.

"I am all for the underdog, ladies and gentlemen, do not mistake that fact." Lem gestured with his forefinger. "But when you are taking food out of the mouths of our hungry children—how much money did he say, Artie?"

"Twenty-one million large, Mr. Howell."

"When you are using money that could be better spent on a pension fund for Ms. Cooper or a fine new robe for the judge or membership at a gym for Artie Tramm"— Lem patted Artie's paunch as the officer passed behind him—"and instead, you are correcting, you are fueling, you are—hell, Ms. Cooper, you're the expert here, what's going on? You, my dear taxpayers, and the United States government, have just declared an end to erectile dysfunction, is that it? Whose lobby is this? Erectile dysfunction is unfair for sex offenders. Watch the ACLU jump in on their side. It's mind-boggling."

"I'll tell you right up front," Artie said, "I keep waitin' for one of those four-hour jobs that I'd have to call my doctor and complain about. Four minutes I'm lucky. I see that ad one more time on TV I'm gonna throw something at the set."

Fred Gertz swept into the courtroom from his robing room. "Who's complaining about what? I must say, you're a happy-looking bunch this morning. How many jurors missing now, Artie?"

"I just checked. We need two regulars and one alternate. Nobody's called with a problem, so we should be fine by nine fifteen."

"Anything to discuss? Any housekeeping?"

Lem and I looked at each other, and I said, "No."

"Shall we bring the prisoner in?" Gertz asked.

Lem walked to the bench for his daily bonding with the judge. "You have to hear this one, Fred. Special Victims Unit locks up a serial rapist last night—a guy on parole for a bunch of attacks Alex got him on years ago. You know what you bought him?"

"Me?" Gertz didn't get it at first. "What did I buy who?"

"We've been paying for his Viagra, Fred. You and I. We've been helping to set him up in business in the hood. Helping him get his groove back."

The two court officers, Oscar and Elsie, had left the room to bring Brendan Quillian in, so that he could take his place before the press, the public, and the jurors were allowed to enter.

"That's expensive stuff," Gertz said with a chuckle. "What does one have to do to get the government to pay?"

More than I needed to know about the usually sober jurist.

I walked to the wall phone that was mounted behind Jonetta's desk. Cell phones were not allowed in court, and this was an internal unit that could only be used to reach extensions within the DA's Office system.

"Rose? Would you tell the boss that Ryan Blackmer will be sending up an urgent notice any minute now? Paul has to pay attention to it and I'm not available till the end of the day. The police commissioner will be trying to get lots of press on this one, and Battaglia needs to know the numbers." I thanked her and hung up the phone.

Oscar Valenti held open the door for Quillian, and I could hear the distinctive jangling of the metal cuffs as Oscar's partner, Elsie, unlocked the prisoner's hands as they paused at the entrance to the court.

"I'll look into it for you, Fred," Lem said.

"That's what they call a stiff dose of medicine," Artie called across the room, the only one of us laughing at his joke.

The levity would be over the minute Gertz banged his gavel and called for the stenographer and jury to be brought in. But the bizarre news of the Medicaid outrage had broken the tension for all of us before the day's serious work began.

It had also put us all off guard.

I heard the gunshot before I saw the weapon in Brendan Quillian's hand. I watched as the petite court officer fell to the floor, shot in the head with her own service revolver.

29

Quillian took a few steps forward, his head sweeping the room so his only good eye could scope the territory. He'd been present enough times to know that the door to the main hallway stayed locked until the prisoner was seated. His only way out was the exit in back that had brought him from the Tombs to the holding pen.

Jonetta Purvis was standing still, frozen in place, screaming at the bloody sight of the woman whose brains had been blown out before us. I watched helplessly as Brendan

Quillian struck Oscar Valenti on the head with Elsie's gun, after the older man instinctively kneeled to look at his partner's wound at the same time he tried to unholster his own weapon.

Then Quillian swung the barrel of the gun in Jonetta's direction. I tackled her to the ground and we both went down behind the desk. There was a huge noise in the high-ceilinged room as he fired again, a bullet striking the wall above our heads.

As I fell on top of Jonetta, I saw Lem Howell vault over the side of the jury box, taking cover behind it. "Give it up, Brendan. Give it up, you damn fool."

The judge must have ducked beneath the bench the minute the first shot rang out. I neither saw him nor heard his voice.

Artie Tramm had drawn his gun and was trying to jog to the rear of the room to unlock the hallway door—or to run out. Quillian moved faster than Tramm. Before the officer was halfway down the aisle, Quillian fired three times at Artie's broad back.

I couldn't see my old friend, but I heard him grunt as at least one bullet struck its mark, and I recoiled as his body hit the floor with a dull thud.

From beneath the kneehole of Jonetta's desk, I saw the defendant turn and go back to Oscar's side.

I had one hand over Jonetta's mouth, trying to stifle her sobs while I propped myself up with the other. I could see Quillian take the man's gun from its leather case and disappear back into the top of the landing beside the holding pen from which he had emerged. After all these months, he knew the enormity of the building as well as I did—a maze of hallways, staircases, and elevator shafts. He'd had scores of opportunities to make note of its labyrinthine passages, and he was undoubtedly scrambling down the one adjacent to the prisoners' elevator as we stayed frozen in place.

The slaughter and turmoil that Brendan Quillian had begun so abruptly ended just as fast.

I pushed myself up as Lem called out the judge's name. I got onto my knees, barefoot, the skirt of my dress ripped at the seam from the tumble with Jonetta.

There was still no sound from the bench, no sign of Fred Gertz.

Oscar was stirring, rolling onto his back and stroking his head.

I started crawling toward Elsie's body.

"Get the hell back, Alex," Lem said. "Fred, are you alive, man?"

Lem ran toward Elsie and crouched beside her. I stood up, thinking I could help him if there was any chance of keeping her alive. "Forget it. She's gone, Alex. Get back with Jonetta."

Judge Gertz clutched the top of the bench with both hands. "Is it safe?"

Everything seemed to be happening at once. I could hear Artie Tramm moan and Lem ran in his direction. "Stay down, Fred. He could be back any minute."

I dashed to the door through which Quillian had entered and slammed it shut, turning the lock. If he encountered other armed officers in the stairwell, he was just as likely to try to get back here and take us all hostage.

"I told you to stay put, Alex," Lem shouted. "That one's not like the front door. Most officers have a key to open that lock—it's useless."

Lem had spent far more time outside those holding pens than any prosecutor had.

"Is Artie—?"

"I got his gun, Alex. Everybody stay calm with me. That door opens again, I got Artie's gun and we'll be fine." Lem raised his arm so Jonetta and I could see it. "It's just your arm, Artie. Don't fight it. Stay down here with me. You'll be kicking ass again in no time, Artie."

I stepped closer to Elsie Evers. Two minutes earlier, this quiet woman had been doing her job, none of us anticipating the deadly threat from the seemingly well-bred defendant who had been so compliant during every other court appearance.

I ignored every principle of crime-scene investigation I had ever learned and expected from other professionals. I knelt beside her, taking her still-warm hand in my own to try to feel a pulse. One look at the back of her head was enough to tell me I wouldn't find one—that it would be better for Elsie if I couldn't find one—but I felt an overwhelming need to minister to her in some human way as her life oozed out on the filthy courtroom floor.

"What are you doing?" the judge asked. "She's dead. Leave it alone."

"Jonetta, would you get my jacket from the back of my chair?"

Someone was rattling the door from the pens.

Jonetta heard it, too, and ducked back beneath the desk.

Lem had grabbed Artie's walkie-talkie to toss to me. "Alex—catch it! Press the talk button and send an SOS."

He sprinted the remaining twenty feet to the main entrance and unlocked the door to the hallway. The two young officers who had been stationed at the metal detector came in with their guns drawn as Lem explained to them what had happened.

I transmitted the message that an armed prisoner had escaped and one court officer was dead. "Lem," I called out. "Someone's trying to get back in over here."

Both officers were on their walkie-talkies, coming toward me to secure the door through which Quillian had fled. "When we heard shots, I called for backup and a bus," one of them said—the NYPD shorthand for an ambulance. "They should be here any minute. Those reporters are all going nuts."

One stationed himself beside the door, watching the knob wiggle, hearing a man's voice yelling to Artie Tramm as he banged at the door. "Artie? Open up. It's me—it's Blakely."

The second officer went around to the back of the bench and put his hand under Fred Gertz's arm to help the shell-shocked jurist to his feet. "Judge, you gotta come with me. I want you at the other end of the room."

"The captain has us in lockdown," the first officer answered Blakely. "I can't let you in till we get backup here. The prisoner went out your way. We got Elsie down. Artie and Oscar are waiting for medics."

I walked to counsel's table and slipped my jacket off the back of the chair. I brought it over to where Elsie lay and covered her head and upper body with it. There would be no shelter from the way the media pundits would blame her for her own death—for allowing Quillian to overpower her, take her gun, kill her, and endanger everyone else, as well as possibly make his escape from the massive building with its dozens of entrances and exits.

I could only offer her a bit of dignity now, in case the reporters and photographers flooded the room when we admitted the rescue team.

"Lockdown?" Gertz shouted. "I want to get out of here now. Right now."

"I'd like you in that last row," the officer said, "so they can remove you as soon as they deal with Artie."

"Not that way. I'm going through my chambers," Gertz said, resisting and pointing to his own exit. "I don't need an ambulance. I don't want any of those people to see me."

The deep red blood stained through the turquoise of the fabric of my suit jacket, turning it to cobalt blue as the silk quickly absorbed it.

As much as the sight of Elsie's gaping head wound had revolted Jonetta, she had not been able to stop staring at it. Her sobs subsided as I put my arm around her and guided her out of the well to a seat closer to the main hallway entrance.

Lem was crouched beside Artie, trying to keep him calm. He was writhing in pain, sweat dripping from his face, drenching his hair and his mustache. The more he rolled around, the more the blood spread through the tear in his dingy shirtsleeve.

I squatted behind Lem's back.

"The great white whale," Lem said.

Artie mustered a laugh.

"That's why he got away, Artie. Brendan Quillian is the great white whale in this friggin' criminal justice system. Damn, if he'd been a brother—or just a lowlife from the Bowery—you'd have been on his ass like every other prisoner. That whole Upper East Side rich-boy attitude was just a veneer. Nobody took him seriously. Nobody saw the risk."

Artie opened his eyes. "Make me a promise, Lem. Tell me you're not gonna represent that bastard for shooting me. For killing Elsie, okay?"

"I think Alex and I are grounded on that one. We're gonna be your star witnesses."

There was a loud banging again, this time from the hallway. The walkie-talkie crackled in my hand. "Open up in there, Part 83. Artie, can you hear me?"

I held the device in front of Tramm. He gulped for breath and answered with a weak "Yeah."

"Open up, dammit. I got four cops and some EMTs here."

"You know who that is? Recognize the voice?" Lem asked.

Artie nodded.

Lem walked to the door and unlocked the large brass bolts.

Two of the medics got right to work on Artie, one ripping open the polyester uniform shirt to examine the wound as the other started taking his vital signs.

The next two asked if we were okay, and we signaled them on to Elsie's body and to Oscar, who still seemed dazed and disoriented.

The four cops, dressed in flak jackets and helmets, positioned themselves around the other door, relieving the court officer who had been the first to arrive. The knocking started again.

"Who's there?" one asked.

"Blakely. Captain Blakely, for chrissakes. Lemme in."

The cops turned to us. Artie nodded again at Lem.

"You alone?" one cop asked, while another motioned to Lem, Jonetta, and me to get down on the floor, in case Blakely had been taken hostage by the escapee.

"Yeah."

Another unlocked the door, and as Blakely entered, we got the all clear to get up.

"Where's Artie?"

They pointed Blakely back to the cluster of people in the aisle of the courtroom, and the crusty, white-haired captain barely stopped to look down as he passed Elsie's body.

"We owe this to you?" Blakely said to Lem Howell. "You the brains behind this operation?"

"I appreciate the thought, Captain. But I was about to whip Ms. Cooper's tail fair and square at the end of this trial, so, the answer to that would be no."

"Has Quillian been caught?" I asked.

Blakely raised his thick, white eyebrows and frowned at me.

"The prisoners' elevator must have been very busy at this hour," Lem said. "I kept thinking he'd be trapped because of that. I was waiting for him to burst back in here."

"Forget the elevator. He used the stairwell. Nobody else seems to have gone that way. He must have run down a few flights. Probably reentered the main corridor on four or five," Blakely said.

The rooms in which misdemeanor cases were heard were on the lower levels of the courthouse. The sixth through ninth floors, in the bizarre architectural scheme of the

WPA building, were occupied by the District Attorney's Office. No access was possible from the courts except where they connected on the seventh floor.

"Then he's somewhere in the building?" I asked. "You know he's still got a fully loaded piece—he took Oscar Valenti's gun with him, too."

"Too bad there are no metal detectors when you exit the damn place," Blakely said.

"Why? You think he can escape? There are hundreds of cops and court officers around at this hour of the day," I said.

"He was out before the word spread—out before any of them knew."

"What do you mean?"

"If Quillian crossed over on the fourth or fifth floors, he must have gone down on the public elevators from there, passing off like a lawyer with the rest of you suits," Blakely said, fingering the lapel of Lem's jacket.

"What makes you think he got away?" I was shocked that a breakout of this magnitude could happen at 100 Centre Street.

"'Cause a man fitting his description just hijacked a car on the corner of White Street, opposite the courthouse steps. Shot the guy who was putting his money in the me-ter and drove off in a black Toyota," Blakely said. "Brendan Quillian's on the loose."

30

Flashbulbs popped as Captain Blakely swung back the wooden door to lead us into the corridor, still full of reporters and press photographers held there since the lockdown two hours earlier. The EMTs had treated the injured court officers, and a deputy medical examiner had declared Elsie dead—long after the fact—before she was loaded into a body bag and removed from the courtroom.

Lem took off his suit jacket. He held it open, and I slipped my arms into it, wrapping it around my dress to cover the blood-stains and the long tears in the fabric. He put his arm around my shoulders as we entered the gauntlet formed by the eager press hounds.

"Hey, Alex! Who'd he shoot at first—you or the judge?" a voice called out.

Court officers and cops formed a human chain, holding back the impatient spectators.

"Lem! Hey, Howell!" It was Mickey Diamond's voice. "Give me three words, Lem. We'll make the headline your signature triplicate."

We both stared straight ahead as we walked, counting the steps left to the elevator doors, half a corridor away.

"'Gunned. Gone. Guilty.'" Diamond was relentless.

"Is it true Judge Gertz is still hiding under the bench?" A local crime reporter thrust his microphone over the linked arms of two cops.

"'Murder. Mayhem. Manhunt.'" Diamond was stuck behind one of the film crews and I could barely hear him now.

Lem stepped up the pace. "Shit. I could write better copy in my sleep. Can you keep up with me? We're almost there."

"You get paid up front, Mr. Howell?" another news jock asked. "You bank your money before Quillian skips town?"

A detective—his gold shield flopped over his breast pocket—was holding the elevator open for us. "I got you from here."

He held up his hand and the cops who had been following us from the rear turned to face the crowd as the doors closed.

"You okay?" Lem asked, letting go of me.

"I will be. It's Elsie—it's what happened to Elsie that just breaks my heart. And you?"

"You know me well enough to understand how much I hate it when I can't see something coming. I thought I had Quillian convinced he was walking out a free man. I was going to blow every argument you had right out of the water."

"Did you talk with him last night?"

"After the funeral? Yeah, he called."

"Did you tell him what McKinney said about the possible exhumation of Bex Hassett's body?"

Howell's face twisted into a grimace, but he wouldn't answer my question.

When the doors opened on the seventh floor, four detectives from the District Attorney's Office Squad were waiting to take both of us upstairs to the Trial Division conference room, one flight above. All friends, all trusted colleagues, they surrounded me in a cocoon as we moved down the hallway and up the dark staircase—a protective shell that would have been more useful several hours back.

The chief of detectives himself was at the head of the table. He greeted both of us and had Laura standing by to get anything we needed. Jude Rutling, the head of the office's elite Homicide Investigation Unit, had been put in charge of the investigation.

"Let's get you comfortable first," the chief said. "Why don't you each go to the restroom. Alex, we'll need you to give us your clothes. Did they get pictures of you—that blood and all—upstairs?"

"Yes. Yes, they did. Crime scene."

"We'll be debriefing you one at a time. Jude can start with Alex, and my men will take you in another office, Lem."

"I'd like some coffee, please," I said, shivering, even though Lem's jacket was still over my shoulders. "May I talk to Laura?"

A detective escorted me down the hall, past Laura's desk, on the way to the ladies' room. Laura reached out to give me a hug and I pushed back. "Wait till I clean myself off. Can you dig anything up in the closet? I used my jeans for that trip to the tunnel last week."

"Marisa's already been over," Laura said, walking into my office to grab a hanger from the closet.

"These should fit."

I took the black track suit into the restroom—the same one in which Carol Goodwin had cut herself a day before. My head was spinning as I looked in the mirror—blood smears had been transferred from my hands to my face, and the layer of dirt that had previously coated the courtroom floor was on my skin and in my hair.

I undressed and changed into Marisa Bourgis's gym clothes. I filled the sink with warm water, leaned over it, and plunged my entire head into the bowl. There were no showers in the women's bathrooms throughout the old offices—built in the days when there had been no women on the legal staff of the district attorney.

I scrubbed my face with brown-paper toweling and ran my fingers through my wet hair. The detective standing guard at the door was startled to see my new look when

I emerged minutes later. He walked me back to the conference room where Jude—and my coffee—and two Major Case Squad detectives were waiting to take me through the details of the morning's events.

Quillian's outburst had been sudden and short. I knew this drill as well as the men who were questioning me and tried to be patient as they went at me again and again for every nuance, every sequence of how each of us in the room had responded to the gunshots and action.

The door opened behind me and I rested my head against the back of the tall leather chair. Laura interrupted the grilling. "Excuse me, Jude. Mr. Battaglia's back from City Hall. He'd like to see Alex."

"We'll be done shortly."

"Right now."

I stood up, grateful for the break, even though I knew I was in for a different kind of interrogation from the boss. "You think the hallways are safe enough for me to make it the next fifty feet by myself?"

"Laura's in charge. But the chief's giving you a detail once you leave this building—Lem Howell, too—till they find Quillian. Two detectives with you round the clock. You've got your choice of someone sleeping at your place during the night. The other one will be in the lobby."

"Ignacia Bliss," I said, smiling at Jude. "Unless Lem picked her first. Or Sue Morley. It's just more comfortable for me to have a woman there."

"I understand. See you later."

Laura walked me across to the executive wing and stopped to fill Rose Malone in on what had been happening, as Rose waved me into Battaglia's suite.

Mike Chapman was sitting at the district attorney's desk, his feet on top of a file drawer and a Cohiba between his lips. "You gotta be the most high-maintenance broad in the universe, Coop. You can't even be in the courtroom without drawing fire."

Mercer Wallace walked toward me and put his arms around me, drawing me tight against his chest. He had always been as easy at expressing emotion as Mike had been restrained. Paul Battaglia was seated at the far end of the long table, holding up a finger to tell me he'd be off his call in a minute.

"And you got that drowned-rat look on top of it," Mike said. "Very becoming. Your only hope is an earthquake in some third-world country that swallows an entire village tonight so you're not on the cover of the papers looking like that."

Mercer whispered to me, "You're shaking, Alex."

"I can't stop it. I'm cold." I didn't need to add that I was also scared.

"Rose had a late lunch sent in. There's some soup here for you."

"What time is it?"

"After two."

"Have they—have they found Quillian yet?"

Mercer shook his head.

"Any other bodies?"

"No," he said, stroking my arm.

I sat at the table and opened the cardboard container of lukewarm tomato soup. My stomach growled as I tried to fill it with something nourishing.

"I really underestimated your trial skills this time," Mike said. "Maybe you were actually gonna pull a rabbit out of a hat and put that boy away."

Battaglia hung up the receiver. He did his best to ask about my well-being—no more anxious than Mike to bring out any emotional reaction—and to confirm the court-room encounter as it had already been reported to him. Then it was on to business.

"I've been talking with the guys here, Alex. It's quite puzzling, this desperate attempt at an escape by Brendan Quillian."

"Attempt my ass, Mr. B," Mike said. "You might take note that he made it."

"Without your snitch, your case didn't appear to be all that airtight."

"No, Paul. It wasn't. But—"

"Well, what the hell do you think spooked him so that he would go to this extreme, at this point in the trial? Now he's got a cold-blooded murder witnessed by Freddy Gertz and Lem and you."

"From what I hear," Mike said, "the justice was really blind this time. Forget about Gertz."

I looked from Mike to Mercer. "What do you two think?"

"We got under his skin somehow," Mercer said. "And I don't believe it had anything to do with Alex's case against him for the killing of his wife."

I turned to Battaglia. "I think the things we've been digging at—things that still seem so remote and unrelated—must have struck Quillian right in the gut."

"Like what?"

"The day we met with his sister—the day before her brother's funeral," I said. "Trish told Brendan when she saw him for the first time in years that she was planning to talk to Mike about the Hassetts."

"Why?"

"She's convinced that Duke Quillian's murder was arranged or committed by the Hassett brothers. And yet, Brendan demanded that she not tell that to the police."

"If there was any truth to her reasoning," Mercer said, "you'd think Brendan would want her to dangle that before our noses. Makes you wonder what he knew—what Trish didn't know—that made him crazy at the thought she might tell us."

"What else?" Battaglia asked.

"I'm in," Mike said. "On the drive back from the funeral with Quillian, I brought up the unsolved case of the murdered teenager, Rebecca Hassett."

"You asked him about it? You questioned him?" Battaglia was annoyed enough to remove his cigar from his mouth and clearly articulate his concern.

"Nah. I just goosed him. I didn't think it would set him off on a rampage. I wanted to see if I could raise some hairs on his neck, and like I told Coop, I think I did."

"Add one more straw to the camel's back," I said. "Quillian called Lem Howell last night. Just the usual daily update, I'm sure. But that was after Lem and I left the meeting with Judge Gertz—and McKinney. I asked Lem if he told Brendan that McKinney had talked about an exhumation. If he mentioned that the girl was named Rebecca Hassett."

"Yes? He said yes?"

"For once Lem didn't have his best poker face on. I'm assuming he mentioned to Brendan that the subject had been raised in front of Gertz, without any way of knowing that it was a follow-up to the bombshell Mike dropped in the car. Lem wasn't going to give up any privileged conversation with his client—so if he doesn't drop a hint of it to whoever is interrogating him now about the shooting, I'm just saying that I think I caught him off guard when I asked about it."

"But this one issue . . . ?"

"Not one, Paul," I said. "Three points, each of them coming from a different direction—his sister, the cop who locked him up, and then his own lawyer."

"I think he was so close to beating the rap on Amanda's case," Mercer said, checking my reaction to Battaglia's dismissal of my effort, "at least in Lem's view, that he was devastated at the idea of being trapped by something more deadly, from his past— maybe something more readily connected to him—than what he faced with this jury."

"Makes you wonder," Battaglia said, re-plugging the cigar in his mouth, "why he didn't try for a clean kill of Alex while he had the chance."

"If what Mercer says is right, Quillian didn't have any reason to connect these past events to me. He just wanted to get out of there—out of the courtroom, out of custody," I said, shredding the napkin with my fingers, the soup stains on it a pale imitation of Elsie's blood.

"You got it," Mercer said.

"Elsie was the weakest link. He just over-powered her and started shooting. He wasn't after her any more than he wanted to kill me. I wasn't an obstacle to his freedom at that moment. Brendan Quillian just wanted to be gone."

We kicked around ideas for more than fifteen minutes. Rose interrupted us when she opened the door, and Battaglia snapped at her before she could speak.

"I told you no calls." He was waiting for the commissioner of correction to tell him how they planned to handle this fiasco before he went public on it.

"It's Judge Gertz, Mr. Battaglia. I thought you might want this one." Rose knew him better than he knew himself.

His lips widened into a broad smile around the cigar stub as he reached for the telephone. "A real profile in courage," he said, winking at Mike. "Freddy, what the hell were you running up there, the O.K. Corral? Where are you now? You got a panic room here in the courthouse I ought to know about?"

Whatever the answer was, and it was a long one, erased Battaglia's smile.

"She's okay. She's here with me now. Naturally, she's shaken up about the woman who was killed, seeing her friends shot and all that. But you know Alex. One hundred percent business when she needs to be."

"More like ninety percent blended Scotch whiskey in her veins and ten percent hair spray that makes her look like she's glued together from the outside," Mike said. "Blow on her gently and I think she'll be down for the count today."

"Lay off it, Mike," Mercer said, putting the lid on my coffee cup. "I'll drive you home as soon as Mr. B lets us go, Alex. Enough with the caffeine."

"You did what?" Battaglia asked, crushing the cigar's remains in his ashtray. "Yeah, I got Chapman here with me. I'll tell him. Thanks, Freddy.

"Now, see, Alex? Sometimes you shouldn't be so stubborn about listening to Pat McKinney. There's an old saw that says, 'All politics is local.' Well, I guess all crime is personal, too."

"He's got me in this mix?" Mike asked.

"Looks like Gertz did some thinking while he was resting under the bench this morning. He's got a real hard-on for Brendan Quillian now, if he didn't have one before today. Wants us to leave no stone unturned in the effort to find Quillian, and to put him behind bars for the rest of his life."

"So?"

"He's already called the Bronx district attorney to tell him about that old murder case—the Hassett girl. He's about to call the chief administrative judge of Bronx County, see if he can move that tough old bastard to order an immediate exhumation. Gertz wants to know what your plans are for tomorrow, Chapman. If he gets the court order, can you be there at the cemetery and get things rushed through at the morgue?"

Mike put his feet on the floor and saluted Battaglia. "I'm on the job, Mr. B."

"Check with the Hassetts, too," Battaglia said. "It goes even easier if you get consent from a family member. I know you told me the father was killed years ago. Is the mother still . . . ?"

"She died recently," I said. "Mike asked Trish about that just before we left her."

"The brothers, then. Contact the brothers. We may not even need the damn judge."

The door opened again and Nan Toth came into the room. "Rose sent me in," she said to Battaglia, talking to him as she walked to take the seat beside me, rubbing my back with her hand and asking how I was.

"You have something new?"

"Lawrence Pritchard just canceled our

meeting. I thought you'd want to know right away."

"What's got him backing off?"

"*Frightened* isn't exactly the word he used. But he won't sit down with me as long as Quillian is on the loose. He's worried about who's going to be shielding Quillian on the outside. Pritchard thinks he's got too many enemies of his own in the sandhog community, so he doesn't want anything to do with cooperating until Quillian's caught."

Battaglia was through with us now. He was waving Mike away from his desk, or, more precisely, from the humidor behind his desk chair. "All right, then. You've all got things to do. Take care of yourself, Alex. Do whatever Mercer thinks is best. You got a mistrial here, so you can rest up before you go at Quillian again. I'm sure they'll have him back in custody before the end of the day."

"I just saw the chief of detectives flying out of the lobby on my way in. Didn't you get the latest word about the car?" Nan asked.

Battaglia held a match to the cigar tip and inhaled as he lit it. "What car?"

"Patrol just found the Toyota that Quillian

stole when he broke out of the courthouse. Abandoned along the East River beneath the FDR Drive. He's on foot now, somewhere loose in the city. All the APBs and highway notices for the stolen vehicle have been canceled."

Mike shook his head. "So now we're just looking for a one-eyed white man—with a couple of guns—who's a subway ride away from freedom."

31

Mercer had me home before five o'clock. Ignacia Bliss had done a midnight tour the night before, so she would not be ready to take a shift safeguarding me until later in the evening. Mercer would stay with me—along with two uniformed cops in the lobby of the high-rise building—until Ignacia arrived.

I had settled in under the comforter on my bed to try to nap for a couple of hours before what would be a long spell in front of the television. The dramatic events of the day would be replayed ad nauseam on the news, while well-meaning citizens would contribute useless interviews whenever they saw anyone who remotely resembled the escaped prisoner.

Court TV anchors had already left messages on my home machine, asking for comments on a retrospective they were planning with comparisons between today's shooting and the Atlanta courthouse massacre of several years earlier. I turned off my telephone before shutting off the lights.

I was awakened by voices in the living room. Mercer was talking to someone, so I got up to wash my face and try to regain some control over my hair before going inside.

"I came by to apologize," Mike said. "I was out of line with—"

"Don't bother. I wasn't even listening. That's the way I've learned to protect myself from your barbed tongue. No apology necessary. Anything new?"

"Correction confirmed that Quillian had more than fifty bucks on him. His commissary money. His protection stash. Whatever. More than enough for a MetroCard or taxi ride."

"And a sweatshirt and baseball cap off

the tourist stands near the seaport," Mercer said. "Board a rush-hour train and be on Long Island in an hour."

"Or Jersey or Westchester or Connecticut."

"Odds are he's staying close. He still doesn't have enough dough to get him very far, and now we know he's got no family out of town. Where's he going to go?"

"That one dead eye could be a giveaway," Mike said. "You might be right, Mercer."

"Am I the only one in this with—with a security detail?"

"Nobody's taking chances with any of you. Artie Tramm's in the hospital for a few days," Mike said. "Even he's got cops around the clock. Lem, too, and Gertz."

"He had his chance at all of us."

"Yeah, but desperate men do desperate things, Coop. If he finds himself trapped, who knows what he'll try? Besides, your theory about Amanda's murder is that Brendan had an accomplice. So what if he's still around?"

"You sleep?" Mercer asked.

"Look at her, man. If she did, she must have been having a nightmare to come out of it looking like that."

"I keep replaying the courtroom scene in my head, hoping for a different ending. Thinking of some way to stop him from getting his hands on Elsie's gun."

"Repeat after me: 'It's not my fault.' How many times have I heard you tell that to your victims?"

"I've planned a little something different for the evening," Mercer said, guiding me away from Mike and into the den. "We'll get you through this."

"I don't want different. I just want calm, quiet—"

"That's what you'll have. I mean a real home-cooked meal instead of takeout. In the privacy of your own apartment. Vickee's coming over, okay?"

Mercer's wife, Vickee Eaton, was a second-grade detective who worked in the office of the deputy commissioner for public information. Her father had been a decorated police officer who had been killed in the field when she was fifteen, and she had split with Mercer years ago for fear she couldn't deal with the dangers to which he was constantly exposed.

They had remarried more than two years earlier, and their baby son, Logan, had become the center of their lives. I hadn't seen Vickee as often as I used to because of the demands of her schedule—the delicate balance of a tough job and motherhood.

"I couldn't ask for anything better. Is she okay about leaving Logan?"

"Her sister's only too happy to babysit. Comfort food—that's what you're going to have. Today was her RDO," Mercer said, referring to Vickee's regular day off. "She roasted a chicken this afternoon after I called her and made mashed potatoes from scratch. Some monkey bread and veggies. She'll bring it on over and reheat it here."

I reached my arms around his neck and kissed him.

"I've already ransacked your wine cabinet for something to go with it. Something smooth, something pricey."

"You've got immunity for that. Anytime."

"I'll set the table," Mike said. "The good stuff, right? You don't have to do anything except try to relax. And use your brain a bit. Figure out who Quillian's connections might be. Who would he trust to give him cover?"

"Sandhogs?" Mercer asked.

"That underground-boys-club shit only goes so far," Mike said, opening drawers to find my silver and china. "He hasn't been linked to any of them for years."

"C'mon. You know better than that. Duke's still a hero to lots of hogs. So was their father," Mercer said. "I'm not so sure he couldn't find some old family friends to lean on."

"We've also got all those pals he did business with," I said. "All those guys who stood up for him during the investigation. The ones who were willing to be character witnesses at the trial despite whatever they knew about how bad his relationship with Amanda had become."

"That's the spirit, Coop. You do the thinking, Mercer and I will take it from there. Dig out those lists of names from your files."

Mike followed us into the den, took off his blazer, and rolled up his sleeves. "Gimme some Trebek, Mercer. Grey Goose and trivia, and I'll be happy."

Mercer poured drinks for each of them while Mike set the table. I stretched out on the sofa with a glass of seltzer.

"Can't we watch some news until the final question?" I asked.

"You know what the news is, Alex. Don't beat yourself up any more."

I closed my eyes and rested—the volume muted—until the last segment of the show, when Mercer clicked on the sound.

"Tonight's category is Royal Blood. Royal Blood," Trebek said. "We'll be back in a minute to see what each of you has wagered. Stay with us."

"Double or nothing," Mike called from the dining room.

"Either way, I'm the loser," Mercer said. "Warriors or princesses, you two have a lock on this one."

"Blood," I said, for no reason at all. It was the only word I heard.

"Paper napkins?"

"No. The linen ones are in the armoire. Second shelf, on the right."

Trebek stepped aside and the final answer was revealed as he read it aloud for the viewers. "'First British king who required his subjects to call him Majesty.'"

Two contestants put on their best puzzled game-faces while the third one began to scribble an answer.

"You know it, Coop?"

"Why, Mike? You got anything in your wallet? Take a stab at it."

"See, Mercer? That means she knows

something," Mike said, coming into the room and perching on the arm of the sofa, behind my head. "Must be a cultured king, not a soldier statesman."

"Same guy who invented the handkerchief and insisted spoons be used at all court events."

"What a wuss."

"'Who was Richard the Second?'" I asked.

I held up my hand for Mike's forty dollars. He grabbed my fingers and squeezed hard before letting them drop—empty.

"Now that's a ridiculous clue," Mike said. "I mean, I could have been a contender if they'd asked it the right way. Like, 'Son of the Black Prince.' No offense, Mercer. Not a homey, bro—just the guy who wore a black cuirass at the Battle of Crécy. Or they could have said, 'British king who lacked the hereditary thirst for battle. First casualty of the Wars of the Roses.' Then she'd have been stumped. Coop doesn't know from history—she just relies on Willy Shakespeare."

"'The worst is death, and death will have his day.'"

"Yeah, well, he's had his day many times

over," Mike said. "And usually when I'm catching cases."

The intercom buzzed and he got up to answer it. "The only thing more miserable than Coop being in a dark mood like this is Coop being in a dark mood like this when she's not drinking."

He came back and smiled at Mercer. "Dinner is served. Vickee's here with the vittles."

I got up and went to the door with Mercer to greet her. She handed the packages to him and put her arms around me.

"Don't get her started again, Vickee," Mike said. "We've barely got the tear ducts and tissues under control. None of this estrogen emo-show, okay?"

"Just help Mercer heat up the meal, Mike. Can you handle that?" Vickee said, turning to him and running her hands up and down his sides. "You better go double on my potatoes, Mr. Chapman. You've dropped too much weight."

"What can I get you?" I asked.

"I'd love some white wine. And your doormen asked me to thank you for their dinner. They said it was delicious—some kind of veal? Now where did that come from, girl?"

"I have no idea what you're talking about."

Mike was holding one of Vickee's shopping bags. "Yeah, I meant to tell you. They wanted me to bring the food up on my way in. The cops said that some guy from a restaurant came by—one of your snooty French bistros, no doubt. Must have been a waiter who was sent to surprise you with food. A care package. Mercer had already told me we were getting a special delivery from Vickee, so I just told the guys to split it up. No note or anything. Your bloody puss was all over the news. Everyone in town knows you had a rough day."

I bit my lip. It was almost worth laughing at the notion of Luc being taken for a waiter. He had probably tried to get through to me with a four-star meal. "Guess so."

"When do we eat?" Mike asked Vickee.

"Half an hour."

"You mind if I call Teddy O'Malley?" he said to me, after depositing the food in the kitchen. "See if he's got any ideas about who might hide Brendan Quillian."

"Go right ahead. I think it would be harder to go undercover with sandhogs than to infiltrate the Mob."

Mercer busied himself in the kitchen with the food and Mike took out his notepad to make a series of calls from the den, where he was watching the local news. Vickee and I curled up on the living room sofa while she listened to me vent about the day while Dr. John sang background about his gris-gris.

At eight thirty, Mercer called us to the table and served the meal.

The breakout of Brendan Quillian seemed as if it had happened in a bad dream. Here, safe in my own home with my loyal friends, it was almost easy to think of murder for hire, domestic abuse, and dynamite blasts as other people's problems. But then I would have a flashback to the face of Elsie Evers on the courtroom floor, and I knew we'd all be back to business as usual by daybreak.

"Take some more, Alex," Vickee said, passing the platter of chicken. "Alex likes the breast. Give her that piece of white meat, Mike, will you? It's her favorite."

"Speaking of that, Coop. You ever do Lem Howell back in your rookie days?"

I laughed and shook my head.

"They were just replaying that shot of him walking you out of the courtroom today, you wrapped in his jacket and him looking at you like he wanted the rest of your dress to just slice off in two."

I pushed my plate away. "I'm full. And if I wasn't, you once again have the flawless ability to take my appetite away."

Mike reached for a third helping of potatoes and tore off a fistful of bread. "You were good buddies, right? Don't you credit him for half of your courtroom success?"

"I had a lot of help from a lot of guys. And from the handful of women who broke me in. And I didn't *do* them all, thanks."

I stood up to clear my place, but Vickee pointed at me and told me to sit.

She came out of the kitchen with a pecan pie and a carton of vanilla ice cream. "Nobody says no to this dish. My mama's recipe and it's the very best."

"Your money on Lem Howell and Coop, Detective Wallace?"

"I spent a lot of time in Ms. Cooper's office in those early years," Mercer said, gnawing on a chicken wing. "I may have to go to the grave with some of the messages that steamed off that telephone when I sat out those long days at her desk while she was upstairs on trial, but Mr. Howell was not among those in hot pursuit."

I wagged a finger at him. "Don't give me up, Mercer. We'll see how good Mike's detecting skills are. I don't have a lot of secrets from you guys, but the ones I do, I'm keeping close to the vest for the time being."

The phone rang and I walked to the den to answer it.

"Alexandra? It's Paul Battaglia. How are you feeling?"

"I'm okay. I'll be fine."

"What were your plans for tomorrow?"

"Well, Judge Gertz wanted to give the jury a couple of days away from the courthouse. He'll probably bring them back on Friday to declare a mistrial. I'd like to go to Elsie's wake, certainly."

"That starts tomorrow night. You'll come with me."

I would have preferred to avoid the political statement and show up without the district attorney, but he might leave me no choice.

"So, for the morning—"

"Exactly. Here's what I'd like. Jefferson just called me," Battaglia said, referring to the Bronx district attorney. "You know where Mike Chapman is?"

"Yes, yes, I do."

"Get in touch with him and coordinate. Jefferson just got an expedited ruling from the administrative judge up there. He's ordered the immediate exhumation of the body of that teenager—what's her name?"

"Hassett. Rebecca Hassett." When I said her name, Mike and Mercer both looked up. The candles on the dining table seemed to flicker with the breeze that wafted through the open windows behind them.

"Tomorrow morning. You and Chapman have to meet the Bronx homicide prosecutor at the grave site. Woodlawn Cemetery. Can you do that?"

"Of course, boss. Sure we can."

"Who knows. May be good for nothing, may give us a clue or two. But the media's all over this case now. Your job is to be there so this doesn't get away from us and wind up on Jefferson's plate in Bronx County," Battaglia said.

"I understand." The district attorney was turning the screws and I could feel the pressure throbbing in my head.

"He'll try to pull it out from under you if

you don't sit on it. Make sure Chapman gets that body to the morgue. You've brought Quillian this far, Alex. Let's not let him slip away from my jurisdiction completely. I want that bastard brought in."

32

"Teddy O'Malley thinks his subterranean empire is a necropolis," Mike said. "But *this* is what I call a city of death."

We had parked in front of the tall wrought-iron gates of Woodlawn Cemetery in the Bronx, four hundred acres of elegantly land-scaped grounds that had been a burial place for New Yorkers since the time of the Civil War. Evan Silbey, the funeral coordinator who would escort us to Rebecca Hassett's grave site, met us there.

Silbey settled into the backseat of the car.

"The word *cemetery* means 'place of sleep,' Mr. Chapman. It's more calming than the word *death*."

"The big sleep, buddy. No disrespect to Raymond Chandler."

"My point is that cemeteries are a very recent concept, historically speaking," Silbey said. "The necropolis style was mainly driven by architecture—funerary monuments just stacked upon each other with no sense of nature. The ancients buried their dead along the roadsides leading out of the cities. Via Appia, if you will."

Mike walked around to the driver's side and got into the car.

"In medieval times, it became the custom to bury people in churchyards, right inside the cities," Silbey went on. He was slightly built and quite pale, with horn-rimmed glasses and the flattest monotone of a voice. "But most urban areas eventually ran out of room. By 1800, many city dwellers wanted more rural retreats that would offer places for meditation and contemplation while visiting the departed, so people could use these grounds as public parks, too."

Silbey handed Mike a map of Woodlawn.

"You got miles of interior roadway here,

haven't you?" Mike asked, unfolding and studying the vast property plan.

"Indeed. And more than three hundred thousand residents. It's quite a large sanctuary in the middle of the city, although this was all farmland when the design was plotted. You know Mount Auburn?"

"In Massachusetts?" I asked. "Cambridge?"

"Yes. That was the first rural cemetery planned in America. The idea was that the arboretum around the graves—the air being cleaned by circulating through the trees—would be a much healthier burial setting. Greenwood, in Brooklyn, was the next park set up on this model. It actually became one of the first tourist attractions in New York."

"Where to?" Mike asked.

Silbey leaned forward and pointed to our location on the map, at the northeast corner of the vast memorial park. "We're right here, at the corner of East 233rd Street. The cemetery runs the entire way down to Gun Hill Road."

"George Washington territory."

"What is?" I asked.

"Seventeen seventy-six. Washington was retreating from the city to Westchester, to make a stand at what became the battle of White Plains. He constructed a redoubt to delay the British troops that were coming after him. That's why it's called Gun Hill—the redoubt commanded the Bronx River valley and the Boston Road."

"I'm impressed, Mr. Chapman," Silbey said. "We're bounded on the west by Jerome Avenue. You know that one, too?"

"Nope."

"A capitalist, not a general. Leonard Jerome. Had a grandson named Winston Churchill." Silbey leaned his small head over the seat back, looking between Mike and me. "You know, Miss Cooper, that even long after we opened these gates here at Woodlawn, women weren't allowed to accompany their loved ones to their graves at most other places like it."

"I can't imagine that."

"Greenwood Cemetery was built before the Brooklyn Bridge was. Between the street congestion in Manhattan and the instability of the little ferries to Brooklyn, it was considered too indelicate for ladies to make the trip. Our resting ground was much more accessible, so women were always welcome. Primrose, Detective Chapman. That's where we're going."

Silbey tried to stretch his fingers to point at a section of the map.

"Primrose? Like the tree?"

"Yes, that's it. Stay to the center—we'll take that main drive."

Mike started off slowly. Ahead and to the right was the sloping hillside that led west from our starting point. From the street off to our left, the usual city sounds of car traffic and honking horns were almost drowned out as a Metro North train rattled by on the adjacent tracks.

A minute later, we had lost the noise as we climbed the gentle rise within the cemetery and were surrounded by the sylvan atmosphere of the plantings and sculptures.

"We want Walnut or Magnolia?" Mike asked at the first fork in the road.

"Follow Walnut. You see, Miss Cooper, the landscape architects used trees not only to be decorative, but for their symbolic meaning as well. Almost all of our plots are named for a variety of tree," Silbey said. "Oaks, you may know, are the symbol of steadfast fidelity. In First Kings of the Bible, Elijah tells us he wants to lie down and die under a juniper. Watch that arrow, Detective Chapman. Don't take Clover."

We were driving deeper and deeper into the cemetery, the narrow roadways bordered by blossoming plants and shrubs, stone bridges arching over ponds, giant family mausoleums in the style of Doric temples standing on hilltops—the most expensive real estate with the best views in this peaceful enclave.

"You know your Greek mythology?" Silbey went on. "Apollo transformed the dead body of his dearest friend into a cypress tree. They're often used to stand guard at gravesides. It's all part of that nineteenth-century Romantic style of philosophy and design."

"Romantic? In a cemetery?" Mike said. "That's looking for love in all the wrong places."

"Turn right here."

We hadn't passed more than ten people on our way. Some individual mourners were walking on pathways, and several gardeners had been tending to stone markers and the flower beds around them. Thick gray clouds moved quickly overhead, casting shadows on the tall monuments. An eerie calm seemed to settle in over this pastoral setting the farther away from the city streets we traveled.

Mike had slowed the car. He was staring at one of the larger granite monuments, a Tuscan canopy supported by a dozen columns, covering a swag-draped sarcophagus, surrounded by a stand of tall pine trees. "How rich do you have to be to get a place here? Some of these things look palatial."

"Oh, Detective Chapman, you're not wrong. We've got our Whitneys and our Woolworths and our Vanderbilts." Silbey poked his head between us again with a new spurt of energy. "This was such an elite place in its heyday. We've got Irving Berlin and Duke Ellington, Herman Melville and Joseph Pulitzer. Mayor La Guardia, of course. And our ladies—like Elizabeth Cady Stanton and Nellie Bly."

"No matter how much money they spent on these shrines to themselves, they're still dead, aren't they?" Mike said.

"Obviously so. These memorials just tell their stories, sir." Silbey sat back in his seat. "That's Primrose, just after the stop sign. You can pull over and park."

"What's this? The low-rent district?"

The headstones in the section we were approaching were on a flat piece of land, far less dramatic than the rolling topography of so much of the park. There were no grandiose monuments here, but rather crowded rows of small markers, set close together.

The strips were bare of the elegant plantings we had passed along the way, shaded simply by tall, old trees that dotted the dirt pathways.

"Some of the more modest graves are in this area. The girl's family," Silbey said, stepping out of the car, checking his notes for the name, "the Hassetts, is it? Looks like they bought the plot about fifty years ago. Not quite the placement some of our rich and famous have, but we've got many local folks like them."

I joined Mike on the side of the road. "The diggers will meet us here?" he asked.

Silbey checked his watch. "It's almost nine. They should be along shortly. Anyone else coming?"

"There'll be a van from the medical examiner's office to take the body away," Mike said. "And maybe a couple of detectives from the Bronx District Attorney's Office. Where is she?"

Silbey crossed the road. "Four rows back in there. G112. It's just a small marker in the ground."

Mike made his way through the narrow footpaths—stopping to kneel in front of the flat stone that said rebecca hassett on it. I watched as he ran his finger over the letters that formed her name and studied the numbers chiseled in it, which noted the few years between her birth and death.

Several generations of Hassetts were here, resting head to foot, fast running out of room in their final resting place. Mike glanced around at the names, then continued walking downhill toward what looked to be another pond, which was bordered in part by an enormous weeping beech.

I walked behind him and stopped when he did, for a second time, at a larger headstone. "Whaddaya know? William Barclay Masterson."

"Who?"

"Gold-topped cane, derby hat, fastest gun in the West. I'd have expected him to be buried on Boot Hill."

"Bat? Bat Masterson?" I remembered the

reruns of the popular fifties TV western starring Gene Barry, but knew nothing about the life of the real deputy marshal appointed by Teddy Roosevelt.

Neither of us heard Evan Silbey come down the dirt path. "He left Dodge City to come back to New York. Bat was a sportswriter for the *Morning Telegraph* when he—"

"Did you see that?" Mike asked, turning to look toward a tall obelisk marker.

"What? The van?" I noticed the morgue car—with its ocme markings on the side panel—coasting to a stop behind our Crown Vic.

Mike shook his head. "Someone was crouching behind the marker opposite the Hassett plot. Somebody waiting for us who wasn't invited to this unpleasant little disinterment." He started to trot down the incline.

"Where's he going?" Silbey asked, his voice rising almost an octave.

I saw a figure in a dark coat dart out from behind the obelisk and cross the road to go down toward the tranquil pond. Mike called out for the person to stop as he began to give chase.

"Mike," I said, in almost a whisper. It seemed so inappropriate to be shattering the quiet of this sanctuary.

He ignored me but had reached the roadway just as the truck carrying four gravediggers pulled up to the intersection.

The person picked up speed as he ran downhill, and Mike lost seconds waiting for the truck to make the turn. Whoever it was did not want to stop to see why Mike was after him.

The branches of the weeping beech hung over the landscape, like hundreds of arms reaching almost to the ground. I lost sight of the black-coated figure when he headed directly for the great tree and slipped under its limbs, disappearing behind it. A garish mausoleum with a green copper roof sat beside the beech and provided cover for him as well.

Ten seconds later, Mike was swallowed up by the foliage, too. Anxiety had overtaken me again. I didn't need any more excitement after yesterday's trauma. I was too late to try to chase Mike and uncertain about what had set him off after the elusive figure.

I cut through the grass between several

markers to get to the curb. I pleaded with Mr. Silbey to send the gravediggers to back Mike up. All four of them—and Silbey himself—looked at me as though I had lost my mind.

"What do you need, Miss Cooper?" one of the morgue drivers asked.

"Mike Chapman—he's gone off after someone. Would you check down there"—I pointed—"and see if he needs any help?"

"Sure. Who was it?"

"I don't know."

"But," the driver said tentatively, "what if it's trouble?"

"It's probably paparazzi," I said. "Mike was worried that someone at the squad might have leaked this to a reporter. We wanted to get the exhumation done without any press around. Please hurry."

We had talked about that possibility on the ride to the cemetery. I hadn't seen a camera in the runner's hand, but now I was actually hoping that the interloper was no more dangerous than a press photographer.

Reluctantly, the driver started walking toward the pond.

Another car pulled up behind our growing caravan. A husky, thick-necked man in a

T-shirt, jeans, and clean work boots—a baseball cap barely fitting the circumference of his wide head—got out and came slowly toward Evan Silbey and me with his head down.

"I thought you weren't expecting anyone else," Silbey said. "Get Chapman back here. Who is this?"

"I don't have any idea," I said.

Then the well-muscled figure lifted his head and kept walking toward the stone that bore Rebecca Hassett's name. All his features were exaggerated—a bulbous nose, strong chin, piercing blue eyes, and sulking expression. It was her brother Bobby.

He wagged a finger in my direction. "Don't think you'll be touching my sister, Miss District Attorney. Not you, not that wiseass cop who's sticking his nose in our personal business every place I go. Let her rest in peace, for God's sake, or I'll be sure you live to regret it." Hassett stepped closer to me and backed me against another headstone. "You leave the poor girl alone."

33

"Look, Mr. Hassett, we've got a court order to do this," I said, trying to glance over my shoulder for any sign of Mike. "I—I know this is an awful thing to have to think about, but it's quite possible that techniques we have now that weren't available when your sister was killed might help us identify—"

Bobby Hassett's face was just inches from mine. His nostrils flared and his bloodshot eyes narrowed as I spoke. His breath had the faint odor of beer as he interrupted my lame explanation. "Don't give me none of that. What difference is it to know who the mutt is who killed the kid? He's lived way too long to make any kind of justice worthwhile."

"A judge has already made a ruling about this," I said, inching backward again.

"I know that. I got a call from the DA's Office last night—"

"My office?"

"The Bronx. Those fools thought they were going to get my permission to do this."

"Well, that would have been necessary if the judge hadn't granted the order," I said, aware that the prosecutor's phone call was what had alerted Bobby to this morning's exhumation.

"An order? Let me see your papers."

Evan Silbey had retreated from this encounter. "Mr. Silbey," I said, "you've got to send your men to find Detective Chapman."

Bobby Hassett grabbed my wrist and pulled me forward. "Get your damn foot off my mother's grave."

I looked down to see the writing on a small flat stone similar to Rebecca's, though not worn by age and exposure to the elements. The woman had been dead less than six months, according to the date. The grass around her little plot was newer than that around the family graves surrounding it.

"The documents are in the car. The detective picked them up early this morning. I'll get them for you."

I was glad to step away from Hassett and even more relieved to see Mike Chapman, leaning on the arm of the morgue driver, limping up the slope that led from the pond.

I didn't stop to get the court order, but jogged directly down to meet the two men.

"What happened?"

"I fell on my rear end, that's all. Glad you weren't there to see it. Twisted my ankle and slid down. Just missed that frigging tree trunk. Could have planted me in old Mr. Woolworth's mausoleum."

"Is it—"

"Nah. I stepped into a pile of goose droppings and my foot went out from underneath. It's just sore. Maybe a sprain."

"You didn't catch up to the guy, did you?"

"Not even close. Not even a good look. Like a gazelle, he was."

I put my arm around Mike's back and let him walk the rest of the way up leaning on me. "A photographer?"

"Not likely. No equipment dangling and no reason to run."

"Well, we've got another spectator," I said. "Bobby Hassett."

"That's a gruesome thought. He wants to watch?"

"He wants to stop us. Someone from Jefferson's office called him last night, trying to get his consent in case the judge didn't go for their application. Tipped him off that something might happen this morning, whether the Hassetts agreed to it or not, and now he's here to try to prevent us from—from doing this."

As soon as Mike heard Hassett's name, he untangled himself from me and straightened up, walking gingerly across the road to get to the family plot.

Mr. Silbey scurried toward Mike. "Please, Detective Chapman. We can't have a scene here."

"I forgot—all your peeps are asleep, aren't they?"

"This man has rights, too, doesn't he?"

Mike kept moving while he looked around us. Birds were chirping in the surrounding trees, the wind occasionally gusted and rustled the leaves, no one else was in sight but those of us who had come to disturb Re-becca Hassett's grave—and her irate brother. There was nothing in this pastoral setting to tell us that we were still in New York City.

"Bobby," Mike said, reaching a hand out to Hassett. "Mike Chapman. Homicide."

"Yeah. I know that." His hands were dug as far as they could go into his jeans' pock-ets.

"Could we step away from here? Would you let me tell you—"

"Not a chance."

I walked to the morgue van and spoke to the patient attendants, waiting for their cargo.

"Call 911. Get Chapman some backup from the precinct, okay?"

They both looked startled, and I had to re-peat the demand, explaining who Hassett was, to get them to make the call.

I opened the door of the department car and removed Mike's folder, looking for the court order. I started back over to where he and Bobby Hassett were going head-to-head.

"I don't understand you," Mike said. "If it was someone I loved—if it were my sister—

and you come along telling me we can maybe solve a crime, find her killer—I don't care if it's fifty years later, I'd be so thrilled to get the motherfucker I'd move heaven and earth."

One eye was on my watch. Forty-five seconds since the 911 call was placed. Officer needs assistance was bound to get a rapid response.

"Yeah, well, you're not moving this piece of earth."

I handed Mike the exhumation order, thinking it might help him to have some law to back up his reason.

He flipped the page to the judge's signature and turned it around so Hassett could read the bottom line. Instead, Hassett swung his arm wildly and knocked the papers out of Mike's hand.

I bent to retrieve them as Mike signaled the quartet of gravediggers to move in. A minute and a half later, and Bobby Hassett was becoming more agitated, his face reddening and his eyes bulging.

The four workmen picked up their tools and began a solemn march toward Rebecca's grave.

Hassett waited until they were alongside

him, then lurched at the first man, trying to take hold of the long wooden handle of his shovel. Mike took a step forward, wincing as his full weight landed on his bad ankle, and grabbed Hassett's right arm.

Bobby Hassett spun on his heel and threw his fist at Mike's face, missing narrowly. The other men backed off as Mike held out both arms to try to calm his opponent down.

It was more than two minutes—two and a half—before the peaceful cemetery air vibrated with the sound of a distant siren.

Hassett punched again, and Mike, unable to dance away on his lame leg, was nailed in the shoulder.

"Don't be crazy, Bobby," I said. "Don't get yourself locked up over this."

He paid no attention to me and lashed out again, without success.

The siren was getting louder. The gravediggers turned their backs to the commotion and huddled together while Evan Silbey ran for the shelter of Mike's car. The driver of the morgue vehicle had stayed on the phone—with the operator, I guessed—to let her know when the cops arrived.

The patrol car came from the west,

speeding down the gently undulating hill. The two officers parked in the middle of the road, running over toward us.

I flashed my gold-and-blue shield—a prosecutorial copy of the NYPD badge—and identified myself. "That's Mike Chapman—Homicide—in the blue blazer."

The younger cop made a beeline for Bobby Hassett, while the older one laughed and took his time. "I worked with Mikey when he was breaking in. I oughta let this one go ten rounds, for all the aggravation he gave me."

The uniformed rookie wrestled Hassett to the ground and restrained him until his partner caught up and rear-cuffed the silent, sullen man.

"Is it a collar, Mikey?" the older one asked, patting Chapman on the shoulder. "You get him for assaulting you, or did you start up with him?"

"No arrest, Jesse. Just let him cool down. I can't blame him for taking a shot at me."

Mike crouched next to Bobby Hassett. "Nice try. I might have done the same thing in your circumstance. Now, we're going ahead with what we gotta do whether you like it or not. Me personally, Bobby? I'd recommend you get in your car and get out of here. You wanna see how we handle this? Then you're doing it from the back of Jesse's RMP, hands behind your back with your mouth shut. I'll let you know every detail of anything we find out. I promise you she'll be in good hands."

Mike paused to get an answer. "What's your call?"

Hassett raised his head off the ground. The radio motor patrol car obviously didn't interest him. "I'll go. Lemme up and I'll go."

Mike nodded at the two cops, who released their prisoner and stepped back while he got to his feet.

We all watched as Bobby Hassett walked to the foot of Bex's grave, lowered himself onto one knee, made the sign of the cross, and bowed his head. Tears fell over the reddened rims of his lids, and with his thick fingers he wiped them off his cheeks. I closed my eyes and thought of the sister he had lost so long ago.

After a minute or so, he stood up, glared at me with whatever energy he had left, and headed across to his car. The patrol car was blocking his way, so he backed up into the intersection and gassed the Toyota as he drove away from us.

Again, Mike waved the workmen on to begin opening the Hassett grave. He talked to the cops and convinced them to stay at the site to make sure no other unexpected visitors interfered with our grim task.

Then he told me to follow him and we walked back to his car. "There's nothing to see, Coop. Might as well wait over here. Let them do what they gotta do."

Just as we leaned against the car, another Crown Vic approached. The two men got out and smiled at me, then introduced themselves to Mike.

"Heads or tails?" I heard one of them say. "Heads we get to keep her, tails she goes downtown with you."

"You're too late, guys," Mike said. "We just got permission from the family."

"What? Who're you kidding?" The detectives looked at each other before the one in charge spoke. "Jefferson said they ain't cooperating. He wants the body, Chapman."

"Bobby Hassett just left us, isn't that right, Ms. Cooper? All you had to do yesterday was talk nice to him, guys. Guess you couldn't even get that right. We reached an understanding with him, didn't we? Like gentlemen."

"We did, actually. I suggest you find him before you embarrass yourselves," I said, returning their smiles and thinking of Battaglia's directive to me. "Mike seemed to have gotten to him this morning. Maybe his technique was a little different than whatever you and your prosecutors told him."

It had taken less than a quarter of an hour for one of the men to strike his shovel against the lid of Rebecca Hassett's coffin. I heard the metal edge crack against the wood and turned to look.

The detectives went over to the guys from the morgue to see what story could be coaxed from them, but since the duo were from Manhattan—not the Bronx satellite office of the medical examiner—they weren't planning to return to First Avenue without the body either.

Another half hour and the diggers were waist-deep in the hole they had made, wedging the wooden box up as they secured it with straps in order to raise it onto the ground. It appeared to be made of simple pine, intact but showing obvious signs of rot on each of the corners.

Mike had gone back over to the grave. He crouched beside the coffin—probably offering a prayer, much as Bobby Hassett had done minutes earlier—then brushed some of the dirt off the worn lid before directing the men to load it into the van for the ride to the morgue.

The driver stood next to the rear door. "Don't you want them to open it here? Take a peek? Make sure it's who you're looking for? That's how we usually do it."

"Nothing's been going according to plan with this. I want her out of here before anybody else shows up, okay? Let's just get her downtown," Mike said. "I'll be right behind you."

We drove slowly up to the corner of the next plot and followed the van as it made a U-turn to retrace its route to Woodlawn's entrance. As we passed the Hassett grave again, the men were filling the hole with the dirt that had been displaced.

Mike paused at the intersection, and my eyes were drawn by the movement of something dark off to my right. The ornate headstone that marked the border of the

Primrose section of the cemetery had a large relief carving on its face—a weeping mother mourning the effigy of her curly-haired child, a sculpted robe covering her arched back.

The wind gusted again. It caught and lifted a piece of the black-sleeved coat of the person hiding behind the tomb—the same motion that must have gotten my attention originally.

"Mike, look over here. I think it's the guy you were chasing. He's come back."

He made the turn and threw the car into park, opening the door as though to give chase.

"Don't do it," I said. "Your leg—it's not worth it. You'll make it worse."

He waved me off and started to lope across the road.

A head appeared around the side of the old granite marker.

"It's not a guy at all," Mike said, stopping in place as I caught up to him. "It's Trish Quillian."

The figure in black ducked under a tree branch and ran headlong into the maze of shrubs and grave sites beyond the roadway. We'd lost her.

"Crazy as a loon that girl is," Mike said. "I bet she's been waiting with Bex—waiting at her friend's grave for something to happen. I sure as hell would like to know why."

34

I smelled the musty odor as I entered the autopsy room at the morgue. I had been to crime scenes where bodies had been discovered in closets or locked rooms after several days, and the stench was unbearable. This was just stale and unpleasant.

Jerry Genco was standing beside the photographer, who was bending over the coffin with his camera, talking to Mike.

"Stop wriggling your nose, Alex. There's nothing much to smell," Jerry said.

As with most forensic pathologists, years

on the job had burned out his olfactory nerves.

"You ready for this?" Mike asked.

I didn't like anything about being present during an autopsy—not the sights nor the sounds nor my inevitable musings about how the deceased would, when alive, have felt about this kind of investigation. I had enormous respect for the work of the doctors who performed the critical task and never ceased to be amazed at how they interpreted the stories that dead bodies revealed to them. I was comfortable knowing Mike would remain in the room for the entire procedure, but it was actually better if I did not make myself a witness to the reexamination.

"I'm not staying," I said, holding up my hand like a stop sign.

At times it was critical to understand the process that would occur. I had never participated in an exhumation, and I knew that Battaglia would have questions that I would have to answer. Perhaps one day, if we were lucky enough to name Bex's killer, a jury would need to know exactly what had transpired, too. So I would stay close by in the event there were developments that would direct the course of our work.

The photographer took a few more shots and walked out of the room. Genco made space for me beside him.

"Aspergillus fungus. That's all it is, Alex," Genco said, offering me a Tic Tac. "The body is pretty well preserved—a combination of the embalming process and luck. What you see is a bit of mold on the surface of the skin. I'd expect it to be there. That's what the odor is."

I looked down at the lifeless remains of Rebecca Hassett. Her skin looked rubbery and discolored against the white satin lining of the coffin, which had been stained by fluids that had seeped into it over the years. The black hair, so lustrous and thick in photographs, was clumped around both sides of her face, which itself had taken on a greenish hue. The once vibrant eyes were closed, probably sewn in place in the funeral home that had prepared her young body for the wake.

I was both horrified and transfixed. I wanted to look away but was drawn to stare at the petite body while images of a life that should have been flashed through my mind.

Her clothing had fared no better. The black cotton sweater and the pleated skirt that draped the thin figure had holes.

Around her neck was a silver crucifix on a chain, and cradled beside the teenager—a reminder of how childlike she still was at the time of her death, despite her defiant independence—was a worn stuffed animal, a brown-and-white bulldog that a family member, I presumed, had placed beside her.

"What happens next?" I asked, reluctantly turning my back to Rebecca.

"We'll lift her out onto the table. Undress her, clean her up. I'll examine the body first, of course. Then the vital organs."

"Were they inventoried?"

"That's the first sign that this case wasn't taken too seriously," Genco said. "I've checked everywhere for a record that the doc kept the neck organs. No luck."

"They'd be useful because the cause of death was asphyxial?" I asked.

"Yes. A careful physician would have put the hyoid bone, the windpipes, the major pieces of the neck, in a formalin jar. They're just not anywhere here in our archives."

Had there been a timely arrest and a trial,

the defense attorney would have been allowed to have his own expert reexamine the body parts at issue.

"And the other organs?"

Genco guided me to the door while he called for his photographer to return and his assistants to move the body. "Just wait out here while we set up. There'll be a bag—a green plastic trash bag, probably—inside the girl's body cavity. That should have all her other organs inside it."

The brain and liver and uterus—everything else that had been removed for analysis during the autopsy at the time of Bex's death—would have been stored within her since then.

Mike and I paced the basement corridor for fifteen minutes until Jerry Genco was ready to proceed. Mike would take his position at the foot of the table while Genco got to work, speaking into the recorder that dangled overhead. I waited in an office down the hall, using the time to catch up with Laura and return calls.

When Genco finished his reexamination of the body, he sent an assistant for me and I rejoined him and Mike as the aides removed the gurney with the girl from the room.

"Pretty straightforward," Genco said. "I'd agree, from what I can see now on the front of the neck and what's left of the strap muscles beneath, that this was a manual strangulation. There's certainly no ligature involved."

"Nothing like a ribbon around her neck?" Mike asked. He was still troubled by the "confession" extracted from the kid named Reuben.

"No. There isn't any injury to the back of her neck. None at all," Genco said. "The pathologist overlooked some other minor trauma, though."

"How significant?" I asked.

"You tell me what isn't significant at an autopsy."

"Inconsistencies?"

"No. More like sloppiness. Laziness, I'd say." Genco sketched a diagram for us. "Some minor bruising on her back—her shoulder blades. The rear of her thighs, too. I'd expect to see those things, since it figures she was lying down when she was killed. Even if she didn't have the ability to resist, she was being pressed against the surface of the ground, and there were bound to be some rocks, stones, or twigs around."

"The doc knew what he had," Mike said. "Guess he thought there was no need to work overtime."

"That's what it looks like. I'll go the whole nine yards," Genco said, pointing to the trash bag. "Check the organs, too, in case he missed anything."

It was early afternoon and Mike's stomach was growling. "You want a sandwich, Jerry? I need some fresh air."

"Ham and cheese."

"Coop?"

"I'll walk with you."

As we started to the door, Mattie Prinzer, the newly appointed chief of forensic biology, walked in. "I heard you two were down here."

"Hey, good to see you. I was going to stop by later on."

"I'll save you the trip. Thought there was something you ought to know."

"You don't have that 'good news' look all over your chops, Mattie. You making life difficult for me?"

"I know you're a guy who likes a challenge, Mike. Is this the child? The girl from Pelham Bay Park?"

"C'mon, Mattie. You get anything off the zipper? You get a profile?"

"I hope inside that thick skull you've kept an open mind, Mike. You have a suspect, don't you?"

Mike feigned indifference and tossed back the hair on his forehead. "Any one of a number of guys, Mattie. I'm in no rush."

"You might need to think outside the box, if you're looking for a guy." Mattie was holding a printout of the DNA results in her hand. She placed it on the countertop near the door. "One of my techs ran this overnight, just as soon as Mercer Wallace brought it in."

"What's the problem?" Mike asked, bending over to study the bands that made up the unique genetic profile of a human being.

I could see where Mattie was going the minute I looked at the page.

The sex of the individual whose blood had been examined was encoded in the DNA results. A male donor's profile was always marked by two peaks that appeared on the line—one representing the X chromosome and the other representing the Y.

"There's only one peak," I said to Mattie.

"Let me see," Mike said, trying to find the telltale image on the page that looked like a hieroglyphic jumble.

"That's it, Alex," Mattie said. "No sign of a Y chromosome anywhere in that little speck of blood, my friend. No question whoever cut herself on that zipper is a woman."

35

"How long have you known this?" Mike asked, his fist resting on the lab results.

"I just found out this morning. The tech didn't want to tell me at first."

"Why not?" Mike said, shaking his head. "We're losing precious time."

"She assumed it was a contaminated result," Mattie said. "Look, that's the problem when you aren't exactly doing a blind test. She knew this was clothing from a female murder victim, and that the original case suspect was a male."

"So she was surprised to have the profile come up as a woman's?" I asked.

"Yes, surprised also when she found that it didn't match the DNA of Rebecca Hassett, from the original samples."

"So what did she do?" I asked.

"Figured it was her own mistake."

Contamination was an enormous problem—an everyday issue—for forensic biologists in every lab in the country. They sneezed and coughed at their workstations, opened vials of fluids that dripped or became airborne, and, in more instances than prosecutors liked to hear, inadvertently compromised investigative results.

"You mean the tech ran the test again?"

"Of course. And compared it to her own DNA sample."

Every person who worked in these offices had to provide his or her own genetic profile, so comparisons could be made against results obtained when contamination was suspected.

"Don't get discouraged so easily. You know what a long shot this was," I said.

"The last thing I expected to find was a woman's DNA on the sweater," Mike said.

"Mattie's right about the blinders you let yourself wear sometimes. We knew there was no sexual assault. We should be thinking other motives, other killers—and even whether that blood was already on Bex's sweater before the night of the murder."

We left Genco's office and crossed First Avenue to walk to the deli. We ate together at the counter before returning to see whether Jerry Genco had completed his careful study of Bex Hassett's remains.

"I should know by now to expect the unexpected."

"That DNA may have nothing to do with the case. The blood wasn't necessarily deposited on the sweater the day the Hassett kid died."

Mike unfolded the copy of the *Post* that he had paid for at the counter. The headline appeared over Brendan Quillian's mug shot: MASSIVE MANHUNT FOR MISSING MOGUL.

"You've got to go back at Trish Quillian," I said. "How did she know to show up at the cemetery this morning? Think—do we have anything with her DNA on it? Have you told

Peterson to get someone to dump her phone? See who's called in to her?"

"That's got to be brother Brendan himself."

"Or Lem Howell, looking for Brendan. He might have spilled the beans. Somebody certainly tipped her off to it."

"Maybe she's just dogging Bobby Hassett's every step," Mike said.

"She was already sneaking around the cemetery before he got there."

We showed our IDs at the entrance and made our way back down to Genco.

"Pull up a couple of stools," he said. "Get off your gimpy foot."

"You're not done yet?" Mike said.

"Not quite. I don't have the luxury of many one-body days."

Rebecca Hassett's internal organs were laid out on separate corkboards, on a stainless steel table along the far end of the wall. A foot square and lightweight, the cork allowed the doctors to cut through the parts without dulling the blades of their knives.

"Is her hair good for information at this point?" Mike asked, looking at a glassine envelope that Genco had prepared for the lab.

"Some drugs stay in it—we'll test for those. Nicotine, for example. Or something like Thorazine, though there was nothing in the history, I take it, to suggest that. But if it's excessive alcohol—and only alcohol— as the first studies showed, it won't give us anything."

"What's next?"

"I've done the spleen and the pancreas. Very decomposed, as I'd expect. I'm working on the kidney now," Genco said, thoroughly absorbed in the samples in front of him. "Quite an experience you had in court, Alex, wasn't it?"

"Dreadful, absolutely dreadful. There aren't words to describe it to you."

"You ever think they'd have you spending a day in the morgue just to keep you out of harm's way?"

"A cemetery *and* the morgue," I said.

"Mike knows how to show a girl a good time."

"What do you look for when you're doing this, Jerry?"

Genco was concentrating on the organs. "The entire point of the exhumation is to examine specimens more carefully than at the autopsy. I dissect each of these things, hopefully for the second time. See? Here's the incision from the original dissection."

I looked over his shoulder. He placed his scalpel an inch away from the previous cut and sliced through the liver, spreading it open on the corkboard like a small piece of fruit.

"Unremarkable," he said. "Nothing of importance."

I sat back down. Mike was next to me, reading the sports pages of the paper.

"Now the kidney," Genco said, moving to the next specimen. "Interesting. There's a small nodule here."

I got up again. "It's only of consequence medically, Alex. Not as evidence. This will go to the lab, of course. It's probably just a benign tumor in the bile duct. We work up microscopic slides of all of this."

I went back to my stool.

"When are they going to get the point about the need for some good middle relievers? Mariano can't do it all by himself," Mike said. "My Yankees pulled out a squeaker last night."

"Peculiar," Genco said, bent over the corkboard.

"Wish it was. I'm afraid it's par for the course this season."

"Sorry. I meant this is peculiar."

"What is?" I asked.

"There's another little lump here."

"Where?"

"I've got the uterus now. Along with the ovaries and fallopian tubes. They're light pinkish when you're alive. Sort of darken with the passage of time."

I stood up again to look.

"There's a bulge here, where I'm slicing. Do you see it?"

"Not really."

"Right next to the point of my scalpel." He adjusted the overhead lamp. "It's a corpus luteum. It's a tiny hemorrhagic cyst in the ovary—where the egg popped out during the menstrual cycle."

"Did the first doctor find it?" I asked. "Should he have noted it?"

Genco shook his head. "Not necessarily, but then if he hadn't cut exactly here in this same spot, he'd have missed it quite naturally. It's very small."

I was fixated on the deft movements of Genco's hand as he guided his instrument back to the fallopian tubes. I winced instinctively as he made another incision.

"Almost to the All-Stars and we're only a game and a half in front of Boston. We better liven up our bats," Mike said.

"There it is, Alex. Do you see now?"

"What, Jerry? What am I looking for?"

"That pea-size bulge, right under my blade."

"Yes, yes, I do."

"It's an embryo, Alex. I'm pretty sure of it. You see how the embryonic substance looks entirely different than the uterus? I'll confirm it under the scope, but I'm certain what you see is fetal tissue."

Mike looked up from the newspaper. "What the hell are you telling us?"

"That your girl Rebecca Hassett was pregnant at the time she was killed."

36

"Don't defend the guy, Jerry. How did a doc miss the kid's pregnancy, can you explain that to me? That fact could have changed the way the entire case shook out. Maybe it gave somebody a motive, maybe it gave—"

"Don't fly off the handle, Mike. It wouldn't have been easy to see. I'd say the fetus wasn't even three months yet—probably just a bit over two. The uterus is barely en-larged. Here—you can see the incision he made—will you look at this, please?" Jerry said. "The pathologist made one cut from front to back—right here—so he didn't see all of the uterus, any more than I did when I made mine. The place where he sliced? There was nothing to show it."

"Why the hell not?"

"Since there was no trauma to the vaginal vault, no signs of a sexual assault at autopsy, a superficial visual of the reproductive organs would be all most docs would have done. Not uncommon. This was a sixteen-year-old girl—eight, maybe nine weeks pregnant. If nobody brought that piece of information in as part of her history, most pathologists doing the postmortem on an asphyxial death might have missed it."

Mike's argument with Jerry Genco faded to background noise. My thoughts were somewhere else.

I was trying to put together what I remembered of the time frame during which Bex Hassett's life had spun so terribly out of control. How much earlier was it that her father had died? When had she started spending all that time away from home? Who was in the pack she was hanging with in Pelham Bay Park? What had caused her to turn against her friend Trish Quillian? Had anyone realized she'd been impregnated just a couple of months before her death?

"I wonder how religious the family was. What if Mrs. Hassett knew her daughter was pregnant and threw her out of the house?" I asked. "Parents have done that with girls who embarrassed them—more often than you think."

"You're a bit tardy with that thought, Coop. About six months too late to ask Mama, according to the headstone on her grave."

"Maybe Bobby knew. Maybe the brothers had some idea. What if that's why he didn't want the exhumation done?"

Mike's eyes narrowed as he considered the idea. "Guess I'll have to talk to him again. Put him back on the list, after I'm done with Trish Quillian."

"You think it throws Reuben DeSoto—the original suspect—back in the mix? What if she'd been sleeping with him and told him he was the father of the baby? He'd have no reason to rape her then—but they might have argued about it. Maybe he did kill her."

"That whole gang she was running with in the park? I guess we'll have to see if we can scare up any of those guys."

Jerry Genco was ready to get us out of his hair. "Odds are this had nothing to do with the girl's death. You know the numbers on teen pregnancy in this country? It's a staggering figure. She had a high-risk lifestyle, this Hassett kid. We see it all too frequently here. Quite sad, really."

The arguments I had made to Judge Gertz about my motion to use an expert on interpersonal violence in Brendan Quillian's trial were triggered now by Genco's dismissal of the relevance of this murder victim's pregnancy.

"The leading cause of death for pregnant women in America is homicide," I said.

Genco was labeling his specimens for storage. "Yeah, I guess that's right."

"Pregnancy—like separation—is one of the two most dangerous times for women in a bad relationship," I went on. "Most of them are killed by the men they'd been intimate with—I hesitate to use the word *lover*. You know that, too."

"And one of the most common causes of death in those circumstances is strangulation," Mike said, looking at me a bit less skeptically.

"So if somebody knew Rebecca Hassett

was pregnant, and that somebody wasn't happy about it, maybe it gives us a new suspect."

"Well, I'll be the first to tell you if I was wrong about the insignificance of this—this pregnancy. I'll call you tomorrow to see if I can give you two any direction," Jerry Genco said. "Maybe we can help figure the paternity. We'll have a preliminary on the DNA of the fetal tissue in twenty-four hours."

37

Ignacia Bliss took over the task of guarding me for the twelve-hour shift starting at 8 p.m. She met me inside the funeral home in the Fort Greene section of Brooklyn, where Elsie Evers's grieving relatives and an honor guard of court officers surrounded the closed coffin. The most skilled technicians in the funeral business couldn't have reconstructed her face well enough to allow anyone to view the slain woman.

My closest friends from the office—Nan, Catherine, and Marisa—had come to the

wake as well, arranging with Ignacia to follow us to my apartment. They were determined to distract me and get a read on my
emotional well-being. Fortunately for me,
Paul Battaglia had become mired in another
matter that required his attention in Manhattan, where the people who vote for him live.

"We're in charge of dinner," Catherine
said. "Go get into your robe."

While I changed and Ignacia went into the
guest room to make some calls, the three of
them poured drinks and opened a bottle of
wine.

Marisa called into the bedroom, "Does
Swifty's deliver? Delicious thought, isn't it?"

"When they get a break in the action, ask
them to send a waiter in a cab with the order. Get something for the two cops in the
lobby, too."

I padded out in a short silk robe and my
ballet slippers. They were listening to television news in the den, and Nan muted it
when she saw me.

"I need to hear it. It's fine."

"Mike and Mercer said we shouldn't let
you—"

I rolled my eyes. "I need my pals around
me, just like this. I don't need a censor."

A seasoned crime reporter was leading off the nine o'clock hour. The chiron below him was running a strip that said breaking news across the bottom of the screen.

"We begin with a story about the many possible sightings of the armed fugitive Brendan Quillian, who broke out of a Manhattan courtroom yesterday in a deadly blaze of gunfire."

In the top right corner, over his head, the news producer had gathered an array of photographs of Quillian that were displayed for several seconds each. Most had been cropped from the social columns, although it was unlikely that the tuxedo-and-bow-tie outfit he was often seen in would translate to someone readily recognizable in casual street clothes.

"The damn eye," I said, sinking into my most comfortable wing chair. "Why don't they use that in their description?"

"Frankly, it never seemed as obvious to me," Marisa said, "the times I've seen him in court."

"He hasn't glared at you the way he fixes on Alex," Nan said.

". . . and tips have continued to come in to police, as well as to our newsroom, from all over the Northeast. Earlier today, Brendan Quillian was reportedly sighted on an Amtrak train to Washington, as well as in a diner in Poughkeepsie, New York," the reporter said. "So as you can imagine, it's quite a task for the NYPD to follow up on all these calls to determine which ones have any credibility."

"Stay with it," the anchor said. "We understand there are Keating Properties offices worldwide, owned by the family of Mr. Quillian's late wife. Is that true?"

"Zap him, will you?" I asked Nan as I sipped my Scotch. "I don't think the Keatings are likely to shelter the bum, here or abroad. Any word on Lawrence Pritchard?"

"He's dug his heels in. He'll be served with a grand jury subpoena, but my guess is we won't get anything from him. He's clammed up as long as Quillian is on the loose."

"Did you get any information on how Artie's doing? And Oscar?"

"Artie's coming along fine. Can't wait to get back to work so he can tell and retell his version of the events. Oscar?" Marisa said. "I think retirement's the next step."

"C'mon, tell us about the wedding," Catherine said. "Everything."

I went through all the details of the weekend, including my meeting with Luc, while we waited for dinner to arrive.

"Why isn't the Frenchman here tonight?" Marisa asked.

"Ignacia'll be out any minute," I said, holding my finger to my lips. "You think it's possible for me to have a romance—even for a couple of weeks—without the homicide squad running a rap sheet on the guy or doing surveillance? Just a head start with a bit of privacy when this madness ends—that's all I'm asking for."

"A Frenchman," Nan said, mocking a sigh. "The three of us married-with-children soccer moms will be living vicariously from the moment you get into bed with him."

"Forget the sex," Catherine said. "Imagine the meals. You may have to take us to France with you to chaperone this deal. Nothing less or I squeal."

Ignacia had taken off her jacket and rejoined us. "A little wine?" Marisa asked.

Ignacia shook her head. "I'll take a rain check, once we find this bastard."

"Anything new from the lieutenant?" I asked. "What are the guys up to?"

"Mike and some of the others are going underground with the sandhogs."

"What do you mean?"

"The squad—everyone's been mobilized. There was a sit-down with the union bosses this afternoon, charting every tunnel and dig and sandhog project in the city. If Quillian leaned on any of Duke's friends to hide him away, our guys will be looking for him down in the holes."

"How about his sister, Trish?" I asked.

"A cop is sitting on her house. Mike wants to talk to her," Ignacia said, putting her feet up on the ottoman. "So far, no luck with her or Bobby Hassett. There's always tomorrow, Alex."

"Trish's phone," I said. "Did he remember to ask Peterson to dump it?"

"Relax," Nan said as the intercom rang to announce the arrival of our dinner. "I did the subpoena this afternoon. You can't run this case anymore, my dear. You're in somebody else's hands now. Sit back and let us worry about it."

The five of us ate dinner together before my friends said good night and Ignacia locked the door behind them. I turned in at eleven, while she was still in the den watching an old movie.

Mercer picked me up at 8 a.m. on Thursday, and I thanked Ignacia as she headed home at the end of her tour.

"You sleeping?" he asked.

"So-so. Anything new?"

"I wish I could tell you something good, Alex. I know you don't like living this way."

We parked around the corner from the Hogan Place entrance and Mercer escorted me up to my office. Laura made sure there was no welcoming committee to overwhelm me on my return and kept McKinney at bay while I dealt with the pileup on my desk.

At ten thirty, Mercer and I made our way up to Part 83.

Fred Gertz was ready for his close-up this time. He had opened the courtroom doors to the press and public half an hour earlier, knowing it would be a capacity crowd. Lem Howell was sitting at counsel table, and an all-new crew of court officers—eight of them now—staffed the room. I didn't recognize the man who had taken Jonetta Purvis's place, but when he looked up as he saw me start down the aisle, most heads in the room turned around to note my arrival, too.

Shortly after, Judge Gertz took the bench. He strode out of the robing room with an uncharacteristically purposeful attitude, as though he were fit to ascend the bench and take his place among the nine Supremes.

He had prepared remarks to deliver and waited until the two officers in front of the press row had quieted everyone.

For almost fifteen minutes, Gertz droned on about the tragic events of Tuesday morning. He explained that he had excused the jury until next Monday, at which time he expected he would have no choice but to declare a mistrial, because of the media coverage that would have been impossible for any New Yorker to miss. He talked about the courage of the court officers and his staff—with an emphasis on the unimaginable loss of Elsie Evers.

Gertz closed his statement with a self-congratulatory description of how he had used the power and dignity of his judicial status to restore calm after the chaos of the shooting.

He thanked Lem and me for our assistance and waved at Lem to remain seated when he tried to stand to put something on the record.

"There will be no interviews of Mr. Howell and Ms. Cooper. They are still involved in these matters, and while I'm not going to gag them, I think it would be most inappropriate if they make any public comments."

Then Gertz walked off as briskly as he had entered, and the reporters raced out to call in their stories.

Lem crossed over to talk to me. "That gets the man his fifteen minutes of fame, I'd guess. Or do you think he didn't want us to talk because he's afraid we might say that when he was hiding in the kneehole under the bench, I didn't quite think he was doing much to restore order in the court?"

"He can't really believe his own statement, can he?"

Lem had clutched my forearm in his usual style. "You okay, Alexandra? I hope you understand that I was as shocked, as surprised, as appalled, as you were by what happened in here with my client."

"I know that, Lem."

"Miss Cooper," the substitute clerk called out. "There's a call for you on the DA's phone over here."

I broke away from Lem and signaled for Mercer to wait for me in the well of the courtroom while I took the call.

"Alex? It's Laura. I've got Jerry Genco on the phone. He said it's urgent. He asked me to patch him through to you."

I was standing in the same place I had been when the door had opened on Tuesday and the defendant had grabbed Elsie's gun to shoot her. I was tethered to the wall by the long beige extension cord, waiting for Genco to come on the line.

"Alex? Forensic biology ran our sample overnight for that prelim I promised you."

"Yes, Jerry?"

"I never expected to have a result as fast as this, but the match comes up in our own linkage database."

"To whom? Can you be more specific?"

"The fetal tissue I extracted yesterday, that's what I submitted to the lab. I don't know much about the old case, but I never thought I'd be ready to give you confirmation on the paternity as fast as this." Genco paused to take a breath. "Rebecca Hassett was pregnant with Brendan Quillian's baby."

38

"God, my heart breaks for that kid," I said to Mercer as I slumped into the chair at counsel table in the empty courtroom. "Why didn't we think of this?"

"Hey, I missed the same signs you did. Mike told me all that talk about how Bex had spent so much time at the Quillians, practically living in their house."

"Of course she wanted to come into Manhattan with Trish the day she went to have lunch with Brendan and meet his fiancée," I said. "No wonder he became so upset when he saw Bex in the rowboat. He probably thought she was going to do something to break up his engagement, act out in front of Amanda Keating. Who knows how long she'd been sleeping with him at that point, on his infrequent visits home?"

"Or playing hooky, slipping into town to meet up with him somewhere. Then she appeared at the church the day of the wedding and went home to the Bronx, all furious with Trish. By then, Bex was pregnant."

"You should have seen that pitiful sight when they opened the coffin yesterday. And I'm thinking she was buried with a stuffed animal like it was a childhood toy."

"And wasn't it that?" Mercer asked.

"A little brown-and-white bulldog? Try Jack the Bulldog, the mascot of the Georgetown Hoyas. A present from Brendan, no doubt. I suppose some family member put it there beside her without having any idea what it stood for."

Mercer and I had been to enough college basketball games at the Garden to recognize the symbol of Brendan's alma mater.

Mercer said, "So if we suppose Brendan knew Bex was pregnant—"

"Of course he knew," I snapped. "He was

calling her house, up until the day of the marriage. He was probably trying to reason with her, checking on whether or not she'd told anyone about it. Wondering how she would be able to deal with it, knowing that terminating a pregnancy wasn't an option with the religious upbringings they'd both had."

"There's his whole golden opportunity—a new life as part of the Keating kingdom— just weeks away from being formalized, and he's messing around with his kid sister's best friend."

"And she's the only one—the only person in the world, little Rebecca Hassett—who stood a chance of getting in the way of Brendan's shot at the entire Keating fortune."

Mercer was leaning against the edge of the table, working the points over and over, and shaking his head from side to side. "Alex, it still doesn't change the fact that Brendan was out of the country on his honeymoon the night Bex was killed."

I tossed my head back and grimaced. "But look at the weight it adds to his desperate breakout this week. Who else stood to know that in a careful reexamination of the body, there was physical evidence that connects him to a murdered teenager?"

Mercer patted my hand. "Look, he may have been afraid an exhumation would reveal the girl's pregnancy. Maybe even tie him to it, since you gotta figure he knows more than the average Joe about DNA after the investigation of Amanda's murder. Somebody was smart enough to kill his wife without a trace of any forensic clues. That still doesn't link him to Bex Hassett's murder."

"Let's let them lock up the courtroom," I said, standing up to leave. "You want to call Mike and break the news to him? I think it's time we sit down with Trish Quillian. Maybe he can have her picked up. And you double-check with your friend Kate Meade."

"I know, I know. Did Kate save anything that proves that Amanda and Brendan were in Europe the night Bex was killed? Souvenir postcards or photographs she might have in a scrapbook somewhere?"

"Exactly. I'd better tell Battaglia about what's been going on at the morgue."

Mercer made his calls to Mike and Kate, then went down to wait for me in the car while I briefed the district attorney. Then we drove together uptown to the Manhattan North Homicide Squad.

Mike was sitting in the lieutenant's office, his feet on the desk. He was wearing the same clothes he'd had on the day before and was unshaved as well. He was eating an egg sandwich and greasy french fries at one o'clock in the afternoon.

"Breakfast?" Mercer asked.

"I think it's yesterday's dinner. We didn't spend much time aboveground. It was a long night with Teddy O'Malley nosing around the water tunnel and a few other sandhog holes." Mike stuck a finger in his ear and wiggled it around. "I can't get that sound of dripping water out of my head. And I was just about to go home for a while when you called."

"Go ahead, then. Mercer and I can handle this."

"If I remember correctly, you and Trish Quillian didn't exactly bond when you met. I'll run this one my way."

He was more likely to have success with her than I was. "Are you going to tell her about Bex? About the baby?"

Mike looked at Mercer. "I don't think so. Not yet. I'm not looking to fuel her up with information. I want to see what she gives us."

Mercer nodded in agreement.

"Maybe this is what old Phinneas Baylor meant about Trish. About saying she should dig for the bones in her own backyard. Maybe these are the bones he meant."

"You have anything to hit her with?"

Mike wiped his hands on his chinos and reached for papers on the desk. "From the phone company. Our boy Brendan finally called his sister after his shooting spree on Tuesday. Here's the incoming right here on the dump of her phone."

"What's that worth?" I asked. "From a booth? From what location?"

"Not so lucky. He called from the cell phone of the guy he carjacked. Only used it once, best I can tell. May have thrown it away after that. But this clocks him in for four and a half minutes with his baby sister. We can start there."

"Is Trish here?"

"Yeah. Across the hall in the captain's office. Roast beef on rye with a root beer. I don't think she's eaten in a week. Two of the guys picked her up at home after Mercer called. Peterson wants a team sitting on her house full-time now in case Brendan makes a guest appearance."

I waited for Mike to finish eating. Mercer left the room and came back with our vending-machine lunch. A choice of entrées—M&M's, red licorice Twizzlers, or a Milky Way—and a soda for each of us.

"Kate Meade seals the deal. Very sentimental type. Saved an album with photographs of the wedding party and letters Amanda wrote on her honeymoon. There's a snapshot of Amanda and Brendan at the Trevi Fountain, with a date stamp on the back. All in sequence with the rest of their travels. Get Brendan Quillian out of your brain, Ms. Cooper. He didn't kill Rebecca Hassett."

Mike rolled up his empty bag and tossed it in the garbage. "Why don't you come with me, Mercer? Alex, you can watch through the one-way mirror. Better you don't set Trish off, okay?"

"She's all yours, Detective."

I took my soda and went off into the room adjacent to the one they would use for the interview. A few minutes later, Mike opened the door for Trish Quillian, who looked nervously around the small, bare rectangular space before sitting down and resting her elbows on the table. She was wearing a black polyester track suit that zipped up the front and clung to her thin frame.

"I have to be getting home, Detective. I've got to be feeding my mother some lunch."

"It's been a pretty rough time for you, Trish, with Brendan going wild on us right on the heels of Duke's funeral. Are you managing okay?"

Trish picked up her head and stared into the mirror. She couldn't see me, I knew, but I was staring right into the hard, sharp features of her unsmiling face. "Is it concern for me now that you sent two cops to pick me up?"

"No. You might say it's concern for your brother."

"For Brendan?" She slowly circled the palm of her hand on the tabletop and looked at Mike. "You're playing me for a fool, aren't you? You make some hokey case about him killing Amanda that wouldn't stand up in a kangaroo court, and now that he's beat you at it, I'm supposed to think you're worried about him?"

Mike sat across from her. "He shot a woman to death at point-blank range, Trish.

Killed a court officer in front of a judge and lawyers and several other decent people. Wounded three others. He stole two guns and he hijacked a car. Brendan's what they used to say was 'armed and extremely dangerous.'"

The lean woman looked a decade older and harder than she had a week ago, rocking in her chair as she continued to trace designs on the wood with her fingertip.

"What do they call it now?" she asked.

"I'd say he's more like a fucking bull's-eye. I'd say your brother's a walking target, Trish, with a great big *X* painted on his forehead. Some cop sees him and knows how trigger-happy he is, Brendan gets nailed by the first shot, before he can even focus the only eye he's got."

One side of Trish Quillian's mouth pulled back, almost in a grin. "My brother's been dead for me a really long time, Detective. You trying to make me think *you* care what happens to him? I gave up worrying about Brendan years ago. Right after he gave up worrying about us."

"I talked to Phin Baylor."

The smile faded. "I'm the one who told you to, wasn't I?"

"He said you shouldn't be pointing fingers at any of the Hassett boys. Phin said there were things about your own brothers—about Brendan and Duke—that we ought to talk about with you."

There was no change in Trish's expression. She kept on rocking back and forth, rubbing her finger around and around on the wooden surface. "Like what?"

"Tell me what else you remember about Brendan. Tell me how he got along with your friends."

"My friends? That's a long way to think." Trish Quillian sat still for more than a minute. "Maybe you know how it is with big brothers, Detective."

She made eye contact with Mike for the first time, and he nodded at her.

"All the guys I went to school with, they looked up to Duke. He was the strong one, he was the street fighter—took on anybody's cause for a friend. Sick as he was, when they thought he was going to die of the cancer, he came back tough as a bull. Wasn't a soul who'd mess with me 'cause they knew Duke would take care of business."

"He hurt people, didn't he?"

Trish's eyes narrowed to the size of slits.

"He never hurt anybody who didn't cause trouble first. And you can be sure no one complained about it to me. I wouldn't have listened." She wagged a finger at Mike as she spoke.

"And Brendan?"

"Boys didn't understand him—him being afraid of the tunnels and the sandhog jobs and all. Liking books so much, inside doing homework most nights while kids were playing on the street. Girls? Well, some of them get kind of stupid around guys like him. He was good-looking—even with the bum eye—and popular with all the fancy girls. From the time he started high school at Regis, he always dressed better and talked smoother than the neighborhood kids. He was something special."

"Your friends, Trish, did he hang out with them?"

She dismissed that thought with a snort. "You must be kidding. Six, seven years difference at that age? I think he liked the attention, liked the girls fawning all over him. But he didn't have any interest in none of them. Just a nuisance, that's all they were to him."

Mike took his time making his approach. "How about Bex?"

"Yeah? What do you want to know about her now?"

"Well, you said she was at your house all the time, am I right?"

"Practically living there. Part of the family. My very best friend."

"And Brendan. Did they get along?"

There was no sign of tension in her face or movements as she answered Mike. She didn't seem to get the significance of his questions.

"I'd say they got along fine. He was good to Bex. Helped her with her homework, even. Things like that. Especially in those few months after her father was killed in that accident—right before Brendan got married—he was trying to be a big brother to her, help her through it."

"They spent time together?"

Trish cocked her head and looked at Mike. "I've just told you what kind of things they did. Family stuff. Schoolwork. Even took her out driving a few times when she got her permit. In old Mr. Keating's car, if I'm not mistaken. He was being good to her, if you don't mind. You're not making something else of it, are you? Sticking Brendan with something else?"

"Not anything—"

"We were kids, Bex and me, Detective. Sixteen years old when he got married to that snooty dame. She hated to lose him, same as I did. Like a brother."

"Think of those last few months, Trish, before the wedding. Was Brendan around?"

"In the city? Sure. He and Amanda had to do Pre-Cana. They had to go to Amanda's church, not ours."

I knew that Pre-Cana was a requirement before Catholic weddings, couples meeting in sessions with a priest to discuss the responsibilities of their marriage, a reminder that it was considered a sacrament of the church.

"Were he and Amanda living together?"

"Before the wedding? Not like you mean. He stayed in the Keatings' home, in the guest room from time to time," Trish said. "My mother used to tell me—like it was the only good example she could draw from the Keatings—what a fine thing it was that Amanda had been raised with such important religious values. She liked that Amanda insisted on keeping herself pure till they were married—that's what Mother called it. 'Pure.' Brendan told her that, she used to say."

I closed my eyes, thinking of Amanda Keating guarding her virginity until her wedding night, while Brendan Quillian found a naive but willing sexual partner in a lost teenager who idolized him.

"So when Bex was angry and upset after the wedding, you didn't think it was because Brendan—like, Brendan had something going on with her?"

"Trust me, Detective. I would have known about something like that. One of them would have told me, I'm sure of it."

Mike sat up straight and Trish Quillian crossed her legs and rubbed her hands together.

"I'd like to trust you, Trish. I'd like to believe what you tell me, but I'm having a hard time with it."

She looked up at Mike's face and pursed her lips. "Why is that?"

"'Cause my damn ankle hurts like hell. I can't concentrate on what you're trying to feed me," he said, ruffling the hair at the back of his neck.

"That's not my fault."

"You Quillians, you're a tough bunch. I'd say it's completely your fault. Wouldn't be this way if I hadn't chased you halfway across the elysian fields yesterday."

"The what?"

"The cemetery, Trish. You were there when we went to—to—uh, to Bex's grave."

The slightest bit of color rose to her sunken cheeks. She looked up at the mirror and then glanced over at the closed door of the room. She began rocking again.

"Now, how did you know that I was going to be at Woodlawn in the morning?"

"It must have been a coincidence. I go there a lot," she said defiantly. "I go there to talk to Bex pretty often. I didn't know any of you was going to be there."

"You ought to bring flowers next time you go. Looks pretty bare next to that little headstone. Aren't you curious about why we had to dig—to disturb her grave?"

"I'm not a curious person, Detective. Since I called you the first time, I'm finding out it's safer to mind my own business." Trish leaned back in the chair and crossed her arms.

"I thought maybe Brendan told you why. I thought maybe Brendan explained the reason we had to take that poor girl back to the morgue and—"

"I don't want to know anything about that part of it. Don't you get that Brendan has nothing to do with this?" She waved a bony hand in front of her face. "I've only seen him at the wake. At the funeral. Brendan and I don't talk."

"Ow!" Mike said, letting out a fake yelp and bending over to grab his ankle. "Every time you tell a lie, my leg just throbs."

"What lie?" She looked again at the door, as if trying to get the nerve to walk out.

Mike leaned in close to Trish Quillian. "Brendan called you on Tuesday. Brendan phoned you after he shot his way out of the courthouse."

Her eyes opened wide and she sat upright. She was speechless.

"What did he tell you, Trish? Bet he didn't mention that there'll be no one left to take care of your mother if you get yourself wound up in helping Brendan get away. You'll be an accessory to this murder. Don't let him drag you into this."

She was looking straight into the mirror now. "There's someone on the other side of that glass, isn't there? Someone watching us and listening."

"You're talking to me," Mike said. "That's all that matters at this point."

"You've tapped my phone then, have you?"

"No, we haven't done that. I wouldn't be needing to ask you what Brendan told you if we had. I wouldn't be asking you where he is."

"Well, I'm not interested in helping you, Detective. You didn't do nothing to help me when I came to you. You haven't done a single damn thing to find who killed Duke."

She stood up. "I can go, can't I? You're not holding me?"

"Yeah, you can go," he said, giving her a card with his cell phone number on it as he got to his feet, too. "But you call me if you get smart about Brendan. And there's one more thing I'd like to ask you for, Trish."

"What's that?"

Mike took a small manila envelope from the pocket of his blazer and removed a Q-tip from it. "Could you just put this inside your cheek for me, dab it around to get some saliva on it?"

The woman appeared to be as taken

aback as I was. She shoved Mike's arm away. "What are you looking for now?" she asked, raising her voice. "You making me some kind of guinea pig, are you? Is this that DNA stuff you're trying to get from me, using me against my own brother? Is that what you're up to?"

Mike was thinking of the speck of blood—with the genetic markers of a woman—that was on the zipper of Rebecca Hassett's sweater.

The Q-tip had dropped to the floor and Trish Quillian had her hand on the door-knob. "You want my saliva, Detective? You and your high-handed girlfriend from the District Attorney's Office, that's what you're after? Like I'm a killer or a criminal?"

She sucked in her hollow cheeks and wet her lips. Then she opened her mouth ever so slightly and spit at Mike, missing the sleeve of his jacket by only inches.

"There's your sample, Detective. Catch me if you can."

39

Mike was on his knees, using a second Q-tip to swab the saliva that Trish Quillian had deposited on the floor of the small room.

"That's quite a smooth interview technique you've developed, Mr. Chapman. Every day I'm on the job with you is a learning experience."

"I've picked up samples from worse places than this, Coop. Where's Mercer?"

"On the phone. He'll be right over."

"I'm whipped. Going home to get some sleep. I'm supposed to start again at mid-

night. Teddy O'Malley's got a whole underground route mapped out again."

"If your ankle is still bothering you so
much, why don't you get it checked out?"

"I'll put it up when I get home. I'm too
tired to wait in an ER just to find out that all
I need is the Ace bandage and Tylenol I've
got in the medicine cabinet."

Mike wasn't the type to complain about
minor physical pain. "Maybe it's worse than
you think. I'll go with you."

"Another time." I followed Mike as he
limped to the lieutenant's office, where Mercer met us. Mike held out the envelope.
"Mind taking this to forensic biology? Have
them work it up? Coop'll explain."

"No problem. Just made one more check
on Duke Quillian. Asked Sloan-Kettering to
pull the records on him to get confirmation
about what Trish originally told you," Mercer
said, dropping his pad on the desk. "Duke
was out of play, too. He was a patient there
for close to two months—still in the hospital
for more than a week after Bex was killed."

"Sounds bad. What kind of cancer?" I
asked.

"Acute leukemia."

"Thanks for making the call," Mike said.

"I've been up and down on these Quillian brothers like a yo-yo. I'm ready for some sleep."

"I think I'll take the rest of the afternoon off," I said.

"C'mon. Let me drop you at the apartment and get this down to the lab," Mercer said.

It was three o'clock by the time I reached home, greeted the cops who were sitting in the lobby for the afternoon shift, and went upstairs. I was looking forward to being alone for several hours—for the first time in days—until Ignacia arrived for the overnight detail.

I put on some soft music, called a few close friends—and my mother—to reassure them that I was okay, and left a message for Luc on his voice mail. It was unlikely that I could keep our Saturday-night dinner date with Brendan Quillian still on the loose.

I spread out on the floor of the den with every map and guide to the city of New York that I could find on my bookshelves, trying to figure out if any place connected to Brendan's sandhog heritage might be a safe haven for my fugitive.

Ignacia arrived with soup and salad, and

we had a quiet dinner together in front of the television. Fatigue and anxiety from the week's events had overtaken me, and I excused myself to go to my bedroom and read a few magazine articles.

I couldn't even concentrate on those, so I closed my eyes. I thought of Luc again—the chiseled features, the sexy accent, the kisses that had aroused me as we walked along the cove a short week ago. I wondered if I would ever have the chance to recreate the electricity of those first hours. And I wondered what it would be like if he were beside me now.

I slept late, and after Ignacia left at 8 a.m., soaked in my bathtub and dressed casually in jeans and a sweater. I wasn't going to court or meeting with any witnesses today, and I didn't expect to be in the office for long. I carried a small bag with my ballet shoes and clothes in it, optimistic that I could sneak away early for a few hours of exercise at the barre.

The patrol car was waiting for me in the driveway when I got downstairs at nine thirty on a cool June morning. I was grateful for the week's end after days scarred by such tragic events.

My cell phone rang just as we pulled onto the southbound FDR Drive at Seventy-third Street.

"Where are you?" Mike asked.

"On my way to the office. And you?"

"Spent half the night again in a warren of subway tunnels filled with homeless men and the other half in something that vaguely resembles a sewer. What does Mattie Prinzer drink?"

"Scotch," I said. "Some kind of fancy single malt. One of those two-hundred-dollar-a-bottle jobs, if I remember correctly. Why?"

"Well, buy her a six-pack of 'em. She stayed up till dawn with my Q-tip."

"And the good news is?"

"She's matched the saliva on the cotton to the blood on Bex Hassett's zipper."

I sat bolt upright. "The same DNA? Trish Quillian's blood is on the sweater her best friend was wearing the night she was killed?"

"Don't get too excited, Coop. It may not be what you think."

I was usually the one curbing Mike's enthusiasm. I'd urge him not to jump the gun, so I thought immediately of the contrary arguments that had to be considered. "I know, I know. The girls were best friends. Trish's blood could have been left on that sweater some other day or time."

"It's not just that—"

"But after more than a decade?" I said. "Don't you think it's fantastic just to get the match? Whatever the issue is about when and how the blood got there, the fact is that Trish Quillian is the only person in the universe with that genetic profile."

"Tell the boys in blue to get you over here to Mattie's office as soon as possible. There were actually *two* people in the universe with Trish Quillian's DNA. That's the first problem we've got to deal with. I'll tell you the other one when you get here."

40

Mattie's small office was tucked away at the end of the hall, past the lab in which forensic biologists sat elbow to elbow at their tables, interpreting data that cooked overnight in the robots—the giant machines capable of running dozens of DNA samples at a time.

"I wanted you to see this for yourself, Alex," Mattie said.

Mike was pacing behind her; three steps in each direction was all that the space allowed. He looked up as I entered, but didn't bother to greet me. "The bastard would never have had the chance to escape."

"What have you got now? I hear you did a brilliant job on Trish Quillian's gob of spit," I said to Mattie. Mike was talking to her about Brendan Quillian, and I didn't understand why.

"That's old news already, Coop. Get with it."

"Last week, the night of the blast in the water tunnel," Mattie said, "we were so proud of ourselves for showing off the mobile lab. Getting the crew up there and having results in less than ten hours."

"The guys did a great job."

"I think so, too. From bits and pieces of flesh, they matched the two sandhogs from Tobago to items they found in their lockers and their home."

"Sorry. I never even focused on those men," I said. "We've all been assuming they were caught in the wrong place at a very wrong time, not that they were the targets of the killer."

"That's quite possible. Yes, one had tissues in a jacket pocket in the shed. Cut himself on a piece of metal a day or two be-

fore the explosion. The other one was identified from his toothbrush."

"And then there was Duke Quillian," Mike
said, locking his thumbs in the rear pockets
of his jeans.

I frowned and looked at Mike for an explanation. "Don't tell me he wasn't down
there in the tunnel? He was certainly identified, too. Wasn't he?"

It was Mattie who spoke. "Yes. Duke Quillian is dead. But the day he was identified, it
wasn't actually done by a DNA analysis of
his blood."

"Why not? I thought . . ."

Mattie spread the reports in front of her.
"For one thing, we had the severed digit,"
she said, pointing to an eight-by-ten blowup of the large finger with its ragged edge.

"They just scraped skin cells off the surface of it, and of course, they also had a
perfect print to match."

"Duke Quillian had no record. No fingerprints on file with the NYPD. Mike checked
that the first day."

"Yes, but the union required all the sandhogs to be fingerprinted after 9/11. It was
mandated as a security issue, for some of
the jobs they had to work on near Ground

Zero—rebuilding subway stations and such," Mattie said. "The prints were delivered to the ME's office within hours of the blast, so that confirmed his death."

"All that confirmed," Mike said, correcting Mattie, "is that it would be a struggle for him to use a rotary phone. It was only one finger."

Mattie shook her head at Mike. "And the dental records. A piece of Quillian's skull was picked up at the scene. That fragment was also matched to his dentist's files."

"So Duke's dead, right?" I asked.

"Very dead, Alex," Mattie said. "And I know we never do things fast enough for Mike, but you've got to remember the backlog we have. No one else was reported missing, so we knew we had the deceased—our three victims—identified."

With the expansion of the capability of DNA to solve crimes—well beyond murders and sexual assaults—the lab was inundated with dozens of investigative requests a day, some of them presenting dozens of samples per case.

"Thousands of pieces of skin and tissue were collected in the debris from the tunnel," Mattie went on. "The techs have been doing extractions on them as fast as they can, in between all the new work that's brought in every day. They've been running samples in the robots. One of my guys got a result yesterday that had him stymied. It didn't make sense to him, so he brought it to me to discuss last night, after Mercer left."

"What didn't make sense?" I asked.

"This—this anomaly."

"Anomaly?"

Mike leaned over Mattie's shoulder. "Yeah, Coop. Anomaly. That's a scientific expression that usually translates as 'Detective Chapman, you're screwed.' Show her."

There were pages of reports from the various biologists who had worked on the tunnel samples. With the tip of her pen, Mattie pointed to the profiles that repeated themselves on different test results.

"Here's Tobagan Number One, as we've called him." His tissue fragments had been identified again and again from remains within the blast site.

She lifted her pen and moved to Tobagan #2, making the same point.

"This," Mattie went on, "is the genetic

profile of Duke Quillian. We obtained it, of course, from the skin cells of the finger that Mike recovered on the first day. It matches skin cells from microscopic pieces of flesh that were in the debris. There's no question that Duke was blown to bits."

"Then what's the anomaly?" I asked.

"You can look at every single blood sample—hundreds of them—that we've been running these last two days to wind up the investigation. Not one of them—not one drop of blood—matches the DNA of Duke Quillian."

"You've got the man's skin, but you don't have his blood?"

"Exactly, Alex."

"Can you explain—"

"It turns out there is DNA from a fourth person," Mattie said, wagging her pen in my face. "A different profile that several techs developed. Something that didn't match to any of the deceased."

"But there are no other reports of missing persons."

"Right, there haven't been any, and it's actually much easier than that, Alex. It's the DNA of a woman in this fourth profile," Mattie said. "One peak only. Again, there's no Y chromosome."

"But there were no women working in the tunnel. It's bad luck—the sandhogs won't have it."

"Don't get ahead of yourself, Coop," Mike said.

"The blood in the tunnel," Mattie said, pushing several pieces of paper toward me. "You can see for yourself what I mean. This profile was sitting on my desk last night, right next to my folder on the Hassett case."

She slid two pieces of paper together— one from Bex Hassett's file and the other from the water tunnel evidence—and pointed to the alleles that aligned with each other at thirteen loci within the cell to create a distinctive genetic profile.

"You want to talk anomaly, Coop? The DNA in that blood sample from evidence in Water Tunnel Number Three—it's a perfect match to the DNA of Trish Quillian."

41

The windows in Anna Borowski's office overlooked York Avenue, the stretch of East Side real estate from the Queensboro Bridge to Seventy-second Street—once tenements—now known as Hospital Row. It had taken us only twenty minutes to get here from the Office of the Chief Medical Examiner forty blocks downtown.

"What made you think to call me?" the doctor, whose medical specialty was blood cancers, asked Mike.

He had known Anna for several years, he

told me on the ride uptown, from the time Valerie was in treatment. Mike had met his fiancée while he was giving blood at the Memorial Sloan-Kettering Cancer Center, where Val had undergone extensive chemo-therapy, as well as her surgery.

"Bad blood, Doc. You know more about it than anyone in town." Mike was looking out at the campus of Rockefeller University on the far side of the street. He turned back to the oncologist and flashed his familiar grin. "I figure I've given you a few pints of my best stuff. That maybe you'd go undercover for me. Get me a peek at the patient's chart, at least."

The tall, handsome woman, dressed in a lab coat, lowered the tortoiseshell frames of her reading glasses from the top of her head and opened the thick sheaf of medical records. "Am I just easy or does that smile work on everyone?" she asked me.

"The perps don't go for it," I said. "Most of the rest of us do."

"Duke Quillian?" Mike asked.

"On the promise your subpoena will fol-low shortly."

"You got it."

She adjusted her glasses and got to work reading the papers in the blue folder.

"Acute leukemia, Mike. His chart begins with the usual symptoms. Fatigue, frequent fevers and infections. Nosebleeds and bleeding gums. By the second or third round of antibiotics, the local doc—a family practitioner in the Bronx—drew some blood to be tested. Got the result, made the diagnosis, and sent Mr. Quillian to us. That's the way the disease typically presents."

"Don't you have to pull all kinds of strings to get into these digs?" Mike asked.

Anna shook her head. "People think that, I guess. Your friend Duke—looks like he had perfectly good insurance coverage from his union. More important than that, there was no medical facility in the Bronx, where he lived, that did transplants in those days. I'm not sure there's one now. This would be the only logical place for him to wind up."

The word *transplant* caught my attention. "Duke Quillian had a transplant?"

"That was the only curable method of treating acute leukemia back in the days when he was ill, especially when the patients were as young as this guy." Anna glanced down at the file. "Mid to late twenties."

"What's the process?" Mike asked.

"The patient is typed for the human leuko-cyte antigen—HLA. And all his family members are typed, too. Did he have siblings, this guy?"

"Yes," we both said.

"There's a one-in-four chance of matching a family member," Anna said. "I've had cases with eight children, and none of them match the patient, although a few of them match each other. There's a second reason we start with family."

"What's that?" Mike asked.

"Donating marrow is an extremely painful process. It's hard to imagine how much it hurts," Anna said, her voice dropping to a whisper. "When you do it for someone you know and love, it's got to ease some of that."

"And if the siblings don't fit?"

"Then we go to the National Marrow Donor Program. Try to find a match from a volunteer donor."

"Does it tell you what happened here?" Mike asked, ready to grab the file from Anna's hand.

"Patient as always, Detective Chapman," Anna said, glancing at me. "Mike would come in every six months to give blood. He'd expect me to have cured someone before he finished his juice and cookies."

She skimmed the pages to find the information we wanted. "Yes, Mike. There was a perfect match to one of Duke's siblings—a sister named Patricia. Seems they refer to her in these records as Trish."

Mike clapped his hands together and flashed me a victory sign. "So Trish was his donor. Duke ended up with her DNA."

"Not so fast, Mike," Anna said. "Yes—and no."

"I'm sorry to say I'm confused, Doctor. I don't understand this."

"Was he in the hospital or not? That's what I want to know," Mike said.

"Let me back it up. After the match was confirmed and the surgical date was set, the patient—in this case, Duke Quillian—was admitted to the hospital. Usually, about nine days before the surgery, the chemo treatment begins. The point of that is to kill off all the old bone marrow cells completely—the ones causing the disease. So from that time—Day minus 9—Duke was right here in Sloan."

"What's the surgery involved?" I asked.

"Two procedures are conducted on the same day, but only one was actually surgical. Trish Quillian would have been in the operating room. Two doctors were harvesting her bone marrow."

I winced. "Harvesting?"

"She's anesthetized, of course, Alex. Facedown on the table. Holes are drilled in her iliac crest," Anna said, pointing to her hip. "A lot of them. Two surgeons go into the holes to draw out three to five cc's of marrow each time. The procedure can require as many as three hundred needles, filling up a container the size of a coffee can. Do you understand how much that is?"

Mike's expression was grim. "Yeah."

"They take what the docs remove directly up to the blood bank for processing, aligning blood types, filtering out the bits of bone from the marrow, and things like that. Runs another hour."

"And Duke?"

"He would have been resting in his room during that process. Once the marrow was ready to be transfused, the docs just brought it to him, hung it on an IV pole, and sent it on its way, to get to work inside his system."

Anna made it sound so matter-of-fact.

"I thought you called it a transplant?"

"In the case of bone marrow, *transplant* and *transfusion* really mean the same thing. The stem cells are quite amazing. They have some kind of internal homing system. Once they're transfused to the patient, they find their way—by themselves—right into the marrow. Like we docs say, the healthy stem cells set up 'housekeeping' exactly where they belong."

"So from that day on, what happens to the patient?" Mike asked.

"Well, that would have been a rough period for Duke Quillian, or anyone else. Trish would have been on her way home in no time, but the next four weeks, Duke would have been under strict quarantine. He would have been isolated from other patients and even visitors—we can't have the transplant patients exposed to infection. He was put on meds to suppress his immune system, to protect against graft-host disease, to do the best to see that he'd accept the new marrow."

Mike was checking the records of the transfusion that Anna had passed to him against the timeline of Rebecca Hassett's murder.

"What do the dates tell you?" I asked.

"This damn record shows Duke Quillian was still a patient here six weeks later, until a full week after Bex was killed," Mike said, his disappointment evident as he slammed the file shut. "Would he have been quarantined till then?"

Anna reached for the thick folder. "You want to get me in trouble with my administration?" she said, trying to get him to lighten up. "We can go through his chart together. It looks like Duke was clear after Day Thirty, as we call it. Day Thirty's the critical point. That's when the DNA tests are done. He had a cautious doctor who was trying to keep him in a safe environment before sending him out in the world."

"What DNA tests?" I asked.

"Routine blood exams to make certain that his sister's bone marrow had not been rejected. That the DNA being produced in Duke was actually from the cells harvested from Trish."

"Anna," Mike said, leaning his elbows on her desk and beaming his most earnest look in her eyes, "was he in quarantine after Day Thirty?"

She took her time, reading through the pages of fine print, vital signs, and nurses' notes. "No. No, he wasn't. He was moved to a room on another floor. His doctor was still doing tests. Didn't want him discharged for another two weeks. Something about Duke's job and the high risk of infection it posed."

Mike was practically in her face. "So just suppose this patient was stir-crazy. Suppose he was hungry for fresh air and a walk in the park. Was he strong enough, healthy enough to do that?"

"Of course. Sure he was. He'd just have to get past hospital security."

"Outbound? Put on his street clothes and walk out the door. You think that's ever a problem?"

"Mike, it's nothing our security would want to hear about."

"I'm talking more than ten years ago, Anna. I'm not getting anyone in trouble today. On the way back in," Mike said, pushing back to talk to me, "Duke's already got his hospital ID and a room number. What's to stop him from waving at the guard and going back to his room? Damn, if he didn't ring for his bedpan during the night, who would have missed him for a couple of hours?"

"Do you have an exact date, Mike?" Anna asked.

Mike told her when Rebecca Hassett was murdered.

She studied the file again, focusing on a specific page. She scratched her forehead before looking at Mike. "I can't say the patient didn't have a window to—to move around. Nurses took his vital signs at the beginning and end of each shift. No other medical procedures were noted."

Mike seemed satisfied with the doctor's answer.

I picked up the file to look at the dates for myself. "What were you saying about DNA tests? How do they figure in this? Trish and Duke—is their DNA the same now?"

"Let me explain it, Alex. Bone marrow is what produces blood. It's the patient's blood that is diseased in Mr. Quillian's kind of diagnosis, and this treatment aims to replace that blood production source entirely, with a healthy one."

"So Trish's bone marrow was transfused to Duke?"

"Right. On Day Thirty, Duke's blood was checked. That's done by DNA probes." Anna turned the file around. "The old method at that time. RFLP, four probes."

Restriction fragment length polymorphism, the original technique used in DNA analysis, had been replaced within the last ten years by PCR, polymerase chain reaction.

"What did that test tell them?" I asked.

"Whether the transplant had been a success. Thirty days out from the procedure, the DNA results on Duke Quillian revealed that all of his blood was produced by his sister's bone marrow. That was great news, for him and his physicians. If he'd been relapsing, there would have been a mix of the donor's DNA—Trish's—with the blood still being produced by the host."

"And for how long do they check it?"

"Six months. One year later. Maybe two or three in all. Someone young and otherwise healthy, like this Duke Quillian character was—well, we'd consider him cured after that. What his medical team would be hoping is that he'd die of old age, with his sister's DNA, his sister's blood," Anna said.

"Not quite the ending he met with," Mike said.

"So it's like identical twins," I said. "From the day of the transfusion on, Trish and Duke Quillian had exactly the same DNA."

"With one twist," Anna Borowski said. "It's only in the blood samples of each of them that their DNA is alike."

"What do you mean?"

"Duke's hair, his skin cells, his saliva—even his sperm—all those tissues retain their original properties. Test any of them and they're still unique to Duke Quillian."

I was thinking of the skin cells from his fingers that didn't match any of the blood extracted from the tunnel debris. Now the discrepancy was beginning to make sense.

"But his blood?" I asked.

"He had a perfect recovery from the leukemia, thanks to the bone marrow transplant from his sister."

"And that means from that moment in time on," I said, "that both of them—Duke and Trish Quillian—had blood with an identical DNA profile."

42

"Just tell the lieutenant we're in the Bronx," I said to the detective who answered in the squad room. "We're picking up Trish Quillian. Mike wants to go at her again, so we'll bring her down this afternoon, if she'll come with us." I hung up the phone.

"I bet she has no idea what the connection was between her brother's blood and her own DNA," Mike said.

"You're right. She was sixteen when they did the transplant. Not many people understood what DNA was back then. I would have thought that once the disease was cured, the patient eventually started producing his own blood again. Especially since all the rest of his DNA was intact."

"Forget the science lesson. She's got to know something more about Duke than she told us. And maybe it's time for her to find out about Bex—and the pregnancy. More bones in her backyard than she ever meant to dig up. I've never been so happy to be spit at in my life."

The quiet street had a series of attached houses. Once tree-lined, now there were twisted stumps and vestiges of dead trunks. Deep potholes rutted the roadway, and the cement in the sidewalks was cracked in many places.

"That's the house," I said, pointing ahead on the left at a small stucco building with brown shutters in sore need of a paint job.

"And there's the detail," Mike said, pulling over and parking in front of a gray Honda in which two detectives were sitting, in the event Brendan Quillian paid a visit.

I started to open my door to get out.

"Hold it, Coop. Slide down, keep your head out of sight if you can."

I knew better than to ask what Mike had

seen as he pulled down the visor above his head and opened the newspaper that was next to him on the front seat to screen his face.

"All clear. He's crossing the street and getting into his car."

When I heard the door slam and the engine start, I lifted my head. Trish Quillian was standing in the doorway, turning to take the mail from the box affixed to the side of the house.

"Who'd I miss?" I asked.

"Teddy O'Malley. I wouldn't think by the way he runs me around those tunnels all night he'd have the strength to make a condolence call."

43

"You got that dark green SUV?" Mike said to the detective in the driver's seat.

"Ford Explorer. I wrote down the plate soon as he headed up the stoop."

"Follow him."

"I got orders to sit on the house."

Mike passed his card to the driver and smacked the hood of the car. "And I'm giving you orders to get off your ass and follow him. I'll take over the sister. Tail him, wherever he goes, and call me every fifteen minutes. Chapman. Homicide."

The two cops looked at each other and drove off after O'Malley's SUV.

"They got as much chance seeing Brendan Quillian coming to call as they do of ever seeing Jimmy Hoffa's body again," Mike said, flipping open his phone and asking to speak to Lieutenant Peterson.

We walked up the steps of the house and I knocked on the door while Mike made his call.

"Loo? Better find out who's got the team sitting on the Quillian crib. I just sent them off on a chase, so I guess you'll need to replace them," he said, pausing to listen to a question from his boss. "O'Malley. My pal Teddy O'Malley. Can't imagine why he'd be dropping in on Trish—especially without letting me in on it—but I told the two flatfoots to tell me what he's up to."

Trish Quillian answered the door in the same black polyester track suit she had worn to the station house, with an apron around her waist.

"Is this a bad time?" I asked.

"There's no good one for seeing you two," she said, untying the apron and balling it up.

"I'm sorry. Were you helping your mother with something to eat?"

"What do you care? She's asleep. Let her be."

"May we come in?"

Trish held the door tightly in place for a moment. Then she stepped back, leading us into the small parlor of the still house. She sat on an ottoman and Mike steered me to the sofa opposite it. The room looked as if it had been frozen in time, like photographs I'd seen of the 1950s—cabbage roses had faded on the fabric of the furniture, worn antimacassars covered the arms of most of the mismatched chairs, photographs of family members and a large framed picture of Pope Pius XII hung on the striped wallpaper, which was rolling up at the seams.

"You didn't finish asking me what you need? You gonna keep interrupting my business every single day?" she said, looking back and forth between us, seeming more fearful than she had before.

"Your mother get many visitors, Trish?"

"You got more sense than that, Detective. Nobody much knows she's alive."

"And you?"

"A regular social club. Don't it look it?"

I took in the family snapshots that represented happier days. Trish Quillian in her Communion dress; Mrs. Quillian with her young brood at the beach in Queens, where Brendan's accident had occurred; Brendan and Duke—I guessed—as teenagers, posing with their father at an assortment of construction sites—subway and tunnel entrances, work yards filled with heavy equipment that towered over the kids, familiar landmarks such as the Brooklyn Bridge, City Hall, and the Empire State Building.

"So, Teddy O'Malley, he just happened to be in the neighborhood?"

The veins in Trish Quillian's neck stood out like blue lines in a road map as her jaw tensed and she glared at Mike.

"You watching me now? You peeking through windows and—"

"We drove up just as Teddy walked down the steps. We've met him, Trish. I recognized him, is all."

"Then you know he's the union rep. We had business, him and me. Business to clear up about Duke. Union benefits is all it is," she said, looking down as she twisted the ties on the apron strings.

Mike leaned his elbows on his thighs.

"You gonna be all right, Trish? Do you and your mother get taken care of?"

She closed her eyes and clamped her lips together, fighting back tears as she shook her head up and down.

From the hallway, up the stairs, I could hear the soft groaning noise that I assumed was coming from Trish's mother. I knew we had to be here asking these questions, but the raw misery of this woman's life was difficult to witness.

She wiped her eyes with the apron. "I got things to do. What is it you want now?"

"Like I said before, we're still looking for Brendan." Mike lowered his voice. "You've talked to him, Trish, haven't you?"

"Why don't you just move right in here, Detective? I'll set an extra place at the table for you. Bring your own whiskey. No, I haven't been talking to him."

Mike stayed on her, gently but firmly. "He called you just hours after the shooting in the courthouse, Trish. Why would you lie for him after all these years?"

She stood up as the groaning sound became louder.

"I've got no need to lie for anyone. I got more important things to do."

"Can you come with us down to the station house?" Mike asked.

"You've had your best shot at me already. Can't leave my mother." She pointed over her head.

"Make arrangements for tomorrow, then. You'll need help, won't you?"

"The help of God, Mike Chapman." Trish walked toward the front door, mustering a laugh. "Wasn't my spit any use for you?"

"It was, actually. Led us right back to Duke. Right to how you saved his life."

The frightened young woman stopped in her tracks. "What about Duke?"

"We learned about the transplant," I said. "We found his medical records from all those years ago. He must have been very grateful to you, Trish."

She bit into her lip again. "Maybe he'd have been grateful if he'd lived a little longer. What's that got to do with my saliva? It's the blood I gave him."

Mike brushed back his hair and tossed his head at me. "You come down to my office tomorrow and I'll explain everything."

He knew he wasn't getting any more from her today. He wanted to tease her to take the next step with us in finding her estranged brother.

Mike put his hand on the door handle to let us out as Trish started up the staircase to her mother. "We'll tell you all about that autopsy, too. Your friend Bex—I guess she kept some secrets to herself back then."

Trish had one hand on the banister, gripping it as she turned slowly in response to Mike's bait.

"What kind of secrets, Detective? There wasn't nothing she didn't tell me."

"I don't mean to shock you when you're already so upset over other things."

"I'm too numb to shock anymore. Speak what you mean."

Mike squared his back against the frame of the door. "Bex Hassett was pregnant when she died, Trish. She was almost three months pregnant."

"Those bastards," she said, rocking back and forth as she stood in place on the second step. "Those little bastards took such advantage of that poor girl. Find them for me, Detective, that's what you can do. Go to the Dominican Republic if you have to and lock their asses up. I'd kill whoever did that to her if I could get my hands on him."

Mike took a step toward her and spoke softly. "Then help us with this."

She was staring down at the step.

"Look at me, will you?" Mike said, waiting for her to lift her eyes to meet his. "It's not what you'd like to think it was. It's your brother Brendan who impregnated Bex Hassett. It's Brendan who was the father of her baby."

Trish Quillian crumpled to the floor as if a baseball bat had slammed against the back of her knees. She slid off the steps onto the landing, the balled-up apron rolling across the scuffed wooden floor.

I grabbed it as I kneeled to help her, and a torn envelope dropped from the apron's pocket.

"Don't!" she shouted at me.

Her mother's mumblings got louder, perhaps because of the commotion we were making.

"Are you okay?" I asked.

"Don't touch that," she said as I picked up the envelope, torn at the corners as though it had been stuffed with something at one time.

I could see a postmark and noted that the recipient had been Duke Quillian. I passed it to Trish, who stretched out her bony thumb—not quite fast enough to cover the return address of her brother Brendan—as she pulled the paper from me and buried it in her lap.

44

"Did you see the date?"

"I couldn't," I said. "She grabbed it too quickly."

We were back in the car in front of Trish Quillian's house.

"But you're sure of the names?"

"Positive. Brendan Quillian was in touch with Duke while he was still working for his father-in-law. The return address was the Keating Properties offices."

"So why was she carrying it around in her pocket today? Why did she have it on her when Teddy O'Malley was here?" Mike asked aloud.

"Maybe Teddy gave it to her. Insurance papers or something like that. Maybe it's just a sentimental letter she's been looking at, something that Brendan wrote to Duke."

"Yeah, Coop, that's one sentimental pair of brothers. Them and the Menendez boys."

"I meant that we don't know—"

"If Brendan wrote a thank-you note to big Duke for offing Amanda, you might have wanted to see that, don't you think? You let go of that envelope faster than the old maid card in a losing game."

"The law is such an impediment to your investigative skills, isn't it?" I looked at my watch. "Tell you what. Stick me in a cab and I'll go down to my office for a couple of hours."

"I'd like to stick you somewhere, but it wouldn't be in a cab. You know Battaglia's rules. One of us has to be glued to your side, like it or not."

Mike drove to the end of Trish Quillian's street. "I got one more idea, as long as we're here in the Bronx. You with me?"

"Depends."

"The Musketeers never said stupid things

like that to each other. Neither would Mercer. You're either in or you're out. It
shouldn't depend on anything. It's not like
I'm gonna throw you to the wolves, Coop."

"In. Okay, I'm in. Whatever you say, my
musketeer. Where to?"

"Back to Fort Schuyler. Phinneas Baylor. I
bet he's given some thought to everything
that's happened since we met him last
week."

He had seemed to know most of the history of bad blood between the Hassetts and
the Quillians and been caught in the middle
of their first deadly tunnel incident. "Good
idea."

"I get 'em every now and then," Mike
said, heading off to the old building on the
edge of Long Island Sound.

Phin was just as we'd left him. A bit more
whiskers on his face, an almost empty sixteen-ounce bottle of beer, and the trusty
cane resting beside him on the bench. The
afternoon sun warmed the ramparts, and he
was leaning back so that his already tanned
face could soak in more rays. He opened his
eyes as he heard our footsteps.

"You imitating me, son? You're limping

worse than me," Phin said, holding out his walking stick to Mike.

"Nah. Just the uneven stones here. Thought I just sprained it, but maybe pulled a ligament. Nothing to complain about to you."

Mike sat next to Phin on the bench while I stood opposite, watching a few kids chase gulls off the battlement.

"So what did you think of the news about Brendan Quillian?"

Phin's expression never changed. He lifted his face to the sunlight and closed his eyes again. "Didn't give it much thought."

"My friend here—Ms. Cooper—she almost got killed by the guy. I'm giving it all the thought I can, Phin."

Baylor took his sunglasses out of his shirt pocket and put them on, but the lenses were so dark I couldn't see whether he opened his eyes.

"I as much as told you they were miserable folk, the Quillians. Much as told you no good comes from being around them."

"That wasn't a choice Coop had, being around Brendan or not."

"Why does everybody think I'm any help?"

"Everybody? Who's everybody?"

Phin didn't answer.

"Guys been coming around asking questions?"

"Yeah."

"Like who?" Mike said.

"Like guys who are willing to pay me for information. Do you pay? I didn't want none of their money, but I've got my needs."

Mike reached into his pocket and pulled out some bills. "I can give you a down payment, Phin. Lots more where this came from."

The old man turned his head and lifted his glasses for a moment.

"Who's been here, Phin?" Mike had a couple of twenties. He handed them to Baylor.

"Bobby Hassett, for one."

"Looking for Brendan, of course," Mike said. "To kill him?"

"Not up to me to figure that out. I don't want no part of any of them."

"But did he tell you anything? Did he tell you what his beef is?"

Phin tapped the great stone floor in front of him with his cane. "How much more of that you got?"

"The green stuff? Coop's my banker. She'll go back to the car and get some cash from her handbag before we leave, won't you, kid?"

"Bobby tried every which way to come at me," Phin said. "Told me a pretty ugly story about Brendan. A personal one. Maybe too private to mention."

"We haven't got time to worry about privacy now, Phin. Brendan's killed one woman already and he's still armed. I need to find him before somebody else gets hurt."

"Yeah, but I got a daughter, too. You don't need to spread these stories."

"Is it about Rebecca Hassett?" I asked. "Did Bobby tell you something—something about her that you're reluctant to tell us?"

Phin lifted the cane onto his lap and studied Mike's face. "You know about Bex?"

"The medical examiner did another—"

"Bobby told me," Phin said, shaking his head from side to side. "They should never have disturbed that grave. No good can come of it."

"So he told you Bex was pregnant when she was killed?"

Phin took a deep breath of the salt air before he answered. "Yeah. Yes, he did."

"How could he know?" I asked Mike, who held up a hand to stop me from going further. I wasn't aware that the medical examiner had released that information to the family yet.

"So it's true then?" Phin was too sharp to miss a beat.

"Yes," I said.

"Well, it wasn't the doctor who told Bobby. He heard it from his own mother." Phin's voice had a slight edge of anger.

"His mother?" Mike asked. "She's dead."

"Bobby was playing on my heartstrings, I guess. I'd known his mother a very long time, like everybody else in our isolated little world. She only died half a year ago. Kept this inside her since it happened."

"What did he tell you?"

Phin Baylor straightened out his bad leg and rubbed his thigh. "The mother was dying for months. Got sick right about the same time you people locked up Brendan Quillian. 'Twas all over the papers, that story about him having his wife killed."

He stopped talking as two mothers walked by with their kids.

"Nobody's told you about the fistfight?" Phin asked.

"No," Mike said.

"I guess it wasn't clocked up to anything more than the long-standing feud between the families," Phin said, reaching out to put his hand on Mike's arm, which was across the back of the bench. "Bobby was pleased as punch when you locked up Brendan for murdering his own wife."

"I kind of liked it myself."

"Well, next time he saw Duke Quillian in the water tunnel, while they were working the dig, young Bobby told him that Brendan was a scumbag. Just tweaking him was all. Nobody in the crowd ever liked Brendan, him being such a snob and all."

"For that, Duke fought him?" Mike asked.

"No, no, son. But Duke gave it to Bobby, in front of half the crew. Back and forth it was about each other's kin, naming every miserable thing each of them had done. Finally, Duke told him his sister—Bex," Phin said, looking down at his feet, "told him that poor dead girl was a whore. A whore who deserved to die. Said that everybody knew it. And that's when Bobby started swinging."

So all those years, Duke Quillian had kept the secret—the one that he shared with his brother, and with Bex—to himself.

"And Bobby hadn't known about his sister's pregnancy?" Mike asked.

"Nope. That's what he told me, just yesterday evening. He went to his mother, practically on her deathbed she was then, to see what she knew."

"What did his mother tell him?" Mike asked.

"I don't like saying these things, son."

"You're almost there, Phin. Tell us what she said."

"I can only go by what Bobby's told me. Is it gospel? I don't know."

"I realize that," Mike said.

Phin's dark glasses masked his expression. "Bobby said his mother was dying— weak and sick and all that. But she actually wanted to talk about Rebecca, was relieved to tell her story."

Phin paused and lifted the rubber tip of his cane to point at me. "You'll excuse me, miss, for talking about this. Mrs. Hassett told Bobby she knew Bex was pregnant— missing her monthly, getting sick every day, starting to act out with all of them. Mrs.

Hassett, now she was just a widow, then, trying to deal with this all by herself. Tried to get her child to talk about it, figure out where they could send her to have the baby—give it up for adoption, give it away. And, well, that's when Bex just started acting all crazy, hanging out in the park, not coming home at night. Yeah, she knew her little girl was pregnant."

"And she knew it was Brendan who was responsible?" Mike asked.

"She thought it, Bobby said. She always believed it. Bex wouldn't tell her mother that, but she was pining away for him when he married that rich girl. And she was calling him all the time, just like Brendan was telephoning Bex right up to the day he went on his honeymoon."

Mrs. Hassett had told her son more facts than she had ever felt comfortable enough to give to the detectives all those many years ago.

Phin hoisted himself up from the bench and walked, leaning on his cane, to look out at the view of the calm Sound and its armada of sailboats.

"So that's what Bobby told *you*," Mike said, walking after him. "Now what is it he was willing to pay to get from you in exchange?"

Phin didn't answer.

"What does he think you know?"

"How to find Brendan Quillian," he said, without looking back over his shoulder.

Mike shrugged his shoulders and held a finger to his temple. "I don't get it. You have any contact with Brendan since he was a kid?"

"Nope."

"You have any idea where he is?"

"Could be in Timbuktu by now. Wouldn't you?"

"Hard to get there—or to Newark—when you bust out of jail with fifty bucks and a blind eye that maybe you could hide for a bit behind sunglasses, but sooner or later someone would spot," Mike said.

"He's got no form of identification for serious travel. No credit cards to use." I wanted Brendan Quillian to be as far away from me as humanly possible, but the reality was that he didn't have the basic resources to let him leave town.

"That's not why Bobby wanted your advice, Phin. He'd go to a frigging travel agent for that. What does he want from you?"

"Same as you do. Where to look. That is, if Brendan was dumb enough to stay in town. Or hiding here until he can figure a way out of the city. You've been huntin' for him, too, haven't you?"

The small boats putting around the Sound had a smooth rhythm that contrasted with the sharp tension that was building between Phin and Mike.

"Day and night."

"Where at?"

"Every place Teddy O'Malley takes me."

Phin laughed.

"What are you snickering at?"

"He's a kid, O'Malley. Where's he had you at?"

"Water Tunnel Number Three—and anything connected to it. The valve control center in the Bronx. The digs in every part of the city. The hole for the new subway on the East Side."

Phin swiveled on his good leg and leaned against the battlement. "Surely he knows Brendan Quillian couldn't be hiding in any of those places."

Mike had hardly slept, chasing after O'Malley to every underground tunnel and construction project.

"Why not? Suppose someone—someone loyal to Duke, maybe even friendly once with their old man—part of the incestuous fraternity you guys make of yourselves—figured a way to shelter him till they could help him get out of town?"

"That's perfectly logical, son. But not in any of the places O'Malley's been going. A wild-goose chase—that's what he's had you do."

"Why's that?"

"'Cause they're all active digs, the spots he's taken you to. There's a place to hide someone in every one of them—that's for certain. But Brendan wouldn't make it in any holes like those. He's spooked, the boy—spooked ever since the explosion that took his eye. He won't make it in a place where they're still blasting, still setting off the dynamite. His nerves would kill him before he got to the end of the first day. I'll bet firing a gun in the courtroom—even though he did it himself to get his freedom—that probably set him on pins and needles all over again."

Mike was nodding his head, absorbing Phin's point.

"Is that what you told Bobby Hassett?" Mike asked, knowing we were at least a day behind the man who hated Brendan Quillian with renewed passion.

"I didn't have to tell him that. He knew it."

"Then what did he want from you?" Mike bored in on the old man. "Exactly what, Phin?"

"What you folks should have been smart enough to think of," Phin said, brooking none of Mike's swagger and poking him in the chest as he answered.

"Okay, so we're ignorant. Give us a hand."

"Some Quillian history," Phin said, now pointing the same finger at his own head. "The Quillians worked on every sandhog job in this city going back five generations. Bridges, tunnels, viaducts, subways, sewers—there ain't nothing below or above the streets of New York that they weren't part of."

"The Hassetts, too," Mike said.

"Yeah. Sometimes they worked the same job sites and sometimes different ones. Bobby's clever enough to know that Brendan Quillian would want to be someplace he'd consider safe."

"Where he'd be comfortable. A familiar setting," Mike said, picking up on Phin's logic. "Maybe a place his father took him to when he was a kid. That's what Bobby was asking about."

Phin Baylor cracked a smile. "Now you're on track."

"You tell him anything? You give him a list of the ones you could remember?"

"I told you I wasn't looking for more trouble, Mike."

"What'll buy us that same list from you, Phin? A hundred bucks?"

"That might get me thinking."

"Start thinking out loud."

"Stay out of all those active tunnels where O'Malley's had you scrambling around. If Brendan Quillian's still in this city, then he's in some sandhog ghost town. An abandoned space. Nothing there but him and the rats."

Mike was listening intently.

"And one thing for sure. He'll need it to be deadly quiet, Chapman. Brendan'll want the place to be silent as a tomb."

45

We paid our informant enough to keep him in cheap beer for a week and started the drive back to Manhattan.

"Pick up Teddy O'Malley and meet us in Coop's office. We should be there by six for some sandhog brainstorming." Mike was on the phone with Mercer. "Peterson put a detail on him when we saw him leave Trish Quillian's house this afternoon. Get in touch with those detectives. They should know exactly where he is and bring him in."

I waited until Mike finished to call

Battaglia and ask him to appeal to the mayor's office to get some juice for what we needed to do. I wanted experts—if not tonight, by tomorrow—from every city agency that had tunnels and construction projects, people who knew exactly where every one of them was. DEP, Transportation, Port Authority. I told Laura to reserve the conference room so that we could spread the crew out with maps in order to chart together every deserted dig in the five boroughs.

Traffic snarled the Deegan Expressway and the Triborough Bridge crossing, slowing the ride back into the city. We were stalled in gridlock just above Canal Street as it approached 7 p.m., both impatient to get to my office and start a fresh look at Brendan Quillian's options.

"It's like Saddam's spider hole, Coop. We're sitting on top of it, somewhere. We just need to find the right opening.

"You got Teddy yet?" Mike called Mercer again to let him know we were getting closer to Hogan Place. "What do you mean those mopes lost him? Jeez. I should have followed him myself. Did you leave a message on his cell?"

Mercer answered and Mike spoke again. "Good."

He listened and then exploded as he pulled the car over to the curb and threw his laminated plaque onto the dashboard. "Shit! How could they lose him in the subway? *There?* It makes no sense. Meet us at the entrance to the City Hall Station . . . Yeah, the East Side one—that old kiosk right across from the Municipal Building. Fifteen minutes, half an hour. Bring company, Mercer. Coop's with me."

Bring company was a command Mike rarely gave. I got chills at the idea that he thought we needed backup.

He took a small flashlight from the glove compartment and stuck it in his rear pants pocket, got out of the car, and started jogging lamely to the intersection of Lafayette and Canal streets, just a block ahead. It was the entrance to the downtown #6 train—the Lexington Avenue local. Pedestrians walking north from the hub of government offices and courthouses slowed our southbound run, and I caught up with Mike as he headed down the steps into the station.

"Stay with me," he called out to me. He

swiped his MetroCard to get through the turnstile, then swiped again so I could get in, too.

"What did Mercer say?"

"Those jerks lost O'Malley after tailing him all afternoon. He left his car a few blocks from the station, then got on the six going downtown. Took it one stop to the Brooklyn Bridge," Mike said. "The dicks got off there, but never saw Teddy again."

"You mean they lost him in the crowd?"

"They told Mercer they saw him on the platform—and no, it wasn't even that busy. But when the group of people cleared, O'Malley was gone."

"Doesn't everybody have to get off the train there? You can't go any farther south, can you?"

The Brooklyn Bridge stop of the IRT #6 train was the last station on the route from lower Manhattan, at the foot of the great bridge, all the way uptown to Pelham Bay Park.

"Not unless you ride the loop," Mike said.

The train pulled into the station and opened its doors to admit us. Tired workers on their way home rested their heads against the windows behind them, while several reading books and newspapers glanced up. I walked briskly behind Mike, moving through three cars to get to the front of the train, behind the motorman's cab. I grasped on to poles and straps as I moved ahead, the train rolling from side to side as it barreled forward.

Mike turned to reach for my hand as we stepped into the front car.

"What's the loop? What are you talking about?"

We were face-to-face. I grabbed on to Mike's shoulder to steady myself.

"Just the kind of place we're looking for, only Mercer didn't have the advantage of our conversation with Phin Baylor. And Teddy O'Malley may have led us there unwittingly."

"Where?"

"City Hall Station. The ceremonial terminal of the first subway system in New York. Maybe the most elegant station ever built."

"But it's closed. It's been closed for fifty years. You've been inside it?"

"It was reopened briefly, to prepare for its centennial in 2004. We had to check it out as part of our Terrorist Task Force duties. The commissioner ordered it shut down again pretty quickly after 9/11. It's directly under City Hall—too risky to chance an attack."

"And the loop?"

"When all the passengers are disgorged from the Number Six at the Brooklyn Bridge platform, the empty train makes a sharp right turn off the local tracks onto a loop. The cars go onto the actual track of the original City Hall Station. That one was way too short to handle the longer modern subway cars, so it's only used for a turnaround."

"Of the Number Six?"

"Yeah, the local makes the tight curve and reappears on the uptown side—completely empty—for the ride north. In the process of looping around, it goes underground deep enough to cross under the express tracks, below grade."

"A typical sandhog job, dug into the bedrock," I said. "And a phantom subway station. There was even a photograph of the Quillian boys at City Hall with their father in the living room of Trish's house."

"You saw that? Fits Phin's theory. Figures Brendan's old man would have gotten them in for a visit. Transit used to give tours of the place until a few years back."

The train jolted to a stop and the motor-man announced the end of the line.

Mike charged forward, displaying his gold shield.

"You gotta get off here, buddy. I don't care who you are. Take your date and go," the motorman said, turning back to his controls and sliding the panel shut behind him.

Mike blocked the closing door with his body. "We're coming with you."

"I can't ride nobody around. It's the rules. You oughta know that," the young man said, his annoyance turning to anger. "-You're making me late."

"And you're making me mad. Move it."

"I could lose my job over this."

"Go slow," Mike said, as the car lurched ahead, around the curve into a darkened tunnel. It was listing to the right side, and I balanced myself against the railing of the first bench.

"Stop it. Right here."

"First you wanna ride with me, now you want me to shut it down. But I can't," the motorman protested.

"I'll bet you can," Mike said, lifting his

jacket back far enough to reveal the revolver on his hip.

Another sudden stop and the doors opened.

"Jump down, Coop. Be careful."

I held on to the door handle and lowered myself to the platform, trying to adjust to the blackness around me. Mike followed as the motorman closed the doors and pulled away, the lights from within the cars flickering to reveal the arched ceilings over the narrow walkway, and the deep blue-and-tan glass lettering of the words CITY HALL.

The last rumblings of the long train grew more distant. There was nothing but darkness around us and the exquisite silence of a tomb.

46

Mike and I stood in place for several minutes without exchanging a word. I was listening for any sound, any noise at all to suggest someone else was anywhere within this great vaulted space. Slowly my eyes began to adjust to the blackness that surrounded us.

I whispered into Mike's ear, "You have a plan?"

He nodded, holding his forefinger over his lips, then pointing to row after row of brick arches overhead. He mouthed a single word: "Echoes."

I didn't think he could get any closer to me, but he leaned in and cupped a hand over my ear. "I know where this leads. Good place to hide."

My pulse was racing and the stillness of the abandoned station was unnerving. "Do you know how to get out once you've found it?"

I could see Mike's white teeth. "I never go in unless I do. And Mercer's up above, watching over you. We move when you hear the sound of the next train."

It was almost six minutes before the headlights of the silver subway car cast a beam that bounced off the curved wall, followed a fraction of a second later by the noise of the steel wheels.

Mike walked quickly, still limping, to a staircase twenty feet ahead and climbed the first few steps, turning sideways and pressing against the handrail as the train passed through. I did the same thing.

I looked above me for the source of whatever natural light seemed to bathe the lower steps. I guessed that the glass skylight in the ceiling must have been situated in the

park in front of City Hall, capturing and filtering the remaining rays that marked the
end of the long June day.

From this vantage point, I could see the
beauty of the original architecture. The tunnel was entirely without angles, the struc-
tural vaults and smooth curves continuing in
a semicircle until they disappeared out of
sight in both directions. Brass chandeliers
without bulbs dangled from the tiled ceiling
that they'd once illuminated. I tried to calm
myself by studying the elegance of the cen-
tury-old design, but Mike tugged on my arm
and I was ready to advance with him deeper
into the darkness again.

Another dozen steps and we reached the
top of the staircase. Mike removed the
flashlight from his pocket and shone it
around the edges of the steel enclosure that
sealed off the exit, pressing against it with
his left hand at the same time.

"Dead end," he said. "C'mon."

He must have seen the anxiety in my troubled expression.

"There's four of these doors
know there's still an opening in on
I've been through there."

He shone the light so that we

scend. "Wait for the next train to go past. I don't want any nosy motorman to see us and decide to stop," he said when we reached the halfway mark.

Minutes later, another local hurtled through the loop to turn and begin its uptown run.

Mike led me along the platform to a second set of steps, also brightened by a second skylight.

He took the first three stairs, then stopped and focused his light on the old cobblestone. "This is the one."

"How do you know?"

"Rat droppings. More likely people have come and gone this way—more likely there's something to eat inside. There are guys who call themselves creepers, Alex. They find these abandoned spaces and make ways to break into them, just for sport. If I had a nose like a rat, I'd have made first grade the year I came on the job. The crawl space is up here. I'm pretty sure of it."

He backtracked and flipped open his phone. "Mercer? Can you hear me?" he said. "Yeah, it's breaking up because I'm in tunnel. Inside the old City Hall Station.

Call Peterson. We mapped this all out for the task force a couple of years back. Have him cover the exits and entrances . . . What? What? Can't hear you."

Mike started up the steps again. He turned and saw me looking over my shoulder at the train tracks. He held up his thumb like a hitchhiker on the road. "Out?"

I caught up to him.

"Look, I can wave down a motorman. Get one to take you out," Mike said softly.

I hesitated but didn't answer.

"It's like a rabbit warren inside. An old wooden ticket booth, subway cars that have rotted out over time, piles of old IRT station signs. If Brendan Quillian is actually hiding here, I promise I'll call in the cavalry. I just think Teddy O'Malley is playing some kind of cat-and-mouse game with me and I want to see what it is."

"I'm a musketeer, aren't I?"

Mike continued up to the top of the tall staircase and I followed. This time, as soon as he flashed his light on the door, the two-foot-square opening at its base became obvious. A trapdoor lifted from the top, on a hinge, as he pressed on it.

"Can you do it?"

"Do what?" I asked.

"Crawl on your belly like a reptile. Four feet. Maybe six."

"Remember me?" I whispered. "I'm the one who's claustrophobic."

"A short shimmy. Then it expands onto this huge mezzanine. Wide-open spaces that you like, with a grand staircase that floats up like a back door to City Hall. Put on your tap shoes and you can do a Busby Berkeley while I see if my hunch about O'Malley is right."

"Won't the mayor be surprised to see us, coming in through his basement?"

"That's why the plan to revamp it didn't work." Mike knelt down and shone the light in. "Not as dusty as you'd think. Transit buffs and creepers sneaking in and out of here all the time."

"But why?"

"Whack jobs. There are antiquated, closed-up stations—not quite as nice as this one—all over town. These train nuts love to make believe it's the good old days. Ten of them camped out here two years ago and threw a party."

Mike was about to kneel down when his cell phone vibrated. "Yeah? Where are you,

Mercer?" He waited for an answer. "Has O'Malley returned your call? Don't you think it's strange that he hasn't? A visit to Trish Quillian, and then he simply goes out of range and we lose him."

There was a longer pause. "Coming in how? Behind us? That'll make Coop happy. Second staircase after the train makes the curve into the station. Tell the loo this might be for nothing, but he's welcome to join us."

"What will I be happy about?"

"Mercer's taking the train into the loop just the way we did. Peterson wants a team ready at the old entrance, just in case we're onto something. And not a peep back from O'Malley. In with me? Those slacks looked ready for the dry cleaners last time you wore them."

"In with you," I said quietly.

Mike stretched out on the floor. "Grab my foot, you'll feel better."

He had become much more reckless since the tragic accident that took Valerie's life. I didn't know how to slow him down, and I didn't want to leave him in this tunnel now. I was tired and confused, and hoping that Mercer would catch up with us quickly.

Mike propelled himself through the short

passageway—the kind I imagined one might find at the base of an Egyptian pyramid—and I followed on my hands and knees, holding on to his good ankle whenever I could. He turned off his flashlight as his head emerged through the narrow space.

Within seconds we had entered the large chamber of the original station. He stood up and helped me to my feet.

Again, as my eyes adjusted to the darkness, I turned slowly in a circle to take in the enormous room that had been the crown jewel in New York's first underground transit system—a little vaulted town beneath the city.

Mike signaled me to stand still and not to speak. Silhouettes of the token booth and a decommissioned "redbird"—one of the old painted subway cars that had been taken out of service years ago—took shape in front of us on the mezzanine level of the original station. Larger chandeliers than those on the platform hung from the interiors of the tall arches against cream-colored tiles that glistened in the background.

But still not a sound to be heard.

Three minutes. Then five passed before

Mike satisfied himself that there was no one in proximity to us and took a few more steps. He had drawn his gun and waved his left arm to motion me to fall in place behind him.

I waited as he approached the token booth. He leaned his back against the outer corner of it, then pivoted around and pointed his gun inside, the way I had seen him do on so many occasions when reconnoitering a dangerous location. It was empty.

Fifteen feet farther into the station was the redbird, left on display from an earlier renovation. The doors were open, and as I got closer, I could see that the dried bamboo strips on the seats had been gnawed through and the stuffing scattered on the floor of the car. But no one was inside.

Mike pointed off to the side and, emboldened by the quiet reception, turned on his flashlight again. There was indeed a grand staircase, and over the span in front of it, the lettering that identified city hall in even larger tiles, surrounded by a bright green ceramic that lightened the drab, earthenware shades of the ones around it.

"That's the way up to the original kiosk

entrance. Let's see if there's still an exit to get out to the street," Mike said.

He leaned on the railing along the wall to support his bad foot, and I climbed beside him. At the top of the landing, he bent over to rub his ankle as I made the turn and started on up. I could see the black wrought-iron framework of a doorway and was glad it was in easy reach, hoping it would be rigged for egress to Centre Street.

I stopped myself when I saw something else—almost like a padded black cushion—blocking the staircase at the very top.

"There's something there, Mike," I said, short of breath—from fear, not exertion.

"Give me the light."

He took the last few steps in pairs and, reaching my side, directed the beam at the floor.

I saw the blood first. Pools of red blood—still wet, and still more oozing from the hulking frame of whoever was lying in front of the doorway.

Mike went even closer and rolled back the shoulder of the large body.

"My God," he said. "O'Malley. It's Teddy O'Malley."

He grabbed Teddy's wrist to feel for a

pulse, but the two bullet holes to the back, as I could see from the blood that had seeped out of the wounds, had done their job. "The man is dead."

47

Mike and I got down the steps as fast as we could travel. When I reached the station floor, I could hear Mercer's voice coming from the direction of the crawl space.

"We're okay. Stay there. We're coming out," I said.

"Brendan Quillian?" Mercer asked.

"I think he killed O'Malley. Don't know if he's still here or not. Maybe he's taken off already—got what he wanted or needed from O'Malley."

Mike reached my side. "Move it, Coop," he said, pushing my back.

For the first time, I heard noise in the great room behind Mike. I looked around, terrified that Quillian might be coming after us.

Rats, three or four of them, were running in the shadows cast across the room by Mike's flashlight. Their tiny claws scratched at the flooring as they raced along.

"They smell the blood," Mike said. "Get out of here."

I scrambled through the crawl space and was met by Mercer, who helped me to my feet and reached for Mike after me. The trapdoor dropped on its hinge and slammed shut.

Before we could speak, I could hear the next train approaching. Mike stepped to the edge of the platform and aimed the flashlight at his badge, his gun reholstered on his hip. This time, he wanted the motorman to stop for us.

The train seemed to brake as it approached the tight curve in the black tunnel, but the driver was probably unable to see Mike's detective shield, so he speeded up again at the sight of the three of us in a place we were not supposed to be.

"You know this tunnel?" Mercer asked Mike. "Any other way out?"

"Yeah, there's a few choices. Probably the easiest is how O'Malley walked in from the Brooklyn Bridge stop. There's an abandoned strip of track you pick up right off the far north end of the platform. Takes you back to civilization."

Mercer speed-dialed the lieutenant on his cell. "Bringing out Mike and Alex. Couldn't get the last train to stop. Motorman must think we look like a politically correct stickup team, trying to hijack him. You think you can do that for us, or do we have to slog our way out through some defunct tunnel Chapman thinks he can find?" Mercer said. "And Teddy O'Malley's dead, inside the station."

Mercer listened to Peterson's response. "Wait up," he said to the lieutenant, "let me ask Mike."

"What'd he say?" Mike asked.

"You want to hold tight here? He'll have a team try to get on with one of the next motormen to pick us up. He'd prefer that to having you tiptoe around the third-rail hot spots. Wants to know if you think Quillian's still around."

"I'm clueless. Tell him to bring in all the backup he's got. Slowly and carefully. There's all kinds of tunnels and passageways inside this place."

"I've got an idea," I said. "Can I talk to him?"

Mercer passed the phone to me.

"Alex, you okay? Battaglia'll have my ass with you being in there," Peterson said.

"Yes, I'm fine. Would you call over to the Fifth?" I asked. The nearby Fifth Precinct station house was on Elizabeth Street, a two-minute ride from our location, with lights and sirens blaring. "Tell whoever's on the desk to send a patrol car to a shop on Bayard called Uncle Charlie's. They all know it."

"What for?"

"As fast as they can go, tell Charlie I need *baozhang*. Hear me? I said *baozhang*. Tell him I need bamboo sticks, as big as he's got. And matches—I want matches, too." I had been reminded of the sticks when I saw the dried-out bamboo seats of the antique train car.

"Alex, what kind of—"

"Trust me on this, Loo. Do it fast."

The three of us were marooned on the

narrow strip of platform until Peterson could get a train to stop and pick us up. The skylight that hung overhead was now sheathed in darkness as night settled over the city.

I was sandwiched between the two men as we waited for an escort out.

"*Baozhang?* I haven't thought of the stuff since you convicted that Asian gang of the Chinese New Year rape. You planning a celebration?" Mercer said.

"I'm celebrating big as soon as we get out of here. No need to wait for the Fourth of July."

"I'm not in the mood for a take-out dinner, whatever the hell you just ordered," Mike said.

"I like her thinking, Mike." Mercer patted me on the back, stroking my shoulder for reassurance.

Off to the south of us came some unexpected noise. Instinctively, Mike raised his arm and the light caught another phalanx of rats—big ones, with long, pink tails, scurrying up and over the edge of the platform, disappearing out of sight around the curve.

Mike started to walk in that direction. "You wait with Coop," he said to Mercer.

"Stay tight, Mike."

He waved off Mercer's admonition.

"You've got the only light. What are you doing?"

Mike stopped.

We both knew that he was looking for Quillian, but Mercer didn't want the killer to be found until some reinforcements arrived. Something had caused the rodents to dance out of their habitat within the old station. If this wasn't their regular feeding time, then perhaps their flight was caused by an intruder.

I looked back to the north, willing a train to arrive, but the evening schedule would bring them less frequently now.

"So there's a side tunnel off to the north," Mercer said, barely loud enough for me to hear. "And what about that way? To the south."

As Mike pointed, we could see to our left the active tracks of the old loop, where the #6 train finished its turnaround. "Over to the right of the raised platform there's another black hole, now abandoned—another sandhog excavation. It's a cylinder—nine feet around—built as a pneumatic mail system almost a century ago."

"Does it open onto this?" Mercer asked.

Mike nodded.

My eyes were playing tricks with me now. The rats were running in our direction, turned back by whatever had disturbed them. The glare from their eyes, like beady little headlights coming toward us, drew my sights to the level of the ground. But along the distant curving wall, something taller—something the size of a human—was moving slowly in the opposite direction.

I didn't want to call the figure to Mike's attention. It couldn't be more than a minute before the next train was due into the loop. I didn't want him going after this desperate man alone.

I looked over my shoulder again but saw no sign of the #6. When I turned my head back, Mike had already spotted the figure under the farthest arch of the platform.

"Quillian! Freeze!" Both Mike and Mercer drew their guns.

"Alex," Mercer said in his firmest voice, "get back up on there."

I retreated to the second step of the staircase, my heart pounding as I watched Mike start to trot lamely toward Quillian.

The fugitive raised an arm. He had a gun, too, and I had no idea how much ammunition he had left, or whether he had discharged any bullets in the days since he'd left the courtroom—before putting two rounds in Teddy O'Malley's back.

"Give it up, Quillian," Mike said. "There's cops on both ends of the tunnel—and a very hot third rail in between."

Mike was too far from Quillian—and it was pitch-black around them—for either to take aim and shoot, but I ached at how exposed both Mike and Mercer were on the narrow platform. Once the train made its approach, they'd be silhouetted in its high beams and at a great disadvantage in the standoff if Quillian fired at them.

"Come over here," I hissed at both of them, but they didn't move.

Brendan Quillian must have been inching farther away, his back against the wall. I couldn't see the movement, but I heard Mike yell at him to stop.

Then his shadow picked up speed as he seemed to reach a corner and round it. Mike barked again and ran away from Mercer and me, slowed by his weak ankle.

He reached the end of the platform and paused before jumping down—practically three feet—to the bed of the train tracks.

His bad leg crumpled beneath him from the impact of his weight. This time Mike screamed in pain as he toppled over and slid against the tracks.

48

Mercer took off in Mike's direction in a flash and Quillian disappeared from sight. I dashed after Mercer and reached the platform's edge just as he jumped down and leaned over beside Mike.

"Go on back, Alex."

I sat and eased myself off the platform. "It's safer being with you. At least you've both got guns."

"This isn't any sprain, man. I'd be surprised if you haven't torn a ligament or broken a bone," Mercer said. "Can you stand? Let me help you up."

Mercer picked his head up, looking for Quillian to reappear, while he tried to help Mike up at the same time. His revolver was still in his right hand.

But as Mike had landed, his good leg had shot out in front of him. It was bent to the side, and his foot was wedged under a tie of the old train tracks, where once tightly packed gravel had loosened and created crevices like the one that now trapped him.

I was on my hands and knees, trying to ease Mike's foot out of the loafer without further twisting it. Mercer attempted to lift him again with one arm, keeping the gun as steady as he could with his other.

I saw the lights of the #6 gleaming on the tracks a second before I heard the blast from its horn. Peterson's cops must have ordered the driver to barrel in at full speed to rescue the three of us from the isolated platform. Only now we were directly in the train's path.

Mike clutched my shoulder again, trying hopelessly to pull himself out from under the grip of the tie. His fingers dug deep into me before he gave up and let go.

"Run, Coop!" Mike yelled at me. "Dammit, girl, run!"

I tugged and tugged, but the heel of his shoe had become stuck between the steel and a rotting piece of wood covered by gravel. I wasn't going anywhere without both men. The sweat was streaming out of my pores as I realized there was every likelihood we'd be crushed to death under the wheels of the subway cars that were racing to bring us to safety.

"Take her, Mercer, will you, for Christ's sake?"

"Make the damn thing stop," I shouted.

Mercer's ebony skin looked as dark as the rest of the station's interior. He picked up the flashlight that had dropped to the ground next to Mike and stood in the middle of the tracks—all that separated Mike and me from the oncoming train—swinging the small beam around and around in a circle until the driver jerked his powerful machine to a sudden halt, inches from where we were huddled together.

49

"What the—?" a young detective asked as he stepped off the front subway car, his shield displayed in his pocket. He was carrying a large brown paper bag in his left hand, his gun in his right. "You guys lost your minds?"

"Mercer Wallace. Special Victims. My partner's got his foot stuck in the track."

"Chapman? That you? You oughta lay off the fancy legwork. You caught your perp?"

"No. Not yet," Mercer said.

"There's more ways out of here than

Osama bin Laden has caves," Mike called out. "Quillian may even know about most of them 'cause he came here as a kid with his old man. Can you get me an EMT? I think I've got a fracture."

I hoisted myself up onto the platform. "I'm Alex Cooper. Did the lieutenant send this bag for me?"

"Yeah," the detective said, handing it over, and taking a matchbook from his pocket. "And these. I'll radio for a bus. We got to make it snappy. The trains will be stacking up behind us. They'll be really restless to get going."

"Make it snappy?" Mike said. "The train gets any closer to me my foot's gonna break in two. I'm not looking for a Phinneas Baylor saw-off-your-ankle-yourself solution."

The detective pulled a walkie-talkie from his pants pocket and stepped back into the subway car, directing the driver to reverse direction by thirty feet—perhaps relieving the pressure on the tracks—while he radioed for a team of paramedics.

I turned to Mercer, who was kneeling beside Mike, using his penknife to jab at the wood. I leaned over, intent on removing the shoe from Mike's foot to ease his obvious pain.

"Nobody move."

I was startled by the sound of Brendan Quillian's voice. He had inched along the darkened tunnel wall and was no more than twenty feet from us, his gun pointed directly at Mike's chest. He was shielded by one of the arches that formed beneath the vaulted ceiling.

"You, Miss Cooper. Take each of their guns and bring them over here to me."

"Don't move, Coop," Mike said, grabbing my wrist with his hand. "He doesn't have enough cartridges to shoot all of us."

"Stay on your knees, Wallace. Tell her to bring me your guns."

Mike's fingers were pressing into my wrist. I looked to Mercer for his reaction and got nothing but a stone-faced stare. His gun was back in his waistband, where he had placed it to work on Mike's foot. He shifted his large body to try to block me from Quillian's line of fire.

The subway car with the young detective was just out of sight around the curve behind us. He couldn't see what was happening.

"We'd be dead already if he had three rounds left," Mike said to Mercer and me, loud enough for Quillian to hear. "Think about it. He wouldn't be talking to us."

Maybe that was true, or maybe he was being cautious until he got close enough to use his ammunition well.

"I just want to get out of here," Quillian said.

"So did O'Malley," Mike said. He was wincing in pain, ready to counter any excuses Quillian threw at him.

"I don't want to kill the three of you, but you know I'm capable of doing it."

"You killed your own child, you sick bastard. I know there's nothing to stop you from shooting us if you had the lead," Mike said. "If that fucking evil eye could see us at this range, maybe you would."

Mike was throwing it all at Brendan, while I couldn't help but think of the irony of his killing the baby he'd conceived with Bex, then never being able to father kids with Amanda.

"How about Teddy O'Malley, Brendan? Did he double-cross you?"

Quillian didn't answer.

"He brought something to you in here that

you needed, didn't he? Food, for one thing? And I bet it was money. I bet he went to your sister's house to get cash for your unexpected trip out of town."

I was trying to figure which direction Quillian wanted to go to make his escape. If he could find the outlet to the street that he was looking for, maybe he'd let us be.

Now footsteps echoed on the platform behind us. The young detective sauntered forward, walkie-talkie in hand, no way of knowing that we'd been joined by Brendan Quillian.

"The bus is coming, Chapman," he called out.

"You!" Quillian shouted from the darkened tracks. "Drop your gun and your radio right there. Get down on your knees. Bend over and put your hands on top of your head if you don't want to see these three get blown up."

"Don't listen to the bastard," Mike called out, but the young cop knew he had walked into a trap he couldn't make sense of, so his equipment clattered to the platform as he followed the killer's orders.

"Duke did all your dirty work, didn't he?" Mike said. "Ever since you were a kid."

"Let me see you lay your guns down and I'll be out of here before there's any more blood, okay?"

Brendan knew as well as we did that he had only minutes before the EMTs—and perhaps Peterson's backup forces—would be in the tube.

Mike was shouting now, calling Brendan a baby killer, the noise reverberating in the tunnel. If Quillian dared to come out from behind the archway, both Mercer and Mike were capable of picking him off.

"That's a lie! I didn't know Duke was going to kill Bex. That was his idea—that was his plan to let me start a new life. He took it on his own to do that when I left the country. I didn't talk to him after that—not for years. I turned my back on the whole damn bunch of them 'cause of what he did."

"Till you needed Duke to kill your wife," Mike said.

I looked up in Quillian's direction. He seemed to be slithering along the wall toward our position, moving to conceal himself behind another arch, one step closer to the long-forgotten mail tunnel Mike had described that branched off at the south end of the platform. Perhaps Brendan had been looking for that since he'd run off after shooting O'Malley.

I knew Mercer would want to take a shot at him if he got within better range, but that he feared drawing fire because I was so close.

I opened the paper bag that Peterson had gotten me from Chinatown and pulled out one of Uncle Charlie's devices. Mercer looked back and tried to push my hand away from it.

"Quillian's only got one eye. Don't stop me. He can't see well enough to shoot unless he gets right on top of us," I said. "And I know you're not going to let that happen."

My hand was shaking as I placed several of the Chinese firecrackers on the ground beside us.

"Keep talking to him, Mike," Mercer said.

"I bet you paid Duke to kill Amanda. When you were ready to bail out of your marriage, but wanted to keep the Keating money, that's when you realized you needed your brother again. Mailed him money—in the envelope Trish showed us today."

Now I remembered what had fallen out of Trish's apron.

"What'd you do, send a cashier's check

to Duke? Left no record in your account but gave him plenty of cash to operate with. Kind of poetic justice that Bobby Hassett sliced off one of Duke's fingers before he killed him, don't you think? Must have tied him up to keep him still, torture him before he died, like someone ought to do to you. Those big fingers of Duke's—the ones that strangled Bex to death? The ones he used to murder Amanda for you?"

The first shot lit up the tunnel as the primer ignited the gunpowder in Brendan Quillian's weapon. The noise sounded as loud as a cannon in the vaulted space. A bullet slammed into the side of the platform just inches over my head.

"Take Coop and run as fast as you can," Mike said softly to Mercer. It looked as if his theory about how much ammunition Quillian still had in his gun was wrong.

"Don't move your hand, Wallace," Quillian said, his head cocked to the side so that his left eye—the good one—could focus on what his two armed adversaries were doing.

Mercer glanced at the red sticks I had lined up. "Okay, Alex. Ready?" he whispered.

I palmed the matchbook and nodded my head.

"If you know Bobby Hassett killed my brother, why don't you arrest him, dammit? He'll be along any minute," Quillian said.

"What?" Mike said, puzzling out the answer. "So Teddy O'Malley double-crossed you? He went to Trish to get the money you wanted, but then he called Bobby Hassett to tell him where you were hiding. Let him even up all the old scores by trapping you in here and finishing you off—his father's death, Bex's murder. Your sandhog instincts are awfully primitive. How'd you know, Brendan? How'd you know Bobby Hassett is coming here?"

Quillian was taking baby steps along the curved wall in our direction. He was angry now, the bad-tempered Brendan Quillian who was responsible for so many deaths.

"'Cause I asked Teddy O'Malley if I could use his cell phone to call Trish. And when I opened it to dial her, I saw the last number he had called before getting here to meet me. It was Bobby Hassett's phone."

"Go ahead, Brendan. Take the tunnel," Mike shouted. Quillian was getting uncomfortably close to the three of us. "We'll let you run before the rest of the cops show up."

"You're not going anywhere, Chapman. That's obvious. But that leaves Mr. Wallace and Ms. Cooper to chase after me. And I don't really like that idea."

Every time he moved, Quillian squinted and tilted his head to adjust the vision in his eye.

"Stand up, Mr. Wallace. Stand up now, will you?"

"No!" I said to Mercer as he lifted a knee, acting as though he were going to obey the command. He was far too big a target to put in Quillian's way.

But as he shifted his weight, Mercer gave me the cover I needed to light the first match. I held it to the wire sticking out of the tip of the firecracker and lobbed it in Quillian's direction. As soon as it was in the air I got two more off, throwing them over Mercer's back and as close to the mouth of the tunnel as I could.

The loud barrage of explosions filled the small tube as the earth seemed to rattle and the hollow vaults burst with a deafening series of blasts. The black hole we were all in, backlit from the subway car that had disappeared behind the curving wall, came alive with a blinding series of colorful streaks and sparks—orange, yellow, green, and a searing white flash.

"Dynamite, Brendan," Mike yelled out as I kept lighting firecrackers and throwing them as near to Quillian as I could. "They'll blast you to kingdom come if you don't make it out of here."

The killer had panicked at the sound and sight of the explosive devices as they landed all around him. It was a combination of every noise, every vibration, every fear that had kept him for all of his young life out of the tunnels in which his father had worked, ever since the accident that had taken the sight of his right eye.

He lifted his gun to shoot in our direction over the other thunderous booms, but fired wildly as he bobbed his head to try to protect his eye from the streaking lights bursting around him.

I watched as he clapped a hand over his left eye, turning away from us before uncovering it to run toward the cylindrical tunnel that led off the side of the platform.

Phin was right—Quillian was so spooked by the noise that he didn't stop to think that the cops would never use real explosives in a subway tunnel.

But the fireworks forced him to the exit he had been seeking—the one Mike said was an old pneumatic mail tunnel—and I had no idea where it led.

50

Within minutes, because of our proximity to both City Hall and One Police Plaza, Peterson had been able to assemble a sophisticated team of sharpshooters to send in to retrieve us. A handful of men in helmets and bulletproof vests, armed with rifles and handguns, surrounded us to learn what had happened, while two transit crewmen who had entered with the police worked to extricate Mike's foot from under the railroad tie.

Mercer pointed with his flashlight at the

narrow tunnel into which Brendan Quillian had fled.

"You know where it ends?" one of the cops asked, while two others, rifles at the ready, positioned themselves on either side of the black hole.

"Murray Street," Mike said, still on his back. "A few blocks west of here. It used to feed into a building that was rented out by the city as a wine cellar."

"I'm Gary Passoni," the group leader said to Mike. "Let's get you topside. The commissioner himself is on this. There's a SWAT team going in from above at every one of those old station exits. They'll find the wine cellar. They've got the maps."

Passoni put his walkie-talkie to his mouth to transmit the information about Quillian's flight into the Murray Street tunnel wing.

Another officer took my arm. "Ms. Cooper? The lieutenant wants you out of here yesterday, okay? You're with me."

"I'd like to wait until Chapman's leg is free."

"Let's go, blondie," Mike called to me from the tracks. "Don't hold up the traffic. I'm bringing up the rear."

I looked back and saw that he was being

helped to his feet by the crewmen. I started to move along the platform with my escort, worried that Mercer was going in the opposite direction, to help the new arrivals find Quillian.

Someone gave a signal that the track was clear, and again the train started a slow approach to meet us.

Before it pulled within range of me, a volley of gunshots rang out, this time from the cylindrical cave into which Brendan Quillian had disappeared.

The men guarding the black hole dropped to their knees, and one screamed out for all of us to get down.

A voice called Passoni's name from within the tunnel.

"Yeah?"

"Hold your fire on that end. I think we hit him after he took a shot at my first man in. My guys are coming toward you, sweeping for him. Stand away."

The police had clearly found the Murray Street entrance and encountered Quillian on his way to a last-ditch effort to escape.

Mercer yelled at the cop holding on to me, "Move her out. Move her out now, understand?"

The man tugged on my arm and I went forward, but continued to look at Mercer, calling out to him, "You get out, too. You don't have a vest, you don't have—"

Passoni held a finger to his lips. I stopped midsentence and could hear the sound of someone whimpering, crying softly, out of sight but not far away.

The two sharpshooters saw something through their night-vision goggles that caused them to lower the aim of their rifles.

Seconds later, Brendan Quillian crawled out of the darkened tunnel, one hand pressed against his throat. He rolled onto his back at the foot of the subway platform.

One cop stepped on his neck, pinning him in place while three others were upon him immediately, wresting a revolver from his hand and searching him for the other gun.

Mercer was on his knees closest to the fugitive when the officer lifted his boot and the gunshot in Quillian's neck spurted blood like a small geyser.

"Get him in the bus!" Passoni shouted, waving his team to carry the dying man to the subway train and out to the ambulance that had been summoned for Mike.

I broke away from the cop who was trying to escort me when I saw Mike hobble toward Quillian.

"How does your fucking neck feel, Brendan?" Mike asked. "At least it's a faster way to die than strangulation."

One of the guys pushed Mike back while they worked to stop the bleeding and lift their prisoner to get him to help. I could see Quillian gasping for breath like a fish out of water, his one good eye darting wildly around at his captors.

He looked harmless now, his long body limp and his face almost gray, as the blood ran out of him.

"What's your hurry?" Mike asked Passoni. "If anyone ever deserved a long, slow, painful—"

"Shut up, Chapman."

"Easy, Mike," Mercer said, stepping back to let four of the men carry the fugitive toward the waiting subway car.

As they passed in front of me, Brendan Quillian's left lid opened wide. He searched the vaulted ceiling above the platform as though hoping to see the sky. He groaned loudly, and his head tossed backward, convulsing several times before he fell still. The fire within his good eye—the left one—went out as he died in the arms of the four cops, deep within one of the blackened tunnels he had feared almost all of his life.

51

The #6 chugged in close again as a second team of EMTs carried Mike onto the empty train for the ride up to Thirty-fourth Street and the Bellevue emergency room.

He stretched out on the long, gray vinyl seat of the brightly lit car. One of the medics had removed his shoes and was sitting at his feet, beginning to examine them to determine the nature of the injury.

"They'll x-ray you, but my guess is you've got a torn ligament. Maybe a fracture, too, the way you said you landed on it when you fell. There's a lot of swelling. You'll have to stay off this for a while."

"Hurts like hell. You got a pillow handy? This bench is hard as a rock. My tail and my head hurt more than my foot."

I laughed and sat down, gently lifting Mike's head and resting it in my lap, brushing the hair back off his face.

He looked up at Mercer. "Has she been useful today or what? Coop earned her stripes. What's up with those firecrackers, kid?"

"Mercer and I met Uncle Charlie a couple of years ago. Kept a bad gang supplied with what the Chinese used to call 'exploding sticks'—*baozhang*."

"What made you think of that?"

"When I saw the bamboo seats on the old redbird inside the terminal, it reminded me of things Charlie told us about firecrackers—that the earliest ones were made of bamboo. It grows so fast that pockets of air and sap get trapped inside. Over fire, the air expands and bursts out with a loud noise. So eventually, the Chinese started wrapping gunpowder in bamboo tubes. I figured if Quillian was anywhere around, the noise would cause flashbacks to his accident—unhinge him—scare him out of hiding."

"How did you know Uncle Charlie would have any?"

"Fourth of July's only a few weeks away. He does a huge business in illegal firecrackers this time of year. And Mercer gave Charlie a pass on our big case—he's a friend for life. Didn't lock him up 'cause he was so cooperative."

The motorman got the signal from the medic and the car moved forward, rounding the rest of the loop before heading up the incline past the northbound side of the Brooklyn Bridge station.

Commuters stepped forward expecting the train to stop and the doors to open, but we were on a private ride with our special patient.

"I thought you hated the subway," Mike said, looking up at me, pressing my hand in his. "You're almost smiling. I know you won't say it, but Brendan Quillian got what he deserved."

"It's over. We're all okay. And I'm almost back, out of the center of the earth. There really is an underground city of death, and I can't wait to leave it."

Mercer was hanging on to the pole as the train continued uptown.

"Marley Dionne—your snitch," Mike said to Mercer. "Is he still at Bellevue?"

"Yeah."

"Talking yet?"

"No way."

"Maybe we'll do a drop-in while I'm waiting to be x-rayed. Dig a little deeper, we're going to prove that Duke Quillian tried to hire him to kill Amanda. Probably through some Jamaican sandhogs. There's got to be a connection there. People like Dionne and that guy Larry Pritchard, they're likely to start talking to us now. Both Duke and Brendan are out of the picture, so they've got to feel a whole lot safer. When the deal fell through with Dionne, I'll bet you Duke kept the contract on Amanda for himself. Delighted in doing it. Brought the whole family breakup back full circle. Duke doing Brendan's dirty work, just like the good old days."

"How'd you figure that out about the cash that O'Malley got from Trish?" Mercer asked.

"Hey, Coop and I had every bank record, phone record, contact that Brendan Quillian made in the year before his arrest. His brother's name never came up a single time. But once we got the story from Trish herself, how Duke had always protected his little brother, done his fighting—it seemed logical to me that Brendan would go to him in the end when he needed the biggest favor of all."

"Kill Amanda but keep the Keating fortune," I said.

"What else would he have to give Duke but money? Trish probably found the stash after he was killed, cleaning out his apartment."

"And Teddy O'Malley?"

"Playing two sides against the middle. Quillians and Hassetts—both families go way back in the business. I tell you it's tribal with those sandhogs. It was a classic blood feud, and O'Malley wasn't any damn good at choosing sides. So he gambled with each of them. He was ready to sell Quillian to the highest bidder, and he lost big."

The train had cruised by the Bleecker Street and Astor Place stations, slowing through the crowded platform at Fourteenth Street, before speeding up again.

"I guess Peterson has the squad looking

for Bobby Hassett right now," Mike said to Mercer. "After the docs check me out, bandage me, you and I can catch up with them."

Mercer shook his head. "By the time they're through with you tonight—thin ankle, thick head, and all—I expect Mr. Hassett will be snug behind bars."

"Screw the hospital. Want to take this damn thing all the way to the end of the line?" Mike asked. I could feel his relief, the tension easing in his body.

"Get me off this chariot, Mr. Chapman. I want to smell fresh air and see the daylight—well, moonlight—as soon as possible. I want to get your ankle taped up so you can take me dancing. I want to be sure that everyone Brendan Quillian hurt throughout his life knows he can't ever do that again. I want to turn on my faucets every day and find the best-tasting water in the world still coming out of them, and be grateful to all the people who've been digging the holes to get it here. I want you to promise me that—"

"Go easy on me, Coop. Way too many demands. Do I have to apologize for taking you into the loop tonight, too?" Mike asked.

"Buy me two drinks and ask me then. If I can hold on to the glass without shaking, without spilling a drop of my Scotch—you'll be forgiven."

"What do you think, Mercer? I got the best seat in the house, don't I?"

The train rocked from side to side and Mike squeezed my hand again.

Acknowledgments

Beneath the streets of New York is a multitude of labyrinthine systems, dug deep into the bedrock of Manhattan Island, which give life to the city above. Subway tubes, gas mains, housing for electrical wiring, sewers and shafts of every variety—as well as the two antiquated tunnels that have carried billions of gallons of fresh water daily, for almost a century, from upstate to the five boroughs—were all built by a small cadre of construction workers known as sandhogs. They have not only created this underground kingdom, but they are the only men ever to see most of it.

I first read about the plans for City Tunnel

Number 3—and those who have died making it—in a riveting article called "City of Water" by David Grann, in *The New Yorker* magazine (September 1, 2003). Two years later, Lesley Stahl and her *60 Minutes* crew took the Alimak cage dozens of stories down and went into the dangerous arms of the tunnel's building site to explore this brilliant feat of modern engineering . . . and led the way for me to follow.

Nonfiction works that provided fascinating historical information include David McCullough's *The Great Bridge*; Paul E. Delaney's *Sandhogs*; Gerard T. Koeppel's *Water for Gotham*; Lorraine B. Diehl's *Subways*; and Edward F. Bergman's *Woodlawn Remembers*.

I lost a great friend when Bohn Vergari died—way too young—and it was his beloved wife, Jane, who suggested to me that I research the lifesaving work of the medical teams at Memorial Sloan-Kettering Cancer Center. My special thanks to Dr. Ann Jakubowski for her wisdom and courage.

Thanks to everyone (and I do mean everyone) at Scribner and Pocket Books, and especially to Colin Harrison, whose guidance and insights are invaluable. Boundless gratitude to my great friend Esther Newberg at ICM, along with her trusty aides, Kari Stuart and Chris Earle.

This book is for Hilary Hale of Time Warner/Little, Brown, who found Alex Cooper shortly after her "birth," and has introduced my books to readers in more places than I ever dreamed possible. Hilary's intelligence and kindness, her editorial eye and firm friendship, have been a treasured partnership for more than a decade.

And once again, to Justin, who—this time—has truly given me his heart.

About the Author

Linda Fairstein, America's foremost legal expert on crimes of sexual assault and domestic violence, led the pioneering Sex Crimes Unit of the District Attorney's Office in Manhattan for twenty-five years, leaving in 2002 to write, lecture, and continue her advocacy for victims of violent crime. A Fellow of the American College of Trial Lawyers and a member of the International Society of Barristers, she is a graduate of Vassar College and the University of Virginia School of Law. Her first novel, *Final Jeopardy,* which introduced the character Alexandra Cooper, was published in 1996 to critical and commercial acclaim. All eight Alex Cooper novels also achieved international bestseller status, and her most recent, *Death Dance,* debuted at #4 on the *New York Times* bestseller list. Fairstein's nonfiction book, *Sexual Violence,* was a *New York Times* Notable Book in 1994. She lives with her husband in Manhattan and on Martha's Vineyard. Her website is www.lindafairstein.com.